Enid Blyton

Magical Treasury

ISBN 978 1 444 93693 3

Hodder Children's Books
An imprint of Hachette Children's Group
Part of Hodder & Stoughton
Carmelite House
London EC4Y 0DZ
An Hachette UK company

Enid Blyton®

Magical Treasury

Compiled by

Norman Wright & Mary Cadogan

Illustrated by

Emma Chichester Clark

Hodder Children's Books

A division of Hachette Children's Group

CONTENTS

Magical Adventures

Extraordinary Objects

Greedy Magic

INTRODUCTION

ENID BLYTON was a born storyteller who effortlessly transported her readers to the enchanted lands of her imagination. There they might encounter giants, witches or even talking teapots in worlds filled with excitement and adventure. In these lands anything was possible. Carpets could grant wishes, rabbits rode on underground railways and you never knew when you might bump into a magic walking-stick! Children were usually the heroes and heroines of these adventures. Whisked through a magic door or down an oversized rabbit-hole to a land of make-believe, they would outwit wizards and rescue fairy princesses from cloud castles before returning home, safe and sound – in time for tea!

In her autobiography, entitled *The Story of My Life*, Enid explained how she created her stories, with the characters and situations coming straight into her mind fully formed: 'I sit in my chair and shut my eyes for a minute or two,' she explained. 'In comes the story I am waiting for, all ready and complete in my imagination.' It was, she said, as if she were watching the tale unfold on a cinema screen. This wonderful gift not only helped her to create stories that were fresh, lively and appealing but also enabled her to write them very quickly.

Enid was born in East Dulwich, London and spent most of her childhood in nearby Beckenham, Kent where her father, Thomas, encouraged her and her two brothers to take a lively interest in the world around them. Young Enid enjoyed going for long countryside walks with her parents, where she became captivated by the wildlife that abounded in the woods and streams close to her home. She delighted too in the meadows and wayside borders with their colourful wild flowers: foxgloves, trefoils, cowslip and many others. She learned everything she could about the natural world around her.

She also loved the countryside tales of many of the plants and animals – and of the magical properties that some were said to possess – and she became enthralled by stories of fairies and woodland folk that, to the small girl with a vivid imagination, seemed so believable. Her interest in folklore was encouraged by her father who could keep her spellbound with stories of leprechauns and 'the little people' that he had heard as a boy from his Irish mother. Enid read everything she could on the subject and in her autobiography she tells us: 'I read every old folk tale I could find, from countries all over the world.' Later, Enid used much of this knowledge to enliven her stories and to educate her readers. She introduced wild flowers and animals into her tales, subtly teaching her readers the traditional – and often magical – stories associated with them.

Even as a child Enid spent much of her time writing and her work often featured the animals and fairy folk that she found so fascinating. As she grew older she began sending stories and poems to magazines and was thrilled when, at the age of thirteen, one of her poems was published in a popular magazine. This encouraged her to continue writing but for the next few years she was unsuccessful in having anything further published.

Despite her early stories being rejected Enid knew that more than anything else she wanted to write for children and every spare minute she had found her busily writing and sending her stories and poems to publishers. Gradually she began to have her work accepted by magazines such as *The Schoolmistress*, *Teachers World* and *Fairyland Tales*. Her energy seemed boundless and in 1922 she succeeded in having a small booklet, entitled *Child Whispers*, published. Two years later she was delighted when her first collection of stories appeared in the bookshops in time for Christmas. It was a large, annual sized volume with stories that Enid knew children would love. It was entitled *The Enid Blyton Book of Fairies*.

In 1926 Enid began writing all the stories for every issue of *Sunny Stories for Little Folks*, a magazine for younger readers. She wrote many types of stories for the magazine but those about magic and enchantment were particularly popular with her readers and Enid happily wrote more and more of what they wanted.

In January 1937 the magazine's title was changed to *Enid Blyton's Sunny Stories* and for it Enid wrote the opening episode of her very first long serial story, entitled *Adventures of the Wishing Chair*. It was hugely popular with readers who were thrilled at Mollie and Peter's many adventures overcoming all sorts of wizardly magic. Equally spellbinding were the serialisations of *The Enchanted Wood* and *The Magic Faraway Tree* that appeared in *Sunny Stories* a few years later. In 1953 Enid stopped writing for *Sunny Stories* and began her own *Enid Blyton's Magazine* for which she wrote yet more tales.

She wrote over three thousand stories for *Sunny Stories* and *Enid Blyton's Magazine*. Many were later collected and published as books. They all delighted her readers but amongst the best loved were those that featured enchanted happenings. In this collection we have gathered together some of the very best of these – including a few that have never before been collected. So turn the pages and let Enid Blyton's magical stories transport you to enchanted worlds where anything might happen – and probably will!

NORMAN WRIGHT AND MARY CADOGAN

Wizards
and
Witches

Very-Young the Wizard

There was once a wizard called Very-Young. He was quite the youngest and smallest of all the wizards, and he was really rather poor at learning magic.

He made a great many mistakes, and all the other wizards laughed at him.

'One of these days you'll work a magic spell on yourself by mistake, and then you'll be in a fine pickle!' they said. 'You must be more careful, Very-Young.'

But Very-Young wouldn't listen to any advice. He thought he knew everything. He went on making spells, stirring up magic in his boiling cauldron over the fire, and muttering enchanted words to himself.

He had one servant, and that was a faithful little rabbit. Most wizards, like witches, have cats for servants, for they are wise, and can keep secrets. But wizard-cats cost a great deal of money and Very-Young couldn't afford one. So he had a rabbit instead, for rabbits didn't want such high wages.

Whiskers was a very tidy, clean servant. He swept and dusted, cooked and mended very well indeed. Sometimes he stirred the cauldron himself, though he was very much afraid of what magic might come out of it.

When he saw that Very-Young often made mistakes, he became alarmed in case the little wizard should do something to harm himself. He was very fond of his master, and wouldn't have had anything happen to him for the world. He asked leave to look into all the magic books, so that he might learn something of magic himself, and perhaps be able to help Very-Young one day.

Very-Young laughed loudly.

'Why, you're only a rabbit!' he said. 'You'll never be able to learn any magic. But you can look at the pictures in my magic book if you like.'

'Thank you, Master,' said Whiskers, gratefully. 'I know I'm only a silly little animal, but who knows, perhaps I might be able to help you one day.'

'Stuff and nonsense,' said Very-Young. 'You couldn't possibly help me, so don't get conceited, Whiskers.'

The rabbit said no more. He waited until his work was done, and then he took down the magic books one by one, and read them all through. He had a good memory, and very soon he knew a great many spells, and could say hundreds of magic words without looking at the book at all.

One day he saw Very-Young mixing spider's web, red mushrooms and the juice from a goose's egg together.

'*Tick-a-too, fa-la-lee-dee, Ta-re, dimon-noo!*'

chanted Very-Young.

'Master! Master!' cried Whiskers, dropping his broom in a hurry. 'You're saying the wrong spell! Instead of making magic to grow a goose that lays golden eggs, you are saying a spell that will turn you into a goose yourself!'

It was quite true. Very-Young had made a mistake. Already feathers had begun to sprout from his shoulders! Hurriedly he began to chant the right spell, and the feathers slowly disappeared.

But instead of being grateful to Whiskers, he was cross with him!

'I should soon have found out my mistake!' he said sharply. 'Get on with your work, Whiskers, and don't interfere in things that you know nothing about.'

Not very long after that Very-Young was told that a wicked goblin was somewhere about. One of the powerful wizards came to give him the news.

'We are all busy,' said the old wizard, 'so you had better work the spell that will get rid of the goblin. Or better still, make some magic that will get him into our power. Then we can make him into a useful servant. Do this tonight, Very-Young. You know how to do so, of course?'

'Of course!' said Very-Young, offended. 'You can trust me to do a simple thing like that! Good morning! The goblin will be in your power before midnight.'

Very-Young at once set to work to get everything ready for the spell. He had to mix green elderberries, powder from a blue butterfly's wings, a small moonbeam, two thorns from a red rose, and a drop of honey all together. Then he had to count from ninety-nine back to one, and stir all the time from left to right.

He had soon got the mixture ready. Then, stirring very carefully, he began to count backwards from ninety-nine. Whiskers watched him.

'Ninety-nine, ninety-eight, ninety-seven,' began Very-Young. He went on counting, and had almost got to twenty, when Whiskers gave a cry of fear.

'Master! You're stirring the wrong way! You are stirring from right to left, instead of left to right! Oh dear, oh dear, you'll put yourself in the goblin's power, instead of getting him into yours!'

Very-Young stopped stirring in fright. Yes, Whiskers was quite right. In a hurry he began stirring the other way – but dear me, you can't do that sort of thing in the middle of a powerful spell! Something is bound to happen!

And something did happen! There came a tremendous *BANG*, a blue-green flame shot out of the cauldron, and all of a sudden Very-Young flew out of the window, and disappeared!

The cauldron overturned, and Whiskers cried out in fear, for a long yellow snake crawled out and vanished up the chimney!

Whiskers crouched in a corner and waited for something else to happen. But nothing did – except that he heard a very peculiar laugh from somewhere, that made him shiver and tremble.

'That was the goblin!' thought the little rabbit. 'He knows that Very-Young has put himself in his power, and he's gone to get him. Oh dear, what a very dreadful thing! If only my dear master had let me help him, nothing of this sort would have happened.'

After a bit he came out of his corner, and tidied up the room. Then he took down a book of magic, and studied it hard. Presently he smiled, and clapped his paws.

'I'll go and rescue my master,' he said. 'I may get taken prisoner myself, but never mind. I'll try, anyway.'

But what had happened to Very-Young? He had flown out of the window, risen as high as the clouds, and then come down bump in a country he didn't know!

'This is a fine thing!' he said. 'Now what am I to do?'

At that moment he heard a horrid laugh, and suddenly there stood in front of him the ugly little goblin whom he had tried to get into his power.

'Ho ho!' said the goblin. 'Now you're in my power, Very-Young. You don't deserve to be a wizard, when you make such foolish mistakes. Come along, I'm going to put you into my cave, and then, when you've starved for a few days, perhaps you will kindly tell me a few of the secret spells you wizards know!'

'Never!' cried Very-Young. 'I won't go to your cave.'

But the goblin knew a little magic too. He muttered a few strange words, and at once Very-Young's feet began to walk in the direction that the goblin wished them to. Soon Very-Young was in an enormous cave, feeling rather frightened.

'Stay there for a week without food,' said the wicked goblin, grinning. 'By the end of that time you'll do anything for me, I know! You'll find a little spring of water trickles into the cave, and you can drink that. Before I leave you I'm going to draw a magic circle round you, and then that will stop you from using any magic you know to call your friends to help you!'

He drew a white chalk circle round poor Very-Young, who watched him in dismay.

'Please set me free,' he begged.

The goblin clapped his hands seven times, laughed mockingly and disappeared. At the same time a great stone rolled over the entrance to the cave – Very-Young was a prisoner! He had nothing to eat, and he could not beg his friends for help. Whatever in the world could he do?

'No one but Whiskers knows I am gone!' he wept. 'And what can a little rabbit do?'

At that very moment the rabbit was speeding towards his master, carrying under one paw a big magic book that he thought might be useful. He guessed that Very-Young had been shot off to the goblin country.

When he got there, he stopped and looked round.

'Now what was that spell I read about the other day?' he wondered. 'If I could think of it, I could soon find my master.'

He had a very good memory, and soon he had thought of the spell, and the magic words that went with it. He pulled three green leaves, and put them in a circle with their ends touching. Then he looked about for a white feather. He blew it into the air, danced round and round on the three leaves, singing a few strange words, and then danced off again. The leaves had vanished!

But the feather was still floating in the air. Just as Whiskers danced off the leaves, it began heading to the west, as if a strong breeze was blowing it.

'Lead me to my master!' cried the rabbit, and at once started off to follow the floating feather.

Soon it brought him to the cave where Very-Young was sitting. Whiskers saw the great stone in front, and felt certain that his master was imprisoned in the cave behind.

'Master, Master!' he cried. 'Are you there? It is I, Whiskers, your little servant.'

'Oh, Whiskers, is it really you!' cried Very-Young, in delighted surprise. 'Oh, can you get me out of here? Can you move that stone?'

Whiskers pushed against the great stone with all his strength; but he could not move it one inch. It was far too heavy.

'I can't move it,' he cried to Very-Young.

'Well, never mind,' said the little wizard, in despair. 'If you could it wouldn't be much use, for I can't move out of this magic circle, and I don't know the spell that would get me out of the goblin's power. If only I had one of my magic books with me, I might be able to do something.'

'Master, I've brought one with me,' cried the little rabbit. 'The one about goblins.'

'Why, that's just the one I want!' cried Very-Young. 'Oh, Whiskers! If only you could get it in to me, somehow!'

Whiskers pushed at the great stone again, but it was no use. He simply couldn't move it at all. Then he had a great idea! Wasn't he a rabbit? Couldn't he burrow like all rabbits do? Surely he hadn't forgotten how to use his paws!

At once he began to burrow in the hillside, just beside the cave entrance. He sent out the earth in great showers, and very soon he had made a tunnel that ran alongside the cave. Then he turned inwards, and in ten minutes he had made a hole into the cave where Very-Young sat.

He leapt out of the tunnel he had made, and ran to his master.

'Here's the book!' he cried. 'Look up what it says about goblins, Master, quickly!'

So Very-Young looked. But he found that it would take many days before he could make a goblin spell, and as he couldn't move out of the magic circle, he didn't know what to do.

'When is the goblin coming back?' asked Whiskers. 'In a week, did you say? Well, Master, we can manage it. Let me get out and get you all the things you want for the spell, and then we'll have everything ready by the time the goblin comes back!'

So in and out of his tunnel went the brave rabbit, fetching night-shade berries, red feathers, yellow toad-stools, and everything else that Very-Young wanted for his spell.

The little wizard discovered from his magic book that the one thing a goblin was frightened of was a green, frilled dragon. His book told him how to make one, so for a whole week he and the rabbit were very busy. Whiskers not only fetched the things needed for the spell, but also bread and meat, for there was no food in the cave at all.

Soon all the things for the spell were neatly piled at one end of the enormous cave. Whiskers put the last one there on the seventh day. Then the two waited for the goblin to come.

Very soon they heard him outside the cave. He shouted a magic word, and the stone flew away from the entrance. Then he strode in. Whiskers had hidden himself, and Very-Young was pretending to be ill and faint.

'Ho-ho!' said the goblin. 'What about a nice hot dinner, Very-Young?'

The wizard pretended to groan.

'Well, tell me a few secret spells and I will give you some bacon and eggs,' said the goblin.

'Here is one,' said Very-Young, raising his head. Then he suddenly began to chant the spell that would turn all the magic things at the end of the cave into a fearful frilled dragon! The goblin listened, thinking that he was hearing a wonderful new spell.

But just as Very-Young got to the last words, a strange thing happened. A rushing, swishing noise was heard at the end of the cave, and suddenly a dreadful bellow rang out. Then two red eyes gleamed, and lo and behold! A great dragon came rushing out!

'A frilled dragon!' yelled the goblin in fright. 'Oh my! Oh my! A frilled dragon! I must go! I shall never come back!'

He leapt six feet into the air, turned into blue smoke, and streamed out of the cave with the dragon after him. Whiskers and Very-Young went too, and the last they saw of the wicked goblin was a thin cloud of smoke far up in the eastern sky.

The dragon soon gave up the chase, and turned back to Very-Young.

'Quick!' whispered Whiskers. 'Change him into something else, or he will eat us.'

Very-Young clapped his hands twice, and uttered a command. At once the dragon became smaller, and when it was as small as a football it turned into a mass of red flames.

Whiskers hurriedly filled a jug with water from the cave, and gave it to Very-Young. The wizard flung it over the flames – and sizzle-sizzle-sizzle! They went out, and nothing was left of the frilled dragon except for a few wet ashes!

'My goodness,' said Very-Young, sitting down on the ground, and heaving a sigh. 'We have been having too many adventures, Whiskers. I shall be glad to get home, and sleep in my soft bed!'

'Poor Master, you must be very tired,' said the kind-hearted rabbit. 'Jump up on my back, and I'll take you home before you can say "Tiddley-winks!" '

So Very-Young climbed up on Whiskers's soft back, and very soon he was safely home.

'I must thank you very much for all you have done for me,' said the little wizard, hugging the delighted rabbit. 'I really think you are cleverer than I am, Whiskers. I shall make you my partner, and you shall wear a pointed hat like me! We will do all our spells together, and then perhaps I shan't ever make a mistake again!'

Whiskers was so pleased. He thanked Very-Young, and said he would always serve him well and faithfully.

'Well, let's go to bed now and have some sleep,' said Very-Young, yawning. 'We haven't slept for a week, and I can hardly keep my eyes open. Then tomorrow we will go out and buy you your pointed hat.'

So they both fell asleep, and all night long Whiskers dreamed happily of wearing a pointed hat and helping Very-Young with his spells.

He is still with the wizard, but now Very-Young is Very-Old, and Whiskers's ears have gone grey with age. Sometimes when all their work is done, they sit one on each side of the chimney corner, and Whiskers says:

'Do you remember, Master, when you made a mistake in your spells?'

Then they both laugh loudly, and wonder where the wicked goblin went to – for he has never been heard of from that day to this.

The Witch
Who Lost Sixpence

There was once an old witch who went for a walk on Bumble Common, and lost a silver sixpence. She had a hole in the bottom of her pocket, and the sixpence fell out and rolled away in the long grass.

When she got home again she looked for her silver sixpence – and it wasn't there. Then she was dreadfully upset, for it was a magic coin, and very useful to her. She went to her cupboard and took out pen and ink. Then she found a big card, and wrote on it:

LOST.
A silver sixpence.
Please return to the witch.

She took the card and pinned it outside her gate. Then she waited for her sixpence to be returned to her.

Now, not long after the witch had pinned up her notice Rollikins the pixie passed by. He saw the notice, and read it. Then he went on his way over Bumble Common, thinking that he would keep his eyes open for a little silver sixpence.

It so happened that he passed the very place where the witch had dropped the sixpence, and the sun shone on the little silver coin and made it bright. Rollikins saw it and picked it up. It looked just like any other sixpence, and he popped it into his pocket.

'I don't see why I shouldn't keep it for myself,' he thought. 'Finding is keeping, people say. Why should I give it back to the old witch? She is a mean old thing, and won't even say thank you, I'll be bound.'

So the naughty pixie went on his way home, and didn't give the sixpence to the witch, as he should have done. He soon arrived home, pushed open his little door, and began to get his tea ready. He laid the table with a blue cloth, cut some bread and butter put out the strawberry jam, and took a ginger cake from its tin. Then he went to see if the kettle was boiling.

The handle was hot, so he took out his handkerchief to hold it. But the money in his pocket was all mixed up with the handkerchief, so he put the coins down on the table, the silver sixpence among them, and then wrapped his handkerchief round the kettle-handle.

He took the kettle to the teapot to pour the water into it – and almost dropped it in surprise! For to his very great astonishment his blue tablecloth had turned to a bright silver one! Rollikins couldn't believe his eyes! How could it have happened? One minute it was pale blue cotton, and the next it was gleaming silver.

Then he suddenly thought of the sixpence. Perhaps that had done it! It

12

must be a magic sixpence! Rollikins picked it up and put it on a white plate. Very slowly, as he watched, the plate turned from white china to shining silver. Rollikins was filled with astonishment.

'No wonder the old witch wanted her sixpence back!' he cried. 'Why, it is as full of silver magic as it can be! What a lucky thing for me that I didn't take it back to her! I shall turn everything in my cottage into silver. Then I shall be very rich indeed!'

So he began. He placed the sixpence on each of his plates, in each of his cups, and on all his dishes. Every one of them changed to silver. Then he placed the sixpence on his dust-pan,

He turned his spoons and forks into real silver, and his six little egg-cups. He put the sixpence on the wooden table-top; and on each of his little wooden chairs. In half a minute they had changed to silver. Rollikins rubbed his hands in delight.

At that moment Whiskers, his fine black cat, jumped in at the window, and stopped in surprise to see the kitchen looking so different.

'Isn't it fine, Whiskers?' cried Rollikins. 'I have found a magic sixpence that changes everything to silver. See, I have turned your dish to silver and your basket too. Won't you feel grand to eat out of a silver saucer and sleep in a silver basket. Why, you will be grander than the Queen's own cat!'

'Thank you, Master,' said Whiskers, and he ran and rubbed his head against Rollikins, for he was very fond of the pixie. Rollikins loved him too, and would have done anything in the world for his beautiful cat.

'Where is the sixpence, Master?' asked the cat. 'Let me see it.'

'There it is,' said Rollikins, pointing to a waste-paper basket which was slowly turning to silver. 'It's in there. Wait a moment, and I will put it on your collar, Whiskers, and change that to silver too. Wouldn't you love to have a silver collar?'

So when the basket had finished turning into silver, Rollikins put the sixpence on Whisker's collar. He watched it slowly changing into silver – and then, oh dear, he noticed something else. Whiskers was changing into silver too! In a trice Rollikins whisked the sixpence off his cat's neck – but it was too late.

Whiskers sat quite still, and in half a minute was a solid silver cat.

Rollikins spoke to him and hugged him, and begged him to say a word – but Whiskers didn't speak or move. He was a little silver cat, very heavy and very bright. Then Rollikins began to cry. He wept and wept and wept. He hugged Whiskers and tried to warm him into life, but it wasn't a bit of good.

The pixie was terribly unhappy. Whiskers was his best friend. He couldn't do without him, he simply couldn't. What a dreadful thing to have turned his best friend into a silver statue that could neither move nor speak!

Rollikins fetched some milk and poured it into the silver dish. He set it before Whiskers, and begged him to have a drink. But the silver cat took no notice at all.

'What shall I do, what shall I do?' wept Rollikins. 'Oh, Whiskers, darling Whiskers, do mew. Don't be silver any more. Be my own, nice, cuddly Whiskers.'

But Whiskers sat and stared with silver eyes, and didn't make a sound.

There came a knock at the door, and Rollikin's next door neighbour came in.

'What's the matter, Rollikins?' he asked. 'I heard you crying. Can I help you? Ooh – what's happened to Whiskers?'

Rollikins told his friend the whole story, and the elf shook his head.

'You were very wrong to keep money that didn't belong to you,' he said, gravely. 'You see what a dreadful punishment has come to you. The only thing you can do is to go and confess to the witch, and tell her you are sorry. Then perhaps she will tell you how to get Whiskers back again.'

'But she will be very angry with me, and she might turn me into silver!' sobbed Rollikins.

'Well, you really deserve it!' said his friend. 'You've turned poor Whiskers into silver, haven't you? The only thing you can do to show you are sorry is to go and confess.'

So Rollikins put the sixpence in his pocket and set out over Bumble Common. He cried all the way, and when he got to the witch's cottage he could hardly see where the bell was. The witch called out 'Come in!' and he pushed open the door and entered.

'What's the matter?' asked the witch.

'P-p-p-please I've got your sixpence,' said Rollikins, and he put it down on the table.

'Well, that's nothing to cry about,' said the witch.

'No, b-b-b-but I've got a confession to make,' stammered Rollikins, and he told the witch all that had happened.

'So you kept my sixpence and used it,' said the witch. 'Well, you've had a good punishment, Rollikins. Goodbye.'

'Oh, but won't you please tell me how to make Whiskers all right again?' begged the pixie, in fright. 'Oh, please don't send me away without telling me what to do.'

'Why should I tell you anything?' asked the witch. 'I don't think you're at all a nice pixie. You keep a sixpence that doesn't belong to you, and then you use the magic in it. You don't deserve any help at all.'

'I'll do anything for you, anything in the world if you'll only get Whiskers back for me,' begged Rollikins, the tears running down his face again. 'I can't bear to think of him being a silver statue and nothing else. It's dreadful.'

The witch sat and thought for a moment.

'Well, listen,' she said. 'You know that fine apple tree of yours that bears hundreds of red apples every year?'

'Yes,' said Rollikins.

'Well, hidden in the trunk near the roots is a magic toad,' said the witch. 'If I had that toad I could make many more spells with its help. If you cut down that apple tree, and give me the toad you find inside, I will change Whiskers back to himself again.'

'Oh dear, oh dear!' groaned Rollikins. 'That apple tree is the finest one in the village. It gives me enough apples to last me all the year, round, witch. It is a shame to cut it down. It will kill it, and then it will never bear any more apples.'

'Well, if you want Whiskers back, that is what you must do,' said the witch.

So poor Rollikins ran home and found his axe. He chopped down his beautiful tree, and saw the toad sitting in the middle of the trunk, just as the witch had said. He popped it into a box and took it to her.

'That is good,' she said, stroking the toad on the back so that it croaked in delight. 'Now go home and stand in the middle of your kitchen. Shut your eyes, clap your hands, and say:

> *'Silver, silver, shining bright,*
> *Fade away from out my sight.*
> *In this house there must not shine*
> *Any silver thing of mine.'*

Rollikins raced home again. He stood in the middle of his kitchen, shut his eyes and clapped his hands. Then he said, very slowly and loudly, what the witch had told him to say. When he opened his eyes he looked at Whiskers.

'The silver's going, the silver's going!' he cried joyfully. 'Oh, Whiskers, you're getting black again!'

In a short time Whiskers was himself, a black furry cat, mewing loudly. Rollikins rushed to him and flung his arms round his neck.

'Oh, Whiskers, I'm so glad you're not silver any more,' he said. Whiskers looked round the kitchen.

'Why, Master,' he said, 'nothing is silver now! Look, the tablecloth has gone back to its blue colour, and my basket is yellow again. All the silver is gone.'

'Hurrah for that!' cried the pixie.

'But, oh, Master, look, your lovely apple tree is down!' cried the cat in dismay. 'How did that happen?'

Rollikins told him, and the cat rubbed his furry head lovingly against the pixie.

'I had to choose between you and the apple tree, Whiskers,' said Rollikins; 'so of course I chose you! But, dear me, I'll never keep anything that doesn't belong to me again.'

And you may be sure he didn't.

The Castle
Without a Door

Once upon a time a wizard came to live just outside Brownie Town. He was called Kookle, and no one knew much about him.

'He's building himself a castle on the hill,' they said to one another. 'He just sits on a stone and says odd words, and the castle grows out of the ground. It is wonderful to watch.'

'But it's a very odd castle,' said Tinker, a fat jolly brownie. 'Do you know

17

that it hasn't any doors at all? How are people going to get in and out, that's what I'd like to know. The windows are far too high up to climb through.'

'That's very funny,' said the brownies, and they shook their heads. 'Perhaps Kookle is up to mischief of some sort.'

It wasn't long before Kookle was very much disliked. He never spoke to the brownies at all, not even when they wished him good day. He turned one of them into a pillarbox one day because the little brownie had accidentally run into him round a corner, and it took Brownie Town a whole week before they could find the right magic to turn the pillarbox back into a brownie.

'He is a horrid wizard,' said the little folk. 'If only we could get rid of him! But what can you do with someone who lives in a castle without any doors? You can't even get in and beg him not to hurt us!'

'He'll do worse mischief yet, you mark my words!' said Tinker.

Now two weeks after that, little Princess Peronel came to stay in Brownie Town with her old nurse, Mother Browneyes. The two of them went walking in Wishing Wood every day.

Then one day a dreadful thing happened. Mother Browneyes came

running back from Wishing Wood in a terrible state, crying and groaning in distress.

'What's the matter, what's the matter?' cried the brownies.

'Oh, oh!' wept Mother Browneyes. 'I was walking in the wood this morning, when who should come up but Kookle the Wizard. And no sooner did he set eyes on pretty little Princess Peronel than he said: "Ha! I will have her marry me!" And oh, brownies, whatever shall we do? He caught her up then and there and carried her off to his castle!'

'Goodness gracious! What a terrible thing!' cried all the brownies in horror. 'Our little Princess with that horrid old wizard! Whatever can we do?'

Well, they decided to go at once to the castle and demand Peronel back. So they trooped off, scores of them, all feeling very angry but frightened too in case Kookle should turn them into beetles or frogs.

They arrived at the castle, and then of course they remembered that it had no doors. They couldn't knock because there was no knocker, and they couldn't ring because there was no bell. They just stood there wondering what in the world they could do.

'Hie! Hie!' suddenly shouted Tinker, the fat little brownie. 'Kookle! Kookle! If you're anywhere in the castle, just listen. Give us back Peronel at once!'

Suddenly the wizard appeared at a window and looked down at the brownies. He laughed loudly.

'Ho!' he cried. 'If you want Peronel, come in and get her. Ho ho ho!'

'We can't!' yelled Tinker in a rage. 'There are no doors!'

'Then go away!' said the wizard. 'If you're not all gone by the time I count ten, I'll turn you into muffinbells! Ha ha! Now – one, two, three …'

But by the time Kookle came to ten, there wasn't a single brownie to be seen. They had all fled down the hill to the town.

'We must do something,' said Tinker. 'We can't let Peronel be captured like this. But unless we find the door of the castle we can do nothing.'

'But there is no door,' said another brownie.

'There must be one that we can't see,' said Tinker. 'The wizard comes in and out, doesn't he? But by some kind of magic he has hidden it from our eyes. We must find out where it is. Then even if we can't see it we shall know where to find it and can turn the handle by feeling about for it.'

'Well, couldn't we go to the castle tonight and feel all round the walls for the door?' said the other brownies.

So that night six brownies went creeping up to the castle. But alas for them! The wizard heard them, and turned them into kittens, so that Brownie Town was in despair to see six little kittens come running back that night instead of six brownies.

Tinker sat in his cottage and thought very hard. He did so want to rescue Peronel, for he thought she was the prettiest little Princess in all Fairyland. But try as he would he could think of no plan.

Next morning when Brownie Town awoke and drew its curtains back, it saw that snow had fallen in the night and all the countryside was white.

'Hurrah!' cried the youngsters. 'Now we can build snowmen, and play with snowballs.'

Then Tinker suddenly had a wonderful idea. He tore out of his cottage to tell the others.

'We will build a big snowman in the field just outside the castle,' he said. 'The wizard will take no notice of that. But, before the moon is out, I will dress myself in a white cloak, and put on the snowman's hat. You will quickly knock down the snowman and I will take his place! Then I will stand there all night to see where the door is when the wizard comes out for his nightly walk!'

'Oh, Tinker, how clever you are!' cried the others. 'That is a wonderful plan!'

'Six of you go and make the snowman now,' said Tinker. 'Make him about my size. Laugh and talk all the time, as if you were really playing and had forgotten all about Peronel.'

So six of the brownies went to the hill on which Kookle's castle stood. The wizard peeped out of a window, but when he saw them building a snowman he took no further notice.

Before nightfall the brownies had built a nice fat snowman just about

Tinker's size. They put a row of stones down his front for buttons, and tied a muffler round his neck. They put a hat with a feather on his head, and stuck a pipe in his mouth.

Then off they went down the hill to Brownie Town. Tinker had been very busy meantime making himself a long white cloak. Mother Brown-eyes had helped him, and together they had sewn six big black buttons down the front. Now the cloak was ready.

So, in the darkness before the moon rose, the seven brownies went silently back up the hill. They quickly knocked the snowman down, and Tinker stood in its place with his long white cloak round him.

The brownies wound the snowman's muffler round his neck, put the snowman's feathered hat on his head and stuck the pipe in his mouth. He was ready!

'Ooh!' said the brownies. 'You do look like a snowman, Tinker! Well, goodbye and good luck to you! The moon is just coming up and we must go.'

They ran off down the snowy hill, and Tinker was left alone just outside the castle. He felt rather lonely and a bit frightened. Suppose the wizard guessed he wasn't a real snowman? Ooh, that would be dreadful!

The moon came up and soon Tinker could see every brick of the castle quite clearly. He stood on the hillside, hat on head, and pipe in mouth, as still as could be, his white cloak reaching down to his heels. He waited for an hour. He waited for two hours. He waited for three, and four and five. At midnight he was so cold that he was shivering.

'Oh my, I do hope the wizard won't see me shivering,' thought Tinker in a fright. 'But I can't stop shaking with the cold!'

Just at that moment the clock down in Brownie Town struck twelve. Tinker heard it – and at the same time he heard a voice inside the castle chanting a long string of magic words. Then he saw the door of the castle appearing! He saw it quite clearly, outlined in green flame, with a knocker and a handle, and a very big letter-box.

As Tinker watched, eyes wide open in surprise, he saw the door swing open. The wizard appeared in the opening, and Tinker hurriedly counted the

number of bricks from the side of the castle to the door. His heart was thumping so loudly he was afraid the wizard would hear it.

Kookle stepped outside, and at the same moment the door disappeared, the place where it had been becoming part of the wall again. Then suddenly Kookle looked towards Tinker!

'Ha, a snowman!' said the wizard. 'Silly little brownies! How they do waste their time! I've a good mind to knock it all down!'

Tinker nearly died of fright. The wizard came right up to him and snatched the pipe out of his mouth. What Kookle meant to do next Tinker didn't know – but just at that moment a witch came sailing through the air on her broomstick.

'Hey, Kookle! It's time to join the big meeting. Come along!' she called.

In a trice the wizard leapt on to the broom with the witch and sailed off into the moonlit sky. Tinker sighed with relief, for he had been very frightened. As soon as the wizard was out of sight he threw off his cloak and ran to the castle. He counted fifty-three bricks from the side, and then felt for the door.

Almost at once he found the handle and the knocker. He turned the handle and the door swung open. He stepped into the castle and shut the door.

'Peronel! Peronel!' he cried. 'Where are you?'

'Here! Here!' cried a tiny voice, far away. 'Oh, who are you? Have you come to save me? I am right at the top of the castle!'

Tinker ran to the winding staircase and raced up it, two steps at a time. He was soon breathless for there were many hundreds of stairs. But up he went, and up and up, hoping with all his heart that Kookle would not return until he had rescued the Princess.

At the top of the castle was a small tower where Peronel was imprisoned. Her door was locked and bolted, but Tinker quickly drew the big bolts back, and turned the key, which the wizard had left in the lock.

The little Princess, very pale and thin, for the wizard had given her only bread and water since she refused to marry him, ran to Tinker and flung her arms round his neck.

'Oh, you dear, brave brownie!' she cried. 'Thank you so much for saving me!'

23

'You're not saved yet!' said Tinker. 'Quick, we must get out of the castle before the wizard comes back.'

Down the hundreds of stairs they ran to the big door, which was easily seen from the inside of the castle. But Tinker couldn't open the door! No matter how he twisted the handle and pulled, that door wouldn't open! The little brownie was in despair.

For two hours he tried, but at last he gave up. Only the right magic words could open it from the inside, he realised.

'I know what we'll do!' said Tinker at last. 'It isn't a very good plan, but it might work. I expect the wizard will see that the snowman is gone and guess that I am here. He will come rushing into the castle in a fearful rage. Now I've got some string here. I'll tie it from this stool to that chair over there, and when the wizard comes in it will trip him up and perhaps we shall just have time to run out of the castle.'

'Yes, that's a good plan,' said Peronel. 'But don't let's try to run all the way down the hill to Brownie Town, because the wizard would surely catch us. Just outside is a rabbit-hole. Sandy, a very nice bunny, lives there, and I know he would let us shelter in his burrow till the danger is past.'

'That's splendid,' said Tinker. He quickly tied the string across the hall just beyond the doorway. Then he and Peronel crouched down in a dark corner near the door.

Suddenly they heard the sound of an angry voice outside. It was the wizard, who had discovered the snowman's cloak on the ground.

'What's this! What's this!' he cried in a fury. 'This is a trick! That snowman was a brownie, and he saw me come from the castle! Well, he can't get out. I'll catch him, yes, I will!'

The door flew open and the wizard rushed in. He caught his foot on the string and down he fell with a crash! The door began to close, but Peronel and Tinker slipped through in a flash. The Princess led the brownie to a rabbit-hole, and the two crept down it. The bunny came to meet them, and they explained to him in a whisper.

'Come this way,' said Sandy. He led them to a little round room, where there was a tiny fire and a jugful of cocoa warming by it. 'Help yourselves to the cocoa, and there are biscuits in that tin. I'm just going to the hillside to see what is happening. Don't be afraid. You are quite safe here.'

So Tinker poured Peronel a steaming hot cup of cocoa, and gave her some sugar-biscuits. Then he helped himself, for he was hungry and cold. They sat there, warm and happy, till Sandy the Rabbit came back.

'Ha!' said Sandy in glee. 'That old wizard is in a dreadful temper. He bumped his head when he fell down and hurt his knee. He tore down the hillside after you, for of course he didn't know you had come here. He couldn't find you, so he's gone back to his castle to bathe his head. I shouldn't be surprised to find that he leaves Brownie Town quite soon.'

All that night the brownie and Peronel stayed with the kind rabbit. Next morning they followed Sandy down many long winding underground passages that led to the bottom of the hill. There they came out into the sunshine and said goodbye to the rabbit.

What a welcome they got in Brownie Town! How all the brownies cheered! And how pleased old Mother Browneyes was to see the Princess again! It really was a very happy morning.

Just as they were all as happy as could be, listening to Tinker's adventures, there came a big BANG! Everyone rushed out to see what was happening and a very strange sight they saw!

Kookle the Wizard, having made up his mind to leave Brownie Town, had worked a spell on his castle. With a big BANG it had risen into the air and was now sailing away to the east, flapping two huge wings that had grown out of the walls.

'Ooh!' said all the brownies in surprise and joy. 'That's the end of the old wizard! He'll never come here again! Let's give a party this afternoon to show we're happy!'

So they did, and the Princess sat next to Tinker, who was happier than he had ever been in his life before. And when Peronel presented him with a lovely gold watch for saving her, you should have heard all the brownies cheer! I do wish I'd been there, don't you?

The Six Red Wizards

Once upon a time there lived six red wizards. They dwelt in a castle together, and dressed in red cloaks and red pointed hats. Their eyes, however, were as green as the eyes of cats, and it was said that all six wizards could see in the dark.

Their castle stood right in the middle of the town of Mumble, where lived many merry little folk – but since the coming of the wizards, the people of Mumble had not been quite so merry as before.

They were afraid of the red wizards. They didn't like their children to play near the castle in case their shouts annoyed the wizards. They didn't like to hold dances on the village green in case the wizards came and stopped them. They wished the wizards would go away.

But this was just what the six red wizards wouldn't do! They were very comfortable where they were, and as they were planning a great deal of magic in their castle they were not going to disturb themselves for anyone.

Now they had a servant called Fum, an ugly, bad-tempered little creature. He had served them for many years, and then, one day, when he had made them an apple pie in which he had put salt in mistake for sugar, the six wizards flew into a temper with him.

Fum let out a howl of rage, picked up the apple pie, and threw it at the wizards. It spilt all over them, and they were half blinded with hot apple juice. Whilst they were wiping their eyes, Fum ran from the room and disappeared.

They hunted all over the castle for him, but he was gone. He knew quite well that he would be turned into a blade of grass, or a dead leaf if they found him – so he had quickly caught up his little bag and off he had sped.

He was full of hate for his six unkind masters. He went into the town of Mumble, and made his way to the big house where the mayor of the town lived. He knocked at the door and asked to see him.

'His Highness will see you in ten minutes,' said the butler. Fum was taken into a little room, and there he waited for ten minutes. Then His Highness the mayor of Mumble came in, looking very grand and important.

But he didn't look so grand and important after he had heard what Fum had to say – for Fum gave away all the wizards' secrets, and frightened the mayor very much.

'The wizards are making a marvellous spell,' said Fum. 'It is nearly finished. When this spell is used, a million soldiers will spring from nothing, and at the wizards' command will march all through Fairyland, destroying every town. They cannot be stopped, for no one can kill them. They will banish the King and Queen, and make everyone their slaves. The wizards themselves will sit on six red thrones and rule the whole of Fairyland.'

'Now this is dreadful!' cried the mayor, his cheeks turning pale. 'Are you sure of this, Fum?'

'Quite,' said Fum. 'Listen, Your Highness. I will take you and three others by a secret way into the castle, and you shall peep through a hole and see the wizards at work, making soldiers out of nothing.'

So that night the mayor and three others were taken by Fum through a secret passage into the castle, and peeped through a hole in the wall. And there, sure enough, they saw one of the wizards standing in a chalk circle, chanting magic words and making soldiers appear out of nothing.

The next day the mayor called a meeting and told the townsfolk all he had seen. He sent a message to the King and Queen themselves, and soon all Fairyland was full of fear.

Then a messenger was sent all through the land proclaiming that if anyone could force the wizards to leave the country, he would be made a Prince and should marry the Princess.

Now it so happened that a wandering seller of lamps and candles heard the messenger proclaiming his news, and he marvelled to think that almost in a night a man such as he might become a Prince and marry a Princess.

The candle-seller went to a pond and looked at himself in the water. He saw looking back at him a young and merry face, with twinkling eyes, and black curly hair.

'Now,' he said, 'why should not I be the man who shall become Prince and win the lovely Princess for a wife?'

With that he made up his mind to try. He journeyed to Mumble, and soon came to the castle of the six red wizards. He stood looking over the wall, wondering what to do.

'Beware!' said an old woman, coming by. 'Over a hundred youths have tried to defeat the wizards this week – and not one of them has succeeded. Do you see that big cage in that window over there, full of birds? Well, the wizards turned each rash youth into a bird, and there they will be for the rest of their lives.'

'Well, I am going to try my luck,' said the youth, and he knocked boldly at the castle gate. It swung open and he went in, carrying his candles and his lamps with him.

He climbed a long flight of steps up to the castle door, which slowly opened as he approached it. He stepped through and found himself in a great hall. The six red wizards sat in a row at one end. The youth went up to them and bowed.

'Would you buy new lamps or candles?' he asked. 'I have come from afar to sell my wares.'

'We want no lamps or candles,' said one wizard. 'But we need a servant. Do you know anything of magic?'

'I have learnt a little,' said the youth.

'Do you work hard?' asked the second wizard.

'Yes, for I have done nothing else all the days of my life,' answered the youth.

'Then you shall be our servant,' said the third wizard.

'Wait,' said the youth. 'I am only used to serving wise and powerful masters. I do not work for weaklings. Prove to me that you are learned in magic, and I will be your servant.'

'Now this is a bold youth to talk so,' said the fifth wizard, angrily.

'Not so,' said the sixth. 'It is all the better for us if he has been used to powerful masters. He will do our bidding well.'

'Prove your power to me,' said the youth.

The wizards began to laugh among themselves, for never before had they met such a bold youth.

'Very well,' said the first one. 'We will show you what we can do.'

They meant to frighten the youth and make him sorry for his bold words, but it was difficult to make him afraid, for he had one of the bravest hearts in the world. He did not tremble when with one accord the wizards turned into roaring lions, nor did he spring back when they changed into a torrent that rushed around his feet.

Then they changed into spiders and began to weave a web round him – but the youth laughed in scorn. They turned into eagles and flapped their wings about his head, but he only smiled. Last of all they made themselves very small and then suddenly very big – but not a shiver or a tremble could they get from the brave candle-seller.

'Ho!' he said, when the six wizards stood once more in front of him. 'That is quite good magic you did – but it is easy to work the magic that you know. Do three things that I command you, and I will be your servant.'

The six wizards frowned.

'What are your three things?' they demanded. 'Have a care lest you try us too far, bold youth. You will perhaps find yourself in the cage with those birds yonder before very long.'

'Then you will lose a good servant,' said the youth. 'Now these are my three tests. First, can you make yourselves invisible?'

The wizards laughed scornfully. They spread out their hands, said a curious magic word, and lo and behold! They had disappeared! Their chairs were empty!

'Very clever!' said the youth. The wizards suddenly appeared again, and sat down in their chairs.

'What is your second test?' asked they.

'The second test is – multiply yourselves by three!' said the youth. In a trice the wizards had turned into eighteen, and surrounded the youth in a ring. He didn't turn a hair, but waved his hand to tell them to become six again.

'Now your last test,' said the wizards.

'Ah!' said the youth. 'This is a test that but few wizards can do.'

He set out six candles in candlesticks on a table. 'Now,' said he, 'turn yourselves into the six flames of my candles!'

With a scornful laugh the wizards disappeared, and in a trice six red flames appeared at the top of the six candles, burning steadily.

'Ha!' said the youth mockingly. 'Very clever!' Then, lightly and easily, he blew at each candle in turn. Puff! Out went one flame. Puff! Out went another. Puff! Out went a third. Puff! Puff! Puff! Out went the fourth, fifth and sixth – and where were the six wizards? Gone out with the candle-flames! They had had no time to take their own shape again, and they were blown out for good.

To this day no one has ever heard of them again.

'Ho ho!' laughed the youth. 'That's the end of the red wizards! Now this castle is mine and all the treasure in it! Tomorrow I shall be made a Prince and the lovely Princess will be mine!'

Then he noticed that the birds in the cage were all clamouring to be set free. He opened the cage door and they flew out. No sooner were they free than each bird disappeared and became the young man he had been before. Then one and all crowded round the youth, and swore to be his faithful servants.

What merry-making there was in the town of Mumble and in the whole of Fairyland that night! The news flew from place to place, and the King and Queen came themselves in great state to see the wonderful youth who had defeated the six powerful wizards.

And next day the wedding bells rang out merrily, for the Princess herself came to marry the youth. When she saw his twinkling eyes and black curly hair she was glad, and smiled at him. He smiled gaily at his lovely bride, and so with glad hearts they were married, and lived happily ever after.

Magic in the Afternoon

Jeffrey had had a most exciting birthday present. It was a box of conjuring tricks of all kinds. When he took the lid off the box he stared in delight at all the things inside.

'Mother! Can I do proper conjuring with these?' he asked. 'Like the conjurer I saw last Christmas at Uncle's party? He put an egg into a bag, then turned the bag inside out and the egg wasn't there any more, do you remember? And he took a shilling out of my ear. I was awfully surprised.'

'Well – you will have to practise very, very hard if you want to do the tricks properly,' said his mother. 'Magic isn't easy, you know. I don't know if you will be able to do good conjuring – but you can try!'

Jeffrey picked up a little book inside the box. It was called 'Magic Made Easy. How to be a Good Magician and Conjure for Others.' His eyes shone as he opened it and looked inside.

'It tells you how to do all the tricks,' he said. 'It even gives magic words to use. Mother, this is the finest present I've ever had. Do you know what I shall do? I shall give a Grand Show as soon as I have learnt to do this magic, and charge threepence a time for people to come to it – and give the money to buy presents for children in hospital! You're always saying I ought to give my old toys to them, but I'd like to buy new ones.'

'Well, we'll see,' said his mother. 'If you can master all the conjuring tricks in that big box, you will really be very clever!'

Jeffrey certainly meant to. He took the box into the garden that afternoon, and began to read the booklet and try to do what it said. He practised waving the wand, and saying a few of the words in the book.

Soon the gardener came up and laughed. 'Ho!' he said. 'What are you doing – making magic to bring me some nice rain for the garden?'

Jeffrey couldn't learn magic when the gardener stood and watched him. He put the things back into the box and went indoors. But his sister Janet was there, and she wanted to learn magic, too, which was a nuisance.

So the next day he made up his mind to take his box of conjuring tricks into the wood, and find a place that was quiet and lonely. Then he could say his magic words and practise wand-waving and tricks as much as he liked.

So, with his box under his arm he went into the green wood, and took a little rabbit-path away to the left. He walked on and on until he came to a quiet, little glade, with three or four big oak trees around.

He sat down on the grass and opened his box. He took out the booklet and began to read it again. He muttered one word over and over and over to get it right.

'Abracadabra, abracadabra.' That was the first word you had to say when you began conjuring. Jeffrey stood up with his wand in his hand, and the little black bag in which he had to put a china egg, just as he had seen the conjurer do at his uncle's party. Now – he had to make the egg disappear. He knew how to, because the bag had an inner pocket, and he just had to slip the egg into it, turn the bag upside down and shake it – and the egg didn't fall out, because it was safely held in the pocket that nobody could see.

'And, as you see,' recited Jeffrey to the trees around, 'er – as you see – the egg, ladies and gentlemen, has completely disappeared!'

He shook the bag again so that it could be seen that no egg was falling out – but alas, the egg did fall out. 'Blow!' said Jeffrey, picking it up. 'I'll have to begin all over again.'

He certainly worked very hard, and it was soon quite plain that it was going to be very, very difficult to be a good conjurer. He put all his things away at last, feeling quite tired.

'I'll come again tomorrow and the next day and the next,' he thought. 'I won't give up – though I've a kind of feeling I'll never be a really good conjurer!'

He was back in the woods again the next day, and the next, as he had planned. He managed the egg trick a little better, but the card tricks were very, very difficult. The cards slid out of his hands so easily and he kept having to pick them up and begin all over again.

'People will laugh at me, they won't clap me,' thought Jeffrey. 'Oh dear – I wish I knew some real magic to help me. Now then – I'll begin properly.'

He stood up straight and waved his wand solemnly. 'Ladies and gentlemen, I am about to work some powerful magic for you. First, let me say the magic words that bring the magic into this wand of mine. Abracadabra, abracadabra, ab–'

He was interrupted by a most exasperated voice. 'This is the third afternoon you've disturbed my nap. For goodness' sake go somewhere else with your silly, old-fashioned magic!'

Jeffrey turned round to where the voice came from, and then stood still in the utmost astonishment. A small door in the nearby oak-tree stood open and a little fellow dressed like a goblin or brownie, stood there, his long beard waving about in the breeze.

He frowned at Jeffrey. 'You and your abracadabra! That's out of date now, surely you know that! Who are you? A young wizard?'

'Er – no. No, I'm not,' said Jeffrey, extremely startled, and wondering if by any chance he was dreaming. 'I'm a boy.'

'I can see that,' said the little fellow. 'But what sort of a boy? You don't look like any kind of goblin or imp. And why come and practise magic here?'

'I'm just a boy,' said Jeffrey, 'and I came here because it is quiet.'

'And I live here because it's quiet – at least it was till you came,' said the cross, little man. 'I'm Bron the Brownie. Have you got to practise magic here? What a silly wand that is! Don't tell me it's magic!'

'Well – it isn't really,' said Jeffrey. 'You see, I'm just trying to learn some conjuring tricks – so I have to have a wand even though it's not really magic.'

'I don't understand all this,' said Bron, pulling at his long beard. 'Why don't you do what we did in my young day – go and learn magic from some good wizard?'

'Ooooh – I'd like to!' said Jeffrey, startled. 'But I didn't know any wizards. I didn't even know there were any left.'

'You are really a most ignorant young fellow,' said the brownie. 'Now look here – if I direct you to a perfectly good wizard I know, will you please stop coming here and waking me up every afternoon with your abracadabra?'

'Yes!' said Jeffrey, perfectly sure now that he was dreaming. Still, he might as well go and see a dream wizard if he could – he might even learn something from him that he would find very useful when he woke up. 'Where does a wizard live?' he asked.

'Come in here,' said Bron, beckoning him to his tree. 'Leave your box there. It'll be safe enough. Now, look – here's my little, round room – it's my sitting-room, and up those stairs is my bedroom. Down those stairs in the corner is a way that goes from this tree underground.'

Jeffrey was too thrilled to say a word. He looked at the small, round room, and then down the stairs that the brownie pointed out to him.

'Go down there, and you'll find yourself in a long passage,' said Bron. 'Pass all the doors till you come to one with a lamp that burns blue then green. Knock at the door and say Bron sent you to learn a bit of magic. That's all.'

'But – who lives there – why – er – what shall I do then – er – do I …' began Jeffrey, feeling rather alarmed.

'Don't make such a fuss!' said Bron. 'I'm sending you to old Wizard Wily. He won't hurt you – he'll tell you a lot of things that will help you – so hurry now and go, because I want to finish my nap. And if I'm asleep when you come back, I warn you, don't wake me, or I'll chase you out of the wood!'

He pushed Jeffrey to the steps. The boy ran down them and came to a dark and winding passage between the tough old roots of the great oak-tree. He went cautiously along it, and came to a door. It had a notice on it. 'Knock once for Mr Cool and three times for Mr Hot.'

This seemed very extraordinary, and Jeffrey was glad he hadn't to knock. He went on and came to another little door that had a small, glass window at the top. Jeffrey peeped through it. He saw a most astonishing sight.

A fire burnt in the room behind the door, all by itself on the bare floor, and as it burnt, strange flowers grew from its flames, and died down and then grew once more. A little pixie-like creature came out of a corner and picked them now and again, and sang a sad, little song as she made them into posies. She suddenly caught sight of Jeffrey looking through the window and pointed her finger at him.

'Peeper!' she cried. 'Peeper!'

Jeffrey fled down the passage at once. He passed three more doors with strange names on them and then came to one that had a little lamp above it, whose flames burnt now blue and now green. Below was a notice.

'Knock for the Wizard. Come in!'

Jeffrey saw a small knocker and knocked. To his horror it made such a loud noise that the knocking echoed all down the passage and back. But nobody answered from inside the door. Jeffrey pushed it open and went inside.

He saw the wizard at once. He sat on a stool and read a most enormous book. He looked up at Jeffrey.

'Oh. So you've come,' he said. 'Sit down. Who sent you?'

'Er – Bron the Brownie, sir,' said Jeffrey. 'To learn a little magic. I – er – I hope I haven't come at an awkward time.'

'Well, I'm expecting my great-great-grandfather at any moment,' said the wizard, who looked like a great-great-great-one himself. 'But I can spare you a minute. Now – where have you got to in the study of magic? Do you want to be a very powerful magician, or just an ordinary one?'

'Well, actually I only want to be able to do a few conjuring tricks,' said Jeffrey. 'I don't know any magic words except abracadabra, I'm afraid.'

'My poor fellow, you are very, very ignorant,' said the wizard. 'Dear, dear – what are things coming to in these days? When I was your age, about five hundred years ago, I could make a dragon come roaring down any chimney, I could take the lightning from the sky and use it to boil my kettle, I could make – but there, what's the use of telling you all this? Look, I'm expecting my very old grand-parent, as I said, so I think I'll just give you a small magic wand, and teach you three magic words. Will that do? The wand will do more or less what you want it to if you blow on it first – like this.'

He took up a little wand and blew down it as if it were a flute. 'There – now take it and wish something!'

Jeffrey took it in trembling fingers. 'I – I wish I wasn't scared!' he said. And hey presto, his fright fell away at once and he was able to smile at the wizard.

'Hm. Quite sensible,' said the wizard. 'Now I'll whisper a few magic words. I can't say them out loud because they're too magic. You only want to use them when you need them. Now – this one makes things vanish. Very useful for conjuring tricks of course.'

He whispered a word so magic that it almost burnt the boy's ear. Then he whispered another that was as cold as ice.

'That word will bring things back after you've made them vanish,' he said. 'And this one will change one thing into another – people always like that, you know.'

He whispered again, and Jeffrey felt himself tremble a little. He looked down in alarm – had the word changed him into anything strange. No – he was still the same!

Just at that moment there was a crash at the door, and a loud voice shouted, making Jeffrey jump almost out of his skin. 'Hey, Wily! Old Gran-Pop's come! Get your visitor out of the way, or I'll change him into a chair and sit on him!'

'Quick – wish yourself away!' said the wizard and pushed the little wand into Jeffrey's hand. The boy wished at once. 'I wish myself back in the wood!'

The room went dark. A whistling sound came like the noise of winds in a storm. Jeffrey covered his head in fright. The noise died away and he looked up cautiously, expecting he didn't quite know what. Was he still in the Wizard's little room? Would the old, old Gran-Pop be there?

No. Nobody was there. He was alone in the wood again, and sunshine was filtering between the trees. Before him was his box of conjuring tricks, open as he had left it. Jeffrey blinked in the bright sunshine and looked all round. Which was the tree that had the little door? He had forgotten! He took up the little wand beside him. Was this the one that the Wizard had given him? Yes, it must be, because the other wand lay in the box. Then it HADN'T been a dream? What were those magic words?

He began to try them out on his tongue and stopped suddenly. He didn't want to wake that cross, old brownie again – though he would have liked to thank him for sending him to the wizard. A glow of excitement crept through Jeffrey. He had a magic wand! He knew magic words! He could give the most wonderful conjuring show in the world.

'Quick! I must get home and write down those words before I forget them!' thought Jeffrey. 'And I mustn't use the wand too much in case I wear out the magic. Oh, what an afternoon! Nobody will believe me if I tell them – but just wait till I give my show – then EVERYONE will believe me!'

And off he went with his box of conjuring tricks, and the tiny wand. I wish he'd lend it to me for just one minute. Oh to have Real Magic – the lucky, lucky boy!

The Wizard's Umbrella

Ribby the Gnome lived in a small cottage at the end of Tiptoe Village. Nobody liked him because he was always borrowing things and never bringing them back! It was most annoying of him.

The things he borrowed most were umbrellas. I really couldn't tell you how many umbrellas Ribby had borrowed in his life – hundreds, I should think! He had borrowed Dame Twinkle's nice red one, he had taken Mr. Biscuit the Baker's old green one, he had had Pixie Dimple's little grey and pink sunshade, and many, many more.

If people came to ask for them back, he would hunt all about and then say he was very sorry but he must have lent their umbrellas to someone else – he certainly hadn't got them in his cottage now. And no one would ever know what had happened to their nice umbrellas!

Of course, Ribby the Gnome knew quite well where they were! They were all tied up tightly together hidden in his loft. And once a month, Ribby would set out on a dark night, when nobody was about, and take with him all the borrowed umbrellas. He would go to the town of Here-we-are, a good many miles away, and then the next day he would go through the streets there, crying: 'Umbrellas for sale! Fine umbrellas!'

He would sell the whole bundle, and make quite a lot of money. Then the wicked gnome would buy himself some fine new clothes, and perhaps a new chair or some new curtains for his cottage and go home again.

Now one day it happened that Dame Twinkle went over to the town of Here-we-are, and paid a call on her cousin, Mother Tantrums. And there standing in the umbrella-stand in Mother Tantrum's hall, Dame Twinkle saw her very own nice red umbrella, that she had lent to Ribby the Gnome the month before!

She stared at it in great surprise. However did it come to be in her cousin's umbrella-stand? Surely she hadn't lent it to Mother Tantrums? No, no – she was certain, quite certain, she had lent it to Ribby the Gnome.

'What are you staring at?' asked Mother Tantrums in surprise.

'Well,' said Dame Twinkle, pointing to the red umbrella, 'it's a funny thing, Cousin Tantrums, but, you know, that's my red umbrella you've got in your umbrella-stand.'

'Nonsense!' said Mother Tantrums. 'Why, that's an umbrella I bought for a shilling from a little gnome who often comes round selling things.'

'A shilling!' cried Dame Twinkle in horror. 'My goodness, gracious me, I

paid sixteen shillings and ninepence for it! A shilling, indeed! What next!'

'What are you talking about?' asked Mother Tantrums, quite cross. 'It's my umbrella, not yours – and a very good bargain it was, too!'

'I should think so!' said Dame Twinkle, looking lovingly at the red umbrella, which she had been very fond of indeed. 'Tell me, Cousin, what sort of a gnome was this that sold you your umbrella?'

'Oh, he was short and rather fat,' said Mother Tantrums.

'Lots of gnomes are short and fat,' said Dame Twinkle. 'Can't you remember anything else about him?'

'Well, he wore a bright yellow scarf round his neck,' said Mother Tantrums, 'and his eyes were a very light green.'

'That's Ribby the Gnome!' cried Dame Twinkle, quite certain. 'He always wears a yellow scarf, and his eyes are a very funny green. Oh, the wicked scamp! I suppose he borrows our umbrellas in order to sell them when he can! Oh, the horrid little thief! I shall tell the wizard who lives in our village and ask him to punish Ribby. Yes, I will! He deserves a very nasty punishment indeed!'

So when she went back to Tiptoe Village, Dame Twinkle went to call on the Wizard Deep-one. He was a great friend of hers, and when he heard about Ribby's wickedness he shook his head in horror.

'He must certainly be punished,' said the wizard, nodding his head. 'Leave it to me, Dame Twinkle. I will see to it.'

Deep-one thought for a long time, and then he smiled. Ha, he would lay a little trap for Ribby that would teach him never to borrow umbrellas again. He took a spell and with it he made a very fine umbrella indeed. It was deep blue, and for a handle it had a dog's head. It was really a marvellous umbrella.

The wizard put it into his umbrella-stand and then left his front door open wide every day so that anyone passing by could see the dog's-head umbrella quite well. He was sure that Ribby the Gnome would spy it the very first time he came walking by.

When Ribby did see the umbrella he stopped to have a good look at it. My, what a lovely umbrella! He hadn't noticed it before, so it must be a new one. See the dog's head on it, it looked almost real! Oh, if Ribby could only get that umbrella, he could sell it for a for a good many shillings in the town of Here-we-are. He was sure that the enchanter who lived there would be very pleased to buy it.

'Somehow or other I must get that umbrella,' thought Ribby. 'The very next time it rains I will hurry by the wizard's house, and pop in and ask him to lend it to me! I don't expect he will, but I'll ask, anyway!'

So on the Thursday following, when a rainstorm came, Ribby hurried out of his cottage without an umbrella and ran to Deep-one's house. The front door was wide open as usual and Ribby could quite well see the dog-headed umbrella in the hall-stand. He ran up the path, and knocked at the open door.

'Who's there?' came the wizard's voice.

'It's me, Ribby the Gnome!' said the gnome. 'Please, Wizard Deep-one, could you lend me an umbrella? It's pouring with rain and I am getting so wet. I am sure I shall get a dreadful cold if someone doesn't lend me an umbrella.'

'Dear, dear, dear!' said the wizard, coming out of his parlour, and looking at the wet gnome. 'You certainly are very wet! Yes, I will lend you an umbrella – but mind, Ribby, let me warn you to bring it back tomorrow in case something unpleasant happens to you.'

'Oh, of course, of course,' said Ribby. 'I always return things I borrow, Wizard. You shall have it back tomorrow as sure as eggs are eggs.'

'Well, take that one from the hall-stand, Ribby,' said the wizard, pointing to the dog's-head umbrella. Ribby took it in delight. He had got what he wanted. How easy it had been after all! He, ho, he wouldn't bring it back tomorrow, not he! He would take it to the town of Here-we-are as soon as ever he could and sell it to the enchanter there. What luck!

He opened it, said thank you to the smiling wizard, and rushed down the path with the blue umbrella. He was half afraid the wizard would call him back – but no, Deep-one let him go without a word – but he chuckled very deeply as he saw the gnome vanishing round the corner. How easily Ribby had fallen into the trap!

Of course Ribby didn't take the umbrella back next day. No, he put it up in his loft and didn't go near the wizard's house at all. If he saw the wizard in the street he would pop into a shop until he had gone by. He wasn't going to let him have his umbrella back for a moment!

Now after three weeks had gone by, and Ribby had heard nothing from the wizard about his umbrella, he decided it would be safe to go to Here-we-are and sell it.

'I expect the wizard has forgotten all about it by now,' thought Ribby. 'He is very forgetful.'

So that night Ribby packed up three other umbrellas, and tied the wizard's dog-headed one to them very carefully. Then he put the bundle over his shoulder and set out in the darkness. Before morning came he was in the town of Here-we-are, and the folk there heard him crying out his wares in a loud voice.

'Umbrellas for sale! Fine umbrellas for sale! Come and buy!'

Ribby easily sold the other three umbrellas he had with him and then he made his way to the enchanter's house. The dog-headed umbrella was now the only one left.

The enchanter came to the door and looked at the umbrella that Ribby showed him. But as soon as his eye fell on it he drew back in horror.

'Buy that umbrella!' he cried. 'Not I! Why, it's alive!'

'Alive!' said Ribby, laughing scornfully. 'No, sir, it is as dead as a door-nail!'

'I tell you, that umbrella is alive!' said the enchanter and he slammed the door in the astonished gnome's face.

Ribby looked at the dog-headed umbrella, feeling very much puzzled – and as he looked, a very strange feeling came over him. The dog's head really did look alive. It wagged one ear as Ribby looked at it, and then it showed its teeth at the gnome and growled fiercely!

My goodness! Ribby was frightened almost out of his life! He dropped the umbrella on to the ground and fled away as fast as his fat little legs would carry him!

As soon as the umbrella touched the ground a very peculiar thing happened to it. It grew four legs, and the head became bigger. The body was made of the long umbrella part, and the tail was the end bit. It could even wag!

'Oh, oh, an umbrella-dog!' cried all the people of Here-we-are town and they fled away in fright. But the strange dog took no notice of anyone but Ribby the Gnome. He galloped after him, barking loudly.

His umbrella-body flapped as he went along on his stout little doggy legs, and his tongue hung out of his mouth. It was most astonishing. People looked out of their windows at it, and everyone closed their front doors with a bang in case the strange umbrella-dog should come running into their houses.

Ribby was dreadfully frightened. He ran on and on, and every now and then he looked round.

'Oh, my goodness, that umbrella-dog's still after me!' he panted. 'What shall I do? Oh, why, why, why did I borrow the wizard's umbrella? Why didn't I take it back? I might have known there would be something odd about it!'

The umbrella-dog raced on, and came so near to Ribby that it was able to snap at his twinkling legs. Snap! The dog's sharp teeth took a piece out of Ribby's green trousers!

'Ow! Ooh! Ow!' shrieked Ribby in horror, and he shot on twice as fast, panting like a railway train going up a hill! Everybody watched from their windows and some of them laughed because it was really a very peculiar sight.

Ribby looked out for someone to open a door so that he could run in. But every single door was shut. He must just run on and on. But how much longer could he run? He was getting terribly out of breath.

The umbrella-dog was enjoying himself very much. Ho, this was better fun than being a dull old umbrella! This was seeing life! If only he could catch that nasty little running thing in front, what fun he would have!

The umbrella-dog ran a bit faster and caught up Ribby once more. This time he jumped up and bit a piece out of the gnome's lovely yellow scarf. Then he jumped again and nipped a tiny piece out of Ribby's leg.

'OW!' yelled Ribby, jumping high into the air. 'OW! You horrid cruel dog! Leave me alone! How dare you, I say? Wait till I get home and find a whip!'

The dog sat down to chew the piece he had bitten out of Ribby's yellow scarf, and the gnome ran on, hoping that the dog would forget about him.

'Oh, if only I could get home!' cried the panting gnome. 'Once I'm in my house I'm safe!'

He ran on and on, through the wood and over the common that lay between the town of Here-we-are and the village of Tiptoe. The dog did not seem to be following him. Ribby kept looking round but there was no umbrella-dog there. If only he could get home in time!

Just as he got to Tiptoe Village he heard a pattering of feet behind him. He looked round and saw the umbrella-dog just behind him. Oh, what a shock for poor Ribby!

'Look, look!' cried everyone in surprise. 'There's a mad umbrella-dog after Ribby. Run, Ribby, run!'

Poor Ribby had to run all through the village of Tiptoe to get to his cottage. The dog ran at his heels snapping every now and again, making the gnome leap high into the air with pain and fright.

'I'll never, never, never borrow an umbrella again, or anything else!' vowed the gnome, as the dog nipped his heel with his sharp teeth. 'Oh, why didn't I take the wizard's umbrella back?'

At last he was home. He rushed up the path, pushed the door open and slammed it. But, alas, the umbrella-dog had slipped in with him, and there it was in front of Ribby, sitting up and begging.

'Oh, you horror!' shouted Ribby, trying to open the door and get out again. But the dog wouldn't let him. Every time Ribby put his hand on the handle of the door it jumped up and nipped him. So at last he stopped trying to open it and looked in despair at the strange dog, who was now sitting up and begging.

'Do you want something to eat?' said the gnome. 'Goodness, I shouldn't have thought an umbrella-dog could be hungry. Wait a bit. I've a nice joint of meat here, you shall have that, if only you will stop snapping at me!'

The dog ran by Ribby as he went hurriedly to his larder and opened the door. He took a joint of meat from a dish and gave it to the dog, which crunched it up hungrily.

Then began a very sorrowful time for Ribby! The dog wouldn't leave him for a moment and the gnome had never in his life known such a hungry creature. Although its body was simply an umbrella, it ate and ate and ate. Ribby spent all his money on food for it, and in the days that came, often went hungry himself. The dog wouldn't leave his side, and when the gnome went out shopping the strange creature always went with him, much to the surprise and amusement of all the people in the village.

'Look!' they would cry. 'Look! There goes Ribby the gnome and his umbrella-dog! Where did he get it from? Why does he keep such a strange, hungry creature?'

If Ribby tried to creep off at night, or run away from the dog, it would at once start snapping and snarling at his heels, and after it had nibbled a bit out of his leg once or twice and bitten a large hole in his best coat, Ribby gave up trying to go away.

'But what shall I do?' wondered the little gnome, each night, as he looked at his empty larder. 'This dog is eating everything I have. I shall soon have no money left to buy anything.'

Ribby had had such a shock when the stolen umbrella had turned into the umbrella-dog, that he had never once thought of borrowing anything else. He felt much too much afraid that what he borrowed would turn into something like the dog, and he really couldn't bear that!

'I suppose I'd better get some work to do,' he said to himself at last. 'But who will give me a job? Nobody likes me because I have always borrowed things and never taken them back. Oh dear, how foolish and silly I have been.'

Then at last he thought he had better go to the Wizard Deep-one and confess to him all that had happened. Perhaps Deep-one would take away the horrid umbrella-dog and then Ribby would feel happier. So off he went to the wizard's house.

The wizard opened the door himself and when he saw Ribby with the dog he began to laugh. How he laughed! He held his sides and roared till the tears ran down his cheeks.

'What's the matter?' asked Ribby, in surprise. 'What is the joke?'

'You are!' cried the wizard, laughing more than ever. 'Ho, ho, Ribby, little did you think that I had made that dog-headed umbrella especially for you to borrow and that I knew exactly what was going to happen! Well, you can't say that I didn't warn you. My only surprise is that you haven't come to me before for help. You can't have liked having such a strange umbrella-dog living with you, eating all your food, and snapping at your heels every moment! But it's a good punishment for you – you won't borrow things and not bring them back again, I'm sure!'

'I never, never will,' said Ribby, going very red. 'I am very sorry for all the wrong things I have done. Perhaps I had better keep this umbrella-dog to remind me to be honest, Wizard.'

'No, I'll have it,' said Deep-one. 'It will do to guard my house for me. I think any burglar would run for miles if he suddenly saw the umbrella-dog coming for him. And what are you going to do, Ribby? Have you any work?'

'No,' said Ribby, sorrowfully. 'Nobody likes me and I'm sure no one will give me any work to do in case I borrow something and don't return it, just as I used to do.'

'Well, well, well,' said the wizard, and his wrinkled eyes looked kindly at the sad little gnome. 'You have learned your lesson, Ribby, I can see. Come and be my gardener and grow my vegetables. I shall work you hard, but I shall pay you well, and I think you will be happy.'

So Ribby is now Deep-one's gardener, and he works hard from morning to night. But he is happy because everyone likes him now – and as for the umbrella-dog, he is as fond of Ribby as anyone else is and keeps at his heels all the time. And the funny thing is that Ribby likes him there!

Animal Magic

The Dog That Went to Fairyland

Once upon a time Peter and Peggy went for a walk in Bluebell Wood. They took their little dog Scamper with them. He was so pleased.

'I shall hunt for rabbits!' he wuffed. 'Nice big fluffy rabbits! I know where they live – down those big holes in the wood.' Scamper always hunted for rabbits in the wood. He put his nose down every hole he came to, scraped very hard, and was very excited.

The children walked happily through the wood. Scamper ran to a very large rabbit-hole and sniffed down it. 'Rabbits!' he barked. 'Down I go!'

And down he went, because the hole really was very large indeed. 'He's gone right down!' said Peggy in surprise. 'Scamper, Scamper, come back!'

Scamper came back, with something in his mouth. Was it a rabbit? No – it wasn't a rabbit. What could it be? The children stared very hard indeed. Then Peggy gave a loud squeal.

'It's a pixie! Scamper has caught a pixie, a real live pixie!'

So he had. The children could hardly believe their eyes when they saw the tiny fairy wriggling hard to get away. Scamper was holding her quite gently in his mouth, but he would not let her go.

'Let me go, let me go!' squealed the pixie angrily. 'You bad, naughty dog, let me go! How dare you catch me like this!'

'Scamper, let the pixie go at once!' said Peter. But Scamper wouldn't! He didn't know he had got a pixie – he thought it was some kind of strange animal. The pixie flew into a temper. 'You're hurting me! Your teeth are digging into me. Let me go, you bad dog, or I'll change you into an earwig!'

'Oh, don't do that,' said Peggy, at once. 'We're very, very fond of Scamper. Keep still, little pixie, and I'll make Scamper let you go.'

Then Peggy took hold of Scamper's mouth and made him open it. Out fell the pixie to the ground. She jumped up at once, still very angry.

'I won't change him into an earwig, but I'm going to punish him somehow!' said the pixie. 'I shall make him very small, and take him off to Fairyland with me! He shall be my prisoner.'

She gave Scamper three light taps with her hand and called out some magic words, that sounded exactly like 'Rikka, rikka, ree, roona, roona, rye!'

And at once Scamper became very small indeed, far smaller than the pixie! She took off her belt, slipped it through his collar – and disappeared down the rabbit-hole with him. Scamper was gone!

'Oh!' cried Peggy, almost in tears, 'did you see that, Peter? The pixie made him small, and now she's taken him away to Fairyland. We shall never, never see dear Scamper again. And I did love him so.'

'It's dreadful,' said Peter. 'And it wasn't really his fault either – he didn't know he had caught a pixie. Oh, poor Scamper – whatever shall we do? I don't see how we can rescue him.'

'Peter,' said Peggy, rubbing her eyes with her hanky, – 'Peter, do you suppose we could go down that rabbit-hole after the pixie? Could we make ourselves small too?'

Peter stared in excitement at Peggy. 'Oh, Peggy – I believe we could! Do you remember those words? What were they?'

'I remember them quite well,' said Peggy. 'Now listen – we'll each give the other three light taps – just like the pixie gave Scamper – and say the magic words at the same time. Then maybe we'll grow small and be able to go down the rabbit-hole. Now – are you ready?'

They each tapped the other, and said the words they had heard the pixie use – 'Rikka, rikka, ree, roona, roona rye!'

And hey presto, they grew so small that even the bluebells beside them were a little taller than they were! 'Now – down the hole we go!' cried Peggy. And down they went.

It was dark down the rabbit-hole. The children ran down it, and then came to a long flight of steps, which surprised them very much. 'It isn't a real rabbit-hole,' said Peggy. 'It must be one of the ways into Fairyland! How exciting, Peter!'

They went down the steps, which were lighted with curious star-shaped lamps hung from the roof. Then they came out into a long, winding passage.

They met a worm, which scared them very much by pushing past them rather rudely.

'Goodness! I thought that worm was a perfectly enormous snake,' said Peter. 'It will be funny to meet animals and insects as big as ourselves!'

'I wish we could meet someone and ask them if they have seen Scamper,' said Peggy. 'Oh, goodness – what's that noise?'

'It sounds like a train!' said Peter, puzzled. 'Oh, look – it really is a train! See, it is stopping in this cave – there is a sort of platform for it!'

Sure enough, a strange-looking train puffed into the cave where the children now stood. It really looked more like a toy train than a proper one. A brownie came up to the children.

'Tickets!' he said. But they hadn't got any.

'We are looking for a pixie and a little dog,' said Peggy. 'Have you seen them?'

'Yes,' said the brownie. 'They caught the train before this. The pixie took a ticket to Toadstool Town.'

'Toadstool Town!' said Peggy. 'Oooh – I would like to see Toadstool Town! Can we take tickets there too?'

'Of course,' said the brownie, and he handed them two enormous yellow tickets. 'Nothing to pay.'

'Oh, thank you,' said Peter. They took the tickets and the brownie went off to give a ticket to a fat little rabbit who had just come on to the platform, dressed in a coat and trousers. It was really very surprising to see him, and to hear him talking.

'We'd better get into the train,' said Peter, so they got into an open carriage with no roof. There was a goblin there, reading a newspaper, a sleepy dormouse, a large rabbit, and a snake who curled himself up into a neat pile. It was funny to travel in a train with such strange passengers.

The train gave a whistle and set off, puffing hard. It ran through tunnels and caves, and at last came out in the open air.

'Fairyland!' cried the children, in delight. 'Oh, Fairyland! Look at the fairies and pixies and goblins and brownies!'

It really was Fairyland. Fairy folk were everywhere, some walking and some flying. It was really most exciting.

The train stopped at a station. 'Pixie Corner! Pixie Corner!' shouted a porter. He was a mouse, and he looked very smart in his porter's uniform.

'We don't get out here,' said Peggy. 'Off we go again. I say, isn't this fun, Peter?'

It certainly was. The train went on through Fairyland, passing pixie villages, fairy palaces with shining towers, little crooked houses, and dear little shops. The children stared in delight.

Then the train ran into a busy market-place and stopped. 'All change! All change!' cried the porter, who this time was a green goblin.

'But we are going to Toadstool Town!' said Peter to the goblin.

'Sorry,' said the goblin. 'You got into the wrong train. This doesn't go any farther. It just turns round and goes back. Take a magic boat. It will sail you off to Toadstool Town all right.'

The children wandered into the fairy market-place. Oh, the things that were sold there! Spells and charms of all kinds! Spells to make you beautiful, spells to make you happy. Magic in a bottle that would make the time go fast or slow, whichever you wished.

All kinds of lovely things were sold in that market by fairies, pixies and goblins. What a noise there was! How they all shouted their wares, and tried to make the children buy!

The children had no money, so they couldn't buy anything in that wonderful market. What a pity!

'We mustn't stay any longer,' said Peggy, at last, after they had watched a doll that could really walk and talk. 'We must find a boat that goes to Toadstool Town.'

A goblin told them where the magic boats were. 'Walk down River Road, and you will see the Blue River at the end,' he said. 'The boats are there. Take which you like.'

This sounded exciting. The children ran down River Road, and there, at the end, was the Blue River, shining and gleaming. It was as blue as forget-me-nots in spring. There were some funny boats there, all in the shape of birds or animals. There was one like a swan, which Peggy liked very much.

'Let's have this one!' she said, and they got in. There were no oars. How did they sail the boat?

'Where to?' said the boat, quite suddenly, and the head of the swan turned round and looked at them.

'Oh – you made me jump, swan-boat!' said Peggy. 'To Toadstool Town, please!'

The swan-boat sailed off down the Blue River. It floated beautifully.

They passed fields of gleaming flowers. They smelt a hundred lovely scents. They saw crowds of fairy-folk flying all around. It was a lovely trip, down the Blue River in the magic boat!

'Look!' cried Peggy, after about half an hour. 'Look, Peter! We are coming to Toadstool Town!'

So they were. The swan-boat floated gently to a tiny wooden pier, and the children got out. 'Thank you,' said Peggy.

'It was a pleasure!' said the swan-boat, turning its head on its graceful neck. Off it went down the Blue River again.

'What a funny place Toadstool Town is!' said Peter. 'All the houses are toadstools!'

'Yes,' said Peggy, in delight. 'Look, the rooms are in the tops of the great big toadstools – and the door is in the stalk! Oh Peter, I do so badly want to go inside a toadstool house!'

'Well, we'll knock at a door and ask if anyone knows where the pixie lives that took Scamper away,' said Peter. So he went up to a neat little toadstool house, which had blue curtains and a blue knocker. He knocked loudly.

'Come in!' cried a voice. Peter opened the little narrow door in the stalk, and saw a tiny staircase leading upwards. In great delight the children went up. They came into an odd-shaped room at the top part of the toadstool. A fairy was there, mending some stockings.

'Oh please excuse us disturbing you,' said Peggy, politely, 'but could you tell us where the pixie lives that has stolen our little dog away?'

'Oh, you mean Silver-Wings,' said the fairy. 'She has gone to the castle of Santa Claus to sell the dog to him!'

'Oh, dear!' said Peter in dismay. 'Why does she want to do that?'

'I expect Santa Claus will turn him into a toy dog and put him into his Christmas sack to give away to someone at Christmas,' said the fairy, darning away busily.

'Oh, he mustn't do that!' cried Peter, in alarm. 'He is our own little dog. He mustn't be given away. Oh quick, tell us where Santa Claus lives and we will go and ask him for Scamper before he turns him into a toy!'

'Well, go through Toadstool Town, and you will see a steep hill in the distance,' said the fairy. 'At the top is a big castle, with an enormous red door. That is where Santa Claus lives.'

'Thank you,' said the children, and they ran down the little stairway and out of the toadstool house. Peggy was so glad she had seen the inside of one.

'There's the castle!' said Peter, as they went through the groups of toadstool houses. He pointed to a hill in the distance. On the top was a fine castle, with towers at each corner. It took some time to get to it. When they reached the hill, what a lot of steps to climb up to the great red door! But at last they were there. They banged on the door with the enormous knocker.

It flew open – and there was Santa Claus himself!

'Well, well, well!' cried Santa Claus, beaming all over his big jolly face. 'A boy and girl to see me! Welcome to my castle. I'm sure you would like to see how all the toys are made, wouldn't you?'

'Oh, yes!' said Peter and Peggy. 'Oh, Santa Claus, we're so pleased to see you.'

'Come along in,' said Santa Claus, and the children went inside the big castle. There was such a noise of hammering and shouting and singing and humming and squeaking and growling. Really, it was most peculiar.

'It's a noisy place, I know,' said Santa, leading the way into a room full of teddy bears. 'Now here are my bears, being taught to growl when they are pressed in the middle. And in the next room you will see railway engines being taught to run round railway lines without falling off. And in the next room there are the humming-tops being taught how to hum … and …'

'Good gracious!' said Peggy, astonished. 'I didn't know that toys had to be taught things like that! Oh, look at that darling bear trying to growl. He's quacking instead!'

The children saw the railway trains rushing round and round their lines. They saw the tops spinning and humming. They watched big rocking-horses learning to rock without rocking right over. They saw toy ducks in a row, practising quacking. They watched dolls learning how to open and shut their eyes. Really, the castle of Santa Claus was a most exciting place!

'Now, you just go into the next room and see the toy dogs and cats and monkeys,' said Santa Claus. 'I'll be back in a minute. I want to teach one or two of these dolls to walk as well as talk.'

The children went by themselves into the next room. It was full of toy animals – and, of course, they were all learning hard! The cats were learning to mew, the dogs were learning to growl and to wag their tails, and the monkeys were learning to squeak and turn their heads from side to side.

And then suddenly Peter and Peggy saw Scamper, their own little dog. He was standing by himself, looking very frightened. Near him were two goblins, waving little silver wands over him.

'Quick! Quick! They are just going to turn Scamper into a toy dog!' cried Peter, and he ran over to the goblins. He took away their wands and spoke to them sternly.

'You mustn't do that. Scamper belongs to us. We don't want him to be turned into a toy dog!'

'You've just saved me in time!' wuffed Scamper, and to the children's surprise they could understand everything he barked.

'There's the pixie who took you away!' suddenly cried Peggy, seeing

Silver-Wings come into the room. 'Run, Scamper, run! She looks so cross.'

Scamper took one look at the cross pixie and ran out of the door as fast as ever he could. He ran to the front door of the castle. It was open and he rushed down the steps. He ran so fast that he lost his footing and rolled over and over for at least fifty steps.

He was puffing and panting and felt very bruised when he got to the bottom. He ran off again. He didn't go to Toadstool Town, but went off the other way, to Goblin Town.

Goblin Town was a strange little place. The houses were all tumble-down and crooked. They were built in a small wood, and some of the houses leaned against the tree-trunks, and one or two even had a tree growing right in the middle of them, sticking out at the roof like a long, tall, green-leafed chimney!

Scamper ran into the village – and then he heard someone crying out loudly. 'Help! Oh, help! Won't someone help me? I'm being taken away by a wicked goblin!'

Scamper pricked up his ears. He ran into the wood and there he saw the prettiest little fairy he had ever seen being dragged along by a sly, green-eyed goblin. In a trice Scamper had rushed up to the goblin and had bitten him on the ankle! The goblin let the fairy go, and ran off into the wood, howling at the top of his voice.

'Oh, thank you, thank you, you kind, clever little dog!' said the fairy, shaking out her mop of golden hair. 'You just came in time.'

'Don't mention it,' said Scamper.

'Come with me and I'll get a wonderful new collar made for you, all shining gold, with your name on it,' said the fairy. Scamper thought that sounded very good.

'The other dogs would think I was wonderful if I wore a collar like that and told them why,' he thought.

'And you shall have the biggest bone you've ever had in your life,' said the fairy. 'Come along. I'm a great friend of Santa Claus, and he will give you both the bone and the collar.'

'But I've just escaped from his castle!' said Scamper. 'They were trying to turn me into a toy dog.'

'Don't worry about that,' said the fairy. 'I'll put that right for you. Now, come along.' So back to the castle the two of them went, and soon they were standing in front of Santa Claus. Peter and Peggy came running up too, glad to see Scamper again.

'Of course your little dog shall have a shining collar and a great big bone!' said Santa Claus, when he heard what the fairy had to say.

So Santa Claus told the goblins nearby to make a most beautiful collar for Scamper, and to find him a giant bone. Just as they were setting to work to make it, there came a great knocking at the front door of the castle.

'Open quickly!' cried a voice. 'The Fairy Queen is here. She has come to visit Santa Claus!'

Well, dear me, what an excitement there was then! Everyone rushed to the front door, Scamper, the goblins, the grateful fairy, Silver-Wings, and all the toys! Santa Claus opened the door.

And there, in a carriage without wheels, drawn through the air by six magnificent butterflies, was the beautiful Fairy Queen herself, her long, shining wings spreading behind her, a smile on her lovely face.

'Oh!' said Peggy. 'Oh, she's simply beautiful.'

'Wuff!' said Scamper. 'I shall give her my new bone. Oh, what a lovely lady!'

'Come in, come in!' cried Santa. 'We've had some adventures today, I can tell you! You must hear the tale of this brave little dog who rescued a fairy from a goblin.' So the Fairy Queen came in, and heard the whole story. 'I shall give a party in honour of these nice children and their brave little dog!' she said. 'It shall be this very night!'

So that night there was a great party on the hillside, under the silver light of the moon. Everybody went, even the toys.

Santa Claus found a shining silver suit for Peter to wear. He really looked like a prince! And as for Peggy, she looked just like a fairy, because Silver-Wings lent her one of her own dresses, and even made her some pretend-wings! They wouldn't fly, which was a pity, but still, they felt simply lovely.

Scamper wore his new, shining collar. He was very proud of it. He had had a bath, and Peggy had brushed his coat well. The Queen was very pleased that he offered her his giant bone, but she said she thought he had better keep it, as she would never be able to eat it all.

They had supper on toadstool tables. They danced on the ground and in the air. They had a band of pixies and goblins to play music for them, and it was lovely to see the toys dancing together – dolls with teddy bears and cats with dogs.

'Isn't this fun?' said Peggy happily to Peter. 'I've just had a dance with a pixie, and his wings were so strong that they carried us both up in the air. Oh, dear – I wish it would last for ever!'

But, of course, it had to come to an end at last.

When the first cock crew, all the fairies and toys stopped dancing. The Fairy Queen smiled at the two children.

'You must go home now,' she said. 'You have been away quite a long time. I will send you home in my butterfly-carriage. You need not go up the rabbit-hole.'

So the children climbed into the lovely carriage, said goodbye to everyone, pulled Scamper in safely, and then off they flew in the moon-light. The butterflies knew the way, of course.

They landed in their own garden – and as soon as their feet touched the grass there, all three of them shot up to their own size once more! It did feel funny.

'We'll creep into bed,' said Peggy. 'I'm so tired now – but very happy.' So they went to bed – and in the morning they thought it must have been a dream. But it wasn't, because Scamper still wore his beautiful shining collar, and he still had his giant bone. It had grown big when he had grown big again. That was lucky for him.

'What a wonderful adventure!' said Peggy. 'What a good thing Scamper went down that hole that led to Fairyland. I hope we find it again.'

Perhaps they will – and then off they'll all go again on another lovely adventure!

Pink! Pink!

Hey-Presto, the wizard, had a wonderful cloak. Whenever he swung it round his shoulders he disappeared at once, because it had very powerful magic in it.

The cloak was most useful to the wizard. He wore it whenever he wanted to be invisible, and then he was able to do all kinds of things.

He could slip into other wizards' castles and watch them at their magic work without being seen. He could go into Witch Green-Eyes' cottage and stand unseen beside her as she stirred spells into her big black pot. He could swing his cloak round him when visitors came that he didn't want to bother about. Nobody could see him then!

'A most useful cloak!' said Hey-Presto, whenever he hung it up in his cupboard, and locked the door. 'An invaluable cloak! I couldn't do without it. I must never, never let my enemies get it.'

One day when he took it out of the cupboard, Miggy, his old servant, saw it. 'Good gracious, master!' she said. 'How can you wear that dirty old cloak? What colour is it meant to be? It's so dirty that I can't even tell if it's blue, red or green!'

'It's pink,' said the wizard, looking at it. 'At least, it's supposed to be pink! It does look dirty, doesn't it? Well, well – I suppose I've used it for over a hundred years now – no wonder it is dirty!'

'It's smelly, too,' said Miggy, wrinkling her nose. 'Pooh! It needs washing, master. Fancy using a thing for over a hundred years and not having it washed. It wants mending too. Look at this hole!'

'Dear me, yes,' said the wizard, quite alarmed. 'It won't do to get big holes in it – bits of me will be seen then, through the holes. Whatever shall I do?'

'I'll wash and mend it,' said Miggy, firmly.

'It's too precious,' said Hey-Presto, clutching it tightly.

'Now listen,' said Miggy, 'that cloak smells so dirty that very soon people will know you are near them, even though you're invisible. You let me wash it. I'll be very, very careful.'

'All right, Miggy. But when you hang it out to dry, please put up a clothes line in the walled garden and make sure the gate is locked,' said Hey-Presto. 'If anyone saw this cloak on the line they might steal it!'

'Oh, master, I'll be as careful of your cloak as if it was made of gold!' said old Miggy, putting it over her arm. 'My word – what a horrible smell! It must be five hundred years old, not one!'

She went off and got a tub full of boiling water. In went the magic cloak, and Miggy soused it up and down in the suds.

'Just look at the dirt coming out,' said Miggy, in disgust. 'Why, there's more dirt than cloak! I'll have to wash it three or four times before it's really clean.'

When she had finished washing it, she could hardly believe her eyes! The cloak was pink – the loveliest pink imaginable!

Miggy shook it out and then called her master. 'Master, come here! Did you ever see such a lovely colour in your life?'

Hey-Presto looked at his cloak. Why, it didn't seem the same one! 'It's the colour of almond blossom!' he said. 'It's the colour of wild roses in the hedge! And yes – it's exactly the colour of the sky when it's pink at sunset time!'

'Yes,' said Miggy. 'Shame on you for wearing it so dirty! I'm going to hang it out to dry and then I'll mend it for you.'

'In the walled garden, mind!' called the wizard, anxiously. 'Nobody can get in there, nobody at all.'

Miggy hurried into the walled garden. She had already put up a washing-line there. She went to the door in the wall and locked it carefully, putting the key into her pocket. Now nobody could get into the garden from outside, and the walls were far too high to climb.

She looked at the clouds racing across the sky. 'Nice windy day – the cloak will dry quickly!' she thought. 'I'll press it tonight and mend it – and I'll see that the master doesn't get it so dirty again. It shan't go for more than twenty years this time before it's washed again.'

She pegged the cloak carefully on the line and watched it flapping in the wind. It would soon be dry!

'I'll fetch it about three o'clock,' she thought and trotted indoors. She kept an eye on it through the kitchen window, and was pleased to see that it was drying nicely.

At three o'clock she went into the garden to unpeg the cloak – but it wasn't there! The line was empty – and three or four clothes pegs lay scattered on the ground!

Miggy gave a scream that brought Hey-Presto out at once. 'MASTER! MASTER! Your cloak's been stolen!'

Hey-Presto came at top speed. He saw the empty washing-line and the scattered pegs and he groaned. He ran to the garden door that led out into the lane, but it was fast locked. No one could have got in that way.

'I kept that cloak under my eye the whole time,' sobbed Miggy. 'I looked out from the kitchen window almost every minute. Nobody could have got in without my seeing them, nobody! They couldn't get out without being seen either.'

'Oh, yes they could,' said Hey-Presto, grimly. 'All the thief had to do was to swing the cloak round his shoulders and he and the cloak too would be invisible at once. He could go where he liked then – even creep in past you through the kitchen, out into the hall and walk out of the front door. Nobody would see him. What am I to do? My wonderful cloak! I MUST get it back!'

'The thief won't always be wearing it, sir, and it's such a bright, glowing pink that it would be very easy to recognise it,' said poor Miggy, very upset indeed. 'Can't you offer a reward, master, to anyone – even to any animal or bird – who finds it or brings news of it?'

'Yes. Yes, I'll certainly do that,' said Hey-Presto. Immediately he sent out hundreds of little pixie heralds, complete with trumpets, to announce his loss and the reward for finding the cloak.

Everyone was excited. The country was searched from top to bottom. But no news came in. Nobody had ever seen the cloak, hardly anyone had even known of it – so how could it have been stolen?

Rabbits searched down burrows. Fish in the rivers hunted here and there. Owls looked in hollow trees, swallows looked in barns. It was no good – nobody saw anything pink that was big enough to be the cloak.

And then one day a chaffinch flew down to Miggy in great excitement. 'Pink!' he called loudly. 'PINK-PINK!'

'What do you mean? Have you found the pink cloak?' cried Miggy. 'Where is it?'

'Pink-pink-pink!' shouted the little chaffinch, fluffing out his pretty chest. 'PINK!'

'I'll come with you,' said Miggy, putting on her bonnet. 'Lead the way, chaffinch. I'm sure you think you've found the cloak!'

'Chip-chip-chip, cherry-erry-erry, chippy, HERE-WE-ARE!' sang the chaffinch, flying up into a tall tree just outside the walled garden. And there, caught on a high branch, and wrapped round and round it, was the magic cloak, as pink as ever, but a little dirty.

'Yes! You're right! It is the cloak!' cried Miggy. 'You clever bird, you VERY clever bird! Wait here till I get a ladder, and don't you DARE to tell anyone else!'

She fetched a long ladder and up and up she went. She unwrapped the cloak from the branch and slipped it round her so that she might use both her hands to climb down the ladder again. At once, to the chaffinch's astonishment, she vanished and the cloak vanished, too!

'Pink!' he called anxiously. Miggy's voice answered him from the ladder.

'It's all right. I'm still here, climbing down the ladder. Wearing the cloak is the easiest way for me to carry it!'

She ran to the wizard, taking the cloak off just as she got to him. 'Master! It's found! Here it is!'

'Where was it?' asked Hey-Presto, startled and delighted.

'Caught up in a tree not far from the walled garden!' said Miggy. 'Nobody stole it! The strong wind must have blown it off the line straight up into the tree, and wrapped it round a branch – and there it's been ever since!'

'But who found it?' asked Hey-Presto, looking to see if the cloak was damaged.

'The chaffinch who nests in that tree,' said Miggy. 'He came and told me. He was so excited he could only say, "Pink! Pink!" But I guessed what he meant, of course.'

'Then he must have the reward,' said Hey-Presto. 'Call him here, the clever bird.'

The chaffinch came. He flew in at the window, calling, 'Pink! Pink!'

'There! He can't say anything but that at the moment,' said Miggy. 'He's been shouting out the news to everyone – he's so proud of himself!'

'Chaffinch, you have earned the reward,' said Hey-Presto, and the little bird flew on to his shoulder. 'You may have a sack of gold – a box of spells – or anything else you can think of.'

The chaffinch whispered a little song into the wizard's ear. Hey-Presto laughed.

'What does he want for a reward?' asked Miggy.

'Nothing! He says money is no use to him – and he's frightened of spells – and as he has a nest of his own, with a dear little wife and four beautiful nestlings, he has got everything he can possibly want,' said the wizard. 'He just wants to know if he can go on telling everyone that he found my pink cloak – he's so very, very proud of that.'

'Well, let him,' said Miggy. 'It's a reward that won't cost you a penny – and he'll be glad that he and all his family can boast about finding your magic cloak. People love boasting – even birds do!'

'You're right,' said Hey-Presto, and he turned to the excited little chaffinch. He spoke very solemnly.

'As your reward for finding my pink cloak you may tell everyone in the world!' he said. 'You may shout the news at the top of your voice year after year!'

And, believe it or not, from that day to this every chaffinch shouts out the news each spring and summer. You must listen, you really must.

'Pink!' he calls loudly. 'PINK, PINK, PINK!' Listen for him, will you, and call out, 'Clever bird! Who found the magic cloak? What colour was it?'

And he will put his knowing little head on one side and answer you at once.

'Pink! PINK-PINK-PINK!'

Old Bufo the Toad

Old Bufo was a toad, fat, brown, and ugly. The only beautiful thing about him was his pair of bright, copper eyes. They were like two shining jewels. Bufo was not allowed in Fairyland. The fairies said he really was much too ugly. He frightened them. So Bufo lived in our world, under a big stone by the streamside. He had a little shop under his stone, and there he worked hard all day long.

What do you think he made? Guess! Yes – toadstools! He was very clever indeed at making these. First he would make a nice sturdy stump, then a pretty curved cap-like top, and then underneath he sewed dozens of tiny frills. So you can see he was a busy fellow.

Now one day the Queen of Fairyland went on a long journey. She visited the Moon. She visited the Land of Dreams. And she visited our world too. She went with six servants, and she wore no crown, for she did not want to be known as she passed here and there.

She called herself Dame Silverwings, and travelled about quite safely in her silver coach, drawn by two white mice.

One day she heard that someone was chasing after her coach to catch her. It was the wizard Tall-Hat. He had found out that Dame Silverwings was no other than the Fairy Queen herself, and he thought that it would be a fine thing to catch her and take her prisoner. He would not let her go until he had been paid ten sacks of gold. Aha! How rich he would be!

A blackbird warned the Queen that Tall-Hat was after her. She hurried on her way – and then alas! a fog came down – and she was lost! On and on went her little white mice, dragging the carriage, but they did not know at all where they were going. When the fog cleared, they were quite lost.

The Queen stepped from her carriage. She was by a stream in a wood. No one seemed to be about at all.

'Is anyone living near here?' she called in her bird-like voice. She listened for an answer – and one came. It was the voice of Bufo, the old toad, that answered. His home was under the big stone nearby. He crawled out and croaked loudly:

'Yes – I, Bufo the toad, live here. Pray come and shelter, if you wish.'

The Queen and her six servants looked at Bufo in surprise, but when they saw his beautiful coppery eyes they trusted him and went to his stone. The Queen was surprised to see such a pretty and neat little shop under the stone – and when she saw the stools she was delighted.

'May I sit down on one of these dear little stools?' she asked. 'Oh, how nice they are! Just the right height, too! I would like to rest here awhile.'

'Then pray rest on my toadstools,' said Bufo. 'I have enough for all of you. And let me offer you each a glass of honey-dew.'

The kindly old toad fussed over his visitors and made them very welcome. The Queen was glad to rest on the quaint toadstool after her long ride.

'I am Dame Silverwings,' she said. 'Which is the quickest way to Fairyland from here?'

'Do you see this stream?' said Bufo. 'Well, on the other side lies Fairyland. There is a bridge a little farther on.'

'Oh, we shall soon be home then,' said the fairy, very pleased. But just as she said that she heard the noise of wings and, peeping from the stone, she saw to her horror the Tall-Hat Wizard himself, looking all round for her. He passed by, and she knew he had gone to the bridge to guard it so that she could not cross to Fairyland.

She began to weep. Bufo the toad could not bear to see her tears, and he begged her to tell him what was the matter. As soon as he heard about Tall-Hat guarding the bridge to Fairyland, he laughed.

'We can easily trick him,' he said. 'You shall cross the stream another way.'

'But there are no boats here,' said the Queen.

'I have something that will do just as well,' said Bufo. He took up one of his toadstools and turned it upside down. 'Look,' he said, 'if I put this into the

water upside down, you can sit on the little frills and hold on to the stalk, then the toadstool will float you across the stream safely. I have seven fine toadstools I can spare for you.'

In the greatest delight the Queen and her servants hurried down to the water with the toadstools. They let them float there upside down. Then one by one they climbed on to their toadstools, waved goodbye to old Bufo, and floated to the opposite side. Once there they were safe!

Tall-Hat waited by the bridge for six weeks – and then heard that the Queen had been safely back in Fairyland all that time. How angry he was! And how Bufo the toad laughed when he heard him go by, shouting and raging! He didn't know that Bufo was peeping at him from under his big stone.

Bufo got such a surprise when he knew that the little fairy he had helped was the Fairy Queen herself. She sent him a gold watch and chain to wear, and an order for as many toad-stools as he and his friends could make. 'They will do so nicely for our parties in the woods,' she said.

So now Bufo and his family make toadstools all day long, and stand them about in the woods for the little folk to sit on, or to use for tables at their parties. And Bufo is allowed in Fairyland, and has a grand time at the palace once a month when he goes to tea with the Queen herself. Nobody thinks he is ugly now, for they always look at his glowing eyes. Have you seen them? You haven't? Well, just look at them next time you see an old toad hopping along.

And don't forget to look at the dear little frills Bufo puts under every toadstool, will you?

'Tell Me My Name!'

The Hoppetty Gnome lived in a little cottage all by himself. He kept no dog and no cat, but outside in the garden lived a fat, freckled thrush who sang to Hoppetty each morning and evening to thank him for the crumbs he put out.

Hoppetty was very fond of this thrush. She was a pretty bird, and the songs she sang were very lovely.

'The sky is blue, blue! And all day through, through,
I sing to you, you!'

That was the thrush's favourite song, and Hoppetty knew it by heart.

Now one day a dreadful thing happened. Hoppetty was trotting through the wood, going home after his shopping, when out pounced a big black goblin

71

and caught hold of him. He put little Hoppetty into a sack and ran off with the struggling gnome over hill and meadow until he came to the tall hill on the top of which he lived. Then he emptied Hoppetty out of his sack, and told him he was to be his cook.

'I am very fond of cakes with jam inside,' said the grinning goblin, 'and I love chocolate fingers sprinkled with nut. I have heard that you are a clever cake-maker. Make me these things.'

Poor Hoppetty! How he had to work! The goblin really had a most enormous appetite, and as he ate nothing but jam cakes and chocolate fingers, Hoppetty was busy all day long at the oven, baking, baking. He was always hot and always tired. He wondered and wondered who this strange goblin was, and one day he asked him.

'Who are you, Master?' he said.

'Oho! Wouldn't you like to know?' said the goblin, putting six chocolate fingers into his mouth at once. 'Well, Hoppetty, if you could guess my name, I'd let you go. But you never will!'

Hoppetty sighed. He was sure he never would guess the goblin's name. Goblins had such strange names. Nobody ever came to the house, no letters were pushed through the letter-box, and Hoppetty was never allowed to go out. So how could he possibly find out the goblin's name? He tried a few guesses.

'Is your name Thingumebob?'

'Ho, ho, ho! No, no, no!'

'Is it Mankypetoddle?'

'Ho, ho, ho! No, no, no!'

'Well, is it Tiddleywinks?'

'Ho, ho, ho! No, no, no!'

Then Hoppetty sighed and set to work to make more jam cakes, for the goblin had eaten twenty-two for breakfast, and the larder was getting empty.

The goblin went out and banged the door. He locked it too, and went down the path. Hoppetty knew he couldn't get out. He had tried before. The windows opened two inches, and no more. The door he couldn't open at all. He was indeed a prisoner. He sighed again and set to work quickly.

And then he heard something that made his heart leap. It was a bird singing sweetly.

'The sky is blue, blue! And all day through, through,
I sing to you, you!'

It was his thrush! Hoppetty rushed to the window and looked out of the open crack. There was the pretty freckled bird, sitting in a nearby tree.

'Thrush!' cried Hoppetty. 'I'm here! Oh, you dear creature, have you been going about singing and looking for me? Did you miss your crumbs? I'm a prisoner here. I can only get away if I find out the name of the goblin who keeps me here.'

Just then the goblin came back, and the gnome rushed to his baking once more. The thrush sang sweetly outside for a few minutes and then flew away.

The bird was unhappy. It loved little Hoppetty. The gnome had been so kind to her, and had loved her singing so very much. If only the thrush could find out the name of the goblin. But how?

The bird made up her mind to watch the goblin and see where he went. So the next day she followed him when he left the cottage, flying from tree to tree as the goblin went on his way. At last he came to another cottage, and, to the thrush's surprise, the door was opened by a black cat with bright green eyes.

'A witch cat!' thought the thrush. 'I wonder if she knows the goblin's name. I dare not ask her, for if I go too near she will spring at me.'

The goblin stayed a little while and then went away. The thrush was about to follow, when the cat brought out a spinning-wheel and set it in the sunshine by the door. She sat down and began to spin her wool.

And as she spun, she sang a strange song.

'First of eel, and second of hen,
And after that the fourth of wren.
Third of lean and first of meat,
Second of leg and third of feet.

> *Fifth of strong and second of pail,*
> *Fourth of hammer and third of nail.*
> *Sixth of button and third of coat,*
> *First of me and second of boat.*
> *When you've played this curious game,*
> *You may perchance have found his name!'*

The cat sang this over and over again, and the thrush listened hard. Soon she knew it by heart and at once flew off to the goblin's cottage. She put her head on one side and looked in at the window. Hoppetty was setting the table for the goblin and was talking to him.

'Is your name Twisty-tail?'

'Ho, ho, ho! No, no, no!' roared the goblin.

'Well, is it Twisty-nose?'

'Ho, ho, ho! No, no, no! And don't you be rude!' snapped the goblin.

'Well, is it Pointed-ears?' asked poor Hoppetty.

'Ho, ho, ho! No, no, no! Give me some more jam cakes!' ordered the goblin.

The next day the thrush waited until the goblin had gone out, and then she began to sing sweetly.

Hoppetty knew that it was his own thrush singing, and he went to the window and listened – but what a peculiar song the bird was whistling! The thrush sang the cat's song over and over again – and suddenly Hoppetty guessed that it was trying to tell him how to find the goblin's name. He frowned and thought hard. Yes – he thought he could!

He fetched a pencil and a piece of paper and sat down. The thrush flew to the window-sill and sang the song slowly. Hoppetty put down the words and then he began to work out the puzzle in great excitement.

'The first of eel – that's E. The second of hen – that's E too. The fourth of wren – that's N. The third of lean – A. The first of meat – M. Second of leg – another E. Third of feet – E again! Fifth of strong, that's N. Second of pail – A. Fourth of hammer – M. Third of nail – I. Sixth of button – N. Third of coat – A.

First of me – M, and second of coat – O! Now what do all these letters spell?'

He wrote the letters out in a word, and looked at it – EENA-MEENA-MINA-MO!

'So that's the goblin's name!' cried the gnome in excitement. 'Oh, I would never, never have thought of that!'

The thrush flew off in a hurry, for she heard the goblin returning. He strode into his cottage and scowled when he saw the gnome sitting down writing instead of baking.

'What's all this?' he roared.

'Is your name Tabby-cat?' asked the gnome, with a grin.

'Ho, ho, ho! No, no, no!' cried the goblin. 'Get to your work.'

'Is it – is it – Wibbly-Wobbly?' asked the gnome, pretending to be frightened.

'Ho, ho, ho! No, no, no!' shouted the goblin in a rage. 'Where are my jam cakes?'

'Is it – can it be – EENA-MEENA-MINA-MO?' cried the gnome suddenly.

The goblin stared at Hoppetty and turned pale. 'How do you know that?' he asked, in a frightened whisper. 'No one knows it! No one! Now you have found out my secret name! Oh! Oh! Go, you horrid creature! I am afraid of you! What will you find out next?'

He flung the door wide open, and Hoppetty ran out gladly, shouting:
'Eena, Meena, Mina, Mo,
Catch a goblin by his toe;
If he squeals, let him go,
Eena, Meena, Mina, Mo!'

He skipped all the way home – and there, sitting on his garden gate, was his friend the thrush. You can guess that Hoppetty gave her a fine meal of crumbs, and told her all about how angry and frightened the goblin was!

'I shall bake you a cake for yourself every time I have a baking day,' he promised. And he did – but, as you can guess, he never again made a jam cake or a chocolate finger!

The Little Walking House

If it hadn't been for Puppy-Dog Pincher the adventure would never have happened. Jill and Norman were taking him for a walk in Cuckoo Wood, and he was mad with joy. He tore here, there and everywhere, barking and jumping for all he was worth.

The children laughed at him, especially when he tumbled head over heels and rolled over and over on the grass. He was such a fat, roly-poly puppy, and they loved him very much.

Then something happened. Pincher dived under a bramble bush, and came out with something in his mouth. It was a string of small sausages!

'Now wherever could he have got those from?' said Jill, in surprise. She soon knew, for out from under the bush ran a little fellow dressed in red and yellow, with a pointed cap on his head. He wasn't much taller than the puppy, but he had a very big voice.

'You bad dog!' he shouted. 'You've stolen the sausages I bought for dinner! Bring them back at once or I'll turn you into a mouse!'

Pincher took no notice. He galloped about with the sausages, enjoying himself very much. Then he sat down to eat them! That was too much for the small man. He rushed at Pincher and struck him on the nose with a tiny silver stick. At the same time he shouted out a string of words so strange that Jill and Norman felt quite frightened. They knew they were magic words, although they had never heard any before.

And then, before their eyes Pincher began to grow small! He grew smaller and smaller and smaller and smaller, and at last he was as tiny as a mouse. In fact, he was a mouse, though he didn't know it! He couldn't think what had happened to him. He scampered up to Jill and Norman, barking in a funny little mouse-like squeak.

The children were dreadfully upset. They picked up the tiny mouse and stroked him. Then they looked for the little man to ask him if he would please change Pincher back to a dog again.

But he had gone. Not a sign of him or his sausages was to be seen. Norman crawled under the bramble bush, but there was nothing there but dead leaves.

'Oh, Jill, whatever shall we do?' he said. 'We can't take Pincher home like this. Nobody would believe he was Pincher, and he might easily be caught by a cat.'

Jill began to cry. She did so love Pincher, and it was dreadful to think he was only a mouse now, not a jolly, romping puppy-dog.

'That must have been a gnome or a brownie,' she said, wiping her eyes. 'Well, Norman, I'm not going home with Pincher like that. Let's go farther into the wood and see if we meet any more little folk. If there's one here, there must be others. We'll ask them for help if we meet them.'

So they went on down the little winding path. Norman carried Pincher in his pocket, for there was plenty of room there for the little dog, now that he was only a mouse.

After they had gone a good way they saw the strangest little house. It had two legs underneath it, and it stood with its back to the children. Norman caught hold of Jill's arm and pointed to it in amazement. They had never seen a house with legs before.

'Oh!' cried Jill, stopping in surprise. 'It's got legs!'

The house gave a jump when it heard Jill's voice, and then, oh goodness me, it ran off! Yes, it really did! You should have seen its little legs twinkling as it scurried away between the trees. The children were too astonished to run after the house. They stood and stared.

'This is a funny part of Cuckoo Wood,' said Norman. 'I say, Jill! Look! There are some more of those houses with legs!'

Jill looked. Sure enough, in a little clearing stood about six more of the houses. Each of them had a pair of legs underneath, and shoes on their big feet. They stood about, sometimes moving a step or two, and even stood on one leg now and again, which made the house they belonged to look very lop-sided.

Jill and Norman walked towards the funny houses – but dear me, as soon as they were seen those houses took to their heels and ran off as fast as ever they could! The children ran after them, but they couldn't run fast enough.

They were just going to give up when they saw one of the houses stop. It went on again, but it limped badly.

'We could catch that one!' said Jill. 'Come on, Norman!'

They ran on and in a few minutes they had caught up the limping house. Just as they got near it the door opened and a pixie looked out. She was very lovely, for her curly golden hair was as fine as spider's thread, and her wings shone like dragonfly wings.

'What's the matter, little house?' they heard her say. 'Why are you limping?'

Then she saw the children and she stared at them in surprise.

'Oh, so that's why the houses ran off!' she said. 'They saw you coming! Could you help me, please, children? I think my house has a stone in one of its shoes, and I'm not strong enough to get it out all by myself.'

Jill and Norman were only too ready to help. Norman held up one side of the house whilst the house put up one of its feet to have its big shoe off. The pixie and Jill found a big stone in the shoe, and after they had shaken it out they put on the shoe again. The little house made a creaking noise that sounded just like 'Thank you!'

'What a funny house you've got!' said Jill to the pixie.

'What's funny about it?' asked the pixie in surprise, shaking back her long curly hair. 'It's just the same as all my friends' houses.'

'But it's got legs!' said Norman. 'Where we come from, houses don't have legs at all. They just stand square on the ground and never move at all, once they are built.'

'They sound silly sort of houses,' said the pixie. 'Suppose an enemy came? Why, your house couldn't run away! Mine's a much better house than yours.'

'Oh, much better,' agreed Jill. 'I only wish I lived in a house like this. It would be lovely. You'd go to sleep at night and wake up in a different place in the morning, because the house might wander miles away.'

'I say, pixie, I wonder if you could help us!' suddenly said Norman. He took the little mouse out of his pocket. 'Look! This was our puppy-dog not long ago and a nasty little man changed him into a mouse. Could you change him back into a dog again?'

'Oh no,' said the pixie. 'You want very strong magic for that. I only know one person who's got the right magic for your mouse, and that's High-Hat the Giant.'

'Where does he live?' asked Jill eagerly.

'Miles away from here,' said the pixie. 'You have to go to the Rainbow's End, and then fly up to Cloud-Castle just half-way up the rainbow.'

'Goodness, we couldn't possibly go there,' said Jill. 'We haven't wings like you, pixie.'

'Well, Dumpy the gnome lives near the Rainbow's End,' said the pixie. 'He keeps pigs that fly, you know, so he might lend you two of them. But I don't know if High-Hat the Giant will help you, even if you go to him. He's a funny-tempered fellow, and if he's in a bad humour he won't do anything for anybody.'

'Well, we might try,' said Norman. 'Which is the way to the Rainbow's End?'

'It depends where there's a rainbow today,' said the pixie. 'I know! I'll get my house to take you there. It always knows the way to anywhere. Come inside and we'll start. You helped me to get the stone out of my house's shoe, and I'd like to help you in return.'

The children went inside the house, feeling most excited. Norman had Pincher the mouse safely in his pocket. Pincher kept barking in his squeaky voice, for he couldn't understand how it was that Jill and Norman had grown so big! He didn't know that it was himself that had grown small.

The pixie shut the door, and told the children to sit down. It was a funny house inside, more like a carriage than a house, for a bench ran all round the wall. A table stood in the middle of the room and on it were some dishes and cups. In a corner a kettle boiled on a stove, and a big grandfather clock ticked in another corner.

The clock had two feet underneath it, like the house, and it gave the children quite a fright when it suddenly walked out from its corner, had a look at them and then walked back.

'Don't take any notice of it,' said the pixie. 'It hasn't any manners, that old clock. Would you like a cup of cocoa and some daffodil biscuits?'

'Oooh yes, please,' said both the children at once, wondering whatever daffodil biscuits were. The pixie made a big jug of cocoa and put some funny yellow biscuits on a plate, the shape of a daffodil trumpet. They tasted delicious, and as for the cocoa, it was lovely – not a bit like ordinary cocoa, but more like chocolate and lemonade mixed together. The children did enjoy their funny meal.

Before the pixie made the cocoa she spoke to her house. 'Take us to the Rainbow's End,' she said. 'And be as quick as you can.'

To the children's great delight the house began to run. They felt as if they were on the sea, or on the elephant's back at the Zoo, for the house rocked from side to side as it scampered along. Jill looked out of the window. They were soon out of the wood, and came to a town.

'Norman, look! There are hundreds of fairy folk here!' cried Jill, in excitement. So there were – crowds of them, going about shopping, talking and wheeling funny prams with the dearest baby fairies inside. The grandfather clock walked out of its corner to the window too, and trod on Jill's toe. It certainly had no manners, that clock.

They passed right through the town and went up a hill where little blue sheep were grazing. Looking after them was a little girl exactly like Bopeep. The pixie said yes, it really was Bopeep. That was where she lived. It was a most exciting journey, and the children were very sorry when they saw a great rainbow in the distance. They knew they were coming to the end of their journey in the walking house.

The little house stopped when it came to one end of the rainbow. The children stepped outside. There was the rainbow, glittering marvellously. It was very, very wide, far wider than a road and the colours were almost too bright to look at.

'Now High-Hat the Giant lives halfway up,' said the pixie, pointing. 'Come along, I'll take you to Dumpy the gnome, and see if he has a couple of pigs to spare you.'

She took them to a squat little house not far from the rainbow. Outside was a big yard and in it were a crowd of very clean pigs, bright pink and shining. Each of them had pink wings on his back, so they looked very strange to Jill and Norman.

'Hie, Dumpy, are you at home?' cried the pixie. The door of the house flew open and a fat gnome with twinkling eyes peeped out.

'Yes, I'm at home,' he said. 'What can I do for you?'

'These children want to fly to High-Hat's,' said the pixie. 'But they haven't wings. Could you lend them two of your pigs?'

'Yes, if they'll promise to be kind to them,' said Dumpy. 'The last time I lent out my pigs someone whipped them and all the curl came out of their tails.'

'Oh, these children helped me to take a stone out of my house's shoe,' said the pixie, 'so I know they're kind. You can trust them. Which pigs can they have, Dumpy?'

'This one and that one,' said the fat little gnome, and he drove two plump pigs towards the children. 'Catch hold of their tails, children, and jump on. Hold on to their collars, and, whatever you do, speak kindly to them or the curl will come out of their tails.'

Jill and Norman caught hold of the curly tails of the two pigs and jumped on. The pigs' backs were rather slippery, but they managed to stay on. Suddenly the fat little animals rose into the air, flapped their pink wings and flew up the shining rainbow. It was such a funny feeling. The pigs talked to one another in little squeals, and the children were careful to pat them kindly in case the curl came out of their tails.

In ten minutes they came to a towering castle, set right in the middle of the rainbow. It was wreathed in clouds at the top, and was made of a strange black stone that reflected all the rainbow colours in a very lovely manner. It didn't seem a real castle, but it felt real enough when the children touched it. They jumped off the pigs' backs and patted them gratefully.

'Stay here, dear little pigs, till we come out again,' said Norman. Then he and Jill climbed up the long flight of shining black steps to the door of the castle. There was a big knocker on it shaped like a ship. Norman knocked. The noise went echoing through the sky just like thunder, and quite frightened the two children.

'Come in!' called a deep voice from inside the castle. Norman pushed open the door and went in. He found himself in a great high room full of a pale silvery light that looked like moonlight. Sitting at a table, frowning hard, was a giant.

He was very, very big, so big that Jill wondered if he could possibly stand up-right in the high room. He was sucking a pencil and looking crossly at a book in front of him.

'Good morning,' said Norman politely.

'It isn't a good morning at all,' said the giant snappily. 'It's a bad morning. One of the very worst. I can't get these sums right again.'

'Well, bad morning, then,' said Jill. 'We've come to ask your help.'

'I'm not helping anyone today,' growled the giant. 'I tell you I can't get these sums right. Go away.'

'We must get his help,' whispered Norman to Jill. 'We'll keep on trying.'

'What sums are they?' Jill asked the giant. To her great surprise High-Hat suddenly picked her up in his great hand and set her by him on the table. When she had got over her fright Jill looked at the giant's book.

She nearly laughed out loud when she saw the sums that were puzzling the giant. This was one of them: 'If two hens, four dogs and one giant went for a walk together, how many legs would you see?'

'I'll tell you the answer to that,' she said. 'It's twenty-two!'

The giant turned to the end of the book and looked. 'Yes!' he said in astonishment. 'You're right! But how did you know that? Do another sum, please.'

Jill did all the sums. They were very easy indeed. The giant wrote down the answers in enormous figures, and then sucked his pencil whilst Jill thought of the next one.

When they were all finished Norman thought it was time to ask for help again.

'Could you help us now?' he asked. 'We've helped you, you know.'

'I tell you, this is one of my bad mornings,' said the giant crossly. 'I never help people on a bad morning. Please go away, and shut the door after you.'

Jill and Norman stared at him in despair. What a nasty giant he was, after all the help they had given him too! It really was too bad.

'I don't believe you know any magic at all!' said Jill. 'You're just a fraud! Why, you couldn't even do easy sums!'

The giant frowned till the children could scarcely see his big saucer-like blue eyes. Then he jumped up in a rage and hit his head hard against the ceiling. He sat down again.

'For saying a rude thing like that I will punish you!' he growled, in a thunderous voice. 'Now listen! You can sit there all the year long and ask me to do one thing after another so that I can show you my power – and the first time you can't think of anything I'll turn you into ladybirds!'

Goodness! Jill and Norman turned quite pale. But in a trice Norman took the little brown mouse out of his pocket and showed it to the giant.

'You couldn't possibly turn this mouse into a puppy-dog, I'm sure!' he cried.

The giant gave a snort and banged his hand on the table. 'Homminy, tinkabooroyillabee, juteray, bong!' he cried, and as soon as the magic words were said, hey presto, the little mouse grew bigger and bigger and bigger, and there was Puppy-dog Pincher again, as large as life, and full of joy at being able to run and jump again. But the giant left the children no time to be glad.

'Next thing, please!' he cried.

'Go to the moon and back!' cried Jill suddenly. In a trice High-Hat had vanished completely.

'Quick, he's gone to the moon!' cried Jill. 'Come on, Norman, we'll escape before he comes back!'

Out of the castle door they ran, Pincher scampering after them. The two pigs were patiently waiting outside on the rainbow at the bottom of the castle steps. Jill and Norman jumped on their backs, Norman carrying the puppy in his arms. Then quickly the flying pigs rose into the air and flew back to the end of the rainbow.

Just as they got there they heard a tremendous noise far up in the air.

'It's the giant, come back from the moon!' said Jill. 'Goodness, what a noise he's making! It sounds like a thunderstorm.'

The pixie came running to meet them.

'Is that High-Hat making all that noise?' she asked, looking frightened. 'Give the pigs back to Dumpy, and climb into my house again with me. The next thing that happens will be High-Hat sliding down the rainbow after you, and we'd better be gone before he arrives. He'll be in a dreadful temper!'

The pigs were given back to the twinkling gnome, and then the children climbed into the walking house with the pixie and Pincher. Off they went at a great rate, far faster than before. Pincher couldn't understand it. He began to bark and that annoyed the grandfather clock very much. It suddenly came out of its corner and boxed Pincher's ears.

'I'm so sorry,' said the pixie. 'It's a very bad-mannered clock. I only keep it because it's been in my family for so many years. By the way, where do you want to go to?'

'Oh, home, please!' begged the children.

'Right!' said the pixie. Just as she said that there came the sound of a most tremendous BUMP, and the whole earth shook and shivered.

'There! That's the giant slid down the rainbow!' said the pixie. 'I knew he would bump himself.'

The house went on and on. When it came to a sunshiny stretch of road it skipped as if it were happy.

'Here you are!' suddenly cried the pixie, opening her door. And sure enough, there they were! They were in their very own garden at home!

The children jumped out and turned to call Pincher, who was barking in excitement. The grandfather clock suddenly ran out of its corner and smacked him as he went.

'Oh dear, I'm so sorry!' cried the pixie. 'It hasn't any manners at all, I'm afraid. Well, see you another day! Goodbye, goodbye!'

The little house ran off, and the children watched it go. What an adventure they had had! And thank goodness Pincher wasn't a mouse any longer, but a jolly, jumping puppy-dog!

'Come on, Pincher!' cried Norman. 'Come and tell Mother all about your great adventure!'

Off they went and, dear me, Mother was surprised to hear their strange and exciting story!

Bufo's One-Legged Stool

Once upon a time the King of Fairyland called all his fairy subjects to his palace. They came flying and running in great excitement, wondering why his Majesty should want them.

The King sat on his beautiful, shining throne, waiting until every fairy was there. Then he held up his hand for silence and spoke to them.

'Fairy-folk,' he began, 'once every year a prize is given to the fairy who thinks of the cleverest idea to make the world more beautiful. Last year, you remember, Morfael won the prize with his golden polish for the buttercups.'

'Yes, we remember!' shouted the fairies.

'Well, this year, I'm going to make a change,' said the King. 'I am going to give the prize to the one who thinks, not of the cleverest idea, but of the most useful! And please tell the rabbits and frogs and birds about it, because it's quite likely they would think of a good idea just as much as you fairy-folk.'

Well, the fairies were most excited. They rushed off telling everyone about it.

'I'm going to think hard for a whole week!' said one.

'And I'm going to use some old magic that will tell me the most useful thing in the world!' said another.

'Let's go and tell all the animals,' shouted a third.

So they visited the grey rabbits and told them. They called out the news to the grasshoppers. They gave the message to Hoo, the White Owl of Fairyland, and he promised to tell all the other birds.

'Now I do believe we've told everyone!' said the fairies.

'No, we haven't. What about ugly old Bufo the Toad, who lives on the edge of Fairyland?' asked an elf.

'Pooh! What's the good of telling him?' cried a pixie scornfully. 'He'll never think of any good idea. Leave him alone!'

But it happened that next door to Bufo lived a brownie called Bron. He had decided to make a beautiful scarf for fairies to wear when the wind was cold. He thought it would be most useful. He was making it of spiders' webs and thistledown, and as he sat in his little garden at work, he sang a little song:

'Oh! I am very wise,
I'm sure to win the prize,
And when I've won the prize, you'll see
How very, very pleased I'll be!'

Bufo the Toad kept hearing him sing this and at last he got so curious that he crawled out of his cottage and asked Bron what prize he was singing about.

Bron told him. 'The King's giving a prize to anyone bringing him the most useful idea this year!' he explained. 'Why don't you try, Bufo?'

'I'm so clumsy!' said Bufo. 'But I'd like to try all the same. Yes, I think I will.'

'I'm making a wonderful scarf for when it's cold!' said Bron proudly. 'It's made of cobwebs and thistledown!'

'My! You are clever!' said Bufo. 'Now I'm going indoors and try to think of something myself!'

He waddled indoors. His cottage was very odd inside. Bufo was so fat and heavy that he had broken all the chairs and his sofa, through sitting on them too hard! So there were none in his cottage at all. He had a big table, and as he really did want something to sit on, he had made himself one large stool. He was so poor at making things, that he thought he had better give his stool just one large fat leg in the middle. He was afraid that if he tried to make three legs to it like Bron's smart little stool, he would never get them the same length. So inside his cottage there was only one table and a one-legged stool.

Bufo the Toad climbed up on to his stool, shut his great yellow eyes, and thought!

At last he opened his eyes. 'I've got an idea!' he cried. 'I'll make an eiderdown of pink rose petals! That will be a most useful thing, and it will smell lovely!'

So he hopped out into his garden and collected all the largest rose petals he could find. Then he begged some spider-thread from a spider friend and began.

But poor Bufo was clumsy. He kept breaking the spider's thread, and the wind blew half his rose petals away.

'Ha, ha!' laughed the rude little brownie. 'Ha, ha! Bufo! It really is a funny sight to see a great toad sewing rose petals! Don't you worry your little old head! I'm going to win the prize, I tell you!'

But Bufo wouldn't give up. He went and sat on his stool again and thought. He thought for three days before he found another idea.

That was really rather a good one. He caught a little pink cloud, and decided to stuff a pillow with it. He thought it would be so lovely and soft for fairies' heads.

Bron laughed to see Bufo poking the pink cloud into a big white pillowcase with his great fingers. He called his friends and they came and watched Bufo and teased him.

'Poke it a bit harder, Bufo!' they called over the fence. 'It's a naughty little cloud, isn't it? It won't let you win the prize.'

Bufo took no notice for a whole day. Then he suddenly got angry, left the half-stuffed pillow on the grass, and hopped to the fence to shout at the rude little brownies.

But alas! As soon as the half-stuffed pillow had no one to hold it, the little pink cloud began to rise in the air, to go back to the sky, and it took Bufo's lovely pillow-case with it!

'Oh, oh, now look what you've made me do!' wept Bufo, trying to jump into the air and catch the pillow. But he couldn't, and the naughty little brownies laughed harder than ever.

Bufo went and sat on his stool again. This time he thought for six weeks. When another idea came, he was so stiff with sitting that he could hardly jump off his stool.

'I'll make some wonderful blue paint, to paint the Queen's carriage with!' he decided. 'I know it wants repainting, so that will be useful.'

He lumbered off with a huge sack. He got the dawn fairies to give him a scraping off the blue of the sky. He asked the blue butterflies for a little powder off their wings. He took one bluebell flower and one harebell. Then he lumbered home again with his sack full of all these things.

When he got indoors, he took a blue shadow, mixed it with honey and water, and poured it into a large paint-pot. Then he emptied his sack into it, and stirred everything up well.

'It's the most glorious blue paint ever I saw!' said Bufo, very pleased. 'This will be useful, I know.'

Now the next day was the day the King had arranged to hold a meeting to judge all the ideas, and everyone in Fairyland was most excited. When the day came, Bufo put his paint outside his cottage door, all ready to take, and then began tidying himself up. Suddenly he heard a terrible yell from Bron, his next door neighbour.

'Help! Help! Arran the Spider is stealing my lovely scarf!'

Bufo rushed out to help, and saw Arran running off with Bron's scarf. He quickly stopped the spider, and took the scarf away.

'He stole some of my thread,' grumbled Arran, running off, frightened. 'I thought I'd come and punish him!'

'Oh, thank you for helping me,' cried Bron. 'If he'd taken my scarf, I wouldn't be able to win the prize.'

'Yes, but it's wrong to take Arran's thread, if he didn't want you to,' said Bufo severely. 'You ought to say you're sorry to him, and give it back!'

He waddled back to his cottage, but, oh! he quite forgot he had put his pot of blue paint outside the door. He walked straight into it, and splish-splash! clitter-clatter! It was all upset.

'Oh! Oh! My beautiful paint!' wept Bufo. 'I've spilt it all, and there's no more time to think of other ideas!'

Some fairies passing by stopped to listen.

'You must take something, Bufo,' they called mischievously. 'The King will be cross with you if you don't.'

Bufo believed them. 'Oh dear! Will he really? But what shall I do? I've nothing else but my stool and a table!'

'Take the stool, Bufo!' laughed the fairies, flying on.

So poor old Bufo the Toad went indoors and fetched his one-legged stool, and joined the crowd of flying fairies. How they laughed to see him waddling along carrying a big one-legged stool.

At last they all reached the palace, and the King soon came to hear and to see the useful ideas that the fairy-folk had brought.

'Here's a wonderful necklace made of raindrops!' cried a fairy, kneeling before the King.

'It is beautiful, but not useful!' answered the King gently. 'Try again.'

'Here's a new sort of polish for the sunset sky!' said the next fairy.

The King looked at it. 'That's no better than the one we use now,' he said. 'Next, please.'

Fairy after fairy came, and rabbits and birds and other animals.

Some had beautiful ideas that weren't useful, some had silly ideas, and some had good ones.

At last Bron's turn came. He showed his beautiful scarf.

'It is lovely, Bron,' said the King, 'but it is not warm enough to be useful. Also I know you have been unkind to Bufo, and you took Arran's thread without asking. I am not pleased with you. Go away, and do better!'

Bron hung his head and crept away, blushing and ashamed.

At last everyone had shown their ideas, except Bufo. He crawled up to the King and put his one-legged stool down.

'I thought of many ideas, but they all got spoilt,' he said. 'Is this one any use? It is a good strong stool, easy to make, and quite nice-looking.'

The King looked at it thoughtfully. Then the Queen leaned forward and spoke.

'Don't you think, Oberon,' she said, 'that it is just the thing we want to put in the woods for fairy seats? Think how easy, too, they would be to put up in a ring for a dance!'

'Well now, so they would!' said the King. 'It really is just what we want. It is certainly the most useful idea we've had given to us today. We could grow these one-legged stools by magic in the woods, and use them for tables or for stools!'

'Then we'll give Bufo the prize!' said the Queen. 'Three cheers for Bufo!'

How surprised the fairies were to see ugly old Bufo win the prize! And oh! How delighted Bufo was! He could hardly believe his ears. He almost cried with joy. He was given a little golden crown to wear, and though he certainly looked rather odd in it, he didn't mind a bit, because he was so very proud of having won it!

One-legged stools were put all about the woods that very day, and they have been used ever since by fairy-folk. Sometimes you find them growing in a ring, and then you'll know there has been a dance the night before.

They are still called toadstools, although it is many, many years ago since Bufo the Toad won the prize. Not many people know why they have such a funny name, but you will be able to tell them the reason now, won't you?

The Rabbit
Who Lost His Tail

Ⅰn the nursery cupboard with all the other toys lived Bun the soft rabbit. He was dressed in an orange tunic and green knickers, and his tail stuck out behind. It was a funny little tail, very short and fluffy, just like a real rabbit's.

Bun often played with Mollie, his mistress. She used to take him into the garden with her, and he sat on a little wooden chair and pretended to have tea. He was a very happy little rabbit.

One day a pixie climbed in at the window and gave Bun a letter. It had a crown printed on the back, so Bun knew that it had come from a King or Queen. He was very much excited and his paws trembled when they tried to undo the envelope.

All the other toys crowded round to see what the letter inside was. Bun unfolded it and read it out loud. It was from the King of Fairyland!

'Dear Bun,

I am having a party under the old beech tree on Wednesday night at moonrise. Please come if you can.

Love from

The King of Fairyland.'

Bun danced for joy. He had always wanted to go to a pixie party, but toys didn't very often get asked.

'Wednesday!' he said. 'That's two days away. Oh, how can I wait?'

Bun was very happy all that day – but the next day something dreadful happened. He lost his tail!

Mollie had taken him out into the garden to play with him and the little boy next door came to play too. But he was rather rough with Bun, and to make Mollie laugh he held the little rabbit up by his tail.

But Mollie didn't laugh. She snatched Bun away from the little boy and scolded him.

'That's not funny!' she said. 'You'll hurt Bun. You're a nasty little boy and I don't want to play with you any more.'

Then the two began to quarrel, and soon they were crying loudly. Mother came out and sent the little boy away. Then she took Mollie indoors.

All that day Bun lay out on the grass. The rain came and made him wet. Then suddenly Mollie remembered him and ran out to fetch him. She sat him in front of the nursery fire to dry, and there he stayed in the warm until Mollie went to bed.

Then, when the nursery was empty and quiet, all the other toys crept round Bun to hear what had happened. He told them all about the little boy who held him up by the tail and the toys exclaimed in horror.

Then suddenly the bear gave a squeak.

'Ooh, Bun!' he said. 'Where is your tail?'

Then all the toys looked at Bun's back, and sure enough his tail was gone. He had no tail at all.

He was upset! He screwed his head round to look at the place where his tail wasn't, and the tears came into his eyes.

'What shall I do?' he wept. 'I can't go to a pixie party without a tail, I really can't. Why, I should feel only half-dressed. Oh, whatever shall I do?'

The toys looked at one another and thought hard.

'I'll run out into the garden and see if I can find your tail for you,' said the clockwork clown. 'If someone will wind me up, I can easily get there and back.'

The teddy bear wound him up and the clockwork clown ran out of the room and down the passage that led to the garden. He hunted everywhere about the grass for Bun's tail, but he couldn't find it. At last he didn't dare to hunt any longer for he was afraid his clockwork would run down, and then he wouldn't be able to get back to the nursery.

'Well,' said the toys, when he went back to them, 'did you find it?'

'No,' said the clown, 'it isn't there.'

Then Bun wept more loudly than ever, and all the toys looked at one another and thought hard again.

'Couldn't one of you lend me a tail?' asked Bun, at last.

'I haven't got one or I would with pleasure,' said the teddy bear.

'What about the baby lamb that lives in the toy stable?' cried the clown. 'He has a fine long tail, and I am sure he would lend it to you.'

'But wouldn't I look funny with a very long tail?' asked Bun. 'My own was so short.'

'Oh, a long tail is better than nothing,' said the teddy, and all the toys agreed. So they went to fetch the baby lamb from the stable and told him what they wanted. He didn't like parting with his tail at first, but when the clown told him all about the wonderful pixie party that Bun had been invited to, he said yes, he would lend his tail just for that night.

'It's only pinned on,' he said, 'so Bun can quite easily unpin it and put it on himself.'

'Well, I'll borrow it tomorrow, and thank you very much,' said Bun, happily. Then all the toys went to sleep, and the nursery was quiet.

The next night the toys fetched the lamb again, and the clown unpinned his tail. It was very long, soft and woolly and felt lovely and warm. Bun turned his back to the clown, and in a trice it was neatly pinned on.

'Ooh Bun!' said the teddy bear, 'you do look fine! A long tail suits you much better than a short one. Everyone will look at you and admire you.'

Bun felt very happy. He took his invitation card, said goodbye to the toys and set off to the big beech tree. The moon was just rising, and as he came near the tree he could see crowds of pixies and elves there.

Bun wondered if Tiptoe, the elf who lived in the foxglove bed, was going to the party too. He was very fond of Tiptoe, and he had often wished that she would marry him and live with him in the nursery. But he had never dared to ask her, for she was very lovely.

Suddenly he saw her. She ran up to him and tweaked one of his big ears.

'Hallo, Bun!' she said. 'I'm so glad you're going to the party.'

'Will you dance with me?' asked Bun, in delight.

'Yes,' said Tiptoe, and then she sneezed three times.

'Oh dear, you haven't got a cold, have you?' asked Bun in alarm. 'What a thin frock you have on, Tiptoe, and the wind is so cold too.'

'Yes, I ought to have put on something warmer,' said Tiptoe, and she shivered, 'but it's too late now. Perhaps I shall get warm dancing.'

The party soon began. The band struck up a merry tune, and all the pixies and elves began to dance. The King and Queen sat on two toad-stool thrones, and clapped when each dance was finished.

Bun enjoyed himself very much, because everyone admired his tail.

'What a beautiful tail!' they said. 'You are a lucky rabbit to have a tail like that! How nice you look! Will you dance with us?'

So Bun danced every single dance, and was so happy that his ears turned bright red inside. But he liked dancing best with Tiptoe. He was worried about her because she did sneeze so, and he felt certain she would get a very bad cold, and be ill.

Suddenly the Queen heard Tiptoe sneezing and she called her to the throne.

'Why didn't you put on a warmer dress?' she said. 'You must really go home, Tiptoe, for you will get a terrible cold.'

'Oh, please, your Majesty, do let me stay!' said poor Tiptoe. 'A-tishoo, a-tishoo!'

Then a wonderful idea came to Bun. He ran up to the Queen and bowed.

'I can lend Tiptoe a fur to put round her neck,' he said. 'Would you let her stay if she wears a fur, your majesty?'

'Certainly,' said the Queen. 'But where is the fur?'

'Here!' said Bun, and he unpinned the long woolly lamb's tail! He put it around Tiptoe's neck, and there she was, as warm as toast, and as pretty as a picture.

How all the elves and pixies cheered! They knew that Bun was proud of his long tail and felt very strange without it, and they thought it was very kind and unselfish of him to lend it to Tiptoe and go without it himself.

After that Bun was more of a hero than ever. All the elves wanted to dance with him, but he danced all the rest of the time with Tiptoe, who had stopped sneezing and felt quite warm with the lamb's tail round her neck.

'I'll see you home,' said Bun, after the party. 'You can wear the fur all the way to the foxglove bed, and when you're nice and warm at home, you can give me the tail to take back to the baby lamb, who lent it to me. I lost my own tail.'

'How sad for you!' said Tiptoe. 'But what a good thing for me, because if you hadn't lost your own tail you wouldn't have been able to lend me this fur, and I should have had to go home early! Tomorrow I'll have a good hunt for your own tail, Bun. Now, good night, and thank you for your kindness.'

Bun said good-night and ran home very happy. He told all the toys what had happened and the baby lamb was very pleased when he heard how useful his tail had been. The teddy bear pinned it on to his back again, and then all the toys settled themselves to sleep.

Next evening there came a tapping at the nursery window and who should it be but Tiptoe!

'Bun!' she called. 'Bun! Come quickly! I've found your tail!'

Bun ran to the window and opened it. There was Tiptoe, and in her hand was Bun's own little short tail.

'Where did you find it?' he asked, in delight.

'A worm had pulled it down into his hole to make himself warm,' said Tiptoe. 'I took it away from him and washed it. Now it is dry and clean, and if you come with me I'll sew it on so tightly for you that you will never lose it again.'

So Bun went to the foxglove bed with Tiptoe and she sewed his tail on for him again with a hundred stitches so that it was very firm indeed.

'You are the dearest elf I ever saw!' said Bun. 'I do wish you would marry me Tiptoe. We could live in the doll's house, and be very happy together.'

'Ooh, let's!' said Tiptoe, and she flung her arms round Bun and hugged him. He had never been so happy in all his life.

They moved into the doll's house, and, oh, what a merry time they had! They gave parties every night, and Tiptoe learnt to cook lovely cakes on the little tin stove in the kitchen. And they always ask the baby lamb to their parties, because if it hadn't been for his long woolly tail Bun and Tiptoe would never have got married!

Fairy
Stories

You Simply Never Know

William had a lovely new kite. He was very proud of it indeed. It had a beautiful tail, and it looked as if it would fly very well indeed.

'I do so hope I don't lose it,' said William to his mother, the first day he took it out to fly. 'It's a big kite – and the wind's so strong it might break the string.'

'Oh, I don't think so, dear,' said Mother. 'But anyway, couldn't you just write your name and address on the kite? Then if it does fly off and somebody finds it, there's a chance they might be honest and bring it back.'

William thought that was a very good idea. He scribbled his name and address on the kite, as neatly as he could.

The kite certainly flew well. It leapt up into the air at once, and tugged and pulled like a live thing. William shouted loudly.

'Here we go! Pull, kite, pull! That's right – go higher and higher! See if you can catch that cloud!'

The kite flew very high. It almost seemed as if it was trying to catch a cloud. William began to find it rather hard to hold the kite. It made him run a few steps!

'Hey, kite! Don't pull me so!' he cried. But the kite flew with the wind and dragged William along again. He came to the stream and fell in! To save himself he let go the kite-string – and away went the kite on its own in the windy sky. It chased the birds. It flew through a cloud. It even raced after an aeroplane.

When William picked himself up, soaked from head to foot, he was cross and upset. 'Look at that! I've fallen into the stream, and I've lost my new kite. The very first time I flew it, too! Thank goodness I put my name and address on it. Perhaps it may be brought back.'

Now the kite flew for miles and miles. It flew over a great wood at last, and then bumped into an enormous tree – a tree that grew so high it touched the clouds.

It was the Faraway Tree, of course, that stood in the middle of the Enchanted Wood. It banged against Moonface's door and lay still outside, tired out.

'Come in!' cried Moonface, thinking the bang was a knock. Nobody came in, of course, so Moonface opened the door. He was most astonished to see a kite there.

'What do you want?' he said, and picked it up. 'What a beauty you are!

Hallo – there's a name and address written here. William Wilson, Redroofs, Limming Village. Do you mean to say you've come all that way?'

The kite wagged its tail. Moonface called down the Faraway Tree. 'Hey, Saucepan Man, are you there? Look what's come to see me!'

Saucepan looked, clanking as he came up to see. He was all hung around with kettles and saucepans as usual.

'Have to take it back,' he said, when he saw the name and address. 'Come along. We'll go now. The boy it belongs to will be very upset if he thinks he has lost it.'

The kite was too big to go down the Slippery-Slip that ran from the top of the Faraway Tree to the bottom, in the very middle of the great trunk. So Moonface walked out on to a broad branch with Saucepan, and threw the kite into the wind. It rose into the air at once, and Moonface and Saucepan hung on to the tail.

The kite took them gently down to the ground. Their weight was too much for it to fly away. Moonface picked up the kite and tucked it under his arm. It was really far too big to go there, and looked very peculiar. Saucepan carried the tail. The string ran on the ground like a long pale worm wriggling in and out.

Through the Enchanted Wood they went and over the ditch that surrounded it. Then they set off to catch the bus that went in the direction of Limming Village. The conductor said that the kite would have to go on top. It was an open-roofed bus so that was all right. Saucepan kept tripping over the tail as they went up the stairs, but at last they were safely sitting on top of the bus with the kite standing quietly beside them.

It was six o'clock before they arrived at Limming Village, and beginning to get dark. Moonface asked where Redroofs was, and then the two of them set off to take the kite to William.

They went to the back door, because they didn't think it was right to take kites to the front door. They knocked and William's mother opened the door.

She didn't see the kite at first. She only saw Moonface's shining round face and Saucepan all hung round with pans, wearing the usual saucepan for a hat.

'What a time to come selling kettles and saucepans!' she said, crossly. 'No, I don't want any.'

'But look – we've brought back....' began Moonface, tugging at the kite.

'So you've got something to sell, too,' said William's mother. 'I don't want anything at all. I don't buy at the door. Go away, please.'

She shut the door. Moonface and Saucepan looked at one another. 'I suppose we do look a bit peculiar to her,' said Moonface. 'We forgot that. We'd better just scribble a message on the kite, leave it here, and go. After all, probably William's mother has never even heard of us.'

So they scribbled a message on the kite, set it down near the kitchen door, gave a loud knock, and went down the path.

It was William who opened the door this time – and the first thing he saw was his kite!

'Mother! My kite – look! Somebody's brought it back!' cried. 'Who was it, do you suppose? Has anyone been to the door?

'Dear me, yes – I wonder if they brought it back,' said his mother 'Two most peculiar-looking people came – one with a round shining face, and one all hung about with pans and kettles, wearing a saucepan for a hat.'

'Mother!' said William, 'oh, Mother – could it have been – no of course it couldn't.' And then he saw the message scribbled on the kite.

'Dear William,

Your kite fell in the Faraway Tree, so we brought it back. It's a beauty.

Yours with love,
Moonface and Saucepan.'

'It was, it was!' shouted William. 'Mother, which way did they go? Mother, I simply must find them. Don't you realise who they were – they're

Moonface and Saucepan from the Faraway Tree. Which way did they go?'

But his mother didn't know. William set off down the path, looking all about in the half-darkness. He heard a clanking noise some way down the road. That must be old Saucepan! He flew down the road after the noise.

The noise had gone round a corner. William rushed round at once. He could see something in the darkness not far off. 'Saucepan!' he yelled. 'MOONFACE!'

The noise stopped. William rushed on eagerly. 'Wait for me, wait!' he cried, and at last he caught up with the noise, which had now begun again.

But what a dreadful disappointment! It was only Jim the farmer's boy going home on Cobber the horse, whose harness was jingle-jangling all the time. It had sounded exactly like the noise old Saucepan's kettles and pans made.

I wish I could tell you that William found Moonface and Saucepan, but he didn't. They were gone, and he could have wept. What a chance, what a wonderful, marvellous chance – and he had missed it. Poor Mother – she would be disappointed, too, when she knew.

All the same, he was lucky, wasn't he? His kite had been brought safely back, he had had Moonface and Saucepan at his back door – and he's still got the little scribbled message on the kite. But oh, what a pity he just missed his two Faraway Tree visitors.

Winkle-Pip Walks Out

Once upon a time Winkle-Pip the gnome did a good turn to the Tappetty Witch, and she was very grateful.

'I will give you something,' she said. 'Would you like a wishing-suit?'

'Ooh, yes!' cried Winkle-Pip, delighted. 'That would be lovely.'

So the Tappetty Witch gave Winkle-Pip a wishing-suit. It was made of yellow silk, spotted with red, and had big pockets in it.

'Now,' said the witch to Winkle-Pip, 'whenever you wear this suit, your wishes will come true – but there is one thing you must do, Winkle.'

'What's that?' asked Winkle-Pip.

'Once each year you must go out into the world of boys and girls and grant wishes to six of them,' said the witch. 'Now don't forget that, Winkle, or the magic will go out of your wishing-suit.'

Winkle-Pip promised not to forget, and off he went home, with the wishing-suit wrapped up in brown paper, tucked safely under his arm.

Now the next day Winkle-Pip's old Aunt Maria was coming to see him. She always liked a very good tea, and often grumbled because Winkle-Pip, who was not a very good cook, sometimes gave her burnt cakes, or jam sandwich that hadn't risen well, and was all wet and heavy.

So the gnome decided to use his wishing-suit the next day, and give his aunt a wonderful surprise. He put it on in the morning and looked at himself in the glass – and he looked very nice indeed. He thought he would try the wish-magic, so he put his hands in his pockets and spoke aloud.

'I wish for a fine feathered cap to go with my suit!' he said.

Hey presto! A yellow hat with a red feather came from nowhere, and landed with a thud on his big head.

'Ho!' said Winkle-Pip, pleased. 'That's a real beauty.'

He looked round his kitchen. It was not very clean, and none of the breakfast dishes had been washed up. The curtains looked dirty too, and Winkle-Pip remembered that his Aunt Maria had said he really should wash them.

'Now for a bit of fun!' said Winkle, and he put his hands in his pockets again.

'Kitchen, tidy yourself, for that is my wish!' he said, loudly.

At once things began to stir and hum. The tap ran water, and the dishes jumped about in the bowl and washed themselves. The cloth jumped out of the pail under the sink, and rubbed itself hard on the soap. Then it began to wash the kitchen floor far more quickly than Winkle-Pip had ever been able to do.

The brush leapt out of its corner and swept the rugs, which were really very dirty indeed. The pan held itself ready for the sweepings, and when it was full it ran outside to the dustbin, and emptied itself there.

You should have seen the kitchen when everything had quietened down again! How it shone and glittered! Even the saucepans had joined in and had let themselves be scrubbed well in the sink. It was marvellous.

'Now for the curtains!' said Winkle-Pip, and he put his hands in his pockets again. 'I wish you to make yourselves clean!' he called.

The curtains didn't need to be told twice. They sprang off their hooks and rushed to the sink. The tap ran and filled the basin with hot water. The soap made a lather, and then those curtains jumped themselves up and down in the water until every speck of dirt had run from them and they were as white as snow! Then they flew to the mangle, which squeezed the water from them. Then out to the line in the yard they went, and the pegs pegged them there in the wind. The wind blew its hardest, and in a few minutes they flew back into the kitchen once more. The iron had already put itself on the stove to heat, and as soon as the curtains appeared and laid themselves flat on the table, the iron jumped over to them and ironed them out beautifully.

Then back to their hooks they flew, and hung themselves up at the windows. How lovely they looked!

'Wonderful!' cried Winkle-Pip in delight. 'My, I wonder what my old Aunt Maria will say!'

Then he began to think about food.

'I think I'll have a big chocolate cake, a jelly with sliced pears in it, a dozen little ginger cakes, some ham sandwiches, some fresh lettuce and radishes, and some raspberries and cream,' decided Winkle-Pip. 'That would make a simply glorious tea!'

So he wished for all those – and you should just have seen his kitchen coming to life again. It didn't take the magic very long to make all the cakes and sandwiches he wanted, and to wash the lettuce and radishes that suddenly flew in from the garden.

'Splendid!' cried the gnome, clapping his hands with joy. 'Won't my Aunt

Maria stare to see all this?'

In the afternoon his old aunt came – and as soon as she opened the kitchen door, how she stared! She looked at the snowy sink, she looked at the spotless floor. She stared at the clean curtains, and she stared at the shining saucepans. Then she gazed at the lovely tea spread out on the table.

'Well!' she cried in astonishment. 'What a marvellous change, Winkle-Pip. How hard you must have worked! I am really very, very pleased with you.'

She gave the gnome a loud kiss, and he blushed very red.

'It's my wishing-suit, Aunt,' he said, for he was a truthful little gnome. He told her all about it and she was full of surprise.

'Well, you be sure to take great care of it,' she said, eating a big piece of chocolate cake. 'And whatever you do, Winkle-Pip, don't forget to go out into the world of boys and girls and find six of them to grant wishes to – or you'll lose the wishing-magic as sure as eggs are eggs.'

Winkle-Pip did enjoy his wishing-suit! He granted wishes to all his friends – and you may be sure that everyone wanted to be his friend when they knew about his new magic suit! Then a time came when he knew that he must go out into our world, for the magic in his suit began to weaken.

So one day Winkle-Pip put on his suit of yellow silk and his fine feathered cap, and walked to the end of Fairyland.

'How pleased all the boys and girls will be to see me!' he said. 'And how glad they will be to have their wishes granted. I am sure they don't see fairy folk very often, and they will go mad with joy to find me walking up to them.'

'Don't be too sure,' said his friend, the green pixie, who had walked to the gates of Fairyland with him. 'I have heard that boys and girls nowadays don't believe in fairies, and are much too busy with their wireless-sets and their Meccanos to want to listen to tales about us. They might not believe in you!'

'Rubbish!' said Winkle-Pip. He shook hands with the green pixie and walked out into our world. He looked all around him and wondered which way to go.

'I'll go eastwards,' he thought. 'It looks as if there might be a town over there.'

So off he went, and after a few miles he came to a little market town. He went along, peeping into the windows of the houses as he passed by, and at last he saw a nursery. A little boy and girl were playing with a beautiful dolls' house, and they were talking about it.

'You know, this dolls' house is very old-fashioned,' said the little boy. 'It's got oil-lamps, instead of electric light. It's a silly dolls' house, I think.'

'Well, I'm sure Grandpa won't have electric light put into it for us,' said the little girl. 'I do so wish he would. That would be fine!'

'Ha!' thought Winkle-Pip. 'Here's a chance for me to give them a wish.'

So he jumped into the window, and walked quietly up behind the children. 'Would you like electric light in that dolls' house?' he asked. 'You have only to wish for it, whilst I am here, and you shall have it.'

The children looked round in surprise.

'Of course I'd like it,' said the girl. 'I wish I could have electric light all over the house!'

In a second the magic had worked, and the dolls' house was lit up with tiny electric lights from top to bottom! How the children gasped to see such a wonderful sight. They found that there were tiny switches beside each door, and when they snapped these on and off the lights went on or out. They began to play with them in great excitement.

Meanwhile the gnome stood behind them, waiting for a word of thanks. The children seemed quite to have forgotten him. He was terribly hurt, and at last he crept out of the window, without even saying good-bye.

'Fancy not thanking me for granting their wish!' he thought, mournfully. 'Well, that was a nasty surprise for me! I thought the children would be delighted to talk to me too.'

Winkle-Pip went on again, and after a while he came across two boys hunting in the grass for something they had lost.

'Where can that shilling have gone?' he heard one of them say. 'Oh, I do wish we could find it, for we shall get into such trouble for losing it, when we get home.'

Up went Winkle-Pip to them. 'I can grant you your wish,' he said. 'I am a gnome, and have my wishing-suit on.'

The two boys looked at him.

'Don't be silly,' said one. 'You know quite well that there are no such things as gnomes – and as for wishing-suits, well, you must think us silly to believe in things like that! You couldn't possibly grant us a wish!'

Winkle-Pip went very red. He stuck his hands in his pockets and looked at the two boys.

'Do you really want to find that shilling?' he asked.

'Yes, rather!' said the boys. 'We wish we could, for we shall get whipped for coming home without it.'

No sooner had they wished than the silver shilling rose up from where it had been hidden in the grass, and flew into Winkle-Pip's hand.

'Here it is,' he said to the boys, and gave it to them. But were they pleased? No, not a bit of it!

'You had it all the time!' they cried, for they had not seen it fly into the gnome's hand. 'You have played a trick on us!'

They set upon the poor gnome and he had to run for his life. He sat down on the first gate he came to and rubbed his bruises.

'Well!' he thought miserably. 'That's two wishes granted and not a word of thanks for either of them. What is the world coming to, I wonder? Is there any politeness or gratitude left?'

After a while he went on again, and soon he heard the sound of sobbing. He peeped round the corner and saw a little girl sitting on the steps of a small house, crying bitterly.

'What's the matter?' asked Winkle-Pip, his kind heart touched by her loud sobs. At first the little girl didn't answer, but just frowned at him. Then suddenly from the house there came a voice.

'Now stop that silly crying, Mary! It was very naughty of you to break your poor dolly like that, just out of temper.'

'I shall break her again if I like!' shouted the naughty little girl, jumping to her feet and stamping hard. The gnome was terribly shocked.

'You shouldn't talk like that,' he said. 'Why, do you know, I came to give

you a wish, and —'

'Silly creature, silly creature!' screamed the bad-tempered child, making an ugly face at him. 'I wish you'd go away, that's what I wish! I wish you'd run to the other end of the town; then I wouldn't see you any more!'

Well, of course, her wish had to come true and poor Winkle-Pip found himself scurrying off to the other end of the town in a mighty hurry. He was soon very much out of breath, but not until he was right at the other end of the little town did his feet stop running.

'My goodness!' said Winkle-Pip, sinking down on the grass by the road-side. 'What a horrid day I'm having! What nasty children there are nowadays! Three more wishes to give away – and, dear me, I do wish I'd finished, for I'm not enjoying it at all.'

As Winkle-Pip sat there, two children came by, a boy and a girl.

'Hallo, funny-face,' said the boy, rudely. 'Wherever do you come from?'

'I come from Fairyland,' said the gnome. 'I am a gnome, as I should think you could guess.'

'Pooh!' said the boy, 'what rubbish to talk like that! There are no gnomes or fairies.'

'Of course not,' said the little girl.

'Well, there are,' said Winkle-Pip, 'and, what's more, I'm rather a special gnome. I've come into your world today to give wishes to six children. I've wasted three wishes, and I'm beginning to think there are no children worth bothering about nowadays.'

'What, do you mean you can grant wishes to us?' asked the boy. 'I don't believe it! Well, I'll try, anyway, and we'll see if what you say is true! I wish for a banana, a pear, and a pineapple to come and sit on your head!'

Whee-ee-ee-ee-eesh! Through the air came flying a large banana, very ripe, a big pear, and a spiky pineapple. Plonk! They all fell on poor Winkle-Pip's head and he groaned in dismay. The children stared in amazement and began to laugh. Then they looked rather scared.

'Ooh!' said the boy. 'He must be a gnome, after all, because our wish came true!'

Winkle-Pip was so angry that he couldn't think what to say. The children gave him one more look and then took to their heels and fled, afraid of what the gnome might do to them in revenge.

Poor Winkle-Pip! He was so distressed and so hurt to think that children could play him such a mean trick when he had offered them a wish, that he hardly knew what to do. He tried his best to get the fruit off his head, but it was so firmly stuck there that it would not move.

'Oh dear! oh dear!' wept the gnome. 'I shall have to let it all stay there, because I can't have any wishes for myself till I have given away the six wishes to boys and girls.'

Presently there came by a little girl carrying a heavy load of wood. She stopped when she saw the gnome, and looked at him in surprise.

'Why are you carrying all those things on your head?' she asked. 'Aren't they dreadfully heavy?'

'Yes,' said the gnome with a sigh. 'But I can't very well help it.' Then he told the little girl all his story, and she was very sorry for him.

'I do wish I could get it off for you,' she said. 'If I had a wish, I would wish that, and the fruit would fly away.'

No sooner had she spoken these words than her wish came true! Off flew the banana, off went the pear, and off jumped the pineapple. They all disappeared with a click, and the gnome shook his head about in joy.

'Hurrah!' he said. 'They've gone. Oh, you nice little girl, I'm so glad you wished that wish. You're the only unselfish child I have met in my journeys today.'

'And you're the first person who has ever called me unselfish,' said the little girl, with a sigh. 'I live with my stepmother, and she is always telling me I am lazy and selfish. I do try so hard not to be.'

'Poor child,' said Winkle-Pip, thinking it was a dreadful shame to make a little girl carry such a heavy load of wood. 'Have you no kind father?'

'No,' said the little girl. 'I have an aunt though, but since we moved she doesn't know where my stepmother and I live. My stepmother didn't like her because she was kind to me, and wanted me to live with her. She said I was nothing but a little servant to my stepmother, and so I am. I wouldn't mind that a bit, if only she would love me and be kind to me.'

Winkle-Pip was nearly in tears when he heard this sad story. 'I do wish I could help you,' he said. 'What a pity your kind aunt isn't here to take you to her home and love you.'

'I do wish she was,' said the little girl, lifting the bundle of wood on to her shoulder again – and then she gave a loud cry of delight and dropped it. Winkle-Pip cried out too, for, what do you think? – hurrying towards them was the kindest, plumpest woman you could possibly imagine!

'Auntie! Auntie!' cried the little girl. 'I was just wishing you were here!'

'Of course,' said Winkle-Pip to himself with a smile, 'that's the sixth wish! I'd quite forgotten there was still another one to give. Well, I'm very, very glad that this little girl has got the last wish. She used up one wish to set me free from that banana, pear, and pineapple, and she deserves to have one for herself, bless her kind heart!'

'Where have you come from, Auntie?' asked the little girl, hugging the smiling woman round the neck. 'Oh, I have missed you so!'

'I've come to fetch you home with me,' said her aunt, kissing her. 'I've had such a time trying to find out where your stepmother took you to. I don't quite know how I got here, but still, here I am, and you're coming straight home with me, and I'm going to look after you and love you.'

'But what about my stepmother?' asked the child.

'Oh, I'll go and see her for you,' said the gnome, with a grin. 'I'll tell her what I think of her. You go home with your aunt and have a lovely time. I'll take your wood back for you.'

So the little girl went off happily, with her aunt holding her tightly by the hand. Winkle-Pip shouldered the bundle of wood and ran off to the little cottage that the child had pointed out to him.

An ugly, bad-tempered-looking woman opened the door, and frowned when she saw Winkle-Pip.

'I've brought you the wood that your little stepdaughter was bringing,' said the gnome. 'She has gone to live with her auntie.'

'Oh, she has, has she?' said the woman, picking up a broom. 'Well, I'm sure you've had something to do with that, you interfering little creature! I'll give you such a drubbing!'

She ran at the little gnome, but he stuck his hands into his pockets, and wished quickly.

'I've given away six wishes!' he said. 'Now my wishing-suit is full of magic for me again – so I wish myself back in Fairyland once more!'

Whee-ee-ee-eesh! He was swept up into the air, and vanished before the angry woman's eyes. She turned pale with fright, and ran inside her cottage and banged the door. She was so terrified that she never once tried to find out where her stepdaughter had gone.

As for Winkle-Pip, he was delighted to get home again.

Over a cup of cocoa he told the green pixie all his adventures, and they both agreed that he had had a most exciting day.

It will soon be time for Winkle-Pip to walk out into our world again – so be careful if you meet him, and do try to use your wish in the best way you can.

The Surprising Blackberry

'Let's go blackberrying,' said Ronnie to Wendy. 'There are heaps of berries on the hill above the village.'

'All right,' said Wendy. 'I'll get the baskets.'

'Bring me back enough to make Daddy a blackberry pie!' said their mother. 'He loves that, and will be so pleased to see it.'

So the children promised to bring back their baskets quite full, so that Daddy could have a pie that evening. Off they went, carrying their baskets in which Mummy had put sandwiches for them.

It was a long climb up the hill, and when at last they reached the big stretch of blackberry bushes, they were both tired.

'Shall we eat our sandwiches now?' said Wendy. 'Then we can pick blackberries hard until it is time to go home.'

'Yes,' said Ronnie. So they sat down and ate their sandwiches. That emptied their baskets, so they at once set to work to pick the blackberries. What a lot there were! Great big, juicy ones, as black as could be! The children ate a lot, and filled their baskets as well.

When they had got a fine load, and their baskets were almost running over with the berries, they sat down for a rest. The sun was very hot indeed, and they found a nice shady place under a tree. They put their baskets down beside them, and lay down flat on their backs.

They were both tired, and in a few moments they were fast asleep. Wendy woke up first and dug Ronnie in the ribs.

'Wake up,' she said. 'We've both been asleep! Hadn't we better start for home?'

'Yes,' said Ronnie, rubbing his eyes. He put out his hand for his basket, and then stared in the utmost surprise! For it was quite empty!

Wendy looked at hers too – and that was quite empty as well! The two children didn't know what to make of it. They were very much upset.

'Someone has been along and stolen our blackberries,' said Ronnie, in a temper. 'Oh, what a mean thing to do! Now Daddy won't have any pie for supper!'

'Who can it be?' asked Wendy.

The two children stood up and looked all round them. There was no sign of anyone. Then suddenly Ronnie sniffed the air.

'Smell, Wendy!' he said. 'Sniff the air!'

Wendy sniffed. Then she turned to Ronnie in excitement.

'That's the smell of blackberry pie!' she said. 'Someone's making it quite near here – and I guess it is with our blackberries!'

The children went in the direction of the delicious smell. It got stronger and stronger, and suddenly they came to a little door set deep in the hillside. It was open, and from inside came the smell of blackberry pie. Someone was singing a little song, and when Wendy peeped in, she saw a pixie standing by a table, setting it with knives and forks.

Ronnie went boldly into the tiny room, and startled the pixie so much that he dropped a knife and fork with a great clatter.

'Where did you get those blackberries for your pie?' asked Ronnie. 'Did you take them out of our baskets?'

Before the pixie could answer a lovely fairy came in through the open door too.

'Is dinner ready?' she began to ask – and then she saw Ronnie and stared in surprise.

'What do you want here?' she said.

'If you please,' said Ronnie, 'I came to find out if the blackberries cooking in that pie over there were stolen from our baskets whilst we were asleep.'

'Oh, how dreadful!' said the fairy. She turned to the pixie and spoke to him sternly.

'Slyfoot,' she said, 'have you been up to your tricks again? Did you take those blackberries from these children, or did you pick them, as I told you to?'

'I t-t-took them from their b-b-b-askets,' stammered the pixie, going very red. 'You see, I hadn't t-t-time to pick them, and —'

'You very naughty little pixie!' cried the fairy. 'Go out of the room this minute, and put yourself straight to bed!'

The pixie burst into tears and left the room howling. The fairy turned to Ronnie and said how sorry she was.

'He is a very naughty fellow,' she said. 'I am always having to punish him. May I pay you for the blackberries he stole?'

'Oh no,' said Ronnie, politely. 'Please don't trouble any further.'

'You see, they were for Daddy's blackberry pie tonight,' explained Wendy, who had come into the little room to see what was happening. 'He will be disappointed, but we can easily get some more tomorrow.'

'Oh dear!' said the fairy, in distress. 'I do hate anyone to be disappointed. Ah, wait a minute! I know what I can do! I have a magic blackberry somewhere which will be just the thing for you!'

She hunted in some drawers and at last brought out a small hard blackberry, not quite ripe. She gave it to Ronnie and told him what to do with it.

'You put it on a dish and say:

"Blackberry small, please will you try

To make yourself into a blackberry pie?"

'Then you will see something surprising!' she said. Ronnie took the berry and thanked her very much. Then they said good-bye and ran off down the hillside, carrying their baskets with them.

'What an adventure, Wendy!' said Ronnie. 'I do wonder what will happen when we say the magic rhyme, don't you?'

Mother was very disappointed when she saw that their baskets were quite empty. But when she heard about their adventure, she could hardly believe her ears.

'Here's Daddy,' she said. 'Now put the blackberry on a dish, and see what happens.'

So, with everybody watching, Ronnie put the little blackberry into a big pie-dish.

'Blackberry small, please will you try

To make yourself into a blackberry pie?' he said.

Nothing happened at first. Then the blackberry suddenly swelled, and broke into six pieces, each of which became a berry, black and juicy. Then they all swelled and six more came from each. This went on till the pie-dish was quite filled. Then, suddenly, so quickly that no one saw how it happened, the dish was covered with a lovely crust. Then steam began to rise from the pie, and the crust turned a golden brown.

It was ready to eat!

'Good gracious!' cried Daddy. 'That is quite the most wonderful thing I've ever seen. We must keep that magic blackberry and use it lots of times!'

But, of course, nobody knew which of the blackberries was the right one! Mummy cut the pie and they peered inside to see if they could see the little hard berry but they couldn't. It was cooked along with the rest!

'Never mind!' said Daddy. 'Let's eat the lovely pie!'

So they did – and they all said it was the finest they had ever tasted in all their lives. By the time they had finished there wasn't even a crumb left!

'Tomorrow I'll go with you to see that little house in the hillside,' said Daddy.

But wasn't it disappointing, when they got there the little door had vanished, and though they hunted everywhere, up and down the hill, they couldn't find it again.

'Never mind, we've had the pie!' said Ronnie. 'Wasn't that blackberry surprising? I wonder which of us ate it!' But none of them ever knew!

The Prisoners
of the Dobbadies

When Peter was just finishing his lessons at twelve o'clock, Nurse came running in at the front gate, looking very red.

'Whatever is the matter, Nurse?' asked Mummy.

'Oh dear, oh dear! I've lost Pamela!' said Nurse, sinking down into a chair and looking very miserable.

'Lost Pamela! Where?' exclaimed Mummy.

'We were in the wood together, and Pamela wanted to play at ball. I threw the ball to her and she missed it. She laughed and ran behind a tree to get it, and then,' said poor Nurse, 'she didn't come back. I looked and called, but it wasn't any good.'

They all set off to look for Pamela, but although they called and called, they got no answer, and had to come home without her.

'She must have gone with the fairies,' said Peter. 'Mummy darling, do let me go and see if I can find her.'

Mummy looked at Daddy.

'Shall we let him go and see?' she asked. 'He really does see fairies, you know.'

'Yes, let him try,' said Daddy.

'Oh, thank you, Daddy!' cried Peter, catching up his hat. 'I'll go now, and I'm sure I'll bring Pamela back again. Goodbye, Mummy!' and, after a hug, Peter ran out into the garden.

He went straight to the wood, and made his way into the darker parts where the trees grew close together. He came to a little clearing at last, and in the middle grew a ring of white toadstools.

'I'll sit down in the middle of this ring,' he said, 'for there must be fairies somewhere about here.'

He sat down and looked around. Presently he heard a little voice.

'Hullo, Peter!'

'Hullo!' he said. 'Where are you? I can't see you.'

'Here I am!' laughed the voice, and, looking round, Peter saw a little yellow fairy peeping from behind a tree.

'Come and talk to me,' begged Peter. 'I want to ask you something.'

The fairy came and sat on one of the toadstools. 'I'm Morfael,' she said. 'What is it you want to know?'

'Can you tell me where Pamela is?' asked Peter.

'Yes, Caryll took her off to Fairyland this morning,' answered Morfael.

'Whatever for?' asked Peter in surprise.

'Well, you see, the Princess of Dreamland is very ill, and the Wise Elf says she will only get better if she hears the laugh of a little mortal girl. We knew Pamela had the sweetest laugh in the world, so Caryll had orders to take her to Dreamland for a time,' explained Morfael.

'Well, I'm going to fetch her back,' said Peter, getting up. 'Mummy wouldn't mind her making the Princess better, I know, but Pamela is too little to be all alone without anyone she knows. Which is the shortest way to Fairyland from here?'

'Down Oak Tree House,' answered Morfael. 'Knock three times. Goodbye! I hope you'll find Pamela,' and away she flew.

'Oak Tree House!' said Peter, looking round. 'Wherever's that?'

All around him grew beech trees, and he walked about a little, until he came to a big oak tree.

'This must be it,' he thought to himself, and knocked three times loudly. A little voice sang a little song:

> *'If a fairy's standing there*
> *Enter in, and climb the stair.*
> *If a mortal child you be*
> *Eat an acorn from the tree.'*

Peter looked for an acorn, and ate the nut inside the shell.

Immediately everything round him seemed suddenly to grow tremendously big, and made him gasp for breath.

'Goodness me!' said Peter, most astonished. 'Why, I've gone small. And oh, how funny! I'm holding on to a grass!'

He looked up at the oak tree. It seemed simply enormous, and its branches looked as if they must touch the sky.

Just in front of him was a little door. It was fitted into the oak tree so beautifully that it was difficult to see it.

Peter pushed at it, and it opened. To his surprise he saw a staircase going up inside the tree.

'What fun!' he said, and carefully shutting the door behind him, he ran up the winding staircase.

At the top he came to a little room, rather like an office, in which sat a gnome with a very big head.

'Good morning,' said Peter politely, 'and thank you for telling me to come in.'

'Good morning,' said the gnome. 'I'm Garin. It isn't often I get a visit from a little boy.'

'I'm Peter, and I'm looking for my sister,' said Peter. 'Could you tell me the way to Fairyland?'

'Yes, certainly. The Yellow Bird will take you straight there,' said Garin. 'But he doesn't come till two o'clock. I'm just going to have my dinner. Will you have some with me?'

'I'd love to,' answered Peter. 'I haven't had any, and I'm terribly hungry.'

'Sit down then,' said Garin. He bustled about, and soon had the strangest-looking dinner ready. Peter enjoyed it thoroughly and told him all about Pamela, and how he was going to look for her.

'Well, I don't think you'll find it quite so easy as you think,' said Garin, looking grave. 'The Dobbadies don't like the Princess of Dreamland, because she won't let them live in her country, they're too mischievous. And if they hear that Pamela is going to cure the Princess, they may take it into their heads to capture Pamela before she gets to Dreamland.'

'Oh dear! Do you really think so?' asked Peter, putting down his glass of honey-dew drink in dismay.

'Well, I don't know,' answered Garin, 'but the Yellow Bird will tell us all the news when he comes. Anyway, I'll give you a piece of advice, which will always be of help to you in Fairyland.'

'Oh, thank you!' said Peter gratefully. 'I'll be sure to remember it.'

'Well, it's this,' said Garin. 'Whenever you feel impatient, or cross, don't think about it, and instead, look round you and see if you can find something beautiful. If you do that you'll be all right – but if you don't, things will go wrong and you won't find Pamela.'

'Well, that sounds easy enough,' said Peter.

'Hark! What was that?'

A noise of footsteps was heard on the stairs.

'Oh, that's only the people who want to go to Fairyland at two o'clock,' explained Garin, clearing away the dinner.

Then into the little room came all sorts of fairies and gnomes, talking and laughing with each other.

Suddenly a little bell tinkled.

'There's the Yellow Bird,' exclaimed Garin. 'Come along, everybody.'

He opened a door, and Peter saw leaves waving in the wind.

'Why, it's the outside of the tree,' he exclaimed.

Everyone walked along a broad branch until they came to where a large and beautiful yellow bird was waiting.

'Good afternoon,' said the Yellow Bird. 'Is everybody here?'

'Yes,' said Garin. 'Get on, Peter. Any news, Yellow Bird?'

'Yes,' answered the bird. 'The Dobbadies have captured the Princess of Dreamland, and a little girl called Pamela, who was with her, and nobody knows where they've gone.'

'Oh dear! Oh dear!' said Peter. 'That's just what you said might happen, Garin. Now what am I to do?'

'Are you Pamela's brother?' asked the Yellow Bird. 'Well, get on my back, and I'll try and think of a plan for you as we go along.'

Peter got on, and all the fairies and gnomes climbed up too. It was a very good thing the Yellow Bird had such a broad back, Peter thought.

Just as they were going to start, someone came running across the branch.

'Stop, stop!' she cried. 'I'm coming too.'

'Hurry up, hurry up, Little Miss Muffet,' called Garin. 'You're very late.'

'I'm so sorry,' panted Miss Muffet, a little girl about the same size as Peter, 'but that horrid spider came and frightened me again and I dropped my bowl and spoon, and had to go back and find them.'

She sat down beside Peter. The Yellow Bird spread his wings and off he flew into the air.

'Goodbye, goodbye!' called Garin.

Peter clung on to the bird's feathers, and thought flying was simply glorious. He was sorry when the Yellow Bird kept stopping at various places, to let the fairies, the gnomes, or the rabbit get down.

At last only he and Miss Muffet were left.

'Have you thought of a plan yet?' asked Peter.

'Yes. I think you had better go to the Hideaway House, and ask the Wise Elf there to help you. He will know what to do,' answered the bird.

'I'll go with you,' said Miss Muffet. 'I've got to get off near there.'

At last the Yellow Bird slowed down and came to a stop.

'Here you are,' he said. 'The Hideaway House is in that wood over there.'

'Oh, thank you,' said Peter, getting off. He helped Miss Muffet off, and they both went into the wood.

Suddenly Miss Muffet gave a scream.

'Oh! Oh! There's that horrid spider again!'

Peter saw an immense brown spider coming towards Miss Muffet.

'Quick, run!' he shouted, catching hold of her hand and dragging her behind a tree.

Then he bravely caught up a dead tree-branch, and turned to face the spider.

'I'm going to kill you if you frighten Miss Muffet any more,' he said, and lifting up his stick, he brought it down on the spider's hairy back with a tremendous whack.

To his great astonishment, the spider sat down and began to cry.

'Oh, oh, oh!' he sobbed. 'You are unkind to me. I'm not really a spider, I'm a fairy changed into one. And I love Miss Muffet, but whenever I sit down beside her, I'm so ugly, I frighten her away. And now you've hurt me dreadfully.'

'I'm awfully sorry,' said Peter, 'but how was I to know that you weren't a spider? Wait a minute, and I'll tell Miss Muffet.'

He ran to where she was hiding.

'It isn't a spider, it's a poor fairy changed into one,' he told her, 'and he loves you and doesn't want to frighten you.'

'Is it really?' asked Miss Muffet. 'Then I don't mind so much. I'll go and stroke the poor thing.'

She ran to where the spider was still crying large tears on to the grass, and stroked him. He stopped crying at once, and cried out:

'A thousand thanks to you, little boy. You have done me a great kindness in making Miss Muffet friends with me. Any time you want help, clap your hands three times, and call for Arran the Spider.'

'Thank you, I will,' said Peter, 'but now, goodbye, I'm going to the Wise Elf in Hideaway House.'

'We'll stay and help you catch it, then,' said Miss Muffet, who seemed to have lost all fear of the spider.

'Catch it! Whatever do you mean?' exclaimed Peter, astonished.

Miss Muffet laughed. 'Ah! You'll see,' she said.

'There's Hideaway House,' said Peter, running towards a little wooden house. But just as he got near to it, it disappeared!

'Oh!' cried Peter, amazed and stopping still. 'It's gone!'

'It's behind you, Peter,' laughed Miss Muffet. Sure enough it was.

'However did it get there?' said Peter, going towards it again. But just as he reached the front door, it vanished again.

'I don't like this sort of house,' said Peter, looking puzzled. 'Where's it gone to now?'

'Over in that corner,' said the spider, pointing to it with one of his eight legs.

'I'll try again,' said Peter, and ran over to the little house, but no – directly he reached it, it disappeared once more.

'This is silly,' stormed Peter, feeling quite cross.

'We'll help you,' said Miss Muffet. 'Directly it comes near us, we'll catch hold of it.'

But try as they would, the Hideaway House always got away, and when they looked round, there it was, standing behind them somewhere.

'It's got a very good name,' said Peter, 'but it's the silliest house I ever saw.'

He stared at the house and frowned hard. He felt very impatient and cross. Then he suddenly remembered Garin's advice.

'He said I was to look round for something beautiful whenever I felt cross,' said Peter to himself. 'Very well, I will.'

He looked all round the wood, and his eye caught sight of something blue.

'What's that?' he said, and ran to see. 'Oh, 'tis a perfectly lovely little flower!' he called to Miss Muffet. 'Come and look, it's the prettiest I ever saw.'

Miss Muffet looked at it.

'It's the rarest flower in Fairyland,' she said. 'What a good thing you saw it! Now, all you've got to do is to pick it, and stand in the middle of the clearing here and shout out to the Wise Elf that you've found the blue Mist-flower! He's always wanting it for his magic spells.'

Peter picked it, and stood upright.

'Wise Elf in Hideaway House!' he called. 'I've found the blue Mist-flower! Do you want it?'

At once the door of Hideaway House opened, and an Elf with large wings, large eyes and large ears stood on the doorstep.

'Come in! Come in,' he called, 'and bring the Mist-flower with you.'

'Goodbye,' cried Miss Muffet and the spider. 'We're so glad you've got the Hideaway House at last!' and off they went into the wood.

Peter ran across to the Hideaway House, and to his delight it stood still this time and didn't disappear. He went inside the front door and found himself in a dark room at one end of which sat the Wise Elf.

'Good afternoon,' he said. 'I am glad to see you.'

'Good afternoon,' said Peter. 'This is a funny sort of house to live in. If I hadn't remembered Garin's advice to stop being cross and look round for something beautiful, I would never have got here.'

'Possibly not,' said the Wise Elf, nodding at Peter. 'Being impatient and cross never did anybody any good. Give me that Mist-flower, please.'

Peter handed it to him.

'Please could you tell me how I can find the Dobbadies?' he asked.

'Well,' said the Wise Elf, putting on a large pair of spectacles, and taking down a book. 'Well, I can tell you which way to go, and as you've been clever enough to find exactly the flower I've been wanting for six months, I shall be glad to show you part of the way. Let me see. Let me see!' and he turned over the pages of his book.

'Ah, here we are,' he said at last, coming to a page on which was a map.

'Yes, I thought so – the Dobbadies live on the north side of Dreamland – now, how can you get there? Ummm-m, um-m-m, let me see. Yes, I think I can tell you.'

'Oh, thank you,' said Peter gratefully.

'You had better go through the Underground Caves to the Sleepy Sloos, then you must get them to take you to the Rushing Lift to Cloudland. From Cloudland you can get straight down to Giant Roffti's, and he will carry you across to where the Dobbadies live. Then you must find out how to rescue Pamela.'

'It sounds rather hard,' said Peter, feeling a little dismayed.

'If you make up your mind to do it, you will do it,' said the Wise Elf, looking over the tops of his spectacles at Peter.

'Then I'm going to do it,' said Peter, jumping up. 'Would you mind showing me part of the way, Wise Elf?'

'Certainly,' answered the Elf. 'I can take you as far as the entrance to the Underground Caves.'

'Thank you,' said Peter. 'I'm really awfully obliged to you.'

The Wise Elf bent down and pulled a mat up from the floor. A trap-door lay underneath.

'Help me pull it up,' said the Elf. He and Peter tugged it upright, and Peter saw a long flight of steps stretching downwards.

The Wise Elf ran down the steps, and Peter followed. After they had gone down about a hundred, they came out into a large passage, which was lighted with green lamps.

'Oh, I do believe it's an underground railway. How lovely!' cried Peter.

'Quite right,' said the Elf. 'Ah, look! The lamps have changed to red. That means the train is coming.'

Then suddenly, gliding out of the darkness, came such a small engine that Peter thought it must be a toy one.

'It's run by magic,' explained the Wise Elf. 'It's stopping for us, so we must get in quickly.'

He helped Peter into a funny-looking carriage. There were no seats, but just fat cushions on the floor.

'Good afternoon,' said the Wise Elf politely to the folk inside. He chose a fat green cushion to sit on, and pointed out a mauve one.

The carriage was full of fairy-folk of all kinds. Goblins, gnomes, fairies, and pixies were there, all chattering gaily to each other.

'Where are you going to?' they asked Peter.

'To the Underground Caves,' he answered. 'Where are you all going to?'

'We're all going to the Gnome King's party,' answered a very beautifully-dressed fairy.

The train ran along quietly, past big bowl-shaped lamps lighting up the passage, and at last came to a stop at a little platform.

'Here we are!' said the Wise Elf. He and Peter got out, and the train went on into the darkness.

'Goodbye, goodbye,' called all the folk who were going to the party.

The Wise Elf went to a door on the platform and opened it. It led into a dark cave, lit only by one lantern in the middle.

'Here I must leave you,' said the Elf. 'If you wait here for a little while, you will see the entrance to the Underground Caves. I hope you will find Pamela. Goodbye.'

'Goodbye!' called Peter, feeling rather lonely as he saw the Elf run back to the platform to catch the next train back.

He waited in the dark cave for about ten minutes and then suddenly saw a shiny silver rope coming slowly down from the ceiling.

'This must be something to do with the cave's entrance,' said Peter, and as the rope reached him, he caught hold of it and gave it a pull.

Immediately one side of the cave split open and formed a great archway, leading into another cave!

'Hurray!' cried Peter, running through. 'Here's the entrance at last!'

He looked all round him, and found he was in a tremendously large cave, lighted with pink lights. No one was there. There was an archway leading into another cave. Peter ran into it. It was lighted with mauve lights, and was smaller than the first.

'Why, this one's got an archway leading into another cave,' cried Peter, 'and they're all empty.'

He ran into the next one and looked all round. It had orange lights and was still smaller.

On and on Peter went, into smaller and smaller caves, each lighted differently. At last he came to the smallest cave of all, which had big blue lamps swinging from the ceiling.

'Oh, there really is somebody here!' said Peter, feeling very pleased.

All around the cave were lying mouse-like creatures with large ears, and all were fast asleep.

'Hullo! Are you the Sleepy Sloos?' asked Peter loudly.

No one stirred.

'I say! I want to go to Cloudland,' called Peter, 'so will you help me, please?'

Still no one stirred, but Peter somehow felt quite certain some of the Sleepy Sloos were awake, but were too lazy to help him.

'Wake up! Wake up!' shouted Peter, shaking the one nearest him.

But it was all no good. Peter felt very cross and most impatient, and was just going to stamp round the cave in a temper, when he suddenly remembered Garin's advice again.

'Oh dear, there isn't anything beautiful to look at here!' he grumbled. But he determined to have a good look round the cave all the same.

'Hullo! What's that?' he said, tugging at something that twinkled in a crack of the cave rock. 'What a beautiful stone! It's a diamond, I do believe.'

'What?'

'What's that?'

'What have you got?'

All the Sleepy Sloos had suddenly woken up and were shouting at Peter.

'Hurray! He's found the magic stone we lost last week! How lovely!' cried they, and crowded round Peter.

'Oh,' said Peter, 'so you've woken up at last! What a good thing I took Garin's advice! If I give you back your stone, will you stay awake long enough to show me the Rushing Lift to Cloudland?'

'Yes, yes, yes!' cried the Sleepy Sloos.

Peter gave them the stone, which glittered and twinkled just as though it were alive.

The Sleepy Sloos took paws and danced in a ring and sang:

> *'Rushing Lift*
> *You must come down*
> *And take this boy*
> *To Cloudland Town.'*

Then crash! The roof of the cave split open and down there came a bright orange chair, swinging on purple ropes.

'Get in, get in,' cried the Sleepy Sloos. 'We want to go to sleep. Goodbye!' and they all settled down again and began to snore.

Peter got into the orange chair, and whizz-z-z! He shot right up into the air at a most tremendous pace! When it stopped, he got out and found himself on a great soft cloud.

'Goodness me! Now where do I go?' he said.

'Where would you like to go?' asked a voice.

'Who are you speaking?' asked Peter, looking all round.

'I'm the cloud. I'll take you wherever you like,' answered the voice.

'Then take me down to Giant Roffti's, please,' said Peter, feeling most astonished to hear a cloud speak.

'Very well. Sit down and hold tight,' commanded the cloud. Peter did so, and felt the cloud slowly sink down, down, down, through the air. It seemed simply ages before it stopped.

'Here we are!' at last said the cloud. 'We're in Roffti's backyard. He'll be in the kitchen, I expect. Goodbye!' And as Peter scrambled off the cloud, it swiftly rose again up into the sky.

Peter was in a huge backyard, full of the largest dustbins he had ever seen. Nearby was a great open door.

'I suppose that's the kitchen,' thought Peter, and walked boldly in.

Inside he found a huge giant busy putting tremendous cakes into an oven. The giant looked very hot and very tired, Peter thought.

'Please,' said Peter, 'could you take me to the Dobbadies?'

'Bless me! Bless me!! Bless me!!!' exclaimed the giant, dropping a tray of cakes in amazement. 'How you made me jump!'

'I am so sorry,' said Peter, feeling very uncomfortable as he saw the cakes rolling all over the floor.

'Oh, never mind,' puffed the giant, looking hotter than ever. 'Accidents will happen!'

'Are you very busy?' asked Peter politely.

'Yes. There's a grand party on in Giantland today and I'm baking some extra cakes,' answered the giant, picking up the dropped cakes.

'What a lot of parties are on today!' said Peter.

'Yes, the Dobbadies are going to this one,' said the giant. 'So it's no good my taking you to see them today.'

'Oh, good!' cried Peter. 'You see, I want to rescue my sister and the Princess of Dreamland from the Dobbadies, and it would be much easier if they're not there!'

'Right! Come along, quickly!' cried Roffti, catching Peter up in one hand. He rushed out into the garden, jumped across a large pond, ran down a dark lane, and into a broad drive. At the end stood a great sparkling palace, with thousands of windows.

'That's where the Dobbadies live!' said Roffti. 'Now, what's your sister's name?'

'Pamela,' said Peter, still dangling in the giant's huge hand.

'Pamela! Pamela! Pamela!' roared the giant.

At a tiny window near the roof a little girl's curly head peeped out.

'There she is!' shouted Peter excitedly. Roffti lifted Peter up and put him on the window-sill. To Peter's great delight there was Pamela, lifting her arms to him in joy.

'Peter! Oh, I am glad you've come!' she cried. 'And here's the Princess, she's a prisoner too.'

Peter clambered into the room, and saw a beautiful lady sitting on a chair, and looking very miserable.

'Cheer up!' he cried excitedly. 'I've come to rescue you while the Dobbadies are at the party!'

'Come on, then,' said Pamela, running to the door.

All three raced down the stairs and out into the garden. 'Hush!' suddenly cried the Princess as a cloppity noise reached them.

'Oh, oh, it's the Dobbadies!' whispered Pamela.

Sure enough it was! There they were, little gnome-like creatures, but with three legs instead of two, pouring into the garden, back from the party early.

'Oh dear! What can I do?' thought poor Peter, looking desperately around. 'I can't fight them all!'

Suddenly he remembered Arran the Spider.

'He'll help me, of course!' he cried, and clapping his hands three times loudly, he cried, 'Arran, Arran the Spider! Come and help me, Arran!'

All the Dobbadies crowded round shouting: 'They're escaping! Catch them!'

Then, just as they caught hold of Pamela and the Princess, Peter gave a shout: 'Hurrah! Here's good old Arran! And he's brought Miss Muffet, too!'

Arran, the huge spider, ran rapidly into the garden, carrying Miss Muffet on his back. The Dobbadies let go Pamela and the Princess with cries of alarm. 'What is it? What is it?' they cried.

'Something that will eat you!' cried Arran, as he jumped at them.

'Oh, oh, oh!' cried the Dobbadies, and fled into the palace for all they were worth.

'Quick!' cried Arran. 'Run whilst you've a chance. Miss Muffet will show you the way, and I'll come last and eat up the Dobbadies that follow!'

Little Miss Muffet ran down a passage into a large cave, and the others followed her. A river ran through the cave, and there was a little boat moored to a yellow post.

'Jump in, jump in!' cried Arran. 'The Dobbadies are coming again.'

All of them jumped in the little rocking boat, and just as a crowd of three-legged Dobbadies came rushing into the cave, Arran pushed off.

'Now we're safe,' he said, as the boat raced off on the underground river. 'There's no other boat for the Dobbadies to take.'

So the Dobbadies were left behind, shouting and screaming because the prisoners had escaped.

'Oh, thank you for coming to our help, Arran,' said Peter, stroking the huge spider.

'Very pleased to,' said Arran. 'You made little Miss Muffet friends with me, and I could never forget that.'

'Where do you want to go to?' asked Miss Muffet.

'Oh, home, please,' said Pamela. 'I've made the Princess well now, and I want my mummy.'

The boat went on and on until at last the river flowed out into open fields.

'Why, we've come to a pond!' exclaimed Peter, as the boat came to a stop.

'And it's our pond, in our garden!' cried Pamela. 'But I know there isn't a river into it!'

'Ah, it's magic, you see,' said Arran. 'It'll be gone tomorrow. Now, goodbye; you'll see us again sometime. I'm going to take the Princess back to Dreamland.'

'Goodbye, goodbye!' shouted Pamela and Peter, running up the garden path.

'Mummy, Mummy!' cried Pamela, as Mummy and Daddy came running to meet them.

'Oh, Peter, you are clever and brave!' said Mummy, when all the story had been told, and everyone had been hugged and kissed a hundred times over.

'Come and look at the magic river, Daddy,' begged Peter, running into the garden.

But alas! It was gone.

'Never mind,' said Peter, 'we've had some glorious adventures, and when the river comes again one day, we'll have some more!'

Lazy Binkity

Once upon a time there was a little Brownie called Binkity. He was very lazy and rather naughty, and was always being scolded by the other Brownies.

'Have you tidied up the Oak Tree Wood?' asked Ding, the chief Brownie, one day.

'No, I haven't, and I'm not going to!' answered Binkity rudely, and ran away before Ding could catch him. He curled up inside a hollow tree, and watched Ding looking for him, until he was tired and went away. Then Binkity came out of the tree and looked around for something to do.

'Silly old Ding!' he said to himself. 'He's always trying to make me work when I don't want to!'

Then he found a squirrel's hoard of nuts hidden under some leaves at the foot of a tree.

'Ha! Ha!' chuckled Binkity. 'I'll hide them somewhere else.'

He dug them up quickly, and put them in a rabbit hole. Then he went to find Bushy the Squirrel, who was asleep in a tree.

'Wake up! Wake up!' he cried. 'It's a lovely day for a scamper!'

Bushy rubbed his eyes and sat up. 'I feel hungry,' he said, and down the tree he scampered.

'I'll eat a nut or two,' said Bushy, scraping up the leaves at the foot of the tree where he had hidden his nuts.

But they weren't there!

'Oh dear, dear, dear!' cried the squirrel. 'Someone's taken them! Whatever shall I do! I must have something to eat in the winter!'

Binkity sat on a twig and laughed to see Bushy looking for nuts that weren't there.

Just then Ding, the chief Brownie, came by, with a crowd of other Brownies, and asked Bushy why he was looking so miserable.

'Someone's taken my nuts,' explained poor Bushy, 'and that horrid little Binkity keeps laughing at me.'

'Here are your nuts!' called a Brownie, who had accidentally found them in the rabbit hole where Binkity had put them. 'Binkity must have put them there, he's always playing tricks!'

Binkity began to feel he had better run away again, and looked round to see where he could go to.

'Binkity!' said Ding very sternly. 'You must be punished. You are lazy and mischievous and never help anyone in anything. I shall send you as a servant to Arran the Spider, and he will make you work really hard and keep you out of mischief!'

Now this was a terrible threat, for Arran the Spider sometimes ate people who didn't work hard enough, and Binkity was dreadfully frightened.

He jumped up, and ran away as fast as ever he could, with all the Brownies after him. It was getting dark, and he hoped that soon they would find it too dark to chase him.

'Catch him! Catch him!' called the Brownies, racing after naughty Binkity.

Binkity rushed right through the wood and out into some fields. Then it began to snow hard, and the snowflakes beat against the Brownie's face till he was cold and tired out. But still he could hear the other Brownies chasing him.

'Ah, there's a cottage!' suddenly panted Binkity, as he saw a light near by. He ran up to the cottage, and quick as lightning changed himself into a puppydog.

All the other Brownies, seeing only a shivering puppy, raced by without stopping.

'Now I'm safe,' thought Binkity, 'but, oh dear, how cold and wet I am!' He began to make a little whining noise, like a puppy.

Presently the door opened and a little girl peeped out.

'Oh, here's a poor little puppy!' she cried, picking Binkity up and taking him in.

She set him down before a fire, and gave him a saucer of milk to lap. When he was quite dry and warm, she took him over to her mother, who was in bed, looking very ill.

'Dear little puppy!' said the mother, stroking him. 'I wonder where he came from, Jean? We must keep him, if no one comes to claim him.'

Binkity lay down by the fire, warm and drowsy, and listened to Jean and her mother talking. Presently he was astonished to hear the mother crying.

'Oh, Jean darling,' she was saying, 'I am so ill I cannot get up again this winter, and that means you will have all the housework to do, and all the washing. You will have to do most of the sewing too, to make money, for I am too tired even for that!' And the poor woman sobbed as if her heart would break.

'Never mind, Mother,' said the little girl bravely, 'I will do my best. Don't cry, we shall be all right.' But Binkity could see that she looked dreadfully worried, and he was very sorry for her.

'I wonder if I could help her,' he thought, 'she has been so kind to me. I daren't change back into a Brownie in the daytime, in case the other Brownies see me. I must still be a puppy, till they have forgotten I was naughty. But at night! Yes! At night, I will change back into a Brownie, and do all the work!'

Binkity was so excited with his idea, that he could hardly wait until the house was dark and still.

When Jean had gone to bed and everything was still, Binkity changed into his own shape again. Then he bustled about the house, making no noise at all. He dusted and washed and tidied till the house was as clean as a new pin. Then, just as dawn came in at the windows, he changed into a puppy again and lay down by the fire.

When Jean woke up and looked round, she could hardly believe her eyes.

'Mother! Mother!' she cried. 'Look, look! The house is clean. There is no work to do! I can spend all the day sewing!'

'Jean, it's a Brownie!' said her mother in delight. 'There must have been one near here, working in the night. Leave a saucer of milk on the hearth every night when you go to bed, and don't peep to see what happens when you're in bed.'

All that day Jean sewed at beautiful tablecloths and curtains, which she sold in the town for money, and when night came she put a saucer of milk on the hearth.

'There! That's for you, whoever you are, little Brownie,' she called.

She patted the puppy and kissed him, never dreaming he was the little Brownie, and then she went to bed.

All that night Binkity, changed into a Brownie again, did the housework, and even baked some bread for Jean! Then at dawn he changed into a puppy again, and lay by the fire.

'The Brownie's been here again, Mother,' said Jean, next morning, delightedly, 'and he's done all the work! Isn't it lovely!'

All through the winter Binkity lived at the little cottage. Jean and her mother loved the little puppy that jumped around them in the daytime, and never guessed he was really a Brownie. And every night, when Binkity became himself again, he did all the housework and worked harder than he had ever worked before in his life. He loved Jean, and was always delighted to see how surprised she was each morning.

In the spring Jean's mother got better, and was able to get up. Binkity began to feel that he would like to live in the woods again, and talk to the birds and animals as he used to do, and to live in his little Tree House.

'I think I must go back now!' he said to himself one night as he was washing the floor. 'Perhaps the Brownies will have forgotten they were going to give me to Arran the Spider. Jean's mother can do the housework now, and I'll see that Jean always has plenty of money.'

So when the dawn came Binkity, instead of changing into a puppy again, slipped out of the cottage and ran back to his home in the woods.

'Oh, it's lovely to hear the birds again, and to talk to the rabbits!' said Binkity, thoroughly enjoying himself.

'Hullo, Binkity!' suddenly exclaimed a voice. Binkity turned round, and to his dismay found it was Ding, the chief Brownie.

'Oh, please don't send me to Arran the Spider!' he begged, kneeling down.

Ding smiled kindly. 'Why, Binkity,' he said, 'I'm ever so pleased with you! I know where you were all the winter, and I've often peeped into the cottage at night, and seen you scrubbing the floors.'

'Oh, have you?' cried Binkity, most astonished.

'Yes, often,' answered Ding. 'You used to be lazy and naughty, but you've learnt to work hard, and to help other people now. We're going to have a party tonight to welcome you back to Oak Tree Town again.'

'Oh, how lovely!' cried Binkity, delighted. He ran off to get himself clean and tidy, thinking it was really much more fun to be a good Brownie than a lazy one.

Jean was very astonished and sorry to find the little puppy was gone that morning, but her mother said it must have been a Brownie living with them. Binkity kept his word, and often used to go and visit the cottage and see that Jean was quite all right, and sometimes leave a shining gold piece under her pillow, for a surprise.

He's never lazy now, and if ever you come across a very neat and tidy wood, look about for Binkity. He's sure to be hiding somewhere about, watching you with his little twinkling eyes!

Can It Be True?

John was lying under a green tree, looking through the swaying branches at the blue sky. His book was beside him, closed, because he had just finished it. It had been a most exciting tale of magic in the olden days.

'Wizards and dragons and brownies and spells!' said John to himself. 'I suppose they're not really true – but how I wish I could find even a tiny bit of magic for myself. Then I'd know.'

The wind ran through the leaves of the trees, making a sound of whispering, and round him tall purple-pink foxgloves swayed to and fro. There were hundreds there, for the wood was famous for its tall, dreamy foxgloves.

John looked at them, and saw that now and again, when the wind blew a little more strongly, the bottom flower of a foxglove slid off and fell to the ground with a tiny thud.

'What a lot have fallen!' he thought. 'They don't look dead or faded, either, as most flowers do when they fall. What a strange name they have – foxgloves! As if foxes could ever wear them – or would want to, on their big furry paws!'

And then John suddenly sat up straight and stared hard between the trees. He had seen something very surprising! A small man was walking along a rabbit-path – a man much smaller than John himself! He had on a little brown tunic, and long brown stockings that covered his legs right up to his thighs. He had a pointed hat that flopped over at the top and a long grey beard. He was humming as he went, and the noise sounded like one of the big bumble-bees that visited the foxglove flowers one by one.

The little man carried a brown bag, and each time he came to a foxglove he picked up the fallen bells and popped them into his bag. He didn't see John till he was almost up to him. Then he started back in surprise, and stopped his bee-like humming.

'Who are you?' said John, in a half-whisper. 'You're surely not a – a brownie, are you?'

'My name is Mr Whiskers,' said the little fellow, looking at John with eyes as green as grass, 'and I live in this foxglove wood.'

'Oh. I see,' said John. 'Don't go away, please. Don't vanish or do anything like that. You – you seem so very real – but you can't be!'

'I'm real enough,' said Mr Whiskers. 'Are you?'

'Yes,' said John. 'Of course I am. Why are you collecting fallen foxglove bells? To sell to foxes?'

'Of course not,' said Mr Whiskers, picking up one by John's foot. 'You've got the name wrong – it isn't foxglove – it's folks'-glove – you've heard of the little Folk haven't you – the fairies and pixies and brownies, and …'

'Yes, they're in my books,' said John. 'But – if the right name is folks'-glove, are they gloves for fairies or brownies then?'

'Yes. Or mittens!' said Mr Whiskers, putting some more into his bag. 'Some pixies are so tiny that they can cover their whole hand with one of these bells, so they use them for mittens. Others sew five together and make them into five-fingered gloves. I sell them easily. There's a little magic in them, too, you know.'

John stared at the tiny fellow and felt a little flame of excitement springing inside him. 'Magic! Oh, how I've longed for a little magic!' he said. 'Is that true?'

'Try it for yourself!' said Mr Whiskers.

'How?' said John.

Mr Whiskers stared at him out of his grass-green eyes. 'Well, now, magic's strange stuff,' he said. 'I don't know if I want to trust you with any. Even to meddle with a little can be dangerous – and there's not very much in foxglove bells. Still – you look a nice lad, maybe you'll use it well.'

'Oh, I will. But tell me, do tell me!' begged John, afraid that this strange fellow would disappear before he had told him any more.

'Now listen!' said Mr Whiskers, setting his bag down beside him. 'You have to choose two unspoilt foxglove bells that have fallen that very day. You have to slip one on each thumb when you're in bed at night, just before you go to sleep. And you have to wish for something – and if you wake in the morning with the bells still on your thumbs, your wish may come true!'

'That's real magic!' said John, and his eyes shone as he looked at the little fellow beside him. 'I'll try it. This very night I'll try it.'

'Foxglove magic is good magic, so it's best not to use it for yourself,' said Mr Whiskers, picking up his bag again. 'Use it for someone you love – and wish hard – so hard that you can feel your heart swelling up with love and kindness. Good wishing is hard work, you know. Well, I must be going on my way. I've still half my bag to fill before I go home. Good-day to you.'

'Good-day,' said John, wondering if the little fellow would suddenly disappear. But he didn't. He went on through the trees, picking up a foxglove bell here and another there, humming like a bumble-bee all the time. He went out of sight at last.

John stood up and looked for two unspoilt fallen foxglove bells – but the little man had picked them all up. So he had to wait till the wind came by and shook the tall pink spires. Thud! A bell fell from the bottom of a foxglove stem and John picked it up. It was cool and smooth, and inside there were dusky spots of colour.

Thud! That was another one. He slipped both into his handkerchief and folded it carefully. Then he set off home. He was happy and amazed and excited. He couldn't possibly tell anyone what had happened to him that afternoon – except perhaps his mother, because he was going to use the foxglove magic for her, of course. If the magic was strong enough to make his wish come true, he would tell her then. But not unless!

And so, as he sits in his bed tonight, he will put a folks'-glove bell carefully on each thumb – and when he lies down he will wish hard and long, a good wish and a kind one. Will it come true? Ah – he may wake with bare thumbs in the morning, the bells fallen in his bed, and all the magic gone! I do hope he won't.

What fun to wear them all night long, and find your wish come true!

The Search
for Giant Osta

Sylfai was reading all by herself in the nursery, when there came a knock at the window.

'Goodness me, whoever's that?' thought Sylfai, getting up to see.

The knocking came again. Sylfai opened the window wide and looked out. 'Mind your head!' cried a little voice, and in flew a fairy dressed in yellow.

'I'm Corovell,' she said, 'and I've come to ask you something.'

'What is it?' asked Sylfai, staring at Corovell in astonishment.

'Well, a friend of mine is lying in a magic sleep in Giant Osta's castle. Giant Osta is dreadfully upset, because he's a good giant, and he thinks Peronel, my friend, must have offended someone and had a spell put on her.'

'But why have you come to me?' asked Sylfai, looking puzzled.

'Well, because the spell can only be broken by someone called Sylfai, and that's your name, isn't it?' asked Corovell.

'Yes, it is. Am I going to Fairyland, then?' said Sylfai, feeling tremendously excited.

'I'll take you now,' said Corovell. 'Shut your eyes and count to three, and hold on to me.'

'One, two, three!' counted Sylfai, holding on tight. Then she opened her eyes.

'Oh!' she cried. 'Oh, why I'm in Fairyland! However did I get here?'

She stood in a beautiful wood, with large toadstools standing about here and there. Corovell stood by her side.

'Now listen, Sylfai,' she said. 'I'm not allowed to come with you. You must find the way to Osta's by yourself. But I'll give you a piece of advice. If ever you feel cross with anyone in Fairyland say something nice.'

'I'll try and remember,' said Sylfai, 'but I wish you were coming with me.'

'Goodbye,' called Corovell, and off she flew.

'Dear me, she hasn't even told me which way to go,' said Sylfai, looking around. 'Well, I shall have to sit down on one of these big toadstools, and wait for someone to come along.'

She chose a large toadstool and sat down. Presently, to her astonishment, she saw a large green frog hop up on to another toadstool, and sit down there.

'Please,' said Sylfai, 'will you tell me the way to Giant Osta's?'

The frog blinked at her, but made no answer.

Then Sylfai saw a large green caterpillar crawl up on to another toadstool and curl itself round.

'Will you tell me the way?' she asked.

Still there was no answer.

Then on a third toadstool up hopped a great green grasshopper. He stared solemnly at Sylfai, but wouldn't speak a word.

Suddenly a cross voice made Sylfai jump. 'Now then!' it hissed. 'Get off my seat!'

Sylfai looked down and saw a long green snake sliding round about her toadstool.

'This isn't your seat!' she said. 'I got here first.'

Then the frog, the caterpillar, and the grasshopper all spoke at once – 'Push her off, push her off, push her off!' they cried in a sort of chorus.

Sylfai was going to say something very cross indeed, when she remembered Corovell's advice, and tried to think of something nice instead.

'Oh, I'm sorry if I am sitting on your toadstool,' she said politely. 'I'll get down.' And off she jumped.

The grass snake wriggled up and curled himself on the top.

'You are polite,' he said, 'instead of being cross and rude. We belong to a Green Club because we are all green and meet here to talk on the toadstools every evening. Can we help you in any way?'

'Well,' said Sylfai, feeling very glad she had been polite, 'can you tell me the way to Giant Osta's?'

The caterpillar raised itself up, and spoke:

'I have eaten cabbages in Osta's garden,' he said. 'I can tell you part of the way.'

'Oh, please do!' begged Sylfai.

'Well, go through the wood until you come to a little wooden house painted yellow. In it there lives a dwarf who will take you part of the way. Tell him Greenskin of the Green Club sent you.'

'Thank you,' said Sylfai, taking a last look at the members of the Green Club, and off she went through the wood.

Presently she came to a wooden house, painted yellow. Sylfai walked round it, looking for the door – but to her astonishment there was no door and only one tiny window, very high up.

Sylfai knocked loudly on the walls.

'Come in, come in,' cried a voice.

'I can't come in, there's no door,' answered Sylfai.

'Come in, come in!' repeated the voice.

Sylfai was just going to say something cross, when she remembered in time.

'Whatever nice thing can I say?' she thought. 'Oh, I know. What a pretty yellow colour your house is!' she called.

'Oh, do you like it? I'm so glad,' said the voice, sounding very pleased. 'As you like the outside, you can see the inside. Climb up the beech tree by the side of the house and get on the roof.'

Sylfai climbed up the tree and clambered on to the roof. 'Well, dear me,' she said, 'there is only one way of getting into this house it seems – and that is down the chimney!'

She climbed into the chimney, let herself go, and whizz! She found herself sitting inside the house, on a big yellow cushion.

'That's the way to come in!' chuckled the dwarf. 'I like my house to be different from other people's!'

'Greenskin of the Green Club told me you would show me part of the way to Giant Osta's,' said Sylfai.

'Certainly,' said the dwarf, a bright-eyed little man. 'Follow me.'

He lifted up a trap-door, sat down on the edge, and dangled his legs down. 'Come after me,' he said, and let himself drop.

Sylfai, feeling a little nervous, did the same. She felt herself gliding down a slippery passage – down and down, with little lamps to light the way whizzing past her.

At last she stopped. She found herself by a dark river, which was flowing silently along.

'Here's a boat!' said the dwarf, pulling up an odd-shaped boat to the side. 'Get in – you don't need any oars. I'll give you a push off. Goodbye!'

Sylfai jumped in and off sped the boat, rocking from side to side. It floated past great caves, cast dimly lit passages, and at last stopped by a little wooden platform. Sylfai got out and looked around.

'Wherever do I go now!' she thought. 'Dear me, what's that?'

She heard a rumbling noise coming down the passage in front of her, and then there rolled a bright green ball round a corner, right up to her feet.

'Oh,' cried Sylfai, 'you're hurting my toes! Do roll off.'

The green ball pressed harder. Sylfai was just going to lose her temper when she remembered Corovell's advice again.

'If you don't mind, please will you move yourself?' she said politely. 'I'd like to see what you are.'

The ball burst open, and out jumped a peculiar creature, with tiny legs, a round body and a round head.

He waved his funny little arms. 'I'm the Crawly-wawly Bumpty,' he said, 'and I always roll on to people's toes, just to see what they say. You're the first person who's ever been polite to me. What can I do for you?'

'What a good thing I was polite!' thought Sylfai. Then she said aloud, 'I don't think you're very kind to hurt people's toes, really, you know. Will you tell me where to find Giant Osta?'

'Oh yes. He lives near here. Go up that passage till you come to a door. Knock and Osta will open it.' The Crawly-wawly Bumpty jumped into his ball again and rolled merrily off.

'What a funny creature!' said Sylfai, as she went along the passage. After a long while she came to a great blue door, with a tremendous handle. She knocked with her knuckles as loudly as she could.

The door swung open, and a giant peered out and said: 'Who is there?'

'It is only Sylfai, come to try and break Peronel's spell,' answered Sylfai, looking in wonder at the huge giant, whose kindly eyes seemed miles above her.

'Oh, splendid!' cried the giant. 'I'll pick you up and take you to Peronel.' And Sylfai suddenly found herself in the giant's hand, being carefully carried along.

Osta put her down in a great high room. At one end lay a beautiful fairy asleep on a couch. Over her hung a purple card, and Sylfai saw written there:

'Here Peronel will have to stay,
Summer, winter, night and day,
Until the spell is killed away
By someone who is called Sylfai.'

'Oh, what a shame!' cried Sylfai, and she gently bent over sleeping Peronel and kissed her forehead. To her delight Peronel opened her eyes and sat up.

'Oh, I've been under a horrid spell,' she cried, 'and I'm so glad to wake again. How kind you are, Sylfai, to kiss me. Oh, there is Corovell!'

Sylfai turned round, and sure enough there was Corovell, smiling at them both.

'Brave little Sylfai!' she said. 'I guessed you would break the spell. Now, let's all go and have a lovely time at the Queen's palace. She wants to see you, Sylfai.'

'I'll carry you all there,' laughed Giant Osta, picking them all up, and off he went with big strides – and you can just imagine the lovely time Sylfai had with the fairies, and what a lot of adventures she had to tell when she got safely home again!

Magical
Adventures

Extraordinary Afternoon

'Well, unless you get back that new bicycle pump of yours, I shan't give you the money to go to the Children's Show at the Town Hall,' said Michael's father. 'That's certain. If I don't teach you to be more careful you'll never learn. I can see that.'

'But, Dad – it's not fair,' said Michael. 'I have been careful of it – but Tom Lane borrowed it without asking me, and now he says he never had it. He's a head taller than I am – I can't go and fight him for it!'

'Don't argue with me,' said his father. 'I won't have it! First you come and borrow my pump, so that I never know where it is – and then I give you five shillings to buy a new one, and a week after you come borrowing mine again because you say somebody borrowed yours! Well, all I can say is, you won't get the five shillings to buy your ticket for the Big Show till you bring me your bicycle pump again. Now go away.'

Well, it was never any use for Michael to argue with his father. He wasn't the kind of father who said one thing and meant another. He stuck to what he said. Michael went away looking very gloomy, and feeling very cross.

'It's not fair,' he told his friend Bob. 'I've got to stop away from the grandest show that's ever been given for children in our town, all because that beast of a Tom Lane took my pump and won't give it back! It's not my fault at all.'

'You can't fight him for it because he's in the top form and about twice as big as you are,' said Bob. 'Haven't you got any money yourself, Michael? Can't you buy yourself a ticket for the Show?'

'No. I've got tuppence, that's all,' said Michael. 'It's no good, I can't go. And there's going to be a Grand Tea, and balloons and crackers and a bran-tub – and Mr Hey Presto, the special conjurer down from London!'

'Yes. My cousin saw him once, and he says he's super,' said Bob. 'Absolutely wizard.'

'Wizard's about right,' said Michael, trying to grin. 'He should be wizard if he's a conjurer!'

'Funny joke!' said Bob. 'Poor old Mike – it's hard luck on you. Everybody's going.'

'Don't rub it in,' said Mike. 'Well, so long – I've got to go and clean my bike.'

He went off by himself, brooding over the unfairness of life. Still, these things happened. It wasn't much good thinking and worrying about them.

He wouldn't get back his bicycle pump, that was certain, so he wouldn't get the money to go to the Big Show. That was certain too. He might as well make other plans for that Saturday afternoon.

'I shan't go near the Town Hall, anyway,' thought Michael. 'I'm not going to watch the others going in, and see Tom Lane gloating over me. I shall go over to the Ponds, and see if the ice is hard enough to slide on.'

So, when Saturday came, he didn't join the throng of excited children going off to wait for the doors of the Town Hall to open. He didn't join in the talk about the Grand Tea, and rejoice in the possibility of cream buns and chocolate éclairs. He stalked off by himself down the lanes towards the Ponds.

He whistled as he went, but he sounded much gayer than he really felt. He was going to miss the tea, the games, the fun – and that marvellous conjurer, Mr Hey Presto. And all because of that beast of a Tom Lane. Well, there just wasn't anything to be done about it. He whistled more loudly than ever.

Just as he came round a corner of the lane, slipping a little in the icy ruts, he heard a crash, then a loud yell and a few more noises.

Michael hurried round the corner at once. What had happened?

A small car lay on its side in the ditch, and behind it, also on its side, was a trailer full of boxes and parcels of different shapes. A man was in the car, struggling to get out. His head was bleeding.

Michael ran up at once. 'I say, sir! Are you hurt?'

'Not much,' said the man, trying to open the door. 'This has got jammed. I'll have to get out of the window. I skidded on the icy road. I say, is my trailer all right?'

'Well – it's on its side too,' said Michael, wrenching at the car door and suddenly getting it open. 'The boxes and things are scattered in the ditch. I can soon get them together for you. Your head's bleeding pretty badly, sir.'

The man produced a large white handkerchief and mopped his head. 'Only a cut,' he said. 'Feel in that pocket over there, boy – in the back of the car – there should be a tin of elastoplast there. I'll just stick a bit on.'

Michael did all he could. He found the elastoplast, cut a piece the right size, and neatly stuck it over the cut when it stopped bleeding. He offered to go and telephone from the nearest place for a breakdown car to come and haul the man's car from the ditch. He picked up all the parcels and put them in a neat pile on the road.

The man sat by the side of the lane for a few minutes, rather white in the face. 'Just the shock,' he told Michael. 'I'll soon be all right.'

The boy was pleased to see him looking much better a few minutes later. He got up and had a look at his car. Then he had a look at the trailer.

'What's the time?' he said, looking at his watch. 'My word! I've got to be in the town at three o'clock. It's not my car that's important – it's the trailer and the things on it. Can we get it upright?'

It was difficult, but they managed it. The man arranged all the boxes and parcels on it. 'Any chance of a car coming by here that we can ask to tow this for me?' he said to Michael. The boy shook his head.

'No, sir. This is a lonely lane. But I don't see why I can't help you to pull it to the town – it's not very far away. I'm pretty strong.'

'You're a very great help, old man,' said the stranger, looking at Michael out of very blue eyes that were set under shaggy, overhanging eyebrows. 'Can't think what I should have done without you. Do you really think you can help to pull the trailer?'

'Yes, easily,' said Michael, and he gave the shaft of the trailer a tug. It had big, tyred wheels and moved at once.

'Right,' said the man, 'I'll take your advice then, and we'll haul the trailer to the town. I can telephone from there about the car – get a garage to send along for it. Well – here we go!'

And off they went, pulling the trailer between them. Michael liked this stranger. He had a clever humorous face, and his blue eyes twinkled continually under his black eyebrows. He and Michael talked as they went.

'Where were you going when you came along?' asked the man. 'Nowhere important, I hope.'

'Oh no – just to the Ponds to slide,' said Michael.

'What! All by yourself!' said the man, surprised.

'Well – there's nobody to go with me this afternoon,' said Michael.

'There's a Big Show on at the Town Hall, you know – Grand Tea and Games, and Presents – and Mr Hey Presto, the London magician is coming.'

'You don't say so!' said the man. 'Well, why aren't you going – or is that an awkward question?'

'Oh no. I'm not going because I've had a bit of bad luck,' said Michael, and he poured out the story of the lost bicycle pump and his angry father.

'You see, it's all jolly unfair,' said Michael. 'And the frightful thing is I can't do a thing about it. I've just got to put up with it. But it makes me boil inside.'

'You've no idea how often these unfair things happen in life,' said the stranger. 'They're always happening! And there are two kinds of people, you know – the kind who kick and growl and sulk, and make things unpleasant for everybody when things seem unfair – and the kind who grin and whistle, and say "Well, that's that! I can't do anything about it, so why worry! It happens to everyone sooner or later." And I must say I prefer the second kind of person – like you!'

Michael went red. Was he really that kind of person? Well, perhaps he was! He certainly hadn't made much fuss – and he had gone along whistling that afternoon. He looked gratefully at the stranger, who twinkled at him and then gave him a broad wink.

'It may be jolly unfair on you, boy, but my word, how glad I am you weren't sitting in the Town Hall waiting for Mr Hey Presto, instead of going along that lane ready to give me a helping hand,' said the man. 'Your bad luck brought me a bit of good luck.'

'Well, I'm glad about that,' said Michael, tugging hard at the heavy trailer, and getting rather out of breath. 'But I wish I could have seen Mr Hey Presto. Have you ever seen him?'

'Oh yes,' said the stranger. 'He's a wonder! Last time I saw him he took a bunch of grapes from behind somebody's ear.'

'Oh – he couldn't possibly do that!' said Michael.

'He did – just like this,' said the man, and to the boy's utter astonishment he put his hand up to Michael's left ear – and brought away a bunch of purple grapes! Michael stopped pulling the trailer, and gaped at the grapes.

'I say,' he said at last. 'I say! How – how did you do that?'

'Bit of a nuisance, really, to carry grapes about with us,' said the man, looking at them. 'Put them in your pocket, will you?' He stuffed them into Michael's pocket, but when the boy put his hand in, they weren't there!

'Another thing Mr Hey Presto did was to pick daisies out of a girl's hair,' said the stranger. 'Like this.'

Michael felt his hair tugged two or three times, and then stared in amazement at some perfectly fresh daisies in the man's hand. Daisies! In winter-time! Michael swallowed once or twice, not knowing what to say. He began to wonder if he was in a dream.

The stranger absentmindedly rolled the flowers up into a ball, and threw them into the air. They fell with a little clang to the ground! Michael looked down in surprise. No daisies lay there – only a little brass chain. A chain!

'Dear me – I meant to make a daisy chain,' said the man, annoyed. 'Not a brass chain. How silly of me!'

Michael found his voice. He clutched at the stranger's arm, a sudden idea lighting up his puzzled mind.

'Sir! Are you the conjurer? Are you Mr Hey Presto?'

The stranger smiled, and his blue eyes twinkled again. 'Guessed it first time! I am the one and only mighty and marvellous Mr Hey Presto, the magnificent magician! But not mighty or marvellous enough to stop myself having a skid on an icy road! Do you think we'll get to the Town Hall in time?'

'Well – we'd better hurry,' said Michael, and he pulled harder at the trailer. 'Gosh – to think it was you! This is a bit of luck for me. Why, sir, any of the boys would give up the whole of this afternoon's treat to be able to help you like this, and talk to you!'

'I suppose you wouldn't care to help me a bit more, would you?' said Mr Hey Presto. 'I'd be very glad if you could give up your afternoon to me.'

'I'll do anything you like, Mr Presto,' said Michael, eagerly. 'I'll go to the garage – go back with the man – help with your car – anything!'

'I didn't mean quite that,' said Mr Presto. 'I meant – could you be my assistant on the stage this afternoon? My own assistant is ill. I was going to ask someone to point me out a really intelligent boy who could act as my assistant instead, today – but it has just occurred to me that I might have this boy you told me about – er, Tom Lane, I think you said – I might have him recommended to me, and that would be a pity.'

'Yes, sir, he might be – he's very clever,' said Michael. He looked at Mr Presto, his eyes shining. 'Would you really let me be your assistant? Oh sir! But I'm not as clever as some of the others. I hope I'd be all right.'

'There's nobody I should like better,' said Mr Hey Presto. 'Nobody. I feel we should get along together very well indeed. But I hope you won't mind – you will have to do a little dressing up.'

This was better than ever! Michael stared at Mr Presto eagerly. 'What kind of dressing-up, sir? I know you have a proper magician's pointed hat and a cloak. What do you want me to have?'

'The same – but smaller,' said the conjurer. 'I've got the things with me, of course. They're on the trailer. Well, well – it's really very nice of you to come to my help again. Twice in one afternoon – a most remarkable boy!'

'Oh no, I'm not really,' said Michael. 'I'm never top of my form, never – only about the middle. This is just a bit of terrific good luck for me.'

'Ah – a little bit of good luck to make up for a few of the unfair things that happen,' said Mr Presto. 'Amazing how often that little bit of luck comes along when we take things the right way – almost like magic!'

Michael was so excited and happy that he hardly felt the weight of the trailer after that. He and the conjurer soon arrived at the back door of the Town Hall.

'It's a pity you couldn't have used some of your magic, sir, to put your car right, when it got into the ditch,' said Michael, slyly, as he helped Mr Presto to unpack some of the parcels from the trailer.

'My boy, how do you know I didn't use my magic to produce a nice helpful, fellow like you to come along and take me and the trailer here?' said Mr Presto. 'Ha – I may be cleverer than you think!'

The next ten minutes were extremely interesting and exciting for

162

Michael. He was taken to the dressing-room by Mr Presto, and given his stage clothes to put on. They were rather thrilling. He had to put on green hose, a red velvet tunic, red leather shoes, a small pointed hat, and a black velvet cloak.

'Do I have a wand like yours?' he asked Mr Presto, who was now looking very magnificent indeed in a set of clothes very like Michael's, but larger, of course, and grander.

'No. I don't trust people with my wands,' said Mr Presto. 'I mean – if a wand got into the hands of the wrong person, he might rush round turning people into white elephants or black dogs or green beetles. You never know.'

He touched a little glass bowl with his own wand, and it immediately became filled with water in which a little goldfish swam. Michael stared, open-mouthed. The magician tapped the bowl again, and the goldfish changed into a water-beetle.

'Just practising a bit to see if the wand is all right,' said Mr Presto. 'Now for a few instructions, Michael. Listen carefully.'

Michael listened with both his ears. It was very, very important to do everything right, he could see that. He nodded his head at the end.

'Yes, sir. I can do all that. I won't forget anything at all. And sir – I don't know how to say it properly – but I do think it's smashing of you to let me have the – er – the honour of coming on the stage with you.'

'Very well put,' said Mr Presto, smiling. 'And now – do I hear the band striking up for us? I do. In we go and make our bows.'

And on to the stage they both went, Michael shaking at the knees suddenly when he saw the rows upon rows of children in the audience. Goodness, he knew scores of them – but not one of them knew him!

The conjurer introduced himself and then waved his wand towards Michael. 'And now let me introduce my valued and clever assistant for the afternoon – Master Mikey-Alley-O!'

Then the show began. Certainly Mr Hey Presto was a very, very marvellous conjurer. He played a jolly tune on a banjo that nobody could see, not even Michael. It was quite invisible. Then when it suddenly began to boom like a drum, he apologised.

'I'm so sorry. This banjo has a way of turning into a drum without my knowing.' And then he beat an invisible drum, which made a terrific noise.

With Michael's help he played ball – and the ball suddenly split in half in the air, and a string of flags unfurled. Mike held one end, Mr Presto held the other. The conjurer folded them all up carefully and put them into his pointed hat. He shook them hard – and out flew two white pigeons, cooing to one another!

'Well – I never know what those flags are going to turn into!' Mr Presto told the astonished audience. 'See – the hat's empty now!' He turned it upside down – and out flopped a white rabbit!

'Dear me! I quite thought it was empty,' said Mr Presto. 'Hold the rabbit, Mikey-Alley-O, will you? Oh dear – what's he turned into now? I should have warned you.'

In some really remarkable way the rabbit seemed to change into a large white teapot as Michael got hold of it. He stood there, his mouth open in surprise, holding the teapot. Everyone clapped and yelled.

'Aha! Now here we have a really wonderful teapot,' said Mr Presto. 'It will pour out gingerbeer, lemonade or orangeade, whichever anyone prefers. Will three boys please come up on the platform?'

Up came three red-faced boys, pushing and shoving. Michael looked at them. One was Tom Lane!

'Your names?' said Mr Presto. They told him. 'Ah – and now you, John, what drink will you have? And you, Harry – and you, Tom?'

John said gingerbeer, Harry said orangeade, and Tom said lemonade. Mr Presto produced three glasses from the air.

'Now – a little warning,' he said. 'Don't drink if you've done anything you're ashamed of lately! Otherwise your drink will be sour. Pour, Mikey-Alley-O!'

Michael tipped up the teapot. All three glasses were filled, and the three boys drank.

'Lovely gingerbeer!' cried John.

'What delicious orangeade!' said Harry.

164

But poor Tom Lane said nothing at all. He made a face. How sour his drink had been! He went soberly back to his seat, teased by the boys. What had he done lately to be ashamed of? There were too many things to remember! Tom stared at the conjurer in awe. What a wonderful man he must be! Michael grinned to himself, and the conjurer gave him a broad wink. Justice had been done for once in a way!

It was a truly wonderful afternoon. When the conjuring was over there was the Grand Tea, and it really was grand too. Michael, still dressed up, sat at the high table with Mr Presto and a few other important people. He was allowed to have three éclairs and four cream buns, so he was luckier than anyone. The crackers were the best he had ever pulled – and as for the balloons, they blew up the size of three footballs!

Michael changed out of his things after tea as he wanted to play in the games. Mr Presto was still there, because he was to give the presents out of the bran-tub at the end of the afternoon. 'There won't be a present for me, sir, because I didn't have a ticket,' Michael explained. 'But that doesn't matter a bit – you can leave me out. I've had the most wonderful afternoon in my life! Thanks most awfully. It was super.'

The boys were amazed to see Michael after tea. Not one of them had guessed he had been Mr Presto's assistant, and Michael didn't tell them because he was absolutely certain they wouldn't believe him. He played in the games and had a fine time. And then came the bran-tub, when every child was to get a present, given to him by Mr Presto.

They lined up in excitement. One by one they went up to the platform to the enormous bran-tub there. Mr Hey Presto, looking very grand, said a few words to each child and made everyone laugh. He dipped his hand into the tub and pulled out a parcel for every boy and girl.

They were fine presents – books, ships, dolls, games. Tom Lane opened his parcel rather nervously, wondering if that extraordinary conjurer had handed him out a present as disappointing as his drink. But no, he had quite a nice one, and was very much relieved.

At last every child but Michael had had a present from the tub. Harry called out to Mr Hey Presto. 'Mr Presto, sir! Mike's been left out! He hasn't got a present!'

'Dear me! Very remiss of me!' said Mr Presto at once. 'Michael, come up to the tub.'

Up went Michael, and everyone clapped him, because they liked him. Mr Presto put his hand into the bran-tub and swept it round and round. He stood up.

'Children,' he said solemnly. 'The bran-tub is empty. Not a present is left. But I can't let this nice boy here go without a gift. Michael, look at me. Let me look into your mind and see what present you would like – and perhaps by my magic I can give it to you!'

He swung the boy round and looked at him, twinkling. Then he turned to the children.

'I have looked into this boy's mind, and I have seen his wish. He would like a new bicycle pump.'

There was a shout from the boys in Mike's class. 'Yes! Yes! He's lost his! Somebody borrowed it and never put it back.'

Tom Lane sat silent, very red indeed. How could this conjurer read people's minds like that? How did he know about Mike's pump?

The conjurer turned to the astonished Michael. 'My boy,' he said, 'I will try to grant you what you wish for. I can only do it in one way. I will show you.'

He picked up his wand, which lay on a nearby chair. He took some brown paper and carefully wrapped up the wand. Everyone watched, holding their breath. What in the world was he going to do?

He tied up the parcel with string. Then he chanted a long string of odd words, holding the tied-up wand between his two hands. The children listened in awe.

'Rimmi-illa-foona-kee,
Jarna-rilly-soona-fee,
Wand-into-a-pump-you'll-grow,
Gift-for-Mikey-Alley-O!'

The conjurer finished his chanting, and, in the midst of a profound silence, he handed the parcel to Michael with a deep bow.

'Mr Presto – sir,' stammered Michael. 'It's your wand. Don't give that to me – why, you said you never let …'

But his words were drowned in excited shouts from the children in the audience.

'Open it, Michael! Open the parcel! Go on, Mike, open it!'

Michael stood there in the middle of the platform, hardly daring to open the parcel. With trembling fingers he undid the string, and then pulled off the brown paper. They fell to the ground.

In his hands Michael held, not a wand – but a gleaming new bicycle pump, silver-new, the finest one he had ever seen. He stared at it in awe!

'The wand's changed into a bicycle pump!' yelled the children. 'Look at that! It was a silver wand, now it's a pump. Three cheers for Mr Presto!'

Michael turned to thank the conjurer – but he wasn't there! He had gone. How strange! Nobody had seen him go, but certainly he had gone. Michael was not a bit surprised. It was all part of his strangeness.

He went down from the platform to show the gleaming new pump to the children. They clustered round him – all but Tom Lane. How marvellous! How wonderful! What a glorious afternoon!

Michael went home excited and thrilled. What a time he had had! He went to show his parents the new pump, and poured out the whole story from beginning to end.

'Well!' said his father, 'it's a very strange way to get a new pump, Mike – but I can't help feeling that you deserve it. You'll have to look out for Mr Hey Presto and thank him properly.'

'I will,' said Mike. 'Goodness – what an extraordinary afternoon!'

The Enchanted Goat

Once upon a time a great fair came to the village of Penny-come-quick. There were roundabouts, swings, coconut shies, conjurers, clowns, and a score of other splendid things. Little Benny Biggles was so excited that he couldn't sleep for thinking of it all.

He went every single day, and of all the wonderful things at the fair there was one that he simply couldn't take his eyes off. This was a wooden goat with wings on each of its heels.

A Chinaman had charge of it, and if anyone paid a sixpence he would make the goat rise into the air, fly round the fair-ground and then come back again to him. Benny could have watched that all day. He thought it was the most wonderful thing he had ever seen.

'I wonder how it does it?' he said to himself. 'Wouldn't I love to ride on it!'

Now no sooner did he think that than his heart began to beat very fast indeed. Why shouldn't he have a ride on the goat?

'I'll just see if I can!' said Benny. So the next day, when the Chinaman was taking sixpences, Benny stood as close to him as he could to see what he did to make the goat fly off.

'It's easy!' said Benny to himself. 'Why, he just pulls one ear back, that's all! I could do that myself!'

When the Chinaman's back was turned, and he was telling everyone about his wonderful goat, Benny crept up to it.

'My goat, he will fly all round the fair,' said the man. 'Give me just one more sixpence and you shall see him go!'

Benny suddenly leapt on the goat's back. All the people cried out 'Oh!' in surprise, and the Chinaman turned round quickly. When he saw Benny on his goat, he ran towards him, shouting out something in a strange language that the boy could not understand.

But before he could get to the goat, Benny pulled back its right ear. In a second the wooden creature rose into the air, all its foot-wings flapping hard. Benny hung on tightly, his breath taken away.

'Ooh!' he cried. 'What an adventure! Go on, goat, go on!'

The goat flew right round the fair-ground, and Benny could see everyone below staring up at him in the greatest astonishment. The people pointed their fingers at him, and shouted to one another.

'See! A little boy is riding the enchanted goat!' they cried.

Benny expected the goat to fly down to the Chinaman after it had gone round the fair-ground once, for that was what it always did. He thought that perhaps the man would scold him, but he didn't mind that! He had had the loveliest ride in all his life!

But oh dear me! The goat didn't go down to the Chinaman! After it had circled round the ground once, it suddenly rose much higher in the air, and started flying straight towards the setting sun! Benny was too surprised to say anything at first, and then he gave a shout.

'Hie! Hie! You're going the wrong way, goat! Take me back to the fair – ground! Hurry up and turn round!'

But the goat took no notice of Benny at all. It went on flying towards the sun, very fast and very straight. Benny began to feel frightened. He clung on tightly, his hair streaming out behind him. Below him he could see fields and hills stretched out very small, like a toy countryside. He saw a train going along a railway line, and it seemed to him to be smaller even than his own clockwork train at home.

'Stop! Stop!' he shouted to the goat. 'You are taking me too far! Turn round and go back to the fair!'

Still the goat took no notice. Benny kicked its wooden sides with his feet, but that didn't do any good either. Whatever was he to do?

On and on went the goat, faster than ever. Soon they came to the sea. When they were right over it, the little boy looked downwards. He saw dark blue water stretching out all around him. No land was in sight at all. Benny had no idea that the sea was so big. He clutched the goat more tightly, afraid that he would fall into the water far below.

The sun sank down into the western sky and darkness came. The stars twinkled brightly, the moon came up, and Benny grew very sleepy. He began to cry, for he was afraid.

'I wish I knew how to stop this goat,' he sobbed. 'I expect it will go on like this for ever and ever, and I'll go round and round the world till I fall off.'

Then he dried his tears and began to think hard.

'If I pull the right ear back to start the goat, perhaps I push it forward to stop it,' he thought. But before he did anything, he peeped downwards to see if they were over land or sea. They were still flying over the water, but Benny could see an island not far off. He decided to try and alight on that.

He pushed the goat's right ear forward. Nothing happened at all. The goat still went steadily on. Then the little boy took hold of the left ear, and pulled that back. At once the goat began to slow down!

'I've found the secret, I've found the secret!' cried Benny in delight. 'Oh, if only I'd thought of that before!'

He peered below him, and saw that the goat had not quite reached the island, but would land in the water round it. So he quickly pushed the left ear forward again, and pulled the right ear back. The goat at once flew straight onwards. When he was exactly over the island, Benny pushed the right ear forward and pulled the left ear back.

The goat flew down to the land. Benny tried to see what it was like, but except that he thought he could make out a huge building of some sort, he could see little. Nearer and nearer to the land came the goat, and at last it was skimming only a few feet above the ground. Then bump! It landed, and stood quite still while Benny got off.

The little boy saw that he was at the edge of a wood, but it was so dark that he knew it was no use trying to find anyone to help him. He must wait till the morning. He stretched his stiff legs, and yawned, for it was long past his bedtime, and he was very sleepy.

Then he felt for the goat's ears. He carefully pushed the left ear forward, and made certain that the right ear was in its proper position too. Then he found a soft patch of heather, and curling himself up in it, he went fast asleep.

It was day when he awoke, and the sun was shining in the eastern sky. Benny looked around him in surprise, for at first he did not remember how he had come there. Then he saw the wooden goat standing near-by, and he remembered everything.

'Ooh, I am hungry!' he said, jumping to his feet. 'I wonder where I can get something to eat. Then I'll jump on to my old goat and go off home. If I fly to the east, I'm sure to get there sometime. As soon as I see the fair-ground beneath me, I shall fly down to it!'

He looked round him. He could hear the sound of the sea nearby, and he remembered that he was on an island. Behind him was a wood, and to the right was a very high hill – almost a mountain. On the very top was an enormous castle with thousands of glittering windows.

'Good gracious!' said Benny in astonishment. 'Whoever lives there?'

He saw a smaller hill near-by, and after carefully hiding the wooden goat under a bush, he started off to go to the top. When he stood on the summit he looked around him. He saw sea on every side, for the island was quite small. It had two hills, the one he was on, and the very high one on which the castle stood. A little wood lay between, and from the very middle of it rose some smoke.

'Someone must live there,' said Benny. 'I'll go and ask them if they would kindly give me something to eat, for I've never been so hungry in all my life before!'

Down the hill he went, and into the wood. He soon found a little path, and followed it. After a while he came to the strangest house he had ever seen. It was quite small, and was built of precious stones glittering so brightly that Benny was almost dazzled. Round it was a circle of white stones.

Benny walked up to the circle. He stood outside, trying to see the door of the cottage – but he could see none, though he walked all round it several times.

'Well, I'll just have to go right up and see where it is,' said the little boy. So he put his foot over the ring of white stones to walk up to the house. But good gracious me! He couldn't put it on the ground again! It was held there in the air, though Benny could not see anyone or anything holding it. Then all at once there came the noise of a hundred trumpets blowing and a thousand bells ringing!

'Oh my! Oh my!' said poor Benny. 'This must be a magic circle or something!'

Suddenly there came a voice from the house. Benny looked, and saw a gnome's head peeping out of a window.

'Who are you?' demanded the gnome. 'You have put your foot in my magic circle, and started all my bells ringing and trumpets blowing. Take your foot out.'

Benny tried to but he couldn't.

'I can't,' he said. 'Please undo the spell or whatever it is. I'm getting so tired of standing on one leg. I'm only a little boy coming to ask for something to eat.'

'Say your sixteen times table then,' said the gnome, sternly.

'Oh, I can't,' said Benny, nearly crying. 'Why, I'm only up to seven times at school, and I don't know that very well yet.'

'Oh, that's all right then,' said the gnome, smiling. 'I thought you were a wizard or a witch disguised as a little boy. If you had been, you would have known your sixteen times table, but as you don't, I know you are a little boy. I've taken the spell off now. You can come into the magic circle.'

Benny's foot was suddenly free. He stepped over the ring of white stones, and went up to the glittering house. He looked everywhere for a door, but he couldn't find one.

'Clap your hands twice, and call out "open, open" seven times!' said the gnome.

Benny did so, and at once a door appeared in the wall and opened itself in front of him. The gnome looked out and pulled Benny inside by the hand. At once the door disappeared again.

'Why do all these things happen like this?' said Benny, puzzled. 'Am I in Fairyland?'

'Not exactly,' said the gnome, setting a big bowl of bread and milk in front of Benny. 'This island was once part of Fairyland – just the two hills and the wood, you know – and a great giant came and built his castle on the top of the biggest hill.'

'I thought giants weren't allowed in Fairyland,' said Benny in astonishment.

'They're not,' said the gnome, putting a hot cup of cocoa by Benny's side, 'but this one was very cunning. He turned himself into a small goblin, and built a tiny castle. Nobody minded, of course, for there are lots of goblins in Fairyland. But one night he changed himself back to his proper shape, a giant as tall as a house, and made his castle grow big too! What do you think of that?'

173

'Go on!' said Benny, eating his bread and milk. 'This is very exciting!'

'Well, the giant was so big and so powerful that the King and Queen couldn't get rid of him,' said the gnome. 'He was a terrible nuisance, because he would keep capturing fairies, and taking them to his castle. Then he would charge the King a thousand pieces of gold to get them back again.'

'The horrid monster!' said Benny.

'Then, as they couldn't make the giant go away,' said the gnome, 'they suddenly thought of putting a spell on the land he owned, and sending it away to the middle of the sea to become an island! So they did that, and off went the two hills and the wood one fine starlight night! They landed in the sea miles away with a terrible splash, and here we are!'

'But how did you come to be here?' asked Benny, puzzled.

'Well, I happened to have built my house in the wood without anyone knowing,' said the gnome, sighing. 'So, of course, I went too, and I can't get back. The giant was in a terrible temper when he found what had happened. He came tearing down to me, and if I hadn't quickly put a spell round my house, he would certainly have turned me into a hedgehog or something like that.'

'And does he live here all alone?' asked Benny.

'No, he has got seven fairies with him,' said the gnome. 'The King didn't know that he had stolen them on the very night his castle was moved, so of course the poor things are still there. I wish I could rescue them, but there is such a powerful spell all round the castle that I couldn't get near it even if I tried all day!'

'What does he do with the fairies?' asked Benny, finishing his bread and milk to the very last crumb.

'They are his servants,' said the gnome, 'and very hard he makes them work, I can tell you. If they are not quick enough for him, he scolds them, and I have often heard them crying, poor things. But they will never be rescued, for no one can get to the castle.'

'What a shame!' said Benny. 'Oh, how I wish I could rescue them!'

'You're only a little boy,' said the gnome scornfully, 'you couldn't possibly do anything.'

Benny looked at the gnome. Then an idea flashed into his head.

'Tell me, Mister Gnome,' he said, 'is there a spell on the castle top as well as all around the walls?'

'Of course not!' said the gnome, staring at Benny in surprise. 'The castle is much too high for anyone to get on the top. Why do you ask?'

'Because I think I can rescue the fairies!' said Benny, his heart beating very fast. 'I've got an enchanted goat here, that I came on, and I believe I could make it fly to the castle roof and if I could only find the fairies quickly, they could mount on its back and I could take them away with me!'

'An enchanted goat!' said the gnome in astonishment, 'then you're not a little boy after all. I'll put a spell on you if you're a witch or a wizard!'

'No, no, don't!' cried Benny, 'I really am a little boy. Listen and I'll tell you how I came here.'

In a few minutes the gnome knew Benny's story. The little boy took him to where he had hidden the goat, and the gnome grew tremendously excited.

'Oh, Benny!' he cried, 'I believe we'll do it! Oh, how grand!'

'Will you come with me?' asked Benny, 'I feel a bit frightened all alone.'

'Of course I will!' said the gnome. Then he and Benny got on to the goat's back, Benny pulled the right ear back, and off they went. They flew high above the castle, and then Benny made the goat go downwards. The castle had a flat roof, and it was quite easy to land there.

'Talk in whispers now,' said the gnome. 'If the giant hears us, we shall be captured at once. Look! there are some steps going down from the roof. You'd better go down them, and see if you can find any of the fairies. I'll wait here.'

Benny ran to the steps. He climbed down them very carefully. They went round and round and down and down. At last he came to the end and found himself in a long passage with doors opening off.

'Oh, dear! Had I better try each one to see if the fairies are inside?' thought Benny. 'No, I won't; I'll go on to those stairs over there, and go down a bit farther. If the fairies do the work for the giant, they may be in the kitchen.'

He went down some more stairs, and then down some more. They seemed to be never-ending. At last he heard a tremendous noise. It came from a room nearby. The door was open, and Benny peeped in. He saw an enormous giant there, lying in the biggest armchair he had ever seen. He was fast asleep, and the great noise Benny had heard was the giant snoring.

'Oh, good!' thought Benny in delight. 'Now I can look about in safety for the fairies.'

He came to a smaller door, and listened. He thought he could hear the murmur of little voices behind, and he opened the door. Yes, he was right! Sitting round a big fire, polishing enormous mugs and dishes was a group of small fairies. One of them was crying.

When the door opened, they all sprang to their feet expecting to see the giant. When they saw Benny, they were so astonished that none of them could speak a word.

'Sh! Sh!' said Benny, 'I've come to rescue you! I've got an enchanted goat up on the roof. Hurry up and come along with me. I'll take you back to Fairyland.'

The fairies were so full of joy that they ran to Benny and hugged him. Then they ran lightly out of the room and up the stairs, treading very softly indeed when they passed the room where the giant slept. Benny followed them, and at last they all reached the roof. The gnome stood there with the goat, and greeted them in delight.

How they hugged one another and smiled for joy! Two of the fairies wept for gladness and Benny had to lend them his handkerchief.

'Come on,' said the gnome, at last. 'We mustn't stop here. If the giant wakes he will be sure to miss you and put a spell on you somehow. Are you all here?'

Benny counted the fairies.

'Good gracious!' he said in dismay. 'There are only six of them! Didn't you say there were seven, Mister Gnome?'

'Oh, where's Tiptoe, where's Tiptoe?' cried all the other fairies. 'We've left her behind! She was watering the plants in the greenhouse, and we've left her behind!'

'Well, call her,' said the gnome. 'If the giant wakes it can't be helped. I

expect she will get up here before he knows there is anything the matter.'

So all together the fairies called.

'Tiptoe! Tiptoe! Come up to the roof at once! Tiptoe!'

A little voice from far below answered them.

'I'm coming!'

Then suddenly there came a thunderous roar. The giant had woken up!

'WHO'S THAT CALLING?' he shouted. 'YOU'VE WAKENED ME FROM MY SLEEP, YOU WICKED FAIRIES! I'LL PUNISH YOU, I WILL!'

'Ooh!' said the fairies, turning pale.

'It's all right,' said the gnome. 'By the time he's looked into the kitchen and called for you a few times, we shall be gone! Look, here's Tiptoe!'

The seventh fairy came running up the steps to the roof. In a trice the others explained everything to her.

'Get on the goat,' said the gnome, 'the giant is getting very angry indeed.'

The fairies began to clamber on the goat – but whatever do you think! There was only room for five of them! The goat was much too small.

'Oh my, oh my!' groaned the gnome. 'I don't think I've time to make it big enough for us all, but I'll try. Stand away everyone.'

He drew a chalk ring round the goat, clapped his hands, and began to dance round and round it, singing a magic song. Little by little the wooden creature grew bigger.

The giant below was roaring more angrily than ever – and then Benny suddenly heard his footsteps coming up the stairs!

'Quick, quick, he's coming!' he shouted. The gnome hastily rubbed out the chalk circle with his foot, and ran to the goat. He pushed Benny on first and then he helped all the fairies on. Last of all he got on himself, though there was really hardly room for him. Just as they were all on, the giant appeared at the opening to the roof.

Benny pulled back the right ear of the goat and at once the animal rose into the air. The giant gave a tremendous roar of anger and surprise, and fell down the steps in astonishment. By the time he had picked himself up, and was ready to work a powerful spell on the goat to bring it back, it was far away in the sky.

Benny was trembling with excitement, and so were all the others. For a long while no one spoke. Then the fairies all began to talk at once, and thanked Benny and the gnome over and over again for rescuing them. Benny listened to their little high voices, and thought them the sweetest sound he had ever heard.

After a long time he looked below him. To his great astonishment he was just over his own home! Away to the right was the fairground, and the music of the roundabouts came faintly to Benny's ears.

'Oh, I think I'll go down here,' said Benny. 'There's my home, and I would like to see my mother and tell her I'm all right. Do you mind if I get off here? The gnome will take you safely back to Fairyland.'

So down they all went, and Benny jumped off the goat at the end of his own garden.

'Goodbye,' he said. 'And would you mind sending the goat back to the Chinaman at the fair? I expect he will be upset not to have it.'

'Certainly,' said the gnome, 'we can easily do that. Well, thank you for all your help, Benny. Goodbye!'

'Goodbye, goodbye!' called the fairies, as the goat once more rose into the air. Benny watched them until he could no longer see them, and then ran indoors to tell his mother all his adventures.

'I must go to the fair tomorrow to see if the fairies have sent the goat back,' said Benny. And the next day off he went. Sure enough, the goat was there – but will you believe it, the gnome had forgotten to make it small again, and it was simply enormous!

The Chinaman was so astonished! He couldn't make it out at all.

'It is a very strange thing!' he said, over and over again. 'Who can tell me what has happened?'

Benny told him – but he needn't have bothered, for the Chinaman didn't believe a word of his story! He took his enchanted goat away after the fair was over, and as far as I know, nobody has ever heard of him since.

Up the Faraway Tree

The children did not tell their father and mother about the happenings in the Enchanted Wood, for they were so afraid that they might be forbidden to go there. But when they were alone they talked about nothing else.

'When do you suppose we could go up the Faraway Tree?' Frannie kept asking. 'Oh, do let's go, Joe.'

Joe wanted to go very badly – but he was a little afraid of what might happen, and he knew that he ought to look after his two sisters and see that no harm came to them. Just suppose they all went up the Faraway Tree and never came back!

Then he had an idea. 'Listen,' he said. 'I know what we'll do. We'll climb up the tree and just see what is at the top! We don't need to go there – we can just look. We'll wait until we have a whole day to ourselves, then we'll go.'

The girls were so excited. They worked hard in the house hoping that their mother would say they could have the whole day to themselves. Joe worked hard in the garden, too, clearing away all the weeds. Their parents were very pleased.

'Would you like to go to the nearest town and have a day there?' asked Mother, at last.

'No, thank you,' said Joe, at once. 'We've had enough of towns, Mother! What we'd really like is to go and have a whole-day picnic in the wood!'

'Very well,' said Mother. 'You can go tomorrow. Father is going off for the day to buy some things we need. And I have things to do here in the cottage. So, as I'll be close by you can take your lunch and dinner and go off by yourselves, if it is fine and sunny.'

How the children hoped the day would be fine! They woke early and jumped out of bed. They pulled their curtains open and looked out. The sky was as blue as cornflowers. The sun shone between the trees, and the shadows lay long and dewy on the grass. The Enchanted Wood stood dark and mysterious behind their garden.

They all had breakfast, then Mother cut sandwiches, and put them in a bag along with three cakes each. She sent Joe to pick some plums from the garden, and told Beth to take two bottles of lemonade. The children were most excited.

Father set off to town, and the children waved goodbye to him from the gate. Then they tore off indoors to get the bag in which their food had been put. They said goodbye to their mother and slammed the cottage door.

Ah, adventures were in the air that morning!

> *'Up the Faraway Tree,*
> *Joe, Beth and Me!'*

sang Frannie loudly.

'Hush!' said Joe. 'We are not far from the Enchanted Wood. We don't want anyone to know what we're going to do.'

They ran down the back garden and out of the little gate at the end. They stood still in the overgrown, narrow lane and looked at one another. It was the first big adventure of their lives! What were they going to see? What were they going to do?

They jumped over the ditch and into the wood. At once they felt different. Magic was all around them. The birds' songs sounded different. The trees once again whispered secretly to one another: 'Wisha-wisha-wisha-wisha!'

'Ooooh!' said Frannie, shivering with delight.

'Come on,' said Joe, going down the green path. 'Let's find the Faraway Tree.'

They followed him. He went on until he came to the oak tree under which they had sat before. There were the six toadstools too, on which the elves had held their meeting, though the toadstools looked rather brown and old now.

'Which is the way now?' said Beth, stopping. None of them knew. They set off down a little path, but they soon stopped; for they came to a strange place where the trees stood so close together that they could go no farther. They went back to the oak tree.

'Let's go this other way,' said Beth, so they set off in a different direction. But this time they came to a curious pond, whose waters were pale yellow, and shone like butter. Beth didn't like the look of the pond at all, and the three of them went back once more to the oak tree.

'This is too bad,' said Frannie, almost crying. 'Just when we've got a whole day to ourselves we can't find the tree!'

'I'll tell you what we'll do,' said Joe suddenly. 'We'll call those elves.

Don't you remember how they said they would help us whenever we wanted them?'

'Of course!' said Frannie. 'We had to stand under this oak tree and whistle seven times!'

'Go on, Joe, whistle,' said Beth. So Joe stood beneath the thick green leaves of the old oak and whistled loudly, seven times – 'Phooee, phooee, phooee, phooee, phooee, phooee, phooee!'

The children waited. In about half a minute a rabbit popped its head out of a nearby rabbit-hole and stared at them.

'Who do you want?' said the rabbit, in a furry sort of voice.

The children stared in surprise. They had never heard an animal speak before. The rabbit put his ears up and down and spoke again, rather crossly.

'Are you deaf? Who do you WANT? I said.'

'We want one of the elves,' said Joe, finding his tongue at last.

The rabbit turned and called down his hole, 'Mr Whiskers! Mr Whiskers! There's someone wanting you!'

There came a voice shouting something in answer, and then one of the six elves squeezed out of the rabbit-hole and stared at the children.

'Sorry to be so long,' he said. 'One of the rabbit's children has the

measles, and I was down seeing to it.'

'I didn't think rabbits got the measles,' said Beth, astonished.

'They more often get the weasels,' said Mr Whiskers. 'Weasels are even more catching than measles, as far as rabbits are concerned!'

He grinned as if he had made a huge joke, but as the children had no idea that weasels were savage little animals that caught rabbits, they didn't laugh.

'We wanted to ask you the way to the Faraway Tree,' said Beth. 'We've forgotten it.'

'I'll take you,' said Mr Whiskers, whose name was really a very good one, for his beard reached his toes. Sometimes he trod on it, and this jerked his head downwards suddenly. Beth kept wanting to laugh but she thought she had better not. She wondered why he didn't tie it round his waist out of the way of his feet.

Mr Whiskers led the way between the dark trees. At last he reached the trunk of the enormous Faraway Tree. 'Here you are!' he said. 'Are you expecting someone down it today?'

'Well, no,' said Joe. 'We rather wanted to go up it by ourselves.'

'Go up it by yourselves!' said Mr Whiskers, in horror. 'Don't be silly. It's dangerous. You don't know what might be at the top. There's a different place almost every day!'

'Well, we're going,' said Joe firmly, and he set his foot against the trunk of the tremendous tree and took hold of a branch above his head. 'Come on, girls!'

'I shall fetch my brothers and get you down,' said Mr Whiskers, in a fright, and he scuttled off, crying. 'It's so dangerous! It's so dangerous!'

'Do you suppose it is all right to go?' asked Beth, who was usually the sensible one.

'Come on, Beth!' said Joe impatiently. 'We're only going to see what's at the top! Don't be a baby!'

'I'm not,' said Beth, and she and Frannie hauled themselves up beside Joe. 'It doesn't look very difficult to climb. We'll soon be at the top.'

But it wasn't as easy as they thought, as you will see!

From THE ENCHANTED WOOD:

The Folk in
the Faraway Tree

*B*efore very long the children were hidden in the branches as they climbed upwards. When Mr Whiskers came back with five other elves, not a child could be seen!

'Hey, come down!' yelled the elves, dancing round the tree. 'You'll be captured or lost. This tree is dangerous!'

Joe laughed and peered down. The Faraway Tree seemed to be growing acorns just where he was, so he picked one and threw it down. It hit Mr Whiskers on the hat and he rushed away, shouting, 'Oh, something's hit me! Something's hit me!'

Then there was silence. 'They've gone,' said Joe, laughing again. 'I expect they don't much like when it rains acorns, funny little things! Come on, girls!'

'This must be an oak tree if it grows acorns,' said Beth, as she climbed. But just as she said that she stared in surprise at something nearby. It was a prickly chestnut case, with hard nuts inside!

'Good gracious!' she said. 'It's growing horse chestnuts just here! What a very peculiar tree!'

'Well, let's hope it will grow apples and pears higher up,' said Frannie, with a giggle. 'It's a most extraordinary tree!'

Soon they were quite high up. When Joe parted the leaves and tried to see out of the tree he was amazed to find that he was far higher than the tallest tree in the wood. He and the girls looked down on the top of all the other trees, which looked like a broad green carpet below.

Joe was higher up than the girls. Suddenly he gave a shout. 'I say, girls! Come up here by me, quickly! I've found something odd!'

Beth and Frannie climbed quickly up.

'Why, it's a window in the tree!' said Beth, in astonishment. They all peered inside, and suddenly the window was flung open and an angry little face looked out, with a nightcap on.

'Rude creatures!' shouted the angry little man, who looked like a pixie. 'Everybody that climbs the tree peeps in at me! It doesn't matter what I'm doing, there's always someone peeping!'

The children were too astonished to do anything but stare. The pixie disappeared and came back with a jug of water. He flung it at Beth and soaked her. She gave a scream.

'Perhaps you won't peep into other people's houses next time,' said the pixie with a grin, and he slammed his window shut again and drew the curtain.

'Well!' said Beth, trying to wipe herself dry with her handkerchief. 'What a rude little man!'

'We'd better not look in at any windows we pass,' said Joe. 'But I was so surprised to see a window in the tree!'

Beth soon got dry. They climbed up again, and soon had another surprise. They came to a broad branch that led to a yellow door set neatly in the big trunk of the Faraway Tree. It had a little door-knocker and a brightly-polished bell. The children stared at the door.

'I wonder who lives there?' said Frannie.

'Shall we knock and see?' said Joe.

'Well, I don't want water all over me again,' said Beth.

'We'll ring the bell and then hide behind this branch,' said Joe. 'If anyone thinks he is going to throw water at us he won't find us.'

So Joe rang the bell and then they all hid carefully behind a big branch. A voice came from the inside of the door.

'I'm washing my hair! If that's the butcher, please leave a pound of sausages!'

The children stared at one another and laughed. It was odd to hear of butchers coming up the Faraway Tree. The voice shouted again:

'If it's the oil man, I don't want anything. If it's the red dragon, he must call again next week!'

'Good gracious!' said Beth, looking rather frightened. 'The red dragon! I don't like the sound of that!'

At that moment the yellow door opened and a small fairy looked out. Her hair was fluffed out round her shoulders, drying, and she was rubbing it with a towel. She stared at the peeping children.

'Did you ring my bell?' she asked. 'What do you want?'

'We just wanted to see who lived in the funny little tree-house,' said Joe, peering in at the dark room inside the tree. The fairy smiled. She had a very sweet face.

'Come in for a moment,' she said. 'My name is Silky, because of my silky hair. Where are you off to?'

'We are climbing the Faraway Tree to see what is at the top,' said Joe.

'Be careful you don't find something horrid,' said Silky, giving them each a chair in her dark little tree-room. 'Sometimes there are delightful places at the top of the tree – but sometimes there are strange lands too. Last week there was the land of Hippety-Hop, which was dreadful. As soon as you got there, you had to hop on one leg, and everything went hippety-hop, even the trees. Nothing ever kept still. It was most tiring.'

'It does sound exciting,' said Beth. 'Where's our food, Joe? Let's ask Silky to have some.'

Silky was pleased. She sat there brushing her beautiful golden hair and ate sandwiches with them. She brought out a tin of Pop Cakes, which were lovely. As soon as you bit into them they went *pop*! and you suddenly found your mouth filled with new honey from the middle of the little cakes. Frannie took seven, one after another, for she was rather greedy. Beth stopped her.

'You'll go pop if you eat any more!' she said.

'Do a lot of people live in this tree?' asked Joe.

'Yes, lots,' said Silky. 'They move in and out, you know. But I'm always here, and so is the Angry Pixie, down below.'

'Yes, we've seen him!' said Beth. 'Who else is there?'

'There's a Mister Watzisname above me,' said Silky. 'Nobody knows his name, and he doesn't know it himself, so he's called Mister Watzisname. Don't wake him if he's asleep. He might chase you. Then there's Dame Washalot. She's always washing, and as she pours her water away down the tree, you've got to look out for waterfalls!'

'This is such an interesting and exciting tree,' said Beth, finishing her cake. 'Joe, I think we ought to go now, or we'll never get to the top. Goodbye, Silky. We'll come and see you again one day.'

'Do,' said Silky. 'I'd like to be friends.'

They all left the dear little round room in the tree and began to climb once more. Not long after they heard a peculiar noise. It sounded like an aeroplane throbbing and roaring.

'But there can't be an aeroplane in this tree!' said Joe. He peered all round – and then he saw what was making the noise. A funny old gnome sat in a deckchair on a broad branch, his mouth wide open, his eyes fast shut – snoring hard!

'It's Mister Watzisname!' said Beth. 'What a noise he makes! Mind we don't wake him!'

'Shall I put a cherry in his mouth and see what happens?' asked Joe, who was always ready for a bit of mischief. The Faraway Tree was now growing cherries all around for a change, and there were plenty to pick.

'No, Joe, no!' said Beth. 'You know what Silky said – he might chase us. I don't want to fall out of the Faraway Tree and bump down from bough to bough, if you do!'

So they all crept past old Mister Watzisname, and went on climbing up and up. For a long time nothing happened except that the wind blew in the tree. The children did not pass any more houses or windows in the tree – and then they heard another noise – rather a peculiar one.

They listened. It sounded like a waterfall – and suddenly Joe guessed what it was.

'It's Dame Washalot throwing out her dirty water!' he yelled. 'Look out, Beth! Look out, Frannie!'

Down the trunk of the tree poured a lot of blue, soapy water. Joe dodged it. Frannie slipped under a broad branch. But poor old Beth got splashed from head to foot. How she shouted!

Joe and Frannie had to lend her their handkerchiefs. 'I'm so unlucky!' sighed Beth. 'That's twice I've been soaked today.'

Up they went again, passing more little doors and windows, but seeing no one else – and at last they saw above them a vast white cloud.

'Look!' said Joe, in amazement. 'This cloud has a hole in it – and the branches go up – and I believe we're at the very top of the tree! Shall we creep through the cloud-hole and see what land is above?'

'Let's!' cried Beth and Frannie – so up they went.

Benny and the Giants

Benny was a little boy tramp. He had no home, no mother and no father. He went about the world doing odd jobs here and there, earning a penny one day, twopence the next, and maybe nothing the day after.

He was often very lonely. He sometimes looked into windows at night-time when the lamps were lit, and wished he had a cosy home where there was someone who loved him.

'Never mind!' he said to himself. 'One day I'll find someone who loves me, and then I can love them back, and we'll have a nice little home together.'

One week Benny found it very hard to get work. Nobody seemed to want any jobs done at all. There were no gardens that needed digging, no wood that wanted chopping, and no horses that wanted holding. Benny got very hungry, and wondered whatever he could do.

Then he suddenly saw a big notice by the side of the road. This is what it said:

DANGER. BEWARE OF GIANTS.

'That's funny,' said Benny. 'Fancy there being any giants about here!'

He looked round, but he couldn't see any. Then he spied a carter coming slowly towards him, with a load of sacks of potatoes. He hailed him, and asked for a lift.

'You'd better not come with me,' said the carter. 'I've got to deliver these potatoes a bit too near the giants' castle, for my liking!'

'I'm not afraid!' said Benny. 'Let me come, do, for I'm tired.'

'Jump up, then,' said the carter.

So up Benny sprang, and sat down in the cart. He began to ask the carter questions about the giants, and the man told him all he wanted to know.

'There's a giants' castle over yonder,' he said, pointing with his whip to the west. 'Two great giants live in it, and it is said that they take people prisoner when they can, and hold them to ransom. I heard they were wanting another servant, but you can guess nobody is likely to go there!'

'Dear me!' said Benny. 'I wonder if they would take me for their servant. Do you think they would?'

'What! Do you mean to say you'd go to live with great ugly giants?' cried the carter in amazement. 'You keep away from them, my boy, or maybe they'll have you for dinner.'

Benny thought about it for a little while, and then he made up his mind. He would try to get a job in the giants' castle. That would be better than starving, anyway, and if he thought the giants were likely to eat him he would run away.

'You'd better come back with me on my cart,' said the carter, when he had delivered his sacks at a little house by the roadside. 'If you get down here, you'll meet the giants, perhaps.'

'That's just what I want to do!' said Benny. He leapt down, thanked the surprised carter, and ran down the road. It wound up a hill, and when he came to the top he saw the giants' castle in the distance.

The sun was setting as he came near it, and the windows glistened and shone.

He walked boldly up to the back door, which was about twenty times as high as he was, and pulled hard at the bell.

The door opened, and a giant servant peered out. He didn't see Benny, who only came about as high as his knee, so he shut the door again. The boy pulled the bell hard, and once more the giant peered round the door, looking very much surprised.

'Hi!' called Benny. 'Look down, not up! Can't you see me?'

The giant looked down in surprise. When he saw Benny he grinned broadly.

'Jumping pigs!' he said. 'What a little mannikin! What may you want, shrimp?'

'I hear the giants want a servant,' said Benny. 'Will I do?'

The giant roared with laughter.

'You!' he said. 'Why, what could you do?'

'Anything!' said Benny, stepping inside. 'Just go and tell the giants I am here, will you?'

The servant gaped at Benny's order, but he turned and trotted off, making a noise like thunder on the wooden floor. Soon he came back again.

'The masters want to see you,' he said. So Benny followed him, looking as bold and brave as could be, but inside he was feeling very trembly indeed.

The two giants who wanted to see him were simply enormous. Their servant seemed quite a dwarf beside them. They picked Benny up, and stood him on a table, looking at him very closely.

'He seems a smart lad,' said one of them in a great booming voice.

'He is neat and clean, too,' said the other. Then he spoke to Benny.

'We have a little guest with us,' he said, with a grin that showed all his big teeth. 'She is not eating very well, and we think that our own servant is too clumsy to prepare her meals as she likes them. We want a smaller servant who will please her better. Can you cook, prepare dainty meals, and generally make yourself useful to our guest?'

'Certainly,' said Benny, thinking that the giants had a little niece staying with them. 'I will do my best.'

So the giants engaged him, and he was told to start on his duties the very next day.

Next morning he prepared a nice breakfast, set it on the smallest tray he could find, and then followed the giant servant to the top of the castle. The servant unlocked a heavy door, and flung it open. Benny went in, carrying his tray carefully.

And then he got such a surprise! For the guest was no niece of the giants', but a lovely little Princess, who was being kept a prisoner by them. He nearly dropped the tray when he saw her.

'Why!' he cried. 'You are no giant! You are a princess! Where do you come from, and how long have you been here?'

'Silence!' shouted the giant servant, cuffing Benny on the ear and nearly stunning him. 'The masters say that you and the Princess must not speak a word to one another, on pain of death!'

Benny said no more. The Princess said never a word in reply, for she was afraid of getting Benny into trouble. But she managed to give him one or two looks, which told him as plainly as could be that she was unhappy and wanted to escape.

Benny followed the giant servant downstairs, thinking very hard. He thought the little Princess was the loveliest thing he had ever seen. Every time he remembered her sweet face a little warm feeling crept round his heart, so he knew he had fallen in love with her, and he was very happy.

'Now, how can I rescue her?' he wondered. 'I must certainly get her away from here!'

'If you think you're going to speak to the Princess, or send messages to her, you can get the idea out of your head!' said the giant servant when they were downstairs again. 'I have orders to prevent anything of the sort.'

Benny said nothing, for he did not want to anger the servant. Instead, he began to think out delicious meals for the Princess. He made a small tray, and looked for the very tiniest dishes and plates in the castle, for he knew the Princess would not like her meals set on dishes as large as tables.

Then he began to think how he might get her away in safety. First of all, how was he to tell her things? He soon thought of a way.

'I'll write my messages on strips of paper,' he said. 'Then I'll make some cakes, and put the paper round them. Both paper and cake will be baked together, which, as anybody knows, is the right way to bake, and then the princess can read my messages in secret! Now how can I tell her what I am going to do?'

That night he made himself a bow and a few arrows. He slipped out into the moonlight and looked for the Princess's window. He soon saw it, for she sat by a lamp sewing, and he could see her golden head, bent over her needle.

He wrote a note, and stuck it on the end of an arrow. Then he shot it up at her window. It just missed it, and fell back again. He shot another, with a second note on it. This time he struck the side of the window, and made a noise. The Princess heard it and raised her head.

Benny shot a third arrow. It flew right in at the window, and landed at the feet of the startled maiden. She picked it up and saw the note.

'This is to tell you that I mean to rescue you,' she read. 'Please tear off the paper you will find round the cakes I bake for you, and you will see my messages written there. Shooting letters with arrows is too dangerous. Take heart, Princess, for I will be your knight. BENNY.'

How glad the Princess was! She ran to the window, and waved her hand in the moonlight. Benny knew that she had read his message, and was content.

Every day he baked her a little cake, and wrote his message on the paper round it. The giant servant used to take a skewer, and poke it through the cake, to see if Benny had put notes inside – but it never came into his head that the boy had been clever enough to write his messages on the paper baked round the cake itself. So he didn't find out the secret.

Benny tried hard to think of some way of escape. It was very difficult, for the two giants always seemed to be about, and as for the giant servant, he never let Benny out of his sight.

Then, one very hot day, Benny's chance came. He heard the sound of carriage wheels, and popped his head out of the window. To his joy he saw that the two giants were in it driving away from the castle.

'That's got rid of two, anyway!' he said. 'Now what about the servant? Ah, I've got an idea! If only it will work!'

'Where have our masters gone?' he asked the servant. 'Will they be long?'

'About six hours,' said the giant, with a yawn.

'Then don't let's do any work this afternoon,' said Benny. 'Let's go to sleep.'

'No,' said the giant, suspiciously. 'You'll run off, if I so much as shut my eyes, I know!'

'Well, I'll do some work, and you just have a nice rest,' said Benny. 'You'll be able to hear me working, so you'll know I'm here all right. I'll wash and scrub the kitchen floor.'

'Very well,' said the giant. 'I'll put my chair right in the middle, then you won't need to disturb me.'

He put his easy chair right in the middle of the vast kitchen, and sat down. Benny got out a pail and cloth, and began to wash the floor. He watched the giant carefully, and soon saw that what he hoped would happen, was happening. The giant was falling asleep.

Then Benny ran to the cupboard, and got out the polish, and a duster. He had an idea. He began to polish the wooden floor of the kitchen as if his life depended on it. The giant occasionally opened his eyes, but seeing Benny busy, shut them again at once. The youth went on with his work, until he had made all the floor shiny and slippery. Then he began to polish the long passage that led out of the kitchen to the hall. The giant heard him, and fell asleep for the sixth time.

When Benny had finished, he crawled on his knees to the snoring giant. He carefully picked the key of the tower-room from the giant's belt, and then began to crawl back again. The giant awoke, opened his eyes, and looked for Benny. At once the boy began to rub his duster on the floor, as if he were still cleaning it. The giant shut his eyes, and began to snore once more.

Benny took his chance. He tore up the stairs to the tower-room, unlocked it, and ran to the Princess. He took her hand, and begged her to come with him.

'The two giants are out,' he said. 'As for the servant, he is asleep – but if he awakes, and tries to come after us, he will find it difficult to get out of the kitchen – for I have polished the floor so highly that he will find it impossible to walk across it!'

The Princess held his hand and together they ran down the stairs. They crept out of the front door, and tiptoed down the steps, afraid of making a noise in case they awakened the giant. But alas! He awoke just at that moment, and heard them!

'Benny!' he called. 'BENNY! Where are you? Come here at once!'

When no Benny came, the giant leapt to his feet and tried to run across the floor – but it was so terribly slippery that he fell on his nose at once! He tried to get up, but he couldn't, for the floor was as slippery as ice. He slid here, and slipped there, and at last managed to stand up again.

Then *plonk*! Down he went once more. It would have been a funny sight to watch if anyone had been there to see. He scrambled and slipped, and slipped and scrambled, and at last got to the door. But then there was the long slippery passage to go down!

The servant gave it up at last. He was so tired of bumping his nose, his knees and his elbows. He simply sat down on the floor and waited.

Soon the two giants came home. They walked to the kitchen to speak to their servant – and crash! Down they both went on the polished floor! They clutched at one another, and slid all over the place, getting mixed up with the surprised servant. At last they all sat still and looked at one another.

'What do you mean by this?' asked the giants, scowling at the servant. 'This is a fine thing to do to the floor.'

'It's not my fault,' said the servant, sulkily. 'Benny did it, and now he's gone, and I don't know where he is. He's taken the key of the tower-room too, so I expect the Princess is escaping with him.'

'Good gracious!' cried the giants, and tried to leap to their feet. But down they went again, and slithered all along the passage. By the time they managed to get to the front door and start chasing Benny and the Princess, it was too late.

Benny was far away. He and the Princess had run for miles. 'They had passed the notice-board that said: 'Beware of Giants,' and were hurrying to the east. Soon they saw a fine carriage rolling along the road, and Benny sprang out to stop it.

'Ho, ho! What's this!' cried the coachman, flicking at Benny with his whip. 'How dare you stop the carriage of the Lord High Chamberlain?'

'Oh!' squeaked the Princess in delight. 'He's my uncle!'

A bearded face appeared at the window, and then the door was flung open.

'Princess! My dear little long-lost niece!' cried the Chamberlain. 'How did you come here? We have lost you for months, and looked for you everywhere!'

The Princess hugged him, and begged to be taken to her parents, the King and Queen. Off rolled the carriage once more, with the Chamberlain, the Princess, and Benny sitting inside.

It was not long before they arrived at the palace. How glad the King and Queen were to see their little daughter once again! They hugged and kissed her, and shook Benny's hand a hundred times.

'You shall have as much gold as you please, and I will make you a noble lord!' cried the King. 'I can never be grateful to you enough.'

'And I'll marry you when I'm old enough,' the Princess whispered in his ear, 'because I love you very much, Benny.'

So Benny took his gold, and became Sir Benjamin Bravehcart. And people do say that next year he is going to marry the Princess, and I shouldn't be at all surprised if it is true!

The Wishing Carpet

Once upon a time there were two children who owned a wishing carpet. A little old woman had given it to them in exchange for a basket of mushrooms. They had met her on Breezy Hill when they were gathering mushrooms, and she had begged them to give her their basketful.

'Here you are, my dears,' she said, when they handed her their mushrooms. 'Here is something in exchange for your mushrooms. It is a magic carpet. Take great care of it.'

They took it home and unrolled it. It was bright blue and yellow, with a magic word written in green round the border. Peter and Betty looked at the carpet in wonder.

'I say!' said Peter. 'Suppose it really is magic, Betty! Shall we sit on it and wish ourselves somewhere else and see what happens?'

'Yes,' said Betty. So they sat themselves down on it, and Peter wished.

'Take us to the big city of London,' he said. The carpet didn't move. Peter spoke again. 'I said take us to the big city of London,' he said, more loudly. Still the carpet didn't move. It was most disappointing. And no matter what the two children did or said it just lay still on the floor and behave like any ordinary carpet.

'It isn't a wishing carpet after all!' said Betty, disappointed. 'That old woman wasn't telling the truth.'

'What a shame!' said Peter. 'Let's roll it up and put it in our toy-cupboard. We won't tell the grown-ups about it because they might laugh at us for believing the old woman.'

So they rolled it up and put it right at the back of the toy-cupboard. They forgot all about it until about four weeks later when they met a very strange-looking little man in their garden.

'What are you doing here?' demanded Peter.

'Sh!' said the little man. 'I'm a gnome. I've come to speak to you about that magic carpet of yours.'

'It isn't a magic carpet at all,' said Peter. 'It's just a fraud. It won't take us anywhere.'

'Show it to me and I'll tell you how to make it take you wherever you want to go!' said the gnome eagerly.

'Come on, then,' said Peter, and he led the way indoors. But on the way Betty pulled at his sleeve.

'I don't like that little gnome at all,' she said. 'I'm sure he is a bad gnome, Peter. I don't think we'd better show him the carpet. He might want to steal it.'

'Don't be afraid,' said Peter. 'I shall have tight hold of it all the time!'

He led the way to the toy-cupboard and pulled out the carpet. He laid it on the floor and then sat on it. The gnome clapped his hands in joy when he saw it and sat down too.

'Come on, Betty,' said Peter. 'Come and sit down as well. This may be an adventure. Oh look, here's Bonzo, the puppy. He wants to come as well! Come on, Bonzo, sit down on the carpet too.'

So Betty and Bonzo sat down beside the gnome and Peter.

'Did you say the magic word that is written round the border of the carpet?' asked the gnome.

'Oh, no!' said Peter. 'I didn't know I had to.'

'Well, no wonder the carpet wouldn't move then!' said the gnome. 'Listen!'

He looked closely at the word round the carpet border, and then clapped his hands twice.

'Arra-gitty-borra-ba!' he said. 'Take us to Fairyland!'

In a trice the carpet trembled throughout its length, and then rose in the air. It flew out of the window and rose as high as the chimney-pots. The children gasped in astonishment and held on tightly, afraid of falling off. The carpet flew steadily westwards.

'Oh!' said Peter. 'So that's how you do it! My goodness, what an adventure! Are we really going to Fairyland.'

'Yes,' said the gnome. 'Keep a watch out to the west. You will soon see the towers and the pinnacles on the borders.'

Sure enough it was not long before the children saw shimmering towers and high-flung pinnacles far away on the blue horizon. The carpet flew at a great speed, and the world below seemed to flow away from them like a river, so fast were they going.

'Fairyland!' cried Betty. 'Oh, how lovely!'

They soon passed over a high wall, and then the carpe rapidly flew downwards to a big square that seemed to be used for a market. And then something dreadful happened.

The carpet had hardly reached the ground when the gnome gave Peter a hard push that sent him rolling off the carpet. Bonzo rolled off too – but Betty was still on it with the gnome.

'Ha ha!' cried the gnome. 'I'm off with Betty! She shall be my servant! I've got the carpet for my own, foolish boy! Arra-gitty-borra-b! Take me to my castle, carpet!'

Before Peter or Bonzo could pick themselves up and rush to reach the carpet, it had once more risen into the air and was flying high above the chimney tops. Peter groaned in despair.

'Oh dear, oh dear, whatever shall I do? Betty felt certain that the gnome was a bad old fellow, and I didn't take any notice of her. Now he will make her his servant and perhaps I'll never see her again!'

Bonzo put his nose into Peter's hand, and much to the little boy's surprise, he spoke.

'Don't worry, Peter,' he said. 'I expect we'll get her back again all right.'

'Good gracious, you can speak!' cried Peter in surprise.

'Well, we're in Fairyland, you see,' said Bonzo. 'All animals can speak there.'

Peter looked round the market square. He saw many pixies, elves and brownies looking at him, and he went up to some of them.

'Could you please help me?' he asked. 'My little sister has been taken away on my magic carpet by a horrid little gnome. I don't know where he's gone to, but I really must get Betty back again. She will be so frightened all by herself.'

'How dreadful!' cried the fairy folk. 'Why, that must have been Sly-One! He lives in a castle far away from here. Nobody dares to go near him because he is so powerful.'

'Well, I must go and find him,' said Peter bravely. 'I've got to rescue my sister. Tell me how to get to Sly-One's castle.'

'The Blue Bird will take you to the land where he lives,' said a pixie. 'There you will find an old dame in a yellow cottage, and she will tell you which way to go text.'

'Oh, thank you,' said Peter. 'Where can I find the Blue Bird?'

'We'll get him for you,' said the little folk. One of them took out a silver whistle from his pocket, and blew seven blasts on it. In a few moments there came the sound of flapping wings and a great blue bird soared over the market place. It flew down among the little folk and they ran to it.

'Blue Bird, we want your help,' they cried. 'Will you take this boy to the Land of Higgledy, where Sly-One the Gnome lives? His sister has been carried off there and he wants to rescue her.'

'Certainly,' said the bird. 'Jump on.'

So Peter and Bonzo climbed up on the Blue Bird's soft feathery back. He spread his broad wings, and flew off into the air. Peter held tight, and Bonzo whined, for he was rather frightened.

'It's a good way off,' said the Blue Bird. 'It will take quite half an hour to get there. Feel about behind my neck and you'll find a box of chocolate biscuits. You may help yourself.'

Peter did as he was told. He soon found the box and opened it. Inside was the finest collection of chocolate biscuits he had ever tasted, and he did wish Betty could have shared them. He gave Bonzo three, and the little dog crunched them all up.

In half an hour's time the Blue Bird turned his head round once more and spoke to Peter.

'We're nearly there,' he said. 'Can you see some of the houses?'

Peter looked down. He saw a very curious land. All the trees and houses were higgledy-piggledly. The trees grew twisted and crooked, the houses were built in crooked rows, and their windows and chimneys were set higgledy-piggledy anywhere.

The bird flew down to the ground, and Peter and Bonzo got off his back.

'Thank you very much,' said Peter. 'It was very good of you to help me.'

'Don't mention it,' said the Blue Bird. 'Take one of my feathers, little boy, and put it into your pocket. It may be useful to you, for whenever you want to know where anything is it will at once point in the right direction.'

'Oh, thank you,' said Peter, and he pulled a little blue feather from the bird's neck. He put it in his pocket, said goodbye, and then looked about for the yellow cottage that the little folk had told him about.

It was just a little way off, standing by the side of a lane. It was all crooked, and looked as if it might tumble down at any moment. An old woman stood at the gate, knitting. Peter went up to her.

'Please,' he said, 'could you tell me the way to the castle of Sly-One the gnome.'

'I should advise you not to go there,' said the old dame, knitting very fast indeed. 'He is a bad lot, that gnome.'

'I know,' said Peter. 'But he's got my sister, so I'm afraid I must go to him.'

'Dear, dear, is that so?' said the old woman. 'Well, little boy, catch the bus at the end of the lane, and ask for Cuckoo Corner. Get off there, and look for a green mushroom behind the hedge. Sit on it and wish yourself underground. As soon as you find yourself in the earth, call for Mr Mole. He will tell you what to do next.'

'Thank you,' said Peter. Then, hearing the rumbling sound of a bus, he ran up the lane. At the top he saw a wooden bus drawn by rabbits. He got in, sat down on a seat with Bonzo at his feet, and waited for the conductor to give him a ticket. The conductor was a duck, and he asked Peter where he wanted to go.

'Cuckoo Corner,' said Peter. 'How much, please?'

'Bless you, we don't charge anything on this bus,' said the duck, giving Peter a ticket as large as a postcard. 'I'll tell you when we get to Cuckoo Corner.'

But Peter didn't need to be told – for at Cuckoo Corner there was a most tremendous noise of cuckoos cuckooing for all they were worth! Peter hopped out of the bus, and looked for the green mushroom behind the hedge. He soon found it.

'I've never seen a green mushroom before,' he said to Bonzo. 'Come on, puppy. Jump on my knee, or you may get left behind!'

He sat down on the mushroom and wished himself underground. Bonzo gave a bark of fright as he felt himself sinking downwards, and Peter lost all his breath. Down they went and down. Then bump! They came to rest in a cave far underground. It was lighted by glow-worms who sat in little lamps all about the cave. Peter jumped off the mushroom.

'Now, where's Mister Mole?' he thought. He looked round but could see no one.

'Mister Mole!' he shouted. 'Mister Mole! Where are you?'

'Wuff! Mister Mole!' Bonzo shouted too.

Suddenly a door opened in the wall of the cave and a mole with spectacles on his nose looked out.

'Here I am,' he said. 'What do you want?'

'Please will you help me?' said Peter. 'I want to rescue my sister from Sly-One the Gnome and I don't know what to do next.'

'Well, this door leads to the cellars of Sly-One's castle,' said the mole. 'Come with me.'

Peter followed the mole through the door, and found himself in a large cellar which seemed never-ending. Boxes and bottles stood all about, and except for the glow-worms in lamps, the place was quite dark.

The mole led him to some steps.

'If you go up there you'll come to the gnome's kitchen,' he said. 'Go quietly, because there is someone there. You can hear footsteps on the floor above, if you listen.'

Peter listened, and sure enough he heard someone walking about overheard. He felt rather frightened. Suppose it should be the gnome?

He went quietly up the steps – and then, oh dear! Bonzo suddenly gave a whine and darted right up them, ahead of Peter. He disappeared through a door at the top, and Peter was left alone. He looked upwards in dismay.

'How silly of Bonzo!' he thought. 'If that was the gnome, he'll be warned, and will be waiting for me at the top! Well, I can't help it! Here goes!'

Quietly he climbed the rest of the steps, and came to the door, which was half open. He listened, and thought that he heard someone crying. He popped his head suddenly round the door – and, oh my, whoever should he see but Betty herself in a large kitchen, crying and laughing over Bonzo, who was licking her face in excitement.

'Betty!' cried Peter, and he ran to her and hugged her. How glad she was to see him!

'That horrid gnome brought me to his castle and took me to this kitchen,' said Betty. 'He says I'm to scrub the floor and cook his dinner. Oh, Peter, how can we escape from here?'

'I'll find a way!' said Peter, bravely – but just as he said that his heart sank almost into his boots, for who should come stamping into the kitchen at that very moment but the horrid gnome himself!

'Ha!' he said in surprise when he saw Peter. 'So you think you'll rescue your sister, do you? Well, you're mistaken. There are no doors to this castle, and only one window, which is right at the very top! You can't get out of there! As for this cellar door which you came here by, I'll lock it this very instant! Now I shall have two servants instead of one! Well, you can start work at once. Scrub the floor, please.'

Peter watched him in dismay. He locked the cellar door with a large key, and then went out of the kitchen, whistling.

Betty began to cry again.

'Don't be frightened,' said Peter. 'There must be some way out!'

He looked round the kitchen. It had no window, and no door led outside. He ran into the hall. That had no door and no window either. There was another room opposite, and Peter looked into it. It was no use – there wasn't a single door that led outside, and not a window to be seen. The rooms were all lighted by candles.

The gnome came into the kitchen again, and when he saw that Peter and Betty had done nothing he fell into a rage.

'Now set to work!' he cried. 'If my dinner isn't ready in ten minutes I'll turn you both into beetles. Fry me some bacon and eggs, make me some tea, and toast me some bread!'

He stamped out of the kitchen and left the children in a panic. Neither of them knew how to fry bacon and eggs. But Bonzo came to the rescue.

'I've often watched Cook,' he said. 'I'll do the bacon and eggs, if you'll make the tea and the toast.'

So all three set to work, and soon the gnome's meal was ready on a tray. Peter took the tray in his hands and went into the hall. The gnome looked over the banisters of the staircase, and told him to bring it up to him. Peter carried it up and the gnome led the way to a tiny room whose walls were lined all around with big magic books.

He set the tray on the table and then ran down to Betty again.

'If we're going to escape, we'd better do it now!' he said. 'The gnome's busy eating.'

'But how can we get away?' asked Betty. 'There's no way we can go.'

'If only we knew where the magic carpet was!' said Peter.

'I say!' suddenly cried Bonzo. 'What about that feather the Blue Bird gave you, Peter? Can't you use that to find the carpet?'

'Of course!' cried Peter, and he took the feather from his pocket. He held it up in the air, and spoke to it. 'Point to where the magic carpet is!' he commanded. At once the feather twisted round in Peter's hand and pointed towards the door that led into the hall.

'Come on,' cried Peter. 'It will show us the way!'

They all went into the hall. Then the feather pointed up the stairs. So up they all went, keeping as quiet as they could in case the gnome heard them. Past the door where he was eating his meal they went, and up more stairs. Still the feather pointed upwards. So up they went. At last they came to a broad landing, and on it stood a big chest. The blue feather pointed to it.

Betty ran to the chest and opened it. Inside lay the magic carpet. With a cry of joy she unrolled it and laid it on the floor. And at that very moment the gnome came rushing up the stairs.

'Ho!' he cried. 'So that is what you're doing!'

'Quick, quick!' cried Peter, pulling Betty onto the carpet. The gnome rushed up to them – and then brave Bonzo rushed at the gnome, growing fiercely.

'Keep back or I'll bite you!' he said.

The gnome crouched back against the wall, frightened.

'Bonzo, Bonzo, come on to the carpet!' cried Peter. 'We must go whilst we can!'

'I can't!' said Bonzo. 'I must keep the gnome safely in a corner whilst you go. Never mind me.'

So Peter spoke the magic word, though he was dreadfully sorry to leave brave Bonzo behind – but he knew that he must rescue Betty whilst he could.

'Arra-gitty-borra-ba!' he cried. 'Take us home again!'

At once the carpet rose from the ground and flew upwards. It went up staircase after staircase, for the castle was very tall. At last it came to a big open window right at the very top and flew out. And just then Peter heard Bonzo barking, and caught the sound of his feet tearing up the stairs.

'Wait, wait!' he said to the carpet. 'Wait for Bonzo!' But the carpet didn't wait. It flew right out of the window and began to sail away to the east. Peter was in despair.

Bonzo appeared at the window – and, oh my, whatever do you think he did? He saw the carpet sailing away, and he jumped! It was the most tremendous jump, and he nearly missed the carpet! As it was, he wouldn't have got there safely if Peter hadn't caught his tail, and pulled him on.

'Oh dear, oh dear!' said Betty, the tears pouring down her cheeks. 'I really thought we had lost you, dear Bonzo, darling Bonzo!'

She hugged him and hugged him, and so did Peter.

'You are the bravest puppy I ever knew,' said Peter. 'Did you bite the gnome?'

'Yes, I did,' said Bonzo. 'He tried to get past me to go after you, so I bit his ankle. He cried out in rage and ran down the stairs to get a bandage. So I tore up the stairs to try and catch you up.'

How happy they all were to be going home together! They passed right over Fairyland, and soon came to their own land. It was not long before they were over their own garden, and the carpet flew down to their nursery window. In a moment they all got off, and danced round in delight.

'Bonzo, can you still talk?' asked Betty.

'Wuff, wuff, wuff, wuff!' said Bonzo.

'Oh, you can't!' said Peter. 'But never mind, we understand your barks. Now 'what shall we do with the magic carpet?'

'If we keep it I'm sure that nasty gnome will come after it again,' said Betty. 'Let's send it away in the air by itself! We shan't want to use it again after all our adventures, I'm sure.'

'All right,' said Peter. He spoke to the carpet. 'Arra-gitty-borra-ba!' he said. 'Rise up in the air and fly round and round the world!'

At once the carpet rose and flew out of the window. It was soon out of sight, and the children sighed with relief.

'That's the end of that!' they said. 'What an adventure! Let's go and tell Mummy all about it!'

The Magic Pinny-Minny Flower

Too-thin the Magician was making a new spell. He had nearly everything he wanted for it – a bowl of moonlight, a skein of spider's thread, six golden dew-drops, two hairs from a rabbit's tail, and many other things – but there was still one thing he hadn't got.

'I must have a blue pinny-minny flower,' said Too-Thin. 'That's the only thing I want – a pinny-minny flower. Now I wonder where I can get one.'

He went out into his garden to think about it. He walked round and round, up and down the paths, and thought hard. The beds were full of spring daffodils, but Too-Thin didn't notice them. A freckled thrush was singing a new song in the almond tree, but Too-Thin didn't hear it. He didn't even know it

209

was spring-time, for he didn't care about things like that.

He frowned and thought harder than ever. He really must have a blue pinny-minny flower, but where to get one he couldn't think.

'I must pin a notice outside my gate, and offer a reward to anyone who can bring me what I want,' said the magician at last. So he wrote out a notice and pinned it on his gate. This is what it said: 'Six sacks of gold will be given to anyone who brings a blue pinny-minny flower to Too-Thin the Magician.'

Then Too-Thin went indoors and began to stir the dewdrops in the bowl of moonlight.

Now many people passed by Too-Thin's gate and read the notice. Nobody knew where to get a blue pinny-minny flower at all. Many of them wrote to witches they knew, and to goblins who lived in mountain caves, asking if they could find a blue pinny-minny flower – but no one could.

One day Higgledy, a tiny cobbler pixie, passed by. He was very poor and lived in a tumble-down cottage with no garden. He often used to peep over the wall that ran round Too-Thin's garden and look at the rows of daffodils there. He wished he could have a garden like it and grow snowdrops, croci and daffodils, and roses in the summer-time.

Higgledy read the notice, and then his eyes opened in surprise.

'Surely Too-Thin does not mean this,' he said. He climbed up to the top of the wall and sat there, looking into the magician's garden. He looked over the doorway of the house, for he had often seen a tiny plant growing in the stones of the pathway there.

The plant was still there, and Higgledy stared in astonishment.

'Why, there's the pinny-minny plant still growing outside the magician's own door,' he said to himself. 'I've often seen it when I've looked over the wall. Can it be that the magician doesn't know it's there?'

He jumped over the wall and ran to the door. Yes, it was a pinny-minny plant right enough. Just as he was thinking of knocking at the door and telling the magician, Too-Thin came out, looking rather cross, for he was in a bad temper.

'Now then, now then,' he said. 'What do you want? Have you come about the eggs?'

'No,' said Higgledy, 'I'm not the egg-man. I've come about the pinny-minny plant.'

'Where is it?' cried the magician. 'Have you brought it with you?'

'No,' said Higgledy, 'you see –'

'Oh, you silly creature!' cried Too-Thin. 'Go and get it at once. Is it in someone's garden? Well, go and pick it! You can pay them for it with the gold I shall give you in return.'

Higgledy laughed. He suddenly bent down and picked a blue pinny-minny flower from the plant by his foot. Then he waved it in the magician's face.

'Here it is!' he cried. 'You passed it every day when you walked into the garden and never saw it! Oh, Too-Thin, you may be clever at spells, but you are very poor at other things! Why don't you use your eyes?'

Too-Thin stared in amazement. Why, here was the very flower he had wanted for so long! And to think it grew in his very own garden and he hadn't seen it! He went very red as he took it from Higgledy.

'You shall have the six sacks of gold,' he said, 'even though the plant grew in my own garden. But you must promise not to tell anyone where you found it, for I don't want to be laughed at.'

'I promise,' said Higgledy. Then the magician sent him to fetch a barrow in which he could wheel home his gold, and whilst Higgledy was gone Too-Thin looked round his garden and saw it for the first time.

'I really must use my eyes more!' he said. 'Why, those daffodils are beautiful! And listen to that thrush! Whatever is the use of being a clever magician if I forget to look at daffodils? Well, well, Higgledy has earned his gold, for he has opened my eyes for me!'

Higgledy was so pleased with his good fortune. He bought a beautiful little cottage with a garden and married a nice little wife. And what do you think he called his new cottage? Why, Pinny-Minny Cottage! So if ever you come across it you'll know who lives there!

Extraordinary Objects

The Grandpa Clock

The Grandpa clock stood up on the landing all day and night, ticking solemnly away by himself. He was a very tall clock, much, much taller than the children, and he was really a grandfather clock, of course – but everyone called him Grandpa because he was so nice.

He didn't like being up on the bedroom landing. He wanted to be down in the hall, and see a bit of life. He wasn't even on the front landing – he was on the back one, where the box room and the guest-room were, so he didn't really see much of anything that went on in the house.

'I wish I was down in the hall!' he thought whenever he heard someone ringing the bell or knocking at the door. 'I wonder who that is? Why can't I be down there and see? And I wish I could go and visit the kitchen. So many people come there. I can hear their voices. The cat goes there a lot too, and I like her.'

But it wasn't a bit of good, the back landing was his place and there he had to stay. Until one exciting day came – and then things were suddenly quite different!

It happened one night that a small imp called Scuttle-About lost his way in the dark, and climbed in at the landing window to take shelter. He heard the tick-tock, tick-tock of the Grandpa clock, and he ran to it.

'Can I get inside you?' he whispered. 'Will you hide me, Grandpa Clock?'

'Yes! I've a door under my big face. Open it and creep inside,' said Grandpa. 'Be careful of my pendulum that swings to and fro, though. It might hit you.'

The imp was very careful of it. He crouched down below it, and felt it just scrape the top of his head as it swung to and fro. Tick-tock, tick-tock!

He took off his Scuttle-About shoes. They were very magic and he could run about fast as a hare in them – but his feet were tired now and he wanted to curl up and rest for the night.

Soon he was fast asleep and snoring a little. Grandpa ticked steadily all the time, feeling most excited to have a little imp asleep just under his pendulum!

'Tick-tock! It's time to be up! Tick-tock! You must hurry away!' ticked old Grandpa, when he heard the birds beginning to sing outside. He knew that Annie the cook would soon be up and about. He didn't want her to see the imp when he ran off again.

Scuttle-About woke up with a jump. He stretched himself and hit the

215

swinging pendulum with his hand.

'Hey, don't do that!' said Grandpa. 'You'll make me go slow! Hurry – I believe I can hear someone coming.'

The imp swung open the door and fled in a fright. Grandpa never saw him again. But Scuttle-About left something behind him – he left his little magic shoes!

And soon the magic in them spread to the old Grandpa clock. He suddenly felt restless. He ticked a little faster. And then, to his enormous surprise, he gave a little jiggety-jig, rocking to and fro as he ticked.

'Strange! I seem to be able to move!' said Grandpa, astonished. 'I'm sure I moved an inch or two then. There! I did it again. Good gracious – I've moved out from the wall!'

It was the Scuttle-About spell in the little shoes working, of course. But Grandpa didn't know that. He just thought that for some strange reason he could move about.

Move about! Why, he had always longed to do that. He had always wanted to go into the hall and into the kitchen. Suppose he could? Just suppose he could get himself downstairs – how exciting that would be!

Well, it was difficult for him to move very much at first, but he soon got used to it. He could only move by rocking himself, or doing a curious little jump that made him tick very fast indeed as if he were quite out of breath.

It took him quite half an hour to reach the front landing. Even that was exciting to him because it was years since he had seen it. There were flowers there, and a big chair, and a chest. Grandpa ticked away to them in a loud voice. 'I'm going downstairs when I've got my breath! I'm going exploring!'

But he didn't get downstairs because at that moment the children's father came out of his room to go and wake the children. He almost bumped into Grandpa, who was just outside his bedroom door.

'Good gracious! It's the Grandpa clock!' he said. 'However did it get here? Has someone been having a joke?'

Poor Grandpa! He was carried straight back to his own place on the back landing. He was bitterly disappointed. He grumbled away to himself, ticking very crossly.

'Tick-tock, what a nasty shock, for a poor old clock!' he ticked. The children soon heard that he had been found outside their father's door, and they came to stare at him.

'Who put you there? Grandpa, don't you start wandering about at night!' they said.

Well, the Grandpa clock wasn't going to stop his bit of travelling if he could help it! Somehow or other he was going to get downstairs! Surely, if the family found him in the hall they would let him stay there? Wasn't that the proper place for a big grandfather clock?

That afternoon, when the children were at school and their mother was resting, the clock felt it couldn't keep still on the dull back landing any longer. He must at least go to the top of the stairs and look down.

So he went to the top of the stairs, rocking himself slowly along, sometimes giving a funny little jump. He couldn't help feeling very excited.

The stairs looked very long and very steep. It wasn't much good thinking of rocking himself down them. He would have to do little jumps down from one stair to the next. So down he went – jump – jump – jump – hop – hop!

It was very dangerous. He nearly missed the stair once or twice, and shivered in fright. But at last he was at the bottom, standing in the hall. How wonderful!

The hall seemed a most exciting place. There were mats and chairs, umbrellas, walking-sticks and a little table with flowers on it. Now, where could the clock put himself so that he could see when people came to the door? He badly wanted to have a bit of company.

The cat had heard the noise Grandpa made coming downstairs, and she came out of the kitchen to see what it was. She was amazed to see the Grandpa clock standing by the hall-table! She went up and sniffed at it. The sniffing tickled Grandpa, and made him jump.

That frightened the cat. She put her tail in the air and fled to the kitchen. The clock heard voices coming from there.

'I must go there and listen,' he thought, so he rocked and hopped to the kitchen door. The cook was out in the scullery talking to the milkman and the baker. Grandpa rocked inside and stood by the cupboard. My, what a thrilling place the kitchen was – and look at that lovely red fire! Grandpa began to wish he lived in the kitchen.

The cook came back. She saw Grandpa at once and gave a scream. 'Milkman! Baker! Help, help! Here's old Grandpa in the kitchen!'

They came rushing in, expecting to see an old man. Cook pointed to the clock. 'There, look! How did he get here? Oh, oh, I feel faint!'

The Grandpa clock was scared. When the milkman and the baker helped the cook to a chair, he rocked himself out of the kitchen and put himself back in the hall. He stood there, feeling very excited. My word, this was life!

The children's mother came running down the stairs. She suddenly saw Grandpa by the hall-table, and stopped in amazement.

'Cook!' she called. 'Who put old Grandpa down in the hall!'

'Oh, Mam! Do you mean to say he's out there now?' cried the cook, looking into the hall. 'He was standing in the kitchen a minute ago!'

'Oh, nonsense!' said her mistress. 'But how did he get into the hall? Help me upstairs with him, Cook. This is most extraordinary.'

The children were surprised to hear what had happened when they got home. First, the cook told them how Grandpa had appeared in the kitchen, then their mother told them how she had seen him in the hall.

'Perhaps old Grandpa is dull and bored, living up on the back landing, where nothing happens and nobody goes,' said Mary. 'Can't we let him live in the hall? He's so nice.'

But back on the landing he had to go. He was really most annoyed. Now he would have to hop all the way downstairs again if he wanted to stand in the hall.

'I'll wait till night comes and everyone is in bed,' he thought, ticking solemnly on the landing. 'Then I'll go down again, and look into all the rooms. That will be most exciting.'

Now, that night, when it was very dark and everyone was asleep, old Grandpa thought he would go downstairs once more. And at the same moment that he thought this he heard a little noise downstairs. Who was it? The cat wandering about? Or mice playing? Perhaps it was that imp coming back again.

Grandpa decided to go and see. So off he went, rocking himself to the top of the stairs. He stood at the top, and heard a noise again. The noise wasn't the cat, or the mice, or the imp. It was a burglar! He had got into the house and was in the hall. Think of that!

Grandpa hopped down the first stair. Then he hopped down the next one – but alas, he missed it! With a really tremendous noise he slid and slithered all the way from the top to the bottom, and landed on the top of the alarmed burglar. He was knocked over like a skittle, and lay on the carpet, quite still.

Then things happened quickly. Doors flew open, lights went on, voices called out. 'What was that noise, what's happening?' And down the stairs poured the whole family.

'Why, my goodness me, here's a man lying flat on the floor and the old Grandpa clock on top of him!' said the children's father, in astonishment. 'Ring up the police, quickly!'

The police came. They took the burglar away. One of them nodded at the old clock, which had now been stood upright in the hall, and was watching everything in the greatest excitement.

'What was your clock doing, knocking burglars down in the middle of the night? Good thing you had him in the hall!'

'Well, we didn't. He lives on the back landing,' said Mary. 'But oh – do, do let him live downstairs in the hall, Daddy, will you? I'm sure he wants to! I'm sure he was coming downstairs and he slipped and fell on top of the burglar. He deserves a reward, Daddy, he really does!'

So now old Grandpa lives downstairs, and loves it. And nobody has discovered to this day that he has a tiny pair of Scuttle-About shoes inside his case! It will be sad if somebody takes them out, won't it? He won't ever be able to wander into the kitchen at night and talk to the cat.

Tick-tock, tick-tock. I believe I can hear him coming!

The Strange Old Shop

The adventures really began on the day that Mollie and Peter went out to spend thirty-five pence on a present for their mother's birthday.

They emptied the money out of their moneybox and counted it.

'Thirty-five!' said Peter. 'Good! Now, what shall we buy Mother?'

'Mother loves old things,' said Mollie. 'If we could find an old shop somewhere, full of old things – you know, funny spoons, quaint vases, old glasses, and beads – something of that sort would be lovely for Mother. She would love an old tea-caddy to keep the tea in, I'm sure, or perhaps an old, old vase.'

'All right,' said Peter. 'We'll go and find one of those shops this very day. Put on your hat and come on, Mollie.'

Off they went, and ran into the town.

'It's a shop with the word "Antiques" over it that we want,' said Peter. 'Antiques means old things. Just look out for that, Mollie.'

But there seemed to be no shop with the word 'Antiques' printed over it at all. The children left the main street and went down a little turning. There were more shops there, but still not the one they wanted. So on they went and came to a small, narrow street whose houses were so close that there was hardly any light in the road!

And there, tucked away in the middle, was the shop with 'Antiques' printed on a label inside the dirty window.

'Good!' said Peter. 'Here is a shop that sells old things. Look, Mollie, do you see that strange little vase with swans set all round it? I'm sure Mother would like that. It is marked twenty-five pence. We could buy that and some flowers to put in it!'

So into the old dark shop they went. It was so dark that the children stumbled over some piled-up rugs on the floor. Nobody seemed to be about. Peter went to the counter and rapped on it. A tiny door at the back opened and out came the strangest little man, no higher than the counter top. He had pointed ears like a pixie. The children stared at him in surprise. He looked very cross, and spoke sharply.

'What do you want, making a noise like that?'

'We want to buy the vase with swans round it,' said Peter.

Muttering and grumbling to himself, the little chap picked up the vase and pushed it across the counter. Peter put down the money. 'Can I have some

221

paper to wrap the vase in?' he asked politely. 'You see, it's for my mother's birthday, and I don't want her to see me carrying it home.'

Grumbling away to himself, the little man went to a pile of boxes at the back of the shop and began to open one to look for a piece of paper. The children watched. To their enormous surprise a large black cat with golden eyes jumped out of the box and began to spit and snarl at the little man. He smacked it and put it back again. He opened another box.

Out of that came a great wreath of green smoke that wound about the shop and smelt strange. The little man caught hold of it as if it were a ribbon and tried to stuff it back into the box again. But it broke off and went wandering away. How he stamped and raged! The children felt quite frightened.

'We'd better go without the paper,' whispered Mollie to Peter, but just then another extraordinary thing happened. Out of the next box came a crowd of blue butterflies. They flew into the air, and the little man shouted with rage again. He darted to the door and shut it, afraid that the butterflies would escape. To the children's horror they saw him lock the door, too, and put the key into his pocket!

'We can't get out till he lets us go!' said Mollie. 'Oh dear, why did we ever come here? I'm sure that little man is a gnome or something.'

The little fellow opened another box, and, hey presto, out jumped a red fox! It gave a short bark and then began to run about the shop, its nose to the ground. The children were half afraid of being bitten, and they both sat in an old chair together, their legs drawn up off the ground, out of the way of the fox.

It was the most curious shop they had ever been in! Fancy keeping all those things in boxes! Really, there must be magic about somewhere. It couldn't be a proper shop.

The children noticed a little stairway leading off the shop about the middle, and suddenly at the top of this, there appeared somebody else! It was somebody tall and thin, with such a long beard that it swept the ground. On his head was a pointed hat that made him seem taller still.

'Look!' said Mollie. 'Doesn't he look like a wizard?'

'Tippit, Tippit, what are you doing?' cried the new-comer, in a strange,

deep voice, like the rumbling of faraway thunder.

'Looking for a piece of paper!' answered the little man, in a surly tone. 'And all I can find is butterflies and foxes, a black cat, and —'

'What! You've dared to open those boxes!' shouted the other angrily. He stamped down the stairs, and then saw the children.

'And who are you?' he asked, staring at them. 'How dare you come here?'

'We wanted to buy this vase,' said Peter, frightened.

'Well, seeing you are here, you can help Tippit to catch the fox,' said the tall man, twisting his beard up into a knot and tying it under his chin. 'Come on!'

'I don't want to,' said Mollie. 'He might bite me. Unlock the door and let us go out.'

'Not till the fox and all the butterflies are caught and put into their boxes again,' said the tall man.

'Oh dear!' said Peter, making no movement to get out of the chair, in which he and Mollie were still sitting with their legs drawn up. 'I do wish we were safely at home!'

And then the most extraordinary thing of all happened! The chair they were in began to creak and groan, and suddenly it rose up in the air, with the two children in it! They held tight, wondering whatever was happening! It flew to the door, but that was shut. It flew to the window, but that was shut too.

Meantime the wizard and Tippit were running after it, crying out in rage. 'How dare you use our wishing-chair! Wish it back, wish it back!'

'I shan't!' cried Peter. 'Go on, wishing-chair, take us home!'

The chair, finding that it could not get out of the door or the window, flew up the little stairway. It nearly got stuck in the doorway at the top, which was rather narrow, but just managed to squeeze itself through. Before the children could see what the room upstairs was like, the chair flew to the window there, which was open, and out it went into the street. It immediately rose up very high indeed, far beyond the housetops, and flew towards the children's home. How amazed they were! And how tightly they clung to the arms! It would be dreadful to fall!

'I say, Mollie, can you hear a flapping noise?' said Peter. 'Has the chair got wings anywhere?'

Mollie peeped cautiously over the edge of the chair. 'Yes!' she said. 'It has a little red wing growing out of each leg, and they make the flapping noise!'

The chair began to fly downwards. The children saw that they were just over their garden.

'Go to our playroom, chair,' said Peter quickly. The chair went to a big shed at the bottom of the garden. Inside was a playroom for the children, and here they kept all their toys and books, and could play any game they liked. The chair flew in at the open door and came to rest on the floor. The children jumped off and looked at one another.

'The first real adventure we've ever had in our lives!' said Mollie, in delight. 'Oh, Peter, to think we've got a magic chair – a wishing-chair!'

'Well, it isn't really ours,' said Peter, putting the swan vase carefully down on the table. 'Perhaps we had better send it back to that shop.'

'I suppose we had,' said Mollie sadly. 'It would be so lovely if we could keep it!'

'Go back to your shop, chair,' commanded Peter. The chair didn't move an inch! Peter spoke to it again; still the chair wouldn't move! There it was and there it stayed. And suddenly the children noticed that its little red wings had gone from the legs! It looked just an ordinary chair now!

'See, Mollie! The chair hasn't any wings!' cried Peter. 'It can't fly. I expect it is only when it grows wings that it can fly. It must just have grown them when we were sitting in it in the shop. What luck for us!'

'Peter! Let's wait till the chair has grown wings again, and then get in it and see where it goes!' said Mollie, her face red with excitement. 'Oh, do let's!'

'Well, it might take us anywhere!' said Peter doubtfully. 'Still, we've always wanted adventures, Mollie, haven't we? So we'll try! The very next time our wishing-chair grows wings, we'll sit in it and fly off again!'

'Hurrah!' said Mollie. 'I hope it will be tomorrow!'

The Giant's Castle

Each day Mollie and Peter ran down to their playroom in the garden, and looked at their wishing-chair to see if it had grown wings again. But each time they were disappointed. It hadn't.

'It may grow them in the night,' said Peter. 'But we can't possibly keep coming here in the dark to see. We must just be patient.'

Sometimes the children sat in the chair and wished themselves away, but nothing happened at all. It was really very disappointing.

And then one day the chair grew its wings again. It was a Saturday afternoon, too, which was very jolly, as the children were not at school. They ran down to the playroom and opened the door, and the very first thing they saw was that the chair had grown wings! They couldn't help seeing this, because the chair was flapping its wings about as if it was going to fly off!

'Quick! Quick!' shouted Peter, dragging Mollie to the chair. 'Jump in. It's going to fly!'

They were just in time! The chair rose up in the air, flapping its wings strongly, and made for the door. Out it went and rose high into the air at once. The children clung on tightly in the greatest delight.

'Where do you suppose it is going?' asked Peter.

'Goodness knows!' said Mollie. 'Let it take us wherever it wants to! It will be exciting, anyhow. If it goes back to that funny shop, we can easily jump off and run away when it goes in at the door.'

But the chair didn't go to the old shop. Instead it kept on steadily towards the west, where the sun was beginning to sink. By and by a high mountain rose up below, and the children looked down at it in astonishment. On the top was an enormous castle.

'Where's this, I wonder?' said Peter. 'Oh, I say, Mollie, the chair is going down to the castle!'

Down it went, flapping its rose-red wings. Soon it came to the castle roof, and instead of going lower and finding a door or a window, the chair found a nice flat piece of roof and settled down there with a sigh, as if it were quite tired out!

'Come on, Mollie! Let's explore!' said Peter excitedly. He jumped off the chair and ran to a flight of enormous steps that led down to the inside of the castle. He peeped down. No one was about.

'This is the biggest castle I ever saw,' said Peter. 'I wonder who lives here. Let's go and see!'

They went down the steps, and came to a big staircase leading from a landing. On every side were massive doors, bolted on the outside.

'I hope there are no prisoners inside!' said Mollie, half afraid.

The stairs suddenly ended in a great hall. The children stood and looked in astonishment. Sitting at an enormous table was a giant as big as six men. His eyes were on a book, and he was trying to add up figures.

'Three times seven, three times seven, three times seven!' he muttered to himself. 'I never can remember. Where's that miserable little pixie? If he doesn't know, I'll turn him into a black beetle!'

The giant lifted up his head and shouted so loudly that both children put their hands over their ears. 'Chinky! Chinky!'

A pixie, not quite so big as the children, came running out of what looked like a scullery. He held an enormous boot in one hand, and a very small boot-brush in the other.

'Stop cleaning my boots and listen to me!' ordered the giant. 'I can't do my sums again. I'm adding up all I spent last week and it won't come right. What are three times seven?'

'Three times seven?' said the pixie, with a frightened look on his little pointed face.

'That's what I said,' thundered the bad-tempered giant.

'I know they are the same as seven times three,' said the pixie.

'Well, I don't know what seven times three are either!' roared the giant. 'You tell me! What's the good of having a servant who doesn't know his tables? Quick – what are three times seven?'

'I d – d – d – don't know!' stammered the poor pixie.

'Then I'll lock you into the top room of the castle till you do know!' cried the giant, in a rage. He picked up the pixie and went to the stairs. Then he saw the children standing there, and he stopped in astonishment.

'Who are you, and what are you doing here?' he asked.

'We've just come on a flying visit,' said Peter boldly. 'We know what three times seven are – and seven times three too. So, if you let that pixie go, we'll tell you.'

'You tell me, then, you clever children!' cried the giant, delighted.

'They are twenty-one,' said Peter.

The giant, still holding the pixie tightly in his hand, went across to the table and added up some figures.

'Yes – twenty-one,' he said. 'Now why didn't I think of that? Good!'

'Let the pixie go,' begged Mollie.

'Oh no!' said the giant, with a wicked grin. 'He shall be shut up in the top room of my castle, and you shall be my servants instead, and help me to add up my sums! Come along with me whilst I shut up Chinky.'

He pushed the two angry children in front of him and made them go all the way up the stairs until they came to the topmost door. The giant unbolted it and pushed the weeping pixie inside. Then he bolted it again and locked it.

'Quick!' whispered Peter to Mollie. 'Let's race up these steps to the roof and get on to our magic chair.'

So, whilst the giant was locking the door, the two of them shot up the steps to the roof. The giant didn't try to stop them. He stood and roared with laughter.

'Well, I don't know how you expect to escape that way!' he said. 'You'll have to come down the steps again, and I shall be waiting here to catch you. Then what a spanking you'll get!'

The children climbed out on to the flat piece of castle roof. There was their chair, standing just where they had left it, its red wings gleaming in the sun. They threw themselves into it, and Peter cried, 'Go to the room where that little pixie Chinky is!'

The chair rose into the air, flew over the castle roof, and then down to a big window. It was open, and the chair squeezed itself inside. Chinky the pixie was there, sitting on the floor, weeping. When he saw the chair coming in, with the two children sitting in it, he was so astonished that he couldn't even get up off the floor!

'Quick!' cried Mollie. 'Come into this chair, Chinky. We'll help you to escape!'

'Who's talking in there?' boomed the giant's enormous voice, and the children heard the bolts being undone and the key turned to unlock the door!

'Quick, quick, Chinky!' shouted Peter, and he dragged the amazed pixie to the magic chair. They all three sat in it, huddled together, and Peter shouted, 'Take us home!'

The door flew open and the giant rushed in just as the chair sailed out of the window. He ran to the window and made a grab at the chair. His big hand knocked against a leg, and the chair shook violently. Chinky nearly fell off, but Peter grabbed him and pulled him back safely. Then they sailed high up into the air, far out of reach of the angry giant!

'We've escaped!' shouted Peter. 'What an adventure! Cheer up, Chinky! We'll take you home with us! You shall live with us, if you like. We have a fine playroom at the end of our garden. You can live there and no one will know. What fun we'll have with you and the wishing-chair!'

'You are very kind to me,' said Chinky gratefully. 'I shall love to live with you. I can take you on many, many adventures!'

'Hurrah!' shouted the two children. 'Look, Chinky, we're going down to our garden.'

Soon they were safely in the garden, and the chair flew in at the open door of the playroom. Its wings disappeared, and it settled itself down with a long sigh, as if to say, 'Home again!'

'You can make a nice bed of the cushions from the sofa,' said Mollie to the pixie. 'And I'll give you a rug from the hall-chest to cover yourself with. We must go now, because it is past our tea-time. We'll come and see you again tomorrow. Good luck!'

The Enchanted Table

Once upon a time there was a strange table. It was perfectly round, and had four strong legs ending in feet like a lion's – paws with claws. Round its edge there was carved a circle of tiny animals – mice, cats, dogs, weasels, rats, pigs, and others.

For many years this table stood in the kitchen of a tailor named Snip, and no one knew of its magic powers. Mrs Snip laid a white cloth on it each meal time and spread it with food and drink. Once a week she polished it. All the little Snip children sat round it three times a day and, dear me, how they kicked it with their fidgety feet! How they stained it when they spilt their tea! How they marked it with their knives, pens and pencils!

One day an old man came to see Snip the tailor. Mrs Snip asked him into the kitchen for a cup of tea, and he suddenly saw the table, with its edge of carved animals and its four paws for feet. His eyes opened wide, and he gasped for breath.

'That table!' he cried. 'It's magic! Didn't you know?'

'How is it magic?' asked Mrs Snip, not believing him at all.

'Look!' cried the old man. He went up to the table and ran his fingers round the carved animals. He pressed first a mouse, then a cat, then a pig, then a weasel, muttering a few strange words as he did so. Then he tapped each of the four paw-like feet with his right hand.

'Mercy on us!' cried Mrs Snip, in horror and surprise. 'Look at that! Why, it's alive!'

'Wait!' said the old man, in excitement. 'Let me show what it can do now!'

He went to the table and put his hands on the middle of it. Then, knocking three times sharply, he said: 'Bacon and sausages! New bread! Hot cocoa!'

And, would you believe it, a dish of bacon and sausages, a loaf of new bread, and a jug of hot cocoa suddenly appeared on that strange table!

Mrs Snip couldn't believe her eyes! She sat down on a chair and opened and shut her mouth like a fish, trying to say something. At last she called the tailor in from the shop.

When she told him what had happened he was amazed.

The old man knocked three times on the table again and said: 'Two pineapples! Stewed mushrooms!'

Immediately two large pineapples arrived, and a heap of stewed mushrooms planted themselves in the middle of the dish of bacon and sausages. They smelt very nice.

'Can we eat these things?' asked Mr Snip at last.

'Of course,' said the old man. They all sat down and began to eat. My, how delicious everything was! The table kept quite still, except that once it held out a paw to the fire, and frightened the tailor so much that he swallowed a whole sausage at once and nearly choked.

'This table is worth a lot of money,' said the old man. 'You should sell it, Snip. It's hundreds of years old, and was made by the gnome Brinnen, in a cave in the heart of a mountain. How did you come to have it?'

'Oh, it belonged to my father, and to his father, and to his father; in fact, it has been in our family for ages,' said the tailor. 'But I didn't know it was magic.'

'I expect someone forgot how to set the spell working,' said the old man. 'Look, I'll show you what I did. First you press this animal – then you press this one – and then this – and this – and all the time you say some magic words, which I will whisper into your ear for fear someone hears them.'

He whispered. The tailor listened in delight.

'And then,' said the old man, 'just put your hands in the middle of the table – so – and think what food you want. Then rap smartly three times on the top of the table and call out for what you'd like!'

'Marvellous!' said the tailor, rubbing his hands together. 'Wonderful! But I shan't sell my table, friend. No, it has been in my family so long that I could not part with it. I will keep it and let it provide food for me and my family.'

'Well, treat it kindly,' said the old man, putting on his hat to go. 'It has feelings, you know. Treat it kindly. It likes a good home. And don't forget to say those magic words once a week.'

'Come and dine with us each Sunday,' said the tailor. 'If it hadn't been for you we should never have found out the magic.'

Well, at first all the tailor's children and friends couldn't say enough about that marvellous table. They simply delighted in rapping on it and ordering meals. It didn't matter what they asked for it came. Even when Amelia Snip, the eldest child, rapped and asked for ice-cream pickles they appeared on the table in an instant.

What parties the Snips gave! Roasted chickens, legs of pork, suet

puddings, mince pies, apple tarts, sugar biscuits, six different sorts of cheese –
everything was there and nobody ever went short.

The table seemed quite content, except that it would keep walking over
to the fire, and sometimes it stroked someone's leg, and made that guest jump
nearly out of his skin.

But one day the table became impatient. Six little Snip children sat
round it, and they were very fidgety. Amelia kicked one table-leg. Albert kicked
another. Harriet spilt her lemonade over it and made it sticky. Paul cut a tiny
hole in it with his new penknife. Susan scratched it with her finger-nails. And
Bobbo swung his legs up high and kicked the underneath of the table very
hard indeed.

The table suddenly lost its temper. It lifted up a paw and smacked
Bobbo hard on his bare leg.

'Ooh!' cried Bobbo, slipping down from his chair in a hurry. 'Horrid
table! It slapped me!'

'How dare you slap my brother!' cried Amelia, and kicked the table-leg
hard. It immediately lifted up its paw, put out its claws, and scratched her like
a cat!

'Ow!' cried Amelia, and she ran to the shop, howling. Soon the tailor and
his wife came back with her, and the tailor scolded the table.

But instead of listening humbly, the table put up a big paw and slapped
Mr Snip! Then it got up and walked over to the fire.

'How many times have I told you that you are not to stand so close to the
fire?' scolded Mrs Snip. 'No one can sit at you if you do that. It's too hot.'

The table ran up to Mrs Snip and with two of its great paws it pushed her
into a chair. Then it shook one of its paws at her crossly and went back to the
fire again. Mrs Snip was very angry.

'Ho!' she said. 'So that's how you're feeling, is it? Well, I'll give you some
work to do.'

She went over to it and rapped smartly on the top three times, calling
out: 'Roast beef! Roast pork! Roast mutton! Steak-and-kidney pie! Suet roll!
Jam sandwich! Currant cake! Plum pudding!' and so on and so on, everything

she could think of! The table soon groaned under the weight of all the food she called for, and its four legs almost bent under their burden.

'There!' said the tailor's wife. 'That will punish you for your spitefulness!'

But the table had had enough of the Snip family. It had never liked them, for they were mean and selfish. So it made up its mind to go away from the house and never to come back.

It walked slowly to the door, groaning again under the weight of all its dishes. Mrs Snip and the tailor guessed what it was trying to do, and they rushed at it to push it back. The table rose up on two of its legs and began to punch with its other two.

Crash! Smash! Bang! Splosh! Every dish on the table slid off to the floor! There lay meat, pudding, pie, cakes, everything, and a whole heap of broken china. My, what a mess!

The table was pleased to be rid of its burden. It capered about and gave Mr Snip a punch on the nose. The tailor was frightened and angry. He really didn't know how to fight a fierce table like this. He tried to get hold of the two legs, but suddenly great claws shot out of the table's paws and scratched him on the hand.

Then the table slapped Mrs Snip and smacked Amelia and Paul hard. Then it squeezed itself out of the door and ran away down the street. It went on all-fours as soon as it left the house, and was so pleased with itself that it capered about in a very extraordinary way, making everyone run to their windows and doors in amazement.

Well, of course, the news soon went round that the marvellous magic table was loose in the land. Everyone secretly hoped to get it, and everyone was on the look-out for it. But the table was artful. It hid when the evening came and thought hard what it wanted to do.

'I will put myself into a museum,' said the table to itself. 'A museum is a place where all sorts of interesting and marvellous things are kept for people to wonder at and admire. I will find a museum and go there. Perhaps no one will notice that I have come, and I shall have peace for a while.'

It wandered out into the street again, and went to the next town. It was a big one, and the table felt sure it would have a museum. So it had – but the door was shut.

The table looked round the building to see if a window was open. Sure enough there was one, but rather high up. However, the table cared nothing for that. It climbed up a drain-pipe with all its four paws, and squeezed itself in at the window. Then it clambered down the wall inside and looked about for somewhere to stand.

Not far away was a big four-poster bed, a square table, and two solid-looking chairs. They had all belonged to some famous man. The table thought it might as well go and stand with these things, so off it went, and arranged itself in front of the chairs. Then it went comfortably to sleep.

But in the morning it was, of course, discovered at once! The museum-keeper saw it first, and perhaps he would not have known it was the lost magic table if the table had not suddenly scratched one of its legs with a paw, nearly making the poor man faint with amazement.

'It's the enchanted table!' he cried, and ran off to spread the news.

Soon the room was quite full of people, all staring and exclaiming, wondering how in the world the table had got into their museum. Then of course began the rapping and the commanding of all kinds of food to appear. The table sighed. It was getting very tired of bearing the weight of so many heavy dishes. It was surprised to think that people seemed so often hungry.

It didn't like being in the museum after all. It was dreadfully cold; there was no fire there, as there had been at the tailor's, and a terrible draught blew along the floor. The table shivered so much that all the dishes on it shook and shivered too.

That afternoon a message arrived from the King himself. He wanted the marvellous table in his palace. It would save him such a lot of money in feasts, he thought, and it would bring him quite a lot of fame.

The table heard the people talking to the messenger, and it felt quite pleased. It would be warmer in the palace, at any rate. It got up and walked to the door. The people ran away as it came near, for they had heard how it had fought the tailor's family and defeated them.

But the table didn't want to fight. It just wanted to get somewhere nice and warm. The museum-keeper tried to shut the door to stop it from going out, but the table pushed him over, and went out, doing a jig to keep itself warm. It meant to walk to the palace.

Everyone thought that it was going to run away again, and men, women, and children followed it to see what it was going to do. They were filled with surprise to see it mounting the palace steps one by one, and entering the palace doors!

'It's gone to see the King!' they cried.

The table walked into the palace, and no one tried to stop it, for all the footmen and soldiers were too surprised to move. The table went into the King's study, and found the King there, writing a letter.

'Who is it? Who is it?' asked His Majesty crossly, not looking up. 'How many times have I said that people must knock before they interrupt me?'

The table went up to the King and bowed so low that it knocked its carved edge on the floor. Then it stood up and saluted with one of its paws.

The King looked up – and in a trice he sprang from his chair and ran to the other side of the room in fright, for he had never seen a table like that before.

The table went over to the fire to warm itself. Soon the King recovered from his fright and called his servants.

'Here is that wonderful table,' he said. 'Take it into my dining-hall, and send out invitations to all the kings, queens, princes, and princesses living near to come and feast tonight. Tell them they shall each have what they like to eat and drink.'

The table went into the gold-and-silver dining-hall, and thought it was very grand indeed, but cold. It pointed one of its paws at the empty grate, but as nobody imagined that a table could feel cold, no notice was taken at all. So the table contented itself with doing a little dance to warm itself whenever it began to shiver, and this amused all the servants very much.

When the time for the feast drew near, the footmen laid a wonderful golden cloth on the table-top. Then they set out golden plates and dishes, golden spoons and forks, and golden-handled knives. How they glittered and shone!

No food was put there, not even bread. No, the table was to supply that.

Soon all the guests arrived, and how they stared to see such an empty table! 'Nothing but a vase of flowers!' whispered King Piff to Queen Puff.

'Take your seats,' said the King, smiling. 'I have brought you here tonight to see my new magic table, as enchanted and as bewitched as any table can be! Behold!'

He rapped three times smartly on the table. 'A dish of crusty rolls! Some slices of new-made toast!' he cried.

Before his guests' wondering eyes these things appeared, and the King bowed a little as if he were a conjurer performing tricks.

'Now, Queen Puff,' he said, 'kindly say what you would like for your dinner, and I will see that it comes. Rap three times on the table before saying.'

Queen Puff did as she was told. 'Celery soup, roast chicken, roast beef, cauliflower, potatoes, and plum pudding!' she said, all in one breath. 'Oh, and ginger-beer to drink!'

One by one all the guests wished for the dinner they wanted and marvelled to see everything appear on the table in a trice, all steaming hot and beautifully cooked. They sat and ate, lost in wonder. Then King Piff had an idea.

'I say,' he said to the King who had invited him, 'won't it give you – er – gold, for instance?'

Everybody there listened breathlessly, for one and all they loved gold, and wanted as much as they could get.

'Well,' said the King, 'I've never tried anything but food. Perhaps it would spoil the magic of the table if we did. We'd better not.'

'Pooh! You mean to try when we're not here, so that you can get as much gold as you want for yourself!'

'Yes, you old miser!' cried Prince Bong, and everyone began to talk at once. The King was horrified to hear himself called such names, and he threatened to call in his soldiers and have everyone arrested.

No one listened to him. They were all rapping hard on the poor table, crying out such things as: 'A bag of gold! A sack of gold! Twenty diamonds! Six rubies! A box of jewels! Twenty sacks of gold! A hundred bars of gold!'

The poor table began to tremble. It had never been asked for such things before, and had always been able to give what was demanded. But the magic in it was not strong enough for gold and jewels. It tried its best, but all it could give the excited people were sacks of cabbages, bags of apples, and bars of chocolate!

'Wicked table!' cried Prince Bong, and drew his sword to slash it. 'Horrible table!' cried Queen Puff, and slapped it hard. But that was too much for the frightened table. It jumped up on two legs and began to fight for itself.

Down slid all the dishes, glasses, plates, and knives! The King found a roast chicken in his lap, and Queen Puff was splashed from head to foot with hot gravy. Prince Bong howled when a large ham fell on his toe, and altogether there was a fine to-do.

The table hit out. Slap! That was for the King. Slosh! That was for Prince Bong. Punch! That was for King Piff. Scratch! That was for Queen Puff. Oh, the table soon began to enjoy itself mightily!

But, oh my, the King was calling for his soldiers, and the table could not hope to fight against guns. It suddenly ran down the dining-hall, jumped right over the heads of the astonished soldiers, and disappeared out of the door. How it ran!

'After it, after it!' yelled the King, who did not mean to lose the magic table if he could help it. But the table had vanished into the darkness.

It stumbled on and on, grieving that it could find no place where it would be treated properly. All it wanted was a room with a warm fire, a good polish once each week, and no kicking.

At last it came to a funny-looking shop, lighted inside with one dim lamp. The table peeped in. What a funny collection of things there was there! Old-fashioned furniture, suits of armour, rugs from far countries, lovely vases, old glasses, beaten-brass trays, strange, dusty pictures – oh, I couldn't tell you all there was.

It was a shop kept by an old man who sold strange things, Outside hung a sign on which was written the word 'Antiques'. The table did not know what that meant. All it knew was that there was a fire at the end of the shop, and that everything looked dusty and old – surely a table could hide here and never be discovered!

It crept in at the door. There was the old man, reading a book as old as himself, and the table hoped he would not look up as it walked softly among the dusty furniture.

'Who's there? Who's there?' said the old man, still not looking up. 'Wait a minute – I must just finish my page, and I'll serve you.'

The table squashed itself into a corner by the fire. It put up one of its paws and pulled down an embroidered cloth from the wall to cover itself. Then it heaved a sigh and stood quite still, enjoying the fire.

When the old man had finished his page he looked up – but there was no one in his shop. How strange!

'I felt sure I heard someone!' he said, rubbing his chin and looking all round, but he could see no one. So he went back to his book, and the table sidled a bit nearer the fire.

From that day to this no one has ever heard of that enchanted table. There it stands, happy and forgotten, in the old furniture shop, warming itself by the fire. If ever you see a round table with little animals carved round its edge, and with four big paws for feet, buy it. It is sure to be the long-lost enchanted table. But do be careful how you treat it, won't you?

The Strange Sailor Doll

One day Peter came to tea with Jill. He had with him a sailor doll, but neither Jill nor Peter played with him. It was much more fun playing with all Jill's exciting toys. She had such a lot, because she had plenty of aunts and uncles, and they gave her toys whenever they came to see her.

Peter liked best of all a little motorcar. It ran very fast across the room when it was wound up, and it had a little hooter that tooted loudly every now and again, all by itself. Peter thought it was wonderful.

'Oh, Jill, I do wish you'd give me this,' he kept saying. 'I never in my life saw such a dear little car – and the way it hoots, too! Honestly, I'd just love to have it for my own. Do give it to me.'

'You're not supposed to ask for other people's toys when you go out to tea,' said Jill.

'I know,' said Peter. 'I know quite well it isn't polite. But I can't help it this time. I say – suppose I give you my sailor doll? Would you exchange this little car for him?'

'Well, I don't much want him,' said Jill, looking at the doll. 'He seems rather ordinary to me. And why ever does he wear gloves?'

'Does he? Well, I never noticed it!' said Peter. 'Perhaps Mummy made him a pair sometime. Oh, do let me give him to you for this car.'

'All right,' said Jill. 'I don't really want him – but then, I don't really want the car either. I've got three others. Take it, and leave the sailor doll.'

And that was how Sailor came to live in Jill's house. The other toys crowded round him that night when Jill had gone to sleep. He looked shyly at them.

'I hope you don't mind me coming here,' he said. 'I'm sorry to leave Peter, really – though he isn't very good with his toys, you know. I like the look of your Jill.'

'She's nice,' said Angela, the big doll. 'Sailor, why do you wear gloves? Take them off. They look silly when you are indoors.'

The sailor doll went rather red. 'I don't take them off even when I'm indoors,' he said. 'I'd rather not, thank you.'

The toys laughed. 'Why? Are your hands cold?' said the ragdoll. 'Poor boy! His hands are cold, so he wears gloves! Ho, ho, ho!'

Sailor soon settled down among the toys. He seemed shy and didn't join in their games very much. The big brown teddy bear teased him about it.

'Hey, Sailor! Why don't you come and play head-over-heels tonight?

The Strange Sailor Doll

Come on! And we're going to play leapfrog too!'

'I don't think I will, thank you,' said the sailor doll, politely.

'He's afraid of getting his gloves dirty!' laughed the teddy bear. 'Take off your gloves, Sailor – yes, and your coat too – and come and play properly. You're always so dressed up and polite.'

But Sailor wouldn't. He went red and walked away to a corner by himself, where he talked to the clockwork mouse, who was timid and shy too.

The toys grew rather impatient with him. He had such a jolly face, and yet he wouldn't be jolly. But they were more impatient than ever one night when he wouldn't join in with their work. They wanted to build a ladder of bricks right up to the windowsill, so that they could climb up and look out.

'Come on, Sailor – do your share!' shouted the ragdoll, impatiently. 'Take off your coat and help us. Keep your silly gloves on if you want to – but you'll be awfully hot if you work in your coat, because these bricks are jolly heavy.'

'If you don't mind, I don't think I will help with the building,' said Sailor.

'Why not? Are you afraid of hard work?' asked the ragdoll.

'No,' said Sailor.

'He's bone-lazy,' said Angela, the big doll. 'Aren't you, Sailor? Too lazy to play and too lazy to work.'

'It's a pity he came to our house,' said the bear. 'He's no good at all. Won't join in anything. He's lazy and I expect he's a little coward too. Let's not have anything more to do with him.'

So after that they didn't speak to Sailor, and he might not have been in the room at all. Only the clockwork mouse spoke to him, and that was brave of him because he knew the others didn't like him for it.

Now, one day Mummy spoke to Jill, and the toys heard what she said. She said: 'Jill, will you put all your oldest toys in this basket, because I'll give them away to Mrs Brown. She has eleven children, and they hardly have any toys.'

'All right, Mummy,' said Jill, and went to her toy cupboard. She took out some bricks, a ball that had a hole in it, an old kite, a train that hadn't any lines, and some other things she never played with.

When she had put them all into the basket and gone out of the room, the

243

toys looked at one another. 'I'm glad I wasn't put into the basket,' said the bear. 'I've heard that Mrs Brown's children are rough and rude. I wouldn't like to be one of their toys.'

'Nor would I,' said Sailor.

'We're not speaking to you, so please don't speak to us,' snapped the ragdoll.

'It's a pity you weren't put into the basket, because you're not really wanted here,' said Angela, unkindly.

'Very well. I'll put myself in!' said poor Sailor, looking as if he were going to burst into tears.

'Do – gloves and all!' said the ragdoll in a very nasty voice. The sailor doll walked over to the basket of old toys and set himself on the top of them, looking very, very miserable.

'You won't be much loss,' said Angela. 'Stuck-up thing, never taking your gloves off, or even your coat, to play our games or help in our work.'

Sailor said nothing at all. The clockwork mouse went and sat beside the basket to show Sailor he still had one friend, but he didn't dare to say anything to him. Still, Sailor was very thankful to see him there. It made him feel a little less lonely.

Suddenly the door opened and in came Jill with Peter. He had come to borrow a book. He carried with him a beautiful toy horse with a real furry coat. He set it down on the floor while he went to look in Jill's bookcase.

All the toys gazed in delight at the toy horse. He was lovely, really lovely. His tail was long and swishy, his ears were cocked up, and his mane was beautiful. He had a little white mark on his brown nose, and bright eyes which looked all round the big room.

'Isn't he magnificent?' whispered Angela to the teddy bear. 'I've never seen a toy horse as grand as he is before!'

'I wish we could talk to him,' whispered back the bear. 'But we daren't while Jill and Peter are in the room.'

Well, would you believe it, when Peter found a book to take home with him, he went out of the room with Jill and quite forgot to take his horse with him. There he stood on the floor, looking very handsome and proud.

The toys went across to him. 'I say! Aren't you fine?' said the bear. 'Let me stroke your coat. It's real hair! And your tail is wonderful. Swish it about.'

The horse swished it, and then he kicked up his heels and galloped round and round the room, neighing in a high little horse-voice.

'Oh! You're grand!' cried all the toys, and even the clockwork mouse squeaked in delight. Then suddenly the little toy horse came to a stop and looked all round. 'I say!' he said. 'I've just remembered something. Haven't you got a friend of mine here, Sailor Doll? Didn't Peter give him to Jill in exchange for a little motor-car that hooted?'

'Yes,' said Angela, the big doll. 'Was he really a friend of yours? How strange! We simply can't bear him and his silly ways. Why, he always wears gloves, and he won't even take off his coat to do anything, work or play!'

'Did you ever bother to find out why?' said the little horse, swishing his tail. 'No, I can see you didn't. Where is Sailor? I simply must go and say how-do-you-do to him! He's a grand fellow!'

The toys were most astonished to hear this. Angela waved to the basket of old toys. 'He's over there, with the old toys that are going to be given away.'

The horse galloped up to the basket. He put his front hoofs up on to the tip of the basket and looked inside. 'Hrrrrrrrumph!' he said. 'Hey, Sailor! Don't you remember Dobbin, the horse in Peter's room? You often used to ride me.'

Sailor stood up, his face shining. 'Oh, Dobbin! It's really you! How is everyone at Peter's?'

'Come out of the basket and I'll tell you all the news,' said the little horse. 'Get on to my back – that's right – and we'll have a little trot together.'

The toys watched Dobbin trotting round the room with Sailor on his back. Sailor looked very, very happy. When the ride was over, he leapt off and stroked Dobbin's white-starred nose.

'How's your arm, old fellow?' said Dobbin. 'Got a new one yet? Does it hurt much?'

'Not much,' said Sailor. 'No, I haven't got a new one, and I'm afraid I never shall.'

'What's the matter with his arm?' said the bear suddenly, walking up.

'Nothing much,' said Sailor, turning away.

'I'll tell you,' said the horse, suddenly. 'I'll tell you quite a lot – and I hope you'll be ashamed when I've finished, you unkind toys!'

'No, don't tell them,' begged Sailor. 'I never tell anyone.'

'You're too modest,' said the horse. 'Listen, toys. When Sailor was in Peter's room, a puppy came gambolling into the room one day. He pounced on our baby doll and threw her up into the air. She screamed like anything. Well, when she fell to the floor, Sailor rushed over and flung himself on top of her so that the puppy couldn't get her again.'

'Go on,' said Angela. 'Tell us the rest.'

'Well,' went on the little horse, 'the puppy was angry, but Sailor wouldn't move – and he lay there, protecting the baby doll, and he let the puppy chew his right arm off!'

Angela screamed. The other toys exclaimed loudly. Sailor went very red.

'But – he's got two arms,' squeaked the clockwork mouse.

'Oh no, he hasn't,' said the toy horse. 'Sailor, take off your coat. Go on – let them see. It's time they knew all this!'

Sailor took off his coat, and the toys looked at him in sad surprise. He had one good arm – but the other was just a piece of stick, glued on to his shoulder!

'Peter's mother glued it on,' said the horse. 'She didn't tell Peter about it in case he scolded the puppy. And she made Sailor a tiny pair of gloves so that nobody would notice one of his hands was only the end of a stick. I tell you, Sailor is a grand fellow, one of my best friends – and if anyone wants to say a word against him, just let them say it here and now! I'll kick them up to the ceiling!'

But nobody wanted to say a word against Sailor. Everyone was ashamed and sad. They all went as red as beetroots, even the ragdoll, and that was difficult for him because he had quite a red face already.

The bear went up to Sailor and held out his paw.

'Sorry, Sailor,' he said. 'Please forgive me. I should have guessed all this.'

Sailor shook hands with his proper hand, and grinned happily. 'It's all

right. I got all funny about my arm. I just felt I couldn't tell anyone it was just a stick.'

'Don't you wear your gloves any more,' begged Angela, and she hugged him. 'We shan't mind your stick-arm a bit. We shall be proud of you whenever we see it!'

Sailor was so happy that he just stood there and smiled all over his face. Everyone came and shook hands with him and said they were sorry, would he be friends with them? Sailor put on his coat again – but he threw the gloves into the pile of old toys in the basket. 'Shan't wear those any more!' he said. 'Listen – here come Peter and Jill again – we must be quiet.'

'They've remembered me and come to fetch me,' said the little toy horse. 'Goodbye, Sailor. I'm glad I came today and put things right for you.'

Peter and Jill came in, and Peter picked up his horse. 'Hallo, there's old Sailor,' he said. 'He looks very happy. Hello, Sailor! How nice to see you again!'

Sailor felt happier than ever. When Jill and Peter had gone out of the room again, he turned head-over-heels twice, just to show the toys that he didn't care about his silly old stick-arm any more.

'Be careful!' said Angela, in alarm. 'You'll break it. Oh – I've got such a good idea!'

'What?' cried everyone.

'Well, I know where there's a box that Jill's Mummy keeps, with all sorts of odds and ends in,' said Angela. 'And I do believe there's an old arm there that once belonged to a broken doll. Couldn't we find it and put it on Sailor? It would be a bit shorter than his own, but that wouldn't matter a bit!'

So they are going to find it tonight and put it on for him. Sailor's so excited and happy that he doesn't know what to do. 'To think I nearly went away with the old toys to Mrs Brown's children!' he keeps saying. 'Well, well – you simply never know what's going to happen!'

The Little Roundy Man

Billy, Joan and Tom were out for a picnic in the woods one day when their big adventure happened. They didn't know it was going to happen at all, and it all began when Joan wanted to play hide-and-seek.

'All right,' said Billy. 'I'll hide my eyes first. Call "Cuckoo" when you are ready.'

He hid his eyes, and waited for the others to shout 'Cuckoo.' Tom ran behind a big bramble bush, and crouched down. Joan found a hollow tree with a hole just big enough to squeeze through. She got in, and called 'Cuckoo! Cuckoo!'

Billy opened his eyes and began to look for the others. He soon found Tom, but didn't catch him, for Tom got home first. Then he looked for Joan.

Now as soon as Joan got into the hollow tree she looked about her, but at first it was too dark to see anything. Then she saw a very odd thing. There was a little shelf in the tree, just about the level of her head – and on it was a pair of little blue shoes!

Joan thought that was very strange indeed. Who would hide shoes in a hollow tree? And who had built the neat little shelf? Perhaps the fairies lived near by and the shoes belonged to them.

Joan began to feel excited. She forgot about the game of hide-and-seek and called to Billy.

'I say, Billy!' she cried. 'There's something funny in this tree. Come and see.'

Billy and Tom went racing over to look. When they saw the little shelf and the shoes on it they were full of surprise. Billy took the shoes from the shelf, and helped Joan out of the tree. Then all three looked at the shoes.

They were very beautiful, made of the softest leather, and were the brightest blue you can imagine. They had silver buckles on, and when Billy turned the shoes upside down, he saw that they had never been worn.

'Do you know, Joan, I believe they would just fit you!' said Tom. 'Do try them on.'

So Joan took off her own shoes, and slipped on the blue ones. They fitted her perfectly. She stood up and began to dance about in them – and then a funny thing happened.

The shoes suddenly began to walk away with her. She felt her feet being taken down the path that led to the heart of the wood. She tried to turn back to the boys, but the shoes kept her feet going to the middle of the wood.

'Joan! Come back!' called the boys. 'Don't go that way! You'll get lost!'

'Help me, help me!' cried Joan in a fright. 'I can't come back! The shoes won't let me! Billy! Tom! Come and hold me so that I can't go any further!'

The boys raced after Joan – but as soon as they were almost up to her the shoes on her feet began to hurry, and somehow or other Joan found herself running faster than she had ever run in her life before.

'Quick! Quick!' she shouted to the panting boys, 'I'm being taken away. These shoes are magic! Oh, catch me, Billy, and take these shoes off!'

But the boys couldn't catch Joan, no matter how they hurried. In a few moments she was quite out of sight in the dark wood, and soon they could no longer hear her cries for help. They stopped and looked at one another.

'Oh my goodness,' said Billy. 'This is a dreadful thing! Where has poor Joan gone to? And oh, Tom – we're quite lost! I don't know where we are a bit, do you?'

'No,' said Tom, looking all round. 'And isn't it dark, Billy? The trees are so thick that not a ray of sun gets through. Oh dear, what are we to do about poor little Joan? It's no good going after her – and if we try to get help we shall only get more lost.'

'Well, we must do something,' said Billy. 'Look, there's a kind of rabbit path over there. Let's follow that and see if it brings us anywhere.'

The two boys went down the narrow, winding path. After a few minutes they came to a curious house. It was perfectly round, and had one chimney at the top. There was a window and a door, and that was all. It was about twice as high as they were, and the boys thought it was the funniest place they had ever seen.

'What shall we do?' asked Billy. 'Shall we knock?'

'Yes,' said Tom, and he walked boldly up to the door. He knocked loudly, like a postman – rat-a-tat-tat, rat-a-tat-tat.

At once the door flew open and a little creature looked out. He was almost as round as his house, and he wore big round spectacles on his funny dob of a nose.

'Now, now!' he said, crossly. 'I thought you were the postman. What do you want?'

'Well, it's rather a long story,' said Billy. 'But we would be so glad if you would help us.'

And he told the little round man all about the shoes that had run away with Joan.

'Dear, dear, dear!' said the little man, and he took his glasses off and polished them. 'You'd better come in and sit down. I may be able to help you a little. This is a very serious matter.'

The two boys went into the round house. It was the funniest place inside, quite round, with no corners at all. There was one room downstairs and one room upstairs. Everything was round. The table was round, the stools were round, the carpet was round and the clock was round. There was a cat by the fire and it was almost round too, it was so fat and sleek.

'Sit down,' said the little man. 'Now I had better tell you at once that I am afraid those blue shoes belong to Candle-shoe the old Magician. He plays a trick with them whenever he wants someone to help him with his spells. He puts them in a hollow tree or under a bush, and whoever finds them and tries them on is straightway led to him in his underground cave. Of course, he wants one of the fairy folk, not a little girl – but if he thinks she will do for him, he will keep her for years to help him with his nasty old spells.'

'Oh my!' said Billy in a fright. 'But whatever shall we do, little man?'

'My name is Roundy,' said the little man. 'Well, I must see what I can do to help you. I will first find out if Joan has gone to the cave. Half a moment. Hie, Tibby, fetch me the magic basin.'

Tibby, the little round cat, at once got up and fetched a basin from a shelf. She filled it with blue water from a jug, and set it on a stool in front of Roundy. He took a peacock's feather and stroked the water gently, whispering a string of magic words all the time, which neither Billy nor Tom could understand. Suddenly the water became still and flat like a mirror. Roundy bent over it and breathed on it. Then he rubbed it clean with a duster.

'Look!' he said. 'You can see your sister now!'

Billy and Tom looked into the basin of blue water, and on the mirror-like surface they saw a picture. In the middle was Joan, very tiny, still walking with the blue shoes on her feet. As they watched, she came to a little door in a hillside. It swung open and she walked through a long, long passage, which got darker and darker. Then suddenly she came to a cave, and there in the middle sat Candle-shoe, the old, ugly magician.

Just at that moment the water seemed to cloud over, and the wonderful pictures vanished. Billy and Tom looked at Roundy in despair, for they could not bear to think of poor Joan in the power of that nasty old magician.

'Yes, it's what I thought,' said Roundy, emptying the water out of the window. 'Candle-shoe has got her. Well, how are we going to rescue her?'

'First of all, where is this cave?' asked Tom.

'Nobody knows,' said Roundy.

'But how can we go there, then?' asked Billy.

'Let me think for a moment,' said Roundy. He sat down on a stool, put his head in his hands and frowned hard. Then he suddenly snapped his fingers, and jumped up.

'I've got it! Look here, we'll find another pair of old Candle-shoe's and put them on. Then they will lead us to the cave, and we shall know where it is.'

'Yes, but the shoes go so fast that whoever is following can't keep up,' said Tom.

'Ah,' said Roundy, 'but I can tell you what to do about that! We'll only put one shoe on, and then we shall go slowly enough for us all to keep up. I'll put the shoe on, and you shall follow me.'

'But how shall we find out where a pair of the shoes has been put?' said Billy. 'We can't go looking in every hollow tree.'

'Oh, that's easy enough,' said Roundy. 'My house will take us to a pair in a twinkling.'

'Your house!' said Billy and Tom together. 'But how can a house do that?'

'Well, you see, it's quite round,' said the little man, smiling. 'It can roll along like a ball, and that's how I get about all over the world.'

'But what about the chimney?' asked Billy. 'That sticks out, you know.'

Roundy opened the door and went outside the house. The boys followed him. He gave a big jump and landed just beside the chimney. He pressed hard on it and it sank down into the house, leaving just a hole where it had stood before. The boys were too surprised to say a word.

'Ha,' said Roundy, jumping down again. 'Mine's a fine little house, isn't it? Now would you like to come inside while my house rolls along, or would you rather follow it, walking behind?'

'Oh, I think we'd rather follow it,' said Tom. 'We should be so dreadfully bumped about inside, shouldn't we? What about you, Roundy? Do you stay inside when your house goes travelling?'

'Oh yes,' said Roundy. 'I don't get hurt because I'm quite round, you see. I just roll about like a ball, and so does Tibby. Now wait a moment … I want to tell the house where to go.'

Roundy leaned against his round house and stroked it as if it were a cat – and to Billy's surprise and Tom's it began to purr!

'Little house, little house,' said Roundy in a loving voice. 'Do you know where Candle-shoe hides his pairs of shoes?'

The house purred more loudly than ever.

'You do?' said Roundy. 'That's good. Then take me to one of those pairs of shoes, little house.'

He popped inside, and slammed the door. The house suddenly began to roll itself away through the wood, just like a great big ball. Billy and Tom stared and stared – it looked very odd indeed. They followed it. It didn't go very fast, and all the time it rolled it seemed to be humming a song. It was the funniest house the boys had ever seen.

It rolled through the wood, and came to the open country. Then it came to a river and bounced into the water. Billy and Tom jumped in too and swam across behind the big ball of a house. The house rolled up the bank on the opposite side and stopped. The door flew open and out came Roundy with a duster.

'I must just dry it before it gets a chill,' he said to the boys. 'Sit in the hot sun for a few minutes, you two, and you will soon be dry.'

The boys sat down and dried themselves, whilst Roundy rubbed and polished his funny little house. Then he popped indoors again, and the house rolled on once more.

It rolled until it came to a green hillside. It came to a stop beside a bramble bush. The door flew open and out ran Roundy.

'There must be a pair of shoes somewhere here,' he said in excitement. So they all looked hard – and sure enough, Tom soon came across them. They were red this time, quite small, and had silver buckles just like the others.

'Ha!' said Roundy, taking them from Tom. 'Now I'll just put one on!'

He popped one on his right foot, and held out his hands to Billy and Tom.

'The magic's working!' he said. 'Come on! My house will follow too. It always goes where I go.'

The boys each took one of Roundy's fat hands, and went with him. The house followed behind, humming its little song.

'You see, wearing only one of the shoes means that I don't go at all fast,' said Roundy. 'I wonder where it is going to lead us to.'

The shoe took him up the hill to the top, and then down the other side. There was a deep pit at the foot, and a flight of stone steps led down to the bottom. Down went Roundy, and the two boys scrambled behind. At the bottom of the pit was a large trap-door which opened as they came near. They went through it, and saw more steps leading downwards. Soon they were in a long dark passage, lighted here and there by tiny lamps. Down they went and down, right into the heart of the earth – and then up, they came, and up, until at last they could see daylight ahead of them once more.

When they came out of the passage into the sunshine they saw in front of them a very steep mountain.

'That must be the mountain the magician lives in,' said Billy to Tom. They made their way towards it, and when they came to the foot they saw a narrow winding path. The magic shoe took Roundy up and up, and at last the three of them saw a door in the hillside, fast shut.

'Hold me whilst I slip off this shoe,' said Roundy. 'I don't want to walk into the cave just yet!'

The two boys held tight whilst Roundy pulled off the magic shoe. He tossed it away, and put on his own. Then he sat down and looked round.

'Well, we're here,' he said. 'The next thing to decide is – how are we going to rescue Joan?'

They all thought for five minutes – and then Roundy began to chuckle.

'I think I know,' he said. 'I'll just play a nice little trick on old Candle-shoe. You two hide yourselves and watch.'

The boys went behind a bush and peeped out to see what Roundy meant to do. He went boldly to the door in the mountainside and knocked loudly seven times. In a moment the door swung open and the magician himself looked out.

'What do you want?' he said crossly. 'Go away or I'll turn you into a grass-hopper.'

'I pray your pardon,' said Roundy, bowing himself to the ground. 'But see, your Highness, I have brought a marvellous house for you to see. Maybe you would like to buy it.'

The magician looked at the round house which at once hummed its song again and turned itself about for Candle-shoe to see. The magician was astonished.

He put on a pair of enormous spectacles and walked over to the house.

'This is a strange affair,' he said to Roundy. 'Never in my life have I seen a house like this.'

'It follows its owner like a dog,' said Roundy. 'It will always come if you whistle. It has a pull-out chimney, and a little round cat to sit by the fire.'

Roundy pulled the chimney out and pushed it in to show the magician, who was more astonished than ever.

'Now buy it, sir, do,' said Roundy. 'Think what a surprise it will be to all your friends, the witches, and think how they will envy you.'

'How much is it,' asked the magician.

'Only four gold pieces,' said Roundy.

'It seems very cheap,' said Candle-shoe in surprise. 'Is there anything wrong with it inside?'

'No, your Highness,' said Roundy. 'Please go inside yourself, and look all round.'

The magician pushed open the door and stepped inside. Roundy gave a great shout of joy, and slammed the door at once. He locked it, and then gave his house a push.

'Roll up and down the mountainside!' he commanded. 'Give the old magician a shake-up, little house!'

At once the house began to roll up the hill and down, and the magician inside began to yell and shout in fright. Roundy paid no heed, and he and the two boys rushed into the cave and began to look for Joan. They went down a long dark passage and soon came to the place where Joan was, for they could hear her calling.

But alas! The door was locked! Billy banged on it and called to Joan.

'Joanie! Joanie!' he shouted. 'Are you all right?'

'Oh, Billy!' cried Joan's voice. 'Have you come to rescue me? Yes, I'm all right, but I've been frightened because that horrid old magician wanted me to help him with his bad spells and I wouldn't.'

'Where's the key to this door?' asked Tom.

'Oh, the magician has got it hanging on his girdle,' said Joan. 'However can you get it?'

The three outside the door looked at one another in dismay.

'Come on,' said Roundy to Billy. 'We'll go and see if we can get it, somehow or other. You stay here and keep Joan cheerful, Tom.'

Off went Billy and Roundy. They came out on the hillside and looked to see what the little house was doing. It was still rolling up and down and the magician was still calling and shouting for help.

'Stop, little house,' said Roundy. The house stopped, and stood still. Roundy ran up to it.

'Hie!' he called to the magician. 'Throw your keys out of the window, quickly.'

'Certainly not!' said the magician, angrily. 'I'm not going to let you have that little girl back again!'

'Little house, roll faster!' commanded Roundy. At once the little house began to roll around faster than ever and Candle-shoe was bumped about inside in a dreadful manner. He begged for mercy, and Roundy stopped the little house again.

'Where are those keys?' he cried. The magician threw them out of the window, and Roundy picked them up in glee.

'Go on, little house, roll around a little more so that Candle-shoe can't get out!' he said, and the house began to roll about gently.

Billy and Roundy ran back through the dark passage to the cave. Roundy fitted the biggest key in the lock and turned it. The door opened and Joan ran out. Billy and Tom hugged her tightly, and Joan began to cry for joy. Then the boys told her who Roundy was, and she hugged the kind little man too.

'Now how are we going to get back?' said Tom.

'Let's look about in the magician's cave,' said Roundy. 'We are sure to find something or other that will take you back safely.'

They looked here and they looked there, and suddenly Roundy gave a shout of joy.

'Here's a witch's broomstick,' he cried. 'We'll take it outside, and if you all sit on it and wish yourselves home you'll be there in half a shake of a duck's tail!'

'But what about you?' asked Billy, as they ran outside into the sunshine.

'You'll see what happens to me when you're safely in the air on your broomstick!' laughed Roundy. 'Hop on!'

They all sat on the broomstick, and then Roundy suddenly clapped his hands twice and called out a magic word. The children wished themselves home, and up in the air rose the broomstick at once. The riders held tight, and looked down to see the last of Roundy.

He commanded the little house to stop rolling, and unlocked the door. At once the magician leapt out – but before he could get hold of Roundy that fat little man had hopped inside the door, banged it, and the little house was scurrying away down the mountainside as fast as an express train!

How the children laughed to see it!

'Hurrah for Roundy!' said Billy. 'He was a fine friend to us! I do hope we see him again some day!'

Their broomstick flew faster and faster, and at last brought them right over their own house. It flew down into the garden, and the three children jumped off. Billy put out his hand to catch the broomstick and take it indoors to show his mother, but he wasn't quite quick enough – for it flew away from him, and mounted up into the air once more, all by itself.

'There it goes!' said Joan. 'Oh, my dears, what an adventure we've had. Quick, let's go in and tell Mummy before we forget anything!'

So in they raced – and Mummy really couldn't believe her ears when she heard all they had to tell!

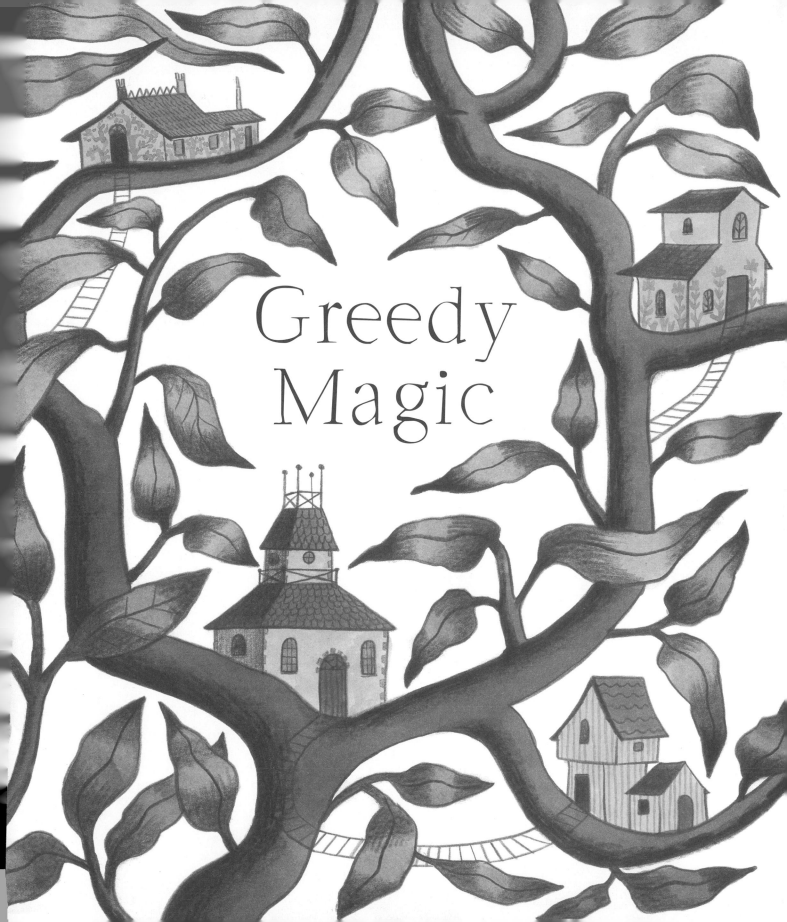

Greedy Magic

Mr Snoogle's Wish

Once old Mr Snoogle, the gnome with the knobbly hands, got hold of a wish.

It happened like this. The Wizard Hurry-By was going past Mr Snoogle's cottage when he tripped over a stone and fell with a crash. He was carrying a sack of magic, and it burst open as it struck the ground.

Out fell a collection of spells, magic wands and marvellous books. Old Mr Snoogle hurried out and helped the Wizard to his feet. Then he picked up everything and put it back into the sack.

'Come in and have a cup of tea – you look a bit pale,' said Snoogle.

'No, thanks,' said Hurry-By. 'I'm in a great hurry. 'Here – take this wish for your kindness – but use it before six o'clock tonight, or it won't be any use!'

He handed Snoogle what looked like a peculiar marble, that ran here and there on the gnome's hand, and changed size and colour every second. Snoogle closed his hand over it at once. His eyes gleamed.

'Oh, thank you, Wizard Hurry-By. I've always wanted a wish. My word – what a surprise!'

Hurry-By was gone in a flash and Snoogle opened his hand cautiously – a wish, think of that! What should he wish for?

He sat down in his front garden to think. Tricky, the pixie, came by and grinned. What was Snoogle thinking about so hard? He picked up a dry pine-cone from beneath a tree and sent it skimming towards Snoogle. It hit him right on the nose!

Up leapt Snoogle in a furious rage. 'It's you again, Tricky, is it!' he shouted. 'Well, let me tell you this – I've just had a Wish given to me by Hurry-By the Wizard – and for two pins I'd wish you away to the moon.'

Tricky felt alarmed. 'No, don't do that,' he said. 'I'm sorry I threw that pine-cone at you! Goodbye!'

He skipped off and soon met a lot of his friends in the market. He told them about Snoogle's wish. They listened in surprise.

'Let's go and help him to wish,' said Hi-Jinks. 'We must stop him from wishing a horrid wish – he might quite well wish all of us into the Land of Nowhere if he feels spiteful!'

So off they went to Snoogle and told him they wanted to help him.

'I don't need help,' said Snoogle, glaring round. 'I'd like to wish you were a lot of wriggling worms, and give you to the birds, that's what I'd like to wish! I've got till six o'clock tonight to use my wish, so just be careful nobody annoys me today!'

'We've only come to help you,' said Tricky. 'We don't want you to waste your wish on anything silly. Why not wish for a great castle on the top of that hill?'

'I might,' said Snoogle. 'Then I'd make you all my servants and you could come and live in the castle.'

Nobody liked that idea. 'Why don't you wish for a million pieces of gold?'

said Hi-Jinks. 'You could buy anything you wanted, then!'

'Where should I put a million pieces of gold?' said Snoogle. 'Anyway, I'd be afraid of robbers.'

'Wish for a beautiful princess for a wife,' said Lo-Jinks.

'And have her living in a cottage?' said Snoogle. 'Please don't be silly. I'm beginning to feel I'd like to wish donkey's ears to grow on each of you!'

'No – that would be a dreadful waste of a wish,' said Tricky, hastily. 'What about a carriage and eight beautiful horses! Think how grand you'd look driving through the market place?'

'And who's going to look after the horses?' said Snoogle, scornfully. 'I'm not going to spend the rest of my life looking after eight horses! Goodness me, it's very, very difficult to think of just one wish. I can't think of one!'

'What about a cupboard that is always full of wonderful food?' said Mr Plump.

'Ho – and have you always on my doorstep asking for something to eat?' said Snoogle. 'Not very clever, Mr Plump. My goodness me – I feel more and more that I'd like to use my wish on you all – I do so dislike you. Let me see – if I wished you were half the size I could easily keep you as little slaves – yes, yes …'

'No, no,' cried everyone and Mr Snoogle grinned to see their fright.

The time went by. It was afternoon – then it was tea-time – and still old Snoogle hadn't thought of a wish to wish. Tricky, Hi-Jinks and the others sat round him, hoping to make him wish something sensible. He really was such an old cross-patch that he might easily wish something horrid just to pay them out for the many silly little tricks and jokes they had played on him!

Five o'clock came – half-past five. Perhaps, just perhaps – Snoogle wouldn't notice the time and six o'clock would come before he had wished. Then the wish would be no use!

'Wish for a suit of gold and silver,' said Tricky. 'You'd look finer than the King then!'

'Who'd mend it for me' said Snoogle, disagreeably. 'Oh my, oh my – so many wishes to wish, and I simply CAN'T make up my mind. What's the time

– good gracious me, ten minutes to six. Oh, I'm getting so tired of thinking. I might just as well wish something horrid and have a good laugh!'

'No, don't,' said Hi-Jinks. 'I've thought of something grand! Wish to be very, very clever, Snoogle!'

'Don't be so silly! I'm clever enough already!' said Snoogle. 'Oh my – it's almost six – I wish I could think of some really grand wishes!'

'You can, you can,' cried everyone, and they winked hard at one another. And sure enough, Snoogle did immediately think of some fine wishes.

'I'll wish to be wise! I'll wish to be a great man! No, I'll wish that everything wrong shall be at once put right. I'll wish that all the sick people in the world shall be well … oh, it's almost six o'clock! Here is my wish – I WISH TO BE GOOD AND WISE!'

Six o'clock struck. Snoogle looked round at the little folk near him. 'Now,' he said, 'I shall be good and wise.' Then he frowned. 'What are you making faces for, Tricky? I'll grab you and give you such a whipping in a minute!'

'Still the same bad-tempered, unfair, mean old Snoogle!' said Tricky, getting up. 'Good and wise! You'll never be that now.'

'But I wished it!' cried Snoogle, jumping to his feet. 'I wished it!'

'Yes – but you wished something else first,' said Mr Plump. 'You wished that you could think of some really great wishes – and that was your one wish gone! It came true, of course – you did think of some really worth-while things but they were too late! You're just exactly the same old silly as you've always been, Snoogle.'

Off they went, chuckling. Snoogle sat down again – and then got up as he saw someone rushing by. It was the Wizard Hurry-By on his way back. Snoogle called to him.

'Hey – give me another wish. I wasted that one, Hurry-By.'

'Sorry – my sack is empty now,' said Hurry-By, rushing on. 'I thought you'd waste it, Snoogle. It serves you right!'

So it did. Snoogle had a fine chance that day, hadn't he – and I'm pretty sure he'll never have another!

265

The Little Singing Kettle

Mister Curly was a small pixie who lived all by himself in Twisty Cottage. His cottage stood at the end of the Village of Ho, and was always very neatly kept. It had blue and yellow curtains at the windows and blue and yellow flowers in the garden, so you can guess how pretty and trim it was.

Mister Curly was mean. He was the meanest pixie that ever lived, but he always pretended to be very generous indeed. If he had a bag of peppermints he never let anyone see it, but put it straight into his pocket till he got home. And if he met any of the other pixies he would pull a long face and say: 'If only I had a bag of sweets I would offer you one.'

'Never mind,' the others said. 'It's nice of you to think of it!'

And they went off, saying what a nice, generous creature Mister Curly was!

Now one day, as Mister Curly was walking home along Dimity Lane, where the trees met overhead, so that it was just like walking in a green tunnel, he saw a fellow in front of him. This was a Humpy Goblin, and he carried a great many saucepans, kettles and pans all slung down his back, round his shoulders and over his chest.

They made a great noise as he walked, but louder than the noise was the Humpy Goblin's voice. He sang all the time in a voice like a cracked bell.

'Do you want a saucepan, kettle or pan?
If you do, here's the Goblin Man!
The Humpy Goblin with his load
Of pots and pans is down the road,
Hie, hie, hie, here's the Goblin Man,
Do you want a saucepan, kettle or pan?'

Now Mister Curly badly wanted a new kettle, because his own had a hole in it and the water leaked over his stove each day, making a funny hissing noise. So he ran after the Goblin Man and called him. The Humpy Goblin turned round and grinned. He was a cheerful fellow, always pleased to see anybody.

'I want a good little kettle, nice and cheap,' said Curly.

'I've just the one for you,' said Humpy, and he pointed to a bright little kettle on his back. Curly looked at it.

'How much is it?' he asked.

'Sixpence,' said the Goblin. This was quite cheap, but mean old Curly wasn't going to give sixpence for the kettle. He pretended to be shocked at the price, and then he gave a huge sigh.

'Oh, I'm not rich enough to pay all that,' he said sadly. 'I can only pay threepence.'

'Oh, no,' said Humpy firmly. 'Threepence isn't enough. You must pay sixpence.'

Well, they stood and talked to one another for a long time, one saying sixpence and the other saying threepence, until at last the Humpy Goblin laughed in Curly's face and walked off jingling all his kettles and pans.

'You're a mean old stick!' he called after Curly. 'I'm not going to sell you anything! Goodbye, Mister Mean!'

Off he went and soon began to sing his song again. Curly heard him.

'Do you want a saucepan, kettle or pan?

If you do, here's the Goblin Man!'

Curly stood and watched him angrily. Then he started walking, too. He had to follow the Goblin Man because that was the way home to Twisty Cottage. But he took care not to follow too close, for he was afraid that Humpy might call something rude after him.

It was a hot day and the Goblin was tired. After a while he thought he would sit down in the hedge and rest. So down he sat – and it wasn't more than a minute before he was sound asleep and snoring! Curly heard him and knew he must be asleep. A naughty thought slipped into his head.

'I wonder if I could take that kettle from him whilst he's asleep! I could leave threepence beside him to pay for it. How cross he would be when he woke up to find that I had got the kettle for threepence after all!'

He crept up to the Humpy Goblin. He certainly was sound asleep, with his mouth so wide open that it was a good thing there wasn't anything above his head that could drop into it. Curly carefully undid the little shining kettle without making even a clink of noise. Then he put three bright pennies on the grass beside the Goblin, and ran off, chuckling to himself for being so smart.

He soon reached home. He filled the little kettle with water and put it on the fire. It really was a dear little thing, and it boiled very quickly indeed, sending a spurt of steam out of the spout almost before Curly had got out the teapot to make the tea.

Just as he was sitting down to enjoy a cup of tea and a piece of cake, someone walked up his garden path and looked in at the door. It was the Humpy Goblin. When he saw that Curly had the kettle on the fire, he grinned all over his face.

'So you've got it!' he said. 'Well, much good may it do you! Kettle, listen to me! Teach Mister Curly the lesson he needs! Ho, ho, Curly, keep the kettle! I don't want it!'

Laughing and skipping, the Goblin went down the path again. Curly felt a bit uncomfortable. What was he laughing like that for?

'Oh, he just tried to frighten me and make me think something nasty would happen,' said Curly to himself. 'Silly old Goblin!'

He cleared away his cup and saucer, and filled up the kettle again. He was washing up the dirty dishes when a knock came at his door, and Dame Pitapat looked in.

'I say, Curly, could you let me have a little tea? I've emptied my tin and it's such a long way to the shops.'

Now Curly had a whole tin full, but he wasn't going to let Dame Pitapat have any. He ran to the dresser and took down a tin he knew was empty.

'Yes, certainly, Dame Pitapat,' he said, 'you shall have some of my tea. Oh, dear! The tin's empty! What a pity! You could have had half of it if only I'd had any, but I must have used it all up!'

Dame Pitapat looked at the empty tin. Then she turned to go.

'I'm sorry I bothered you, Curly,' she said. 'It was kind of you to say I could have had half, if only you'd had any tea.'

Then a funny thing happened. The little kettle on the stove sent out a big spurt of steam and began to sing a shrill song.

'Mister Curly has plenty of tea!

He's just as mean as a pixie can be!

Look in the tin on the left of the shelf

And see what a lot he has for himself!'

Then the kettle took another breath and shouted, 'Mean old thing! Stingy old thing! Oooooh, look at him!'

Dame Pitapat was so astonished that she stood gaping for quite a minute. She couldn't think where the song came from. She had no idea it was the kettle on the stove. But Curly knew it was, and he was so angry and ashamed that he could have cried.

Dame Pitapat went to the shelf and took down the tin that stood on the left. She opened it, and sure enough, it was full to the brim of tea.

'Oh, look at this!' she said. 'Well, Curly, you said I could have half of any tea you had, so I shall take you at your word. Thanks very much.' She emptied half the tea out into the tin she had brought and went out of the cottage, looking round curiously to see if she could spy who had sung that song about Curly. But she didn't think of looking at the kettle, of course.

Curly was so angry with the kettle that he decided to scold it severely. But before he could do that someone poked his head in at the window and called him.

'Mister Curly! Will you lend me your umbrella, please? I've lost mine and it's raining.'

It was little Capers, the pixie who lived next door. He was always lending Curly things, and now he had come to borrow something himself. But Curly was in a very bad temper.

'My umbrella's lost too,' he said. 'I'm so sorry, Capers. You could have it if only I had it myself, but it's gone.'

'Oh, well, never mind,' said Capers. 'It's nice of you to say you would have lent it to me.'

Before he could go the shining kettle gave a tiny hop on the stove and began to sing again.

'Mister Curly has got an umbrella,
He's such a mean and stingy fella,
He says he hasn't got one at all
But just you go and look in the hall!'

Then it took another breath and began to shout again at the top of its steamy voice, 'Mean old thing! Stingy old thing! Oooooh, look at him!'

Capers was so surprised to hear this song that he nearly fell in at the window. He stared at Curly, who was looking as black as thunder and as red as a beetroot. Then Capers looked through the kitchen door into the tiny hall – and sure enough Curly's green umbrella stood there.

Capers jumped in at the window and fetched the umbrella. He waved it at Curly.

'You said I could have it if only you had got it!' he cried. 'Here it is, so I'll borrow it! Many thanks!'

He ran off and left Curly nearly crying with rage. The pixie caught up a stick and ran to catch the kettle – but that small kettle was far too quick for him! It rose up in the air and put itself high up on a shelf for safety. Then it poured just a drop of boiling water on to Curly's hand, which made the pixie dance and shout with pain.

'You wait till I get you!' cried Curly, shaking his stick.

Someone knocked at his front door. Curly opened it. Rag and Tag, the two gnomes, stood there smiling.

'Mister Curly, we are collecting pennies for poor Mister Tumble whose house was burnt down yesterday,' they said. 'You are so generous that we thought you would be sure to give us one.'

Curly knew that there was no money in his pockets, so he pulled them inside out quickly, saying, 'Oh yes, you shall have whatever money I have, Rag and Tag. Goodness, there's none in this pocket – and none in that! How unfortunate! I haven't any pennies to give you, and I should have been so pleased to have let you have all I had.'

'Well, that's very nice of you to say so,' said Rag and Tag. 'Never mind. Thank you very much for trying to be generous!'

Before they could go, that little kettle was singing again, spurting out great clouds of steam as it did so!

'Although he says he hasn't any,
Curly's got a silver penny!
Look in his purse on the table there
And take the money he well can spare!'

Then, taking another breath, the kettle shouted with all its might, 'Mean old thing! Stingy old thing! Oooooh, look at him!'

Rag and Tag stared all round the kitchen to see where the voice came from, but they couldn't see anyone but Curly. It couldn't be the pixie singing, surely! No, he looked too angry and ashamed to sing anything!

The gnomes saw the purse lying on the table and they ran for it. Inside was a silver sixpence. They took it and put it into their box.

'Well, Curly,' they said, 'you said we might have any pennies you had, if you'd had any – and you have, so we'll take this silver one. Goodbye!'

Out they went, giggling together, wondering who it was in the cottage that had given Curly away.

As for Curly, he was so angry that he caught up a jug of milk and flung it straight at the kettle, which was still high up on the shelf. Crash! The kettle hopped aside and the jug broke in a dozen pieces against the wall behind. The milk spilt and dripped on to Curly's head. Then the kettle began to laugh. How it laughed! It was a funny, wheezy laugh, but you can't think how angry it made Curly!

He took up a hammer and flung that at the kettle too – but once more it slipped to one side, and oh, dear me, *smash*! went a lovely big jar of plum jam up on the shelf. It all splashed down on to Curly, so what with milk and jam he was a fine sight. The kettle nearly killed itself with laughing. It almost fell off the shelf.

Curly went and washed himself under the tap. He felt frightened. What was he going to do with that awful singing kettle? He must get rid of it somehow or it would tell everyone the most dreadful tales about him.

'I'll wait till tonight,' thought Curly. 'Then, when it's asleep, I'll take it and throw it away.'

So he took no more notice of the kettle, and as no other visitors came that day the kettle was fairly quiet – except that sometimes it would suddenly shout, 'Mean old thing! Stingy old thing! Ooooooh, look at him!' Then Curly would almost jump out of his skin with fright, and glare at the kettle angrily.

At nine o'clock Curly went to bed. The kettle hopped down to the stove and went to sleep. Curly waited for a little while and then he crept out of bed.

He went to the stove and took hold of the kettle. Ah, he had it now! The kettle woke up and shouted, but Curly had it by the handle. The water in it was no longer hot, so that it could not hurt Curly.

The pixie hurried outside with the kettle and went to the bottom of his garden. There was a rubbish-heap there and the pixie stuffed the struggling kettle right into the middle. He left it there and went back delighted. He climbed into bed and fell asleep.

But at midnight something woke him by tapping at the window.

'Let me in!' cried a voice. 'Let me in! I'm dirty and I want washing!'

'That's that horrid kettle!' thought Curly, in a fright. 'Well, it can go on tapping! I won't let it in!'

But the kettle tapped and tapped and at last it flung itself hard against the glass, broke it and came in through the hole! It went over to Curly's bed and stood itself there.

'Wash me!' it said. 'I'm dirty and smelly. You shouldn't have put me on that nasty rubbish-heap!'

'Get out of my nice clean bed!' cried Curly angrily. 'Look what a mess you are making!'

But the kettle wouldn't get off, and in the end the angry pixie had to get up and wash the kettle till it was clean again. Then he banged it down on the stove and left it.

Next day the kettle sang songs about him again, and Curly kept hearing it shout, 'Mean old fellow! Stingy old fellow! Ooooooh, look at him!' till he was tired of it. So many people had heard about the strange things happening in the pixie's cottage that all day long visitors came to ask for different things, and poor Curly was nearly worried out of his life.

'I'll drown that kettle in my well tonight!' he thought. So once more he took the kettle when it was asleep and threw it down the well. Splash! Ha, it wouldn't get out of there in a hurry!

But about three o'clock in the morning there came a tap-tap-tap at the window, which had now been mended. It was the kettle back again!

'Curly! Let me in! I'm c-c-c-c-cold and w-wet! Let me in!'

Curly was afraid his window would be broken again, so he jumped out of bed and let in the shivering kettle. To his horror it crept into bed with him and wouldn't go away!

'It was cold and wet in the well!' said the kettle. 'Warm me, Curly!'

So Curly had to warm the kettle, and how angry he was! It was so uncomfortable to sleep with a kettle, especially one that kept sticking its sharp spout into him. But he had to put up with it. In the morning he put the kettle back on the stove and started to think hard whilst he had his breakfast.

'I can't get rid of that kettle,' he said to himself. 'And while it's here it's sure to sing horrid things about me every time anyone comes to borrow something. I wonder what it would do if I let people have what they ask for? I'll try and see.'

So when Mother Homey came and begged for a bit of soap, because she had run out of it and the shops were closed that afternoon, Curly gave her a whole new piece without making any excuse at all. Mother Homey was surprised and delighted.

'Thank you so much,' she said. 'You're a kind soul, Curly.'

The kettle said nothing at all. Not a single word. As for Curly, he suddenly felt very nice inside. It was lovely to give somebody something. It made him feel warm and kind. He made up his mind to do it again if he felt nice the next time – and to see if that wretched kettle said anything.

He soon found that the kettle said never a word unless he was mean or untruthful – and he found, too, that it was lovely to be kind and to give things away; it was nice even to lend them.

'I've been horrid and nasty,' thought Curly to himself. 'I'll turn over a new leaf and try to be different. And that old kettle can say what it likes! Anyway, it boils very quickly and makes a lovely pot of tea.'

Very soon the kettle found little to say, for Curly became kind and generous. Once or twice he forgot, but as soon as he heard the kettle beginning to speak he quickly remembered, and the kettle stopped its song.

And one day who should peep in at the door but the Humpy Goblin, grinning all over his face as usual.

'Hallo, Curly!' he said. 'How did you like the kettle? Was it cheap for threepence? I've come to take it back, if you want to get rid of it. It was a mean trick to play on you, really, but I think you deserved it!'

Curly looked at the smiling Goblin. Then he took his purse from his pocket and found three pennies. He held them out to the Humpy Goblin.

'Here you are,' he said. 'You wanted sixpence for the kettle and I was mean enough to leave you only threepence. Here's the other threepence.'

'But – but – don't you want to give me back the kettle?' asked Humpy in surprise. 'I left a horrid singing spell in it.'

'Yes, I know,' said Curly. 'But I deserved it. I'm different now. I like the kettle too – we're great friends. I try to be kind now, so the kettle doesn't sing nasty things about me. It just hums nice, friendly little songs.'

'Well, well, well, wonders will never end!' said the Goblin Man, astonished. 'Don't bother about the other threepence, Curly. I don't want it.'

'Well, if you won't take it, let me offer you a cup of tea made from water boiled in the singing kettle,' said Curly. Humpy was even more astonished to hear the pixie being so kind, but he sat down at the table in delight.

Then he and Curly had a cup of tea each and a large slice of ginger cake – and they talked together and found that they liked one another very much indeed.

So now Mister Curly and the Humpy Goblin are the very greatest friends, and the little singing kettle hums its loudest when it boils water for their tea. You should just hear it!

Gooseberry Whiskers

T here was once a rascally gnome who sold fine paint-brushes to the fairies. No brushes were half as good as his, for the hairs in them were so fine and strong. 'Where do you get them from?' asked the elves one day. But the gnome wouldn't tell them.

'It's a secret,' he said. 'Perhaps I make them out of moonbeams drawn out long and thin, and snipped off in short pieces!'

'You don't!' cried the elves. 'Oh do tell us your secret!'

But he never would – and the reason was that he was afraid to. He got the hairs from sleeping caterpillars, and such a thing was not allowed in Fairyland, as you may guess. Many caterpillars were covered with soft fine hairs, and by pulling a few from this one and a few from that, the little gnome soon had enough for a new brush.

One spring-cleaning time there was a great demand for his brushes. All through May the elves came to buy from him and the gnome could hardly find enough caterpillars to pull hairs from!

He began to pull more than a few hairs from each. Once he took quite a handful, and the caterpillar woke up with a squeak.

Another furry caterpillar woke up one morning to find that he was quite bald. He hadn't a single hair left and he shivered with cold.

When the Queen passed by the stopped in surprise.

'But who could have taken your hairs away?' she asked the caterpillar. 'No one would do such a naughty thing.'

'Please, your Majesty, someone must have done it last night,' said the caterpillar.

'And half my coat is gone too!' said another.

'And about thirty of my finest hairs have disappeared as well!' cried a third.

'This must be looked into,' said the Queen, sternly.

She called to her guards and spoke to them. 'Twelve of you must remain here to look after these caterpillars,' she commanded. 'You can hide under the hedge, and watch for the thief. Catch him and punish him well.'

The caterpillars crawled to their leaves. Now at last they would be safe! The twelve guards looked about for good hiding-places, and then played a game of snap until night-time, for they felt sure there would be no sign of the thief until darkness fell. The caterpillars were so interested in the game that they called 'Snap!' when they shouldn't, and made the guards quite cross.

'Don't interfere,' said the captain. 'We are playing, not you. You eat your juicy leaves, and don't disturb us or we will leave you to the robber!'

When night came the soldiers squeezed themselves into their hiding-places and kept watch. The night was dark, and it was difficult for them to see an inch in front of their noses. Just the night for a robber to come!

Time went on. No thief. Ten o'clock came, eleven o'clock. Still no thief. The guards began to yawn. Surely the robber would not come now.

But at that very moment the little gnome was out on his rounds, looking for furry caterpillars. He was hunting under the leaves, down the stalks, on the ground, and everywhere. He didn't know that anyone was lying in wait for him.

He was very silent. His feet made no sound as he crept along, and he didn't even rustle a leaf.

'Where are all the caterpillars tonight?' he thought. 'I can't seem to find any!'

From bush to bush he went, feeling along the leaves, and at last he really did find a large furry caterpillar, peacefully sleeping.

'Good!' thought the gnome. 'This one has a fine crop of hairs! I can make a fine brush from them.'

He grabbed a big handful from the back of the sleeping caterpillar, and pulled hard. The caterpillar woke up with a loud squeak. 'Eee, eee, eee!' it cried.

At once all the guards sprang up and shouted loudly. 'The robber, the robber!'

The gnome fled away in terror, holding all the hairs in his hand. The guards ran after him, and went crashing through the woods into the palace gardens. Up and down the paths they went, searching for the thief. Where was he? Where had he gone?

The little gnome had found a prickly hiding-place under a big gooseberry bush. He crouched there in fright, wondering what would happen to him if he was found. In his hand he still held the caterpillar hairs. Whatever could he do with them?

'The guards mustn't find them in my hand,' he thought. 'And I daren't throw them away, for they are sure to be found. What can I do?'

He put out his hand and felt about. He touched two or three big fat gooseberries – and then an idea came to him. He would stick the hairs on them, for surely no one would think of looking on the fruit for caterpillar hairs!

In a trice he was sticking the hairs on the green smooth surface of the gooseberries. He made them all hairy and whiskery, and just as he had finished, somebody came down the path near-by, and flashed a lantern on to him.

'Here's someone!' they cried. 'Here's the thief! Quick, come and get him!'

The gnome was dragged out and searched. No hairs were found on him, but in his pocket were two brushes that he had forgotten about – and they were made of caterpillar hairs!

'Turn him out of Fairyland for ever!' cried the captain. 'That will teach him not to steal!

So the gnome was taken to the gates of Fairyland. They were shut behind him, and out he went, weeping bitterly.

No one has heard of him since – but from that day to this gooseberries have always grown whiskers. If you don't believe me, go and look for yourself!

The Golden Enchanter

Once upon a time there lived in Shining Palace a great enchanter. He had thick golden hair, a golden beard, and always dressed in tunics and cloaks made of cloth-of-gold. So he was known as the Golden Enchanter.

He was very, very rich. All his plates, dishes, and cups were made of the purest gold. The very chairs he sat upon were gold, and the table where he sat for his meals was made of such heavy gold that it could never be lifted.

In his cellars were sacks upon sacks of gold, but nobody ever saw them except the Enchanter, for only he had the key to those dark cellars.

Shining Palace was very beautiful. Its walls were built of gold, and there were very many windows, all shining and glittering in the sun that shone every day on the palace. The Enchanter loved the sun. He used its golden beams in his magic, and many a bright sunbeam he had imprisoned in his heavy bars of gold.

The Golden Enchanter was generous and kind-hearted. He gave much of his gold away, and the people loved him. But other enchanters were jealous of his riches.

The Green Magician who lived on the next hill envied him very much, and tried to learn his secrets. The Hobbledy Wizard was jealous of him too, and wouldn't even speak to him when he met him. But the Golden Enchanter didn't mind. He felt sure that his gold was safe, locked up in the strong cellars.

One day there came to Shining Palace a little, lean man, whose eyes were a strange green. He asked to see the Enchanter and he was taken before him.

'Sir,' he said, bowing down to the ground, 'I have worked for Wily-One, the greatest of magicians, but he has turned me away after twenty years' service. So now I come to you to ask for work. There is not much that I do not know, for Wily-One was clever and taught me most of his secrets!'

'Wily-One was wicked,' said the Golden Enchanter sternly. 'I heard that he had been driven away.'

'That may be true,' said the green-eyed man. 'But listen to all the things I can do, O Enchanter, and I think you will find that I may be very useful to you.'

Then, in a long string, the lean man recited all the marvellous spells he could make, and, as he listened, the Enchanter's eyes opened wide.

'I do not know how it was that Wily-One the Magician trusted you so much as to tell you all the secret spells,' he said. 'Only enchanters are supposed to know them. Well, you must have proved yourself trustworthy to him, so I will engage you to help me. Start tomorrow.'

The green-eyed man bowed again, and a strange smile came over his face. The Golden Enchanter did not notice it or he would have wondered about it, and guessed the lean man's secret. For he was no other than Wily-One, the great magician, himself! He had been driven away from his castle, and had had to wander hungry and homeless about the country.

Then he had thought that he would disguise himself and go to the

Golden Enchanter to beg for work. Once he was in the Shining Palace, surely he could steal the keys to the cellar and help himself to enough gold to make him rich again.

He was delighted when the Enchanter engaged him as his chief helper. Day after day he did magic for him, made strange spells, caught sunbeams for gold, and sang magic words as he stirred the big cauldron on the fire. But he could not get permission to go down into the cellars where the sacks of gold were kept. The Enchanter kept his keys guarded carefully, and slept with them under his pillow. He thought that his new servant was very clever, but he did not like him, nor trust him.

The green-eyed servant lived in a small cottage not far from the palace. One day he found a trap-door in the floor, and lifting it up, spied a small cellar underneath.

'I will keep my potatoes there,' he said to himself, and he went down the steps. But when he got there an idea came to him that made him shiver with delight.

'I will use my magic to bore a passage from this cellar to the cellars of Shining Palace,' he thought, and he set to work. All day long he worked for the Golden Enchanter, but half the night he worked for himself, bewitching a spade to dig deep into the earth, making a tunnel through the darkness.

At last the tunnel was finished. Wily-One crept through it and came to the small hole leading right into the cellars of Shining Palace. He was delighted. He was just about to crawl through when he heard the sound of footsteps. He crouched down in fear and saw that it was the Golden Enchanter himself, dragging a new sack of gold into place. As Wily-One hid behind the crumbling wall of earth, something tickled his nose. He wanted to sneeze, but he dared not. He held his nose tightly between his finger and thumb, and made the tiniest noise imaginable.

The Golden Enchanter had very quick ears, which could even hear the grass grow in the spring-time. He heard the tiny noise and wondered what it was. He thought it must be the click of a beetle's wings. He dragged the sack into place, and then went to another cellar.

Wily-One thought that he had better not try to steal any gold that night whilst the Enchanter was about. So, very quietly he turned and crept back along the dark tunnel to his cottage. He went to bed and dreamed all night long of the large sack of gold he would have on the morrow.

The Enchanter had a great deal of work to do the next day, for there was a very fine and delicate spell he was making. It was mostly made of cobwebs and the whiskers of gooseberries, and all the windows had to be shut in case the wind should blow in and upset the spell.

The green-eyed servant was helping. His eyes shone strangely and his cheeks were red with excitement. He kept thinking of that night, when he would once more have gold of his own and be rich. He would go far away to another country, build himself a fine castle, and be a magician once again.

The Golden Enchanter wondered why his assistant's eyes shone so green, and why his hands trembled when he carefully arranged the cobwebs in the right order.

'What's the matter with you this morning?' he asked. 'You don't seem yourself.'

'I'm all right!' said Wily-One.

'Now for goodness' sake don't sneeze or breathe too hard,' said the Enchanter, giving the last touches to the spell. 'If you do, all these cobwebs will have to be arranged again.'

But one of the gooseberry whiskers must have got up Wily-One's nose, for all of a sudden he wanted to sneeze.

He held his nose tightly between his finger and thumb and stopped the sneeze, making only the very tiniest noise, the same noise that he had made the night before in the cellar.

And the Golden Enchanter remembered the noise.

'So that's what that little noise was last night!' he thought to himself. 'It was this green-eyed servant of mine stopping a sneeze. It wasn't a beetle's wings clicking! Oho! I shall have to look into this. Perhaps this clever servant of mine is not what he seems.'

The more he thought about it, the more the Enchanter felt sure that his servant was really a magician – and suddenly he guessed Wily-One's secret! Of course – he was Wily-One himself, disguised! Wily-One had those strange green eyes too. However could he, the Golden Enchanter, have been tricked like this?

'I'll hide in the cellars tonight and see what he is up to,' thought the Enchanter. So that night very early he hid behind his sacks and waited. Just as he had guessed the green-eyed servant crept along the tunnel, climbed into the cellar, and caught up a sack of gold!

'Hi!' shouted the Golden Enchanter. 'Put that down, you robber! I know who you are! You're Wily-One, the wicked magician who was driven away from his castle!'

Wily-One leapt through the hole and scuttled along the tunnel to his cottage. There he shut down the trapdoor and bolted it so that the Enchanter could not follow him. Then he took a magic broomstick he had once stolen from a witch, and rode away on it, taking the sack of gold with him.

But following him he saw a little bird, whom the Enchanter had ordered to chase Wily-One, for he did not like to leave his palace unguarded. He would call out his guards, bid them surround the palace whilst he was gone, and then follow the wicked magician himself. Meanwhile the little bird tracked Wily-One for him.

Wily-One landed at last in a broad field, so sleepy that he could fly no longer. Dawn was just breaking. He saw the little bird who had followed him wheel round and fly off towards Shining Palace.

'Well, by the time you come back with the Golden Enchanter I shall be gone!' he said. He looked at the sack of gold and decided that he had better bury it instead of taking it with him, for it was heavy. So he bewitched a strong stick and bade it make little holes all over the field. When that was done, he bade each piece of gold hide itself there. In a very short time the thousands of golden pieces were hidden all over the field, and there was none to be seen.

And at that moment Wily-One saw the Enchanter running towards him! He changed himself into a rabbit and ran away at top speed.

The Enchanter turned himself into a fox and a breathless race began. Just as the rabbit was almost caught Wily-One changed himself into a lark. Up and up into the sky he rose, hoping to get away from the Enchanter.

But the Enchanter turned himself into an eagle and soared swiftly after the lark. Down the sky they went, the lark trying its hardest to escape. But with a downward rush the eagle was upon it, and both dropped to the earth. As they touched the ground Wily-One turned himself into a tiny mouse, hoping to hide among the bracken. But the Enchanter turned himself into a big black cat and began to hunt the mouse here and there. Smack! It clapped its great paw on to the mouse's back, and knowing himself so nearly caught Wily-One changed swiftly into a snake and tried to bite the cat.

The Enchanter changed back into his own shape and struck the snake with a stick. It glided away and came to a deep pond. The Enchanter followed and lifted his stick again. Hey presto! Wily-One changed into a big fish and slipped silently into the water.

The Enchanter became an otter and slid into the water after him. Round and round the pond they swam, the fish twisting and turning in fear lest the otter should bite him in the neck.

Just as the otter pounced, the fish leapt into the air and changed into a brown bear. He clambered out of the water and ran to the mountains. The otter climbed out after him and changed into a bear too. He raced after his enemy, growling fiercely.

Wily-One saw a cave in a hillside and ran inside. In a trice the Golden Enchanter changed from a bear back to his own shape and laughed loudly. He took a great stone and rolled it in front of the cave, pinning it there by the most powerful magic he knew.

'Well, there you are, and there you may stay!' said he. 'I would never let a wicked magician like you free, for you do so much harm. No, here you will stay for hundreds of years and perhaps you will find time to repent.'

With that he left him and went back to Shining Palace. He did not bother to look for the stolen gold, for he had so much that he hardly missed it.

But one day he happened to pass the field where Wily-One had hidden the gold – and he stared in wonder and delight! Each little gold piece had taken root and grown! The plants had flowered in thousands all over the field and were waving their bright golden heads in the sunshine.

'I've never seen anything so beautiful in my life!' said the Enchanter. 'I hope the seeds will spread so that the flowers may be seen by everybody!'

They did spread – they spread all over the world, and now each summertime you may see fields full of the bright gold flowers that once grew from the stolen gold. Do you know what we call them? Yes, buttercups, of course!

As for Wily-One, he is still in the cave, and long may he remain there!

The Tower
in Ho-Ho Wood

There were once two little girls called Mary Ann and Mary Jane. Mary Ann's mother was dead, and her father had married again. Her stepmother had a little girl of her own, just the same age as Mary Ann. She was called Mary Jane. Now the stepmother was jealous of Mary Ann, for she was a pretty child, and merry and kind-hearted. Mary Jane, her stepsister, was plain, and so sulky and bad-tempered that no one liked her. Whenever anyone came to play in the garden, it was always merry Mary Ann they asked for, and never sulky Mary Jane.

It wasn't long before Mary Ann found that she was expected to do all the work of the house, whilst her lazy stepsister lay in bed late and put never a finger to a pot or pan. Mary Ann didn't mind. She went about singing gaily, and did all her work as well as she could.

But Mary Jane couldn't bear Mary Ann to be happy. She hated to hear her stepsister singing merrily. So one day, when Mary Ann had been making gooseberry jam, she crept into the kitchen and upset the pan so that all the jam was spilt on the floor and was wasted. No one saw her do this, and she ran out of the kitchen quickly.

When the stepmother came in to see what the noise was, she found poor Mary Ann crying bitterly to see her jam wasted, and such a terrible mess to clear up.

'Did you upset that, you careless girl?' cried her stepmother, and without waiting to hear the answer, she boxed her little step-daughter's ears.

'I didn't do it!' sobbed Mary Ann. 'I'm sure it was bad-tempered Mary Jane, who did it to make me unhappy.'

'How dare you tell stories like that!' cried the stepmother, angrier than ever. 'You are a very naughty little girl.'

Poor Mary Ann! She spent the whole morning clearing up the mess, and then she had to go without her dinner as a punishment for spilling the jam – though of course it was really Mary Jane who had done it.

Mary Ann forgave her stepsister, and tried to be nice to her – but the more she tried the more Mary Jane hated her. Mary Ann grew prettier and sweeter, and at last the stepmother thought that she really must send her away, for her own daughter looked so cross and ugly beside Mary Ann that everyone noticed the difference.

But how could she send her away? The father would be sure to want to know where she was, and he would go and bring her back, for he was fond of

Mary Ann. At last, after a great deal of thinking, the stepmother thought of a plan. She would send Mary Ann to the Ho-Ho Wood for some wild strawberries – and then perhaps she would never come back, for the Little Folk lived there, and had forbidden any mortal to set foot in their wood.

So one morning she called Mary Ann to her, and gave her a basket.

'See,' she said, 'I want some wild strawberries to make a pudding for your father. Take this basket, and go to the Ho-Ho Wood where there are plenty. Do not come back until you have your basket full, or I will punish you.'

'But stepmother, the Little Folk will not let us set foot in Ho-Ho Wood,' said Mary Ann, in a fright. 'They will be very angry with me if they catch me, and perhaps they will turn me into a frog!'

'Do as I tell you,' said the stepmother, angrily. 'You will come to no harm. Fetch the strawberries, and let me hear no more words from you.'

With that she pushed Mary Ann out of the door and slammed it behind her. The little girl didn't know what to do. At last she decided to go towards Ho-Ho Wood, and see if there were any strawberries on the borders. So off she went, carrying her basket.

She soon came to the wood. It was thick and dark. Mary Ann hunted along the edge for strawberries, but she could see none. Just inside the wood there were plenty – she could spy them through the trees. But Mary Ann didn't want to go there without permission, for she knew that the Little Folk would be angry.

She walked along the borders of the wood, wondering if perhaps she would see a gnome or a brownie whose permission she might ask. But she saw no one. Suddenly, as she turned a corner, she saw a little house in front of her, set on the edge of the wood. It was very small and very crooked. The little garden was set with brilliant flowers, and at the end of it stood an old well.

As Mary Ann walked up to it, she saw an old dame going down to the well with two big buckets.

'I might ask her if I would be allowed in the wood,' thought Mary Ann, so she went in at the gate. 'Good morning,' she said politely to the old dame.

'Dear me, how you made me jump!' said the old woman, and she dropped her buckets to the ground, and sat down in a fright on the wall nearby. 'I didn't hear you coming.'

'Oh, please forgive me,' said Mary Ann, very sorry. 'Let me draw your water for you. The buckets are heavy for you to carry.'

So she let the buckets down into the well one after the other and filled them with water. Then she carried them into the cottage for the grateful old dame.

'You are a kind little girl,' said the old woman. 'Now tell me what I can do for you.'

Mary Ann told her all about how she had been sent to get wild strawberries from Ho-Ho Wood.

'But I am afraid to go into the wood in case the Little Folk are angry with me,' she said.

'I will help you,' said the old woman. 'See, take this needle and thread, this bottle of water, and this little golden key. You will be quite safe with all these.'

'But what shall I do with them?' asked Mary Ann, in surprise.

'You will see when the time comes,' answered the old woman. 'You will be safe in Ho-Ho Wood, little girl, for you have a kind face and heart, and such folk are always welcome in the wood. It is only unkind, selfish people that come to grief.'

Mary Ann thanked the old dame very much, and then made her way to the wood. She stepped over the ditch that edged the wood, and found herself among the trees. She began to hunt for strawberries, and soon she found some. She was picking them happily, when she heard a noise behind her, and she looked round.

She saw a gnome looking at her crossly.

'What are you doing here?' he asked. 'This wood is private. I shall take you prisoner unless you can do something for me.'

'What shall I do?' asked Mary Ann, frightened.

'Can you sew six buttons on my new coat?' asked the gnome, showing her six little red buttons. 'I haven't got a needle.'

'Yes!' said Mary Ann, gladly, and she took the needle and thread that the old dame had given her, and quickly and neatly sewed the buttons on the gnome's coat, whilst he stood still in front of her.

'Oh, that is beautiful!' said the gnome, pleased. 'Wait a moment, little girl.'

He took a wand from his pocket, and waved it at Mary Ann. In a trice her ragged dress was gone, and in its place appeared a lovely one of gold and silver, set with little rubies all along the hems. Her socks changed to silken stockings, and her shoes to golden slippers with diamond buckles. How pleased and astonished she was!

'Oh, thank you!' she cried. 'What a lovely dress!'

'If you want fine strawberries go down that little path to the right,' said the gnome. 'There are some lovely ones there.'

So Mary Ann ran down the little path and soon found some very big strawberries. She had begun to pick them when a bent old wizard in a big pointed hat came striding by. He looked very hot indeed, and he was very much out of breath, for he panted like a steam-engine.

When he saw Mary Ann he stopped.

'What are you doing here?' he asked, angrily. 'Don't you know this wood is private?'

He looked so fierce that Mary Ann was frightened. Then she suddenly remembered the bottle of water that the old woman had given her. She took it out of her pocket, and held it out to the wizard.

'You look hot and thirsty,' she said. 'Drink some of this water.'

'Thank you,' said the wizard, and he took it. He drank every drop and was delighted.

'Nicest water I've ever tasted,' he said. 'You are a kind little girl. Take this in exchange for the water.'

He gave her a little bag and then marched off through the trees. Mary Ann looked at the bag. It was full of gold. She emptied the gold pieces out into her hand – and lo and behold, as soon as the bag was empty it filled itself again, and when Mary Ann looked into it she saw many more gold coins waiting for her!

'It's a magic bag!' she said in excitement. 'Oh, now I shall be rich! I shall have as much gold as I want! I can buy presents for everybody!'

She went on picking the strawberries, and wandered here and there through the wood. Suddenly she came to a little tower, which had in one side a tiny door. Mary Ann thought it was a curious place. It had no windows except one small one right at the top. The little girl put her hands to her mouth and called loudly.

'Does anyone live here?'

At that an ugly, untidy-looking youth put his head out of the window. When he saw Mary Ann standing below in her beautiful dress he was astonished. He thought he had never in his life seen anyone so lovely.

'I have been locked up here,' he said, mournfully. 'I was riding through the wood, not guessing that it belonged to the Little Folk, and the goblins caught me and imprisoned me. I have been here for a month, and I cannot get out. The door is locked fast.'

'I think I can set you free!' cried Mary Ann, joyfully, and she felt in her pocket for the little golden key that the old dame had given her. She slipped it into the lock of the tiny door, and turned it. The door opened easily, and Mary Ann called up the spiral stairway in front of her.

'Come quickly, you are free!'

Down the stairs came the youth. He was certainly very ugly, for his nose was far too long, one eye was blue and the other brown, and his hair was thin and straggly. His clothes were dirty and ragged, and he limped badly. Mary Ann thought he was a pedlar.

'I cannot thank you enough,' he said. 'You are the kindest maiden I have ever seen. Now I wonder if my steed is anywhere near here so that we may ride away from this wood in safety.'

He looked about, but all he could see was a thin donkey munching some thistles.

'This will do to carry us,' he said. 'Will you ride with me out of the wood? I know the way.'

Now Mary Ann found that she was lost, for she did not know which path to take. So, though she did not like to ride with such a dirty ragged-looking youth, she said yes, she would go with him. She did not like to hurt his feelings by saying he was too dirty. So up she jumped behind him on the donkey and together they rode through the wood.

As soon as they had reached the borders of the wood a very strange thing happened. The donkey suddenly turned into a magnificent black horse! It cantered along, its long mane flowing in the wind, its harness glittering with silver and gold.

Mary Ann was most astonished. She thought she would ask the pedlar if he had seen what had happened – and what a surprise she had! Instead of the ugly, dirty, ragged youth, she saw a handsome prince with thick curling hair, two bright blue eyes, and a merry smile. His nose was no longer too big and his teeth were white and even.

He was dressed in a tunic and cloak of satin embroidered with gold thread, and by his side hung his sword. He looked at Mary Ann and smiled.

'I am no longer an ugly pedlar!' he said. 'I have changed back to my right form. It was kind of you to ride with me when you thought I was ugly and ragged. You have a sweet face and a kind heart. Will you marry me and be my Queen?'

Mary Ann was so happy that she could hardly say yes. She fell in love at once with the handsome prince, and whispered that she would be glad to marry him. So they jogged along together very happily to Mary Ann's home.

How astonished the stepmother and Mary Jane were to see Mary Ann coming back dressed in gold and silver, sitting behind a handsome young prince! They could not believe their eyes. She jumped down from the horse and told them all that had happened.

'We will have a fine wedding!' she said. 'I have enough money in this magic purse to pay for everything. And when the wedding is over I shall go to live with my prince in his beautiful castle! Oh, look, here are your strawberries, stepmother. See what fine ones grow in Ho-Ho Wood!'

The next week the wedding was held, and folk from near and far came to it. Everyone said that the bride was the prettiest, kindest-looking maid in the kingdom, and when the prince rode off with her all the guests cheered and waved their hands in delight.

Only two people were angry and upset about Mary Ann's good luck, and they were her stepmother and stepsister.

'Now Mary Ann is the grandest lady in the land, and we are nobodies,' said Mary Jane, crossly.

'Listen, daughter,' said the mother. 'I have a plan. Why should not you go to pick strawberries in Ho-Ho Wood, and do all that Mary Ann did? Perhaps you also will come back with a prince and a purse of gold.'

'Very well,' said Mary Jane. She took a basket and set off. She looked for the tiny cottage in which lived the old dame Mary Ann had told her about, and soon she saw it. The old woman was going up the path to the well, and Mary Jane stepped into the garden, banging the gate so hard that the old woman jumped and dropped her two buckets.

But instead of being sorry, Mary Jane laughed loudly, for she had no manners at all.

'You looked funny when you dropped your buckets,' said the rude little girl.

'Please fill them for me,' said the old dame. 'You gave me such a fright that I am not able to let them down into the well.'

So Mary Jane let the buckets down, and drew them up full of water. But she put them down so carelessly that they spilt over the old dame's feet and made her shoes and stockings wet. Mary Jane said nothing, but stood looking at the old dame.

'What do you want?' asked the old woman, crossly, wiping her shoes dry.

'I want the needle and thread, the bottle of water and the golden key,' said Mary Jane. 'You gave them to my sister, and she got a golden dress, a purse of gold and a handsome prince who married her. I want the same.'

The old dame laughed a low laugh. She went to her cottage and came back again with something in her hands.

'Here you are,' she said to Mary Jane, and she put into the little girl's hand a needle and thread, a bottle of water and a golden key. Then she chuckled again and went back to her cottage.

Mary Jane was delighted. Now she would soon get the same wonderful things as her stepsister! She ran down the path and into the wood. It wasn't long before she saw a gnome looking at her crossly.

'What are you doing?' he asked. 'This wood is private. I shall take you prisoner unless you can do something for me.'

'I know what you want me to do!' said Mary Jane, whipping out her needle and thread. 'Come here and I'll sew the buttons on!'

The gnome handed her six buttons in silence. She sewed them on one after another, and very badly she did it too, for she was lazy with her needle, and always made Mary Ann do her mending for her. Three times she pricked the gnome and made him jump, and he looked as black as a thunder-cloud when she had finished.

'Now wave your magic wand and change my dress!' said Mary Jane. The gnome waved his wand – but alas for Mary Jane! Instead of a beautiful gold and silver frock appearing, she found that her little cotton dress had changed to a thick, ugly one of grey wool, with patches here and there, and a big hole in the skirt.

How upset she was! But she had to wear it, for her cotton frock had disappeared. She went on into the wood, crying bitterly. Soon she became thirsty, and she looked about for a stream to drink from. But all she could find was a muddy ditch, and she did not want to drink from that!

'I know what I will do,' she said. 'I will drink the water out of the bottle, and fill it with ditch water. I am sure the old wizard won't know the difference!'

So she drank all the water from the bottle, and then filled it up with dirty ditch water. She had hardly finished doing so when she saw the bent old wizard coming along.

'What are you doing here?' he asked, angrily. 'Don't you know that this wood is private?'

'Drink some of this water,' said Mary Jane. 'You look hot and thirsty.'

She handed the wizard the bottle and he put it to his mouth to drink – but as soon as he tasted it he knew that it was ditch water and he was angry.

He emptied it on the ground.

'Give me a magic purse,' said Mary Jane.

The wizard took a bag from his pocket, and handed it to Mary Jane. Then he stalked off without a word. The little girl opened the bag eagerly – but oh, what a disappointment! Instead of being full of gold, it was full of earwigs that jumped out as soon as she opened it! She threw the bag down in horror, but after a while she picked it up again.

'Perhaps it will get full of gold coins soon,' she thought. 'Mary Ann's might have been full of earwigs at first.'

So she carried it off with her. Soon she came to the little tower in the wood, and leaning out of the window at the top was a pedlar, ugly, dirty and ragged, with a long nose and one eye blue and the other brown. In a trice Mary Jane fitted her key to the door and opened it. The youth came running down the stairs.

He found his donkey in the bushes and together they mounted the scraggy little beast. When they came to the edge of the wood, Mary Jane watched eagerly to see if the donkey changed to a horse – but to her great disappointment he remained a donkey. She looked up to see if the pedlar were a handsome prince – but alas! he was still an ugly pedlar dirty and ragged.

'I see you have a magic bag there,' he said. 'What does it contain? Golden coins?'

'Yes,' said Mary Jane, untruthfully. When the pedlar heard that, he thought that he would marry Mary Jane and then he would be rich. So he asked her to marry him and she said she would, for she felt sure that he would turn into a handsome prince sooner or later.

Soon they arrived at her home. The mother was very much disappointed to find that her daughter had such an ugly dress on, and that the purse was full of earwigs. She bade Mary Jane keep the earwigs secret, or perhaps the pedlar would not marry her, and then when he turned into a prince, she would be sorry.

So Mary Jane said nothing about the earwig-purse, but made all arrangements for the wedding. It was to be the very next day, for the pedlar would not wait. So on the morrow there was a wedding, and though Mary Jane told everyone that she was really marrying a prince and not a pedlar, no one believed her. They could not think that a prince would marry such a plain bad-tempered maiden.

After the wedding the two mounted the donkey, and rode off. Mary Jane thought they were going to a palace, and she looked out for it for many hours. But at last she was tired and asked the pedlar when they would get to the palace.

'Palace? What palace?' he asked, in surprise.

'Why, your palace!' said Mary Jane. 'You are a prince, aren't you, and all

princes live in palaces!'

'I am no prince,' said the youth. 'I am a pedlar and nothing else, as well you know. I have no money and therefore I married you, for I knew you had a bag of gold.'

'I haven't!' said Mary Jane, and she began to cry. The pedlar snatched the bag, and opened it. Out fell a crowd of earwigs, and he flung the purse in horror on the ground.

'You have deceived me!' he said, angrily. 'I would never have married such a bad-tempered maid if I had known you had no more gold than I. Now you will have to work hard for your living, for I am no prince, and never said I was.'

Then began a hard life for Mary Jane, for she had to work hard from morning to night and do what the pedlar bade her. No longer could she be lazy, and if she sulked and frowned, she was scolded. So soon she began to learn her lesson and tried to smile and be as sweet-tempered as Mary Ann had been.

As for Mary Ann, she was living happily with her prince in his palace. All her people loved her, for her heart was as kind as her face was sweet. And one day when a pedlar and his wife came riding by her gates, she called out in surprise – for they were her stepsister and the pedlar she had married!

Mary Ann forgot how unkind Mary Jane had been to her – she forgot her selfishness and bad temper. She ran out to meet her, and hugged her lovingly. Mary Jane was humble now, and her eyes were kind. She was no longer the horrid girl that she had once been. She kissed Mary Ann, and then curtsied low to her.

'You must come and live here,' said Mary Ann. 'There is a dear little cottage near by. You shall have it – and your husband shall be our tinker and mend all the pots and pans!'

She was as good as her word, and soon Mary Jane and her pedlar were settled happily in a dear little cottage. So everything came right, and as far as I know they are all living happily together to this very day!

Princess Goldie and the Goblin

Once upon a time there was a very clever goblin called Boody. He had six hundred magic books, and he knew more spells than any goblin in the land. But there was one spell he wanted to know which he couldn't seem to find out.

'How can I make old people young?' he wondered. 'How can I make old eyes shine again, and bent limbs straight? If only I knew that, I should make my fortune!'

He read his magic books every day, and he asked every witch and wizard he knew if they could help him. But no one could.

Then one day he decided to try and make a spell that would do what he wanted. So he got together six fresh violets, picked at sunrise, four hairs from a lamb's tail, a smile from a month-old baby, a kitten's whisker, and many other things. He put them all together into a big blue pot, and made a fire of young twigs on the hillside. Every morning at break of day he stirred the mixture seven times and chanted magic words.

Well, when the spell was made he gave a little sip to Hoity-Toity, his old black cat. Imagine his delight when Hoity became as frolicsome as a kitten, and was just like he used to be ten years back.

'Now I have found the right spell!' cried Boody the goblin. 'Now I shall make my fortune!'

The next day and the next he spent in writing all about how he had found his famous spell, and what he had put into it. But alas! When the third day came Hoity-Toity the cat was no longer young and sprightly. He looked as old as ever, and wouldn't even mew when Boody said 'good morning!' to him.

'Oh, dear, there's something wrong with that spell after all!' said Boody in dismay. 'I have left out something important – now what can it be?'

He thought and thought, and looked up all his magic books – then suddenly he came across just the thing he wanted.

He found that the golden hairs of a seventeen-year-old princess had a great power in spells of the sort he was making. Boody worked excitedly, trying to find how many he would need. At last he discovered it.

'If I stir into my mixture a golden hair fresh plucked from the head of a seventeen-year-old princess, every morning for a month, I shall make the spell quite perfect!' cried Boody. 'Oh, this is splendid!'

But after a while he began to frown. Where could he get twenty-eight golden hairs, and what princess would give him them?

He didn't waste much time in finding out. He called his little servant, Peepo, to him, and bade him go swiftly on bats' wings to every princess in the world, and see if he could find one aged seventeen who had golden hair.

In an hour's time, Peepo came back.

'Master,' he said, bowing low, 'I have visited every court in the world. There are five princesses aged seventeen, and three of these have golden hair.'

'Good!' said Boody, 'we have three to choose from then.'

'Not so, Master,' said Peepo, 'one of the princesses will be eighteen tomorrow, and another is dyeing her hair black to please the King she is going to marry.'

'Oh my!' groaned Boody, 'well, what about the third?'

'She is just seventeen,' said Peepo, 'and her hair is like the sunshine itself. But, Master, you will never get her father, the King, to consent to the princess giving you any of her golden hairs, for he has banished all the goblins from his kingdom, and will not let one live there, no matter how harmless he is. A goblin did him a bad turn once in his youth, and this is his revenge.'

Boody sat thinking. It was too bad that he could not get just the last thing he wanted. He knew that it was of no use going to ask the King's consent – and there was another thing that he had not told Peepo. The princess whose hairs he used would lose all her beauty at the end of a month, and appear to be an old, old woman.

The cunning little goblin would not give up his plans. He meant to get those golden hairs somehow. He lay awake all night long, and when day dawned he had made up his mind what to do. He would capture the princess and bring her to his cave! Then every morning he would pluck a golden hair from her head, and thus he would be able to complete his spell.

The next day he set out. He was invisible, for around his shoulders was a wide cape made from witch's shadows. Anyone wearing such a mantle could be seen by neither man, woman nor child. Only animals could see him, and they shrank back in fear.

At noon he reached the palace where Princess Goldie dwelt. She was in her room alone, threading some blue beads to wear that evening. Boody ran unseen up the stairs, entered the room of the princess, and flung his wide cloak around her. In a moment she was invisible! She screamed in fright, and her maidens came running in at once.

'Help me! Help me!' cried the princess. But though the maidens looked here and there, they could see nothing. Boody carried the princess down the stairs, and the footmen there started in astonishment to hear their princess's voice calling to them, though they could see no one.

'It's a horrid little goblin who's taking me away!' cried Goldie. 'Oh, come and save me!'

The King came rushing out when he heard his daughter's voice, and all the soldiers ran here and there. But nobody could do anything, for the princess and Boody were invisible.

In four hours Princess Goldie was safely in the goblin's cave. He rolled a great stone over the entrance, and then carried her down the long winding passage to his rocky home. Peepo was there, and stared in amazement to see the lovely princess in his master's arms.

'I have got her,' said Boody in delight. 'It will be your task, Peepo, to look after her, and see that she does not escape. Every morning I will take a golden hair, and then in a month's time, my marvellous spell will be finished.'

Goldie was put in a little underground room with a bed and a chair. She was frightened and miserable, and she hated the ugly little goblin. She was so tired that she fell asleep, and did not wake until dawn the next day. Just as she awoke, the goblin came in.

'Give me a hair from your head,' he said.

'No, I won't,' said Goldie. 'You shan't have a single one, you horrid little man. How dare you take me away from my palace? When my father knows, he will come and rescue me, and then you will be punished.'

Now never in all his long life had Boody been spoken to like that, and he was very angry.

He snatched a hair from Goldie's shining head, and pulled it out.

'There!' he said, 'I've got it! And every morning for a month you will have to give me one. At the end of that time you will lose your youth and beauty, and that will punish you for your rudeness to me, Boody the Great Goblin!'

'Great fiddlesticks!' cried the princess, and she slapped the goblin's face.

How angry Boody was! He ran out of the little room in a rage, longing to spank the princess, but not daring to stop in case he missed the dawn.

As soon as he had gone the princess began to cry. She tried the door, but it was fast bolted. She kicked at it, and hammered on it with her fists, but she could not open it. Then at last she heard the bolts being slipped out, and she saw Peepo coming in.

When he saw the tears on the face of the lovely princess, he stopped in dismay.

'Don't cry, Princess Goldie,' he said. 'You have only got to be here a month. Nothing will happen to you, and you will be taken back quite safely to your palace.'

'Something will happen to me!' sobbed the princess. 'That horrid goblin told me that at the end of the month I shall lose all my youth and beauty!'

Peepo stared in horror. What! Would this lovely maiden become old and ugly just because his master wanted to use her hair for his spells? Peepo's heart was full of sadness. He had never seen such a beautiful maid before, and he could not bear to think that she should be unhappy.

Goldie saw his sorrowful face, and she ran to him. She put her arms around his neck, and spoke beseechingly to him.

'Please, please help me to get away,' she said. 'You have such a kind face, and I am so unhappy.'

Peepo went red with delight to feel Goldie's arms round his neck. No one had ever hugged him before or been kind to him. As long as he could remember he had been servant to Boody, and had done his bidding. The goblin had been rough and unkind to him, and Peepo had often been miserable.

'I would like to help you, Princess,' he said in a whisper, 'but I am so afraid of Boody the goblin. If he finds out that I want to help you, he would turn me into a toad and put me in the middle of a tree for a hundred years. He would, really.'

'Well, couldn't you go and find someone who isn't afraid of Boody, and could come and rescue me?' asked Goldie. 'Oh please do go, Peepo, and tell someone where I am.'

'All right,' said Peepo, beginning to tremble when he thought of Boody's anger when he found out. 'I'll go tonight when Boody is asleep.'

So that night when the goblin was snoring away in his hard bed, Peepo slipped out into the starlight. Where should he go, and whom should he tell? He had only a little while, for dawn came early, and the goblin was always awake then.

He ran down the hillside and came to the lane at the bottom. Up it he ran and then sped on until he came to a little cottage. Here dwelt an old man and his wife with their young son.

Peepo rattled at the shutters and called softly. The old man awoke and sent his son to see what was the matter. The boy was astonished to find a tiny dwarf under the window.

'What do you want?' he asked.

'I come with a message from the Princess Goldie,' whispered Peepo, fearful lest the bats should hear and tell the goblin about him. 'She is shut up in one of his caves, and every day for a month he is going to take one of her golden hairs for a new spell of his. At the end of that time she will lose all her youth and beauty, so she must be rescued quickly.'

The boy listened in surprise. Then suddenly he reached out his hand and grabbed hold of Peepo's shoulder. He dragged him through the window and looked at him by the light of his candle.

'Why don't you rescue her yourself?' he asked.

'I daren't,' said Peepo. 'The goblin, my master, is too powerful. But please let me go now – I must be home by dawn or the goblin will see I have been out and will punish me.'

But the boy would not let him go. He kept him there, asking question after question till Peepo was full of terror lest he should be out too late to get back unseen.

At last the boy lifted him out of the window again, and Peepo ran for his

life. Alas for the little servant! Boody was just coming out of the cave as Peepo came in. He saw by the little dwarf's face that he had been betraying him, and he pounced on him.

In a trice Peepo was turned into a toad, and Boody shut him up in a tree for a hundred years. Then he went to the Princess, took one of her golden hairs, and told her what he had done to Peepo.

'That is your fault,' he said to the weeping maiden. 'Do not hope that you will be rescued. I have placed a magic circle outside your door, and whoever steps into it will dissolve at once into smoke!'

He left the frightened princess and went up to the top of the hill with her golden hair. Goldie was in despair. She felt quite certain that no one could save her, and all day long she wept her pretty eyes out.

Now the boy who had listened to Peepo was a very sharp lad. He determined to find out if the story that the little dwarf had told was true. Without being seen by Peepo, he followed after him as he ran back to the cave. He saw Boody catch him, and watched in horror as the poor little servant was turned into a toad.

The lad ran off as soon as he could, and made up his mind to fetch help. So that day he walked across the hills to where a large palace stood. In it dwelt the Chancellor of that land, a very powerful man. The boy saw him, and told his story.

'I will ride straight to the King,' said the Chancellor. 'I will ask him if he has heard of any princess being missing from the countries round about. If your tale is true, you shall be well rewarded for your trouble.'

The Chancellor started off with his swiftest horses. He soon arrived at the King's palace, and told him what he had heard. No sooner had he finished than a courier was seen riding at top speed into the court-yard.

'Perhaps this messenger bears the news!' said the King. Sure enough, he did! He came with a letter from the King of a neighbouring country.

'My daughter, Princess Goldie, has been stolen by a goblin,' said the letter. 'There are goblins in your kingdom. I pray you to seek out every one and see if my daughter is hidden anywhere in your land.'

Now the King's son, Prince Merry, had been listening to all that had been said. He was young and handsome, brave and daring. He knew Princess Goldie, and thought her the sweetest little maiden in the world. When he heard that the goblin had taken her away, he leapt to his feet and drew his sword.

'I shall go and find her!' he cried.

'Sit down, Merry,' said the King, 'you are too young – besides, these goblins are very powerful. You might find yourself turned into a snail or a spider.'

But Merry would not listen. He strode out of the palace, and leaping on his swiftest horse, he rode to the cottage, where lived the little boy who had heard the dwarf's tale the night before. He bade the child get up behind him, and then he rode to where the nearby mountains raised their heads to the sky.

'This is where the goblins live,' said the boy. 'I have often seen them running about. And do you see that highest hill, your Highness? It is there that every morning a goblin goes to stir something in a great bowl, for I have often lain on the hill opposite and watched him.'

Merry rode to the hill the boy pointed to, and the lad showed him where he had seen the dwarf changed into a toad the night before. Merry looked closely at the cave opening, and decided that it would be folly to try and force an entrance that way. The goblin would hear him easily, and before he knew what was happening he would be bewitched in some way.

He rode round to the back of the hill, and dismounted. He looked carefully at the hillside, and scraped the earth with his foot. It was very sandy and came away easily.

'I have an idea,' he said to the lad. 'I believe I could dig through this hill, and come into the goblin's cave from the back. But how I wish I could think of some way by which I might put him off his guard!'

'Your Highness,' said the boy, red with excitement, 'I know. The goblin has no servants now – shall I go and offer myself as one? If he took me, I could find out exactly where the princess is and let you know. I could try and think of some way, too, that would make him keep such a sharp look-out in front of his hill that he would quite neglect the other side of it!'

'Brave boy!' said the prince, 'go at once and try your luck. Come back to me here tonight, and tell me what happens.'

The boy went. The goblin saw him and was pleased to be able to get another servant so quickly, for few people cared to work for goblins. He would not let the lad go into the princess's room, but the boy soon found out exactly where it was.

'Keep a good look-out,' said the goblin. 'See that no stranger comes peering round here, and tell me at once if you see anyone.'

The boy grinned to himself. He meant to give the goblin so many false alarms that he would have too much work to do in watching the front of his cave to bother about the back of the hill.

So all day long he rushed in and out to the goblin crying out this, that and the other, so that Boody was in such a fright he thought only of the front entrance to his cave. If so much as a tiny pebble fell down the hill the lad would tear in, shouting – 'Master! Master! There is a rumbling, roaring sound! Can it be a wizard?'

When night came the boy stole out to see the prince. Merry had begun digging into the hill, and the boy was able to tell him about how far he would have to go before he came to the deep cave where lay the golden-haired princess. All through the night the prince dug hard. He slept the next day, but when night came he again began to dig. Soon he had made quite a long tunnel in the hill, and he thought he must be coming near to where the cave of the princess was.

Then a dreadful thing happened. As he tunnelled a rock fell from the roof of the passage he had made, and struck him on the head. He fell in a faint, and lay on the ground until the boy came creeping out for his nightly talk. He saw the prince lying there, and hastily dragged him out on the hillside where the air was clean and cool.

He saw that Merry was badly hurt, so he fetched a cottager and bade him carry the prince to his home and tend him. This the man was glad to do, for he saw that the young man was of royal rank.

For three weeks Merry lay ill. Then he got back his strength, and when the lad came to see him, he dressed and went out with him.

'Oh, your Highness! Are you strong enough to go on with the digging?' asked the boy. 'There are only two nights left before Boody the goblin takes the twenty-eighth hair from the head of the princess. Then she will lose all her youth and beauty, and great misery will be her lot.'

'I shall be in time!' said the prince. He took off his coat and began to go on with his tunnelling. All night long he worked furiously. Then, just before dawn, he knew he must be somewhere near the cave – for he heard a harsh voice speaking nearby.

'One more morning, Princess Goldie – and my spell will be finished!'

He heard the princess weeping, and put his hand on his sword in rage to think that such a horrid little goblin should have power over Goldie.

He did not dare to dig any farther that day, in case the goblin should hear him. But when night came he set carefully to work.

Goldie did not sleep that night. She was so afraid of the morning, and what it would bring her. As she lay on her bed, weeping, she heard a curious scraping noise. What could it be?

She sat up and listened. Was it a mouse? A rat? Or perhaps a rabbit? No, it could not be any of those, for it was too loud. Oh, was it someone coming to save her?

She watched the wall of the cave behind which the noise seemed to come. It grew louder. Whatever was behind it was getting nearer. Goldie's heart beat fast. She lighted her candle, and watched to see what was going to happen.

Suddenly the prince put his pick right through the wall of the cave. A great hole came, and he put his head through.

'Goldie!' he said. 'Oh, you poor little princess! I am Prince Merry, and I have come to save you!'

'Sh! Sh!' said Goldie. 'You are only just in time. The goblin may be here at any moment. Have I got time to go with you?'

But even as she spoke the goblin was coming to the cave to pluck the twenty-eighth golden hair from her head. Prince Merry heard him, and leapt behind the great door that shut up the entrance to the underground room. Boody opened it, and at once the prince sprang at him.

'Ha!' he cried. 'I have you, you wicked old goblin!'

Boody gave a scream, and dropped on his knees. He was terrified of the gleaming sword that the prince was holding above his head.

'Mercy! Mercy!' he cried.

'Not an ounce of mercy shall I show you!' said the prince, sternly. 'You shall die!'

'Oh wait a minute!' cried Goldie, suddenly remembering the little servant Peepo who had been turned into a toad for trying to help her. 'Tell him to change Peepo back into his right shape again.'

The prince took firm hold of Boody's collar and made him lead the way up the winding passages to the entrance of his cave. Then he made him get the toad from the tree and change it back into Peepo. How glad the little servant was! He ran to the prince and kissed his feet.

'Now for your punishment!' said Merry to the trembling goblin. He raised his bright sword – but suddenly there was a tremendous BANG! And Boody had vanished! Everyone gaped in astonishment – but no matter where they looked, the goblin was not there!

'He's gone for ever,' said Peepo. 'He'll never come back. Hurrah! Now let's go and be happy!'

Off they all went to the King's palace, taking the boy with them too, for he had helped greatly in the rescue. He was made a nobleman, and Peepo the dwarf became the prince's own servant, which made him very proud indeed.

As for the prince and princess, you can guess what happened to them. They were married to each other and lived happily ever after.

ACKNOWLEDGEMENTS

All efforts have been made to seek necessary permissions.

The stories in this collection first appeared in the following publications:

'Very-Young the Wizard' first appeared in *Sunny Stories for Little Folks*, issue 86, 1930.

'The Witch Who Lost Sixpence' first appeared in *Sunny Stories for Little Folks*, issue 105, 1930.

'The Castle Without a Door' first appeared in *Sunny Stories for Little Folks*, issue 109, 1931.

'The Six Red Wizards' first appeared in *Sunny Stories for Little Folks*, issue 110, 1931.

'Magic in the Afternoon' first appeared in *Enid Blyton's Magazine* issue 17, Vol. 3, 1955.

'The Wizard's Umbrella' first appeared in *Sunny Stories for Little Folks*, issue 202, 1934.

The Dog That Went to Fairyland was first published as a standalone book by the Brockhampton Press in 1944.

'Pink! Pink!' first appeared in *Enid Blyton's Magazine* issue 9, Vol. 2, 1954.

'Old Bufo the Toad' first appeared in *Enid Blyton's Sunny Stories*, issue 36, 1937.

'Tell Me My Name!' first appeared in *Enid Blyton's Sunny Stories*, issue 8, 1937.

'The Little Walking House' first appeared as 'The House with Six Legs' in *Sunny Stories for Little Folks*, issue 190, 1934.

'Bufo's One-Legged Stool' first appeared in *Teachers World*, issue 1004, 1923.

'The Rabbit Who Lost His Tail' first appeared in *Sunny Stories for Little Folks*, issue 113, 1931.

'You Simply Never Know' first appeared in *Enid Blyton's Sunny Stories*, issue 480, 1950.

'Winkle-Pip Walks Out' first appeared in *Sunny Stories for Little Folks*, issue 135, 1932.

'The Surprising Blackberry' first appeared in *Sunny Stories for Little Folks*, issue 100, 1930.

'The Prisoners of the Dobbadies' first appeared in *The Enid Blyton Book of Fairies* published by George Newnes in 1924.

'Lazy Binkity' first appeared in *Fairyland Tales*, issue 57, 1923.

'Can It Be True?' first appeared in *Enid Blyton's Magazine*, issue 13, Vol. 3, 1955.

'The Search for Giant Osta' first appeared as 'Fanny in Fairyland' in *Fairyland Tales*, issue 43, 1922.

'Extraordinary Afternoon' first appeared in *The Christmas Stocking* published by Blandford Press in 1949.

'The Enchanted Goat' first appeared in *Sunny Stories for Little Folks*, issue 89, 1930.

'Up The Faraway Tree' first appeared in *Enid Blyton's Sunny Stories*, issue 95, 1938. Reproduced here with the kind permission of Egmont.

'The Folk in the Faraway Tree' first appeared in *Enid Blyton's Sunny Stories*, issue 96, 1938. Reproduced here with the kind permission of Egmont.

'Benny and the Giants' first appeared in *Sunny Stories for Little Folks*, issue 84, 1929.

'The Wishing Carpet' first appeared in *Sunny Stories for Little Folks*, issue 106, 1930.

'The Magic Pinny-Minny Flower' first appeared in *Sunny Stories for Little Folks*, issue 109, 1931.

'The Grandpa Clock' first appeared in *Enid Blyton's Sunny Stories*, issue 520, 1951.

'The Strange Old Shop' first appeared in *Enid Blyton's Sunny Stories*, issue 1, 1937. Reproduced here with the kind permission of Egmont.

'The Giant's Castle' first appeared in *Enid Blyton's Sunny Stories*, issue 2, 1937. Reproduced here with the kind permission of Egmont.

'The Enchanted Table' first appeared in *Sunny Stories for Little Folks*, issue 164, 1933.

'Adventures of the Strange Sailor Doll' first appeared in *Enid Blyton's Sunny Stories*, issue 6, 1937.

'The Little Roundy Man' first appeared in *Sunny Stories for Little Folks*, issue 108, 1930.

'Mr. Snoogle's Wish' first appeared in *Enid Blyton's Magazine*, issue 15, Vol. 2, 1954.

'The Little Singing Kettle' first appeared in *Sunny Stories for Little Folks*, issue 187, 1934.

'Gooseberry Whiskers' first appeared in *Sunny Stories for Little Folks*, issue 92, 1930.

'The Golden Enchanter' first appeared in *Sunny Stories for Little Folks*, issue 146, 1932.

'The Tower in Ho-Ho Wood' first appeared in *Sunny Stories for Little Folks*, issue 112, 1931.

'Princess Goldie and the Goblin' first appeared in *Sunny Stories for Little Folks*, issue 90, 1930.